DINAH.

NEW YORK:
CHARLES SCRIBNER, 124 GRAND STREET,
1861.

JOHN F. TROW,
PRINTER, STEREOTYPER, AND ELECTROTYPER,
48 & 50 Greene Street,
New York.

DINAH.

CHAPTER I.

CHARLES.—HIS MOTHER.—MR. POMPNEY.—HIS ANCESTOR, THE PIONEER.

In a stately theatre of woods and waters in my country, at a proper bucolical distance from the sounding of the sea, there stands a summer house, to which two or three years ago as the lustre of the season was mounting to its noon, came a lady and her son to retire awhile from the gilded artificialities of city life. The patient vicar who is intrusted with the care of the human flock, must have laughed a little when he came to look over these people, who were expending the busiest portion of their time chiefly in meditating upon the disagreeable necessity of passing through the remainder.

The house stands in a bosky silence; the broken accents of the waters and the conversation of the birds seem no louder than a reposing poet would dream those of lazy-land to be; though sometimes, of course, the storms come by here, roaring on high like ocean shells to the infant's ear. On the romantic fields about, a while ago, a native genius whose soul was sick with a multitude of parallelograms tried to subdue nature to an angular harmony. With some gentle touches of a rounded growth, the goddess accepted his landscape poem, and incorporated it as a fair chapter of her greater work around, which was to be read further in the scenic horror of the mountains in the distance and the waving forests rising over each other on the sides thereof in theatric grandeur.

The proprietor of this farm, at that period, was a gentleman by the name of Pompney, whose grand American ancestor was the pioneer who first settled the grant upon which the farm stands, and whose grandfather, it was reported, (as he had returned to this place enriched with the money of romantic marine adventure,) had been a sea-cook, and whose father, in consequence, was a terrible "son of a sea-cook." From this extraordinary derivation of his blood, he had become so saturated with pride of lineage that he went to the expense of keeping a poet to bring forth family traditions, (the same individual who discovered his genius in other walks of art, and sowed the grounds about with broken-nosed statues, &c.) After an apprenticeship in seventeen variations of the pirate and twenty-six of his son, this ingenious native's talents culminated in the invention of an epic in poetic prose concerning the pioneer. The next day after his arrival, while wandering in the garret, (for sinister purposes, perhaps,) Charles discovered this manuscript. Its commencement amused him. It was represented that one morning somewhere between the years 1600 and 1700, Sir Guy de Pompion, of Norman blood, left the white cliffs of his native home in the good ship Hottentot, (it being hinted that he was also in a state of intoxication,) to found for aye his noble race in the wilds of the New World—one of the rare instances where there were not three brothers of the original family who came over, but only one. On the voyage a severe storm arose, but throwing some of the steerage passengers overboard, they lightened the ship and she reached America in safety. In his native land, his nature had been almost decomposed by some unexpected remarks from the lady of his soul. Having asked her one day, in the high jinks of his feelings, if she would have him for better or worse, she replied that she had come to the conclusion, from a minute investigation of his weaknesses, that it would only be for worse, and she had better not; that she thought she could never become acclimated to him, for instance, (probably alluding to his fondness for tobacco and Hollands.)

In consequence of this unexpected confession, being desirous of getting as far into the woods as possible, he started off and finally reached these green forests with a grant of the lands about, and a suit of his ancestor's armor in his trunk, under the weight of which, when clad therein, he was continually falling down. Here he erected a stone house of the composite order, which was a decided proof, from its unrequired irregularity, that necessity was not the mother of invention in his case; being assisted in the work by the circumambient sons of the forest, who at the same time freely extended to him their succor in the consumption of the well-known energetic beverages of the day. Indeed, as long as there were any of these in his rundlets, the eccentric aborigines were very friendly and polite; but whenever his kegs smelt of emptiness, they were accustomed to declare war against him immediately, to surprise him, and take him prisoner, armor and all.

After a life of vicissitude in this respect, in which it seemed he was continually being captured, and continually ransoming himself with new stocks of the incendiary waters, he was finally slaughtered by a princess while, in the afternoon silence of a summer-day, he was dreaming in quiet sorrow at a window, of one who was far away. In this wild daughter of the woods whom he took to himself with all the solemnity of disappointed affection, he fancied, faithful creature, a rapturous contrast to her whom he left in his cradle-home. However, (to abbreviate an elongated narrative,) for the purpose of furthering some social plan, in spite of his upraised and wounded wrist, she insinuated into his soul a flinty dagger, and he died, leaving an heir of course.

After the poet had ingeniously manufactured this stirring tradition, of which the foregoing are the dry bones without the flesh of the poesy or even their own enamel, he submitted it to his friend, the descendant of this heroic pioneer. In the trueness of first thoughts the old gentleman immediately ducked down into ecstasies of admiration at it; but afterwards, in the inebriety of reflection, came to object with growing firmness to the disagreeable inference therefrom of being descended from a red Indian; and although the male siren who sung the song, endeavored to persuade him in a silvery manner that he might trifle with the chastity of history enough to make this spendthrift female a beautiful Dutch girl taken captive in infancy from the Albany settlements, this only seemed to make the matter more unsatisfactory; and indeed, towards the close of his career, the old gentleman, who had evidently experienced a sad reverse in his natural feelings, seemed disgusted with all the legends.

However they are ambered in the belief of many farmers about the neighborhood, who love to dwell particularly upon this one of the pioneer—affirming further that he and his murderess are accustomed to rise, the one from his sarcophagus by the side of the church, and the other from her charnel-wigwam in the ancient Indian burial-ground, and wander in wrangling about the neighboring country, or even to the house again; for, in expanding it from its humble origin, as the pioneer's dwelling, into a lofty modern romance, its successive owners had preserved in the morning freshness of a new architecture the sunset hue of the old tradition about it. Further, the inhabitants of the country have the more shadowy tradition that the spirits of the poor aborigines in whose midst the pioneer dwelt, on still summer days in the woods of the estate, are yet accustomed to sit down in grisly files to grand shadowy banquets, in ghostly continuance of some mysterious piety of their earthly lives. Noises not easily accounted for have been heard at unusual hours in different places of the neighborhood, and mysterious and wildly attired beings also have been frequently met, who could give no satisfactory account of themselves, and who also generally managed to disappear in the most unexpected and, as it were, unearthly manner, without a proper explanation of their presence. The fact that, on several of these occasions spoons and other utensils have been missed from the neighborhood, has corroborated the possibility of these supernatural feasts—being taken without doubt by these ghostly beings for use at the same. So reason, in a triumphant manner, the Atlases of these traditions.

But let us chase from our minds all unseemly levity and idle thought. I will desecrate no longer the solemn dignity of these ancient woods and their legends. The chill of doubt, the flush of pride, the sparkle of courage, the convulsion of remorse, the grandeur of fidelity, the hopes and fears of human hours, are also parts of a mystery.

CHAPTER II.

THE NOCTURN.

There was nothing stirring in the silence of the night but the spoilt child of the winds, idling from the west in his dallying way. All the rest of the household had retired, and their limbs long since were palsied in the exquisite idiocy of sleep, while Charles, the weary bearer to himself of the empty tales of this world, sat bent upon his bed with one boot off, listening in an ecstasy of revery to his own genius as she expatiated upon the absurdities of this mortal state. His mind reverted to the past, the darkness and the breeze in these lofty groves a hundred years back! "So that is the romantic window in which the wild pioneer sat when the Indian slew him! Pshaw! the old fellow's romance is as insipid as reality is nowadays!" Still reflecting, as he disrobed himself, upon the tradition of the pioneer, he fell down upon his pillows, and after a lengthy period of the night expended in the varied gymnastics of restlessness, or in sound repose, his consciousness finally reached that state in which, though the soul has no longer its royal intercourse with the outer world, the imagination still makes use of the immediate objects of the senses in the structure of its airy figments.

The night had now sunk into such a deep stillness that thought even would have seemed noisy; the breeze moved the lacery of the curtains only in the hushed fairy way which some women's hands have, and that dark illumination, coming from the yet unarisen moon, which may be fancied to be, it is so faint, no more than the feeble effort of unhappy Darkness to assimilate her character to that of her brighter sister, had raised in feeble relief the various objects in the chamber, when the door of the room opened, and a person, with head bowed down upon his bosom, coming quietly in, walked slowly and irregularly to the window where the ancient pioneer left his life. There, with the air which people have when they reflect deeply upon some secret sorrow, he sank into the chair which stood by its side, and remained in that melancholy attitude. The dream, if it were not reality, was such a cunning counterfeit that the recumbent young man endeavored, though in vain, to shake off the rigid spell which entranced his limbs, while the drops of perspiration gathered upon his brow. If, indeed, this were creature of reality, with his soul thus wrapt far away in the ethereal depths of sorrowful abstraction, he had given up the wish, or the power had been suddenly wrested from him, of consummating the earthly errand which brought him hither, whether of deadly violence or of softer crime. Just as the closing mist of sleep shut out this witch-like vision from his mind, the young man seemed to understand that a purring cat was rubbing her back against the chair of the phantom as if for recognition.

Soon the clouds of unconsciousness floated away again, and disclosed to his disordered intelligence a curious series of dissolving phantasmagoria. While he seemed to himself to be struggling to scrutinize the indistinguishable lineaments of his visitor half-turned towards him, they appeared to become dis-limned or changed with wild rapidity into novel and grotesque shapes, although the same single expression of sadness, curiously enough, remained through them all, being perhaps the substratum of the thought which cunningly furnished forth the whole scene. This change succeeded also in the form as well as the face of the visitant. As it had first seemed the figure of a youth struck motionless with sudden remorse at his unexecuted intention, it now changed to that of an aged man bowed with years of degradation and misery. Then it assumed the romantic form of the hoofed fiend or satyr doing his worst and mocking sorrow, to be transformed as quickly into a phantom statue—the classic form of the emotion of sorrow chiselled out of the sleeper's eccentric brain. As rapidly as this disorder had taken place in the whole scene did it flit into sudden composure. The sleeper thought he saw the mystery more as if raising his countenance to gaze in vacancy upon the obscure scenery outside, and receive upon his brow the gentle air which came in wooingly. Had the spirit of the pioneer thus wandered again from his bed of dust to seek the sorrowful scene of his earthly existence? A deep sigh and a feeble, suppressed muttering escaped his unearthly lips, and wringing those real hands whose dusty counterparts were crumbling beneath the sod, he started but to sink again at the bitterness of feelings which it seemed were to live forever in his bosom. Here a new actor, apparently of the other sex, entered the scene, for a still image standing suddenly by the door discovered itself to the consciousness of the sleeper as the fatal sweetheart of the past. With the habiliments of woman thrown loosely around her and thus retained by one hand, which was disclosed with the face and bosom, the stooping shoulders and bare feet only by a whiter reflection, she seemed to have stopped for a startled moment to listen breathlessly in the silence, in playing over again the watch of her purposed victim in the old tragedy. And now apparently casting a rapid glance about the room, a glance which, from the movement of her head, seemed to the sleeper to rest for an anxious moment upon him, she sped rapidly, with firm but noiseless steps, to the mysterious personage in the embrasure. From his lips there dropped a singular babble of surprise and—— Here the shadows again fell like a curtain over the soul of the sleeper. The forms as they stood there, and the whole scene, faded at once into nothingness.

But his limbs stirred, for his entranced dream was breaking up, and he was emerging from the shadowy into the real world again. Disenthralled from the bond of his trance, he leaped in faint bewilderment upon the floor, and seizing the pitcher of water from its basin with a sleepy inspiration of defence, he rushed instinctively to the door and cried an alarm, in a voice weak with excitement. He glanced around the room, and down the shadowy corridor, along which the wind gently sighed, but could distinguish no moving object. The light of the rising moon stole through the leaves, and into the casement at the distant end. Amid her clear beams, he saw at the head of the staircase a cat who appeared unalarmed at his presence, as though consciously protected by friends, human or witch, to whom she seemed to be mewing lightly her adieux.

Had the instinctive cry of the young man been heard by any of the inmates of the household, they would, of course, have already spoken. But as the wide hall led away from the modern part of the remodelled house to the rough stone reminiscence of the pioneer, whose chamber Charles had selected for its coolness as his sleeping apartment, he was so far separated from the rest of the household that his voice had not been heard. He had at first turned back into his chamber, but now as he was walking towards the staircase, a dull, unearthly utterance suddenly broken off fell on his ear and stopped him in surprise. It seemed a clear reality indeed, but still an inarticulate babbling sound suddenly stopping, as when a drunken man asks an improper question, and his lips are abruptly sealed by the hand of the impatient listener. A slight creaking appeared to take place on the lower part of the staircase, to which he approached in bewilderment, and something like a secret anxious whisper was borne along to his ear. The doors of the hall beneath were customarily left open at night in the summer season, to take advantage of the cooling draughts of air, but naught there attracted his attention excepting upon the glass panels of one of them the half of the door-post's shadow cut by the planet's oblique flood. There was no creature to be seen, though he plainly heard a retreating pattering noise, the footfalls of the now alarmed pussy.

"By Jove! what is this?" said he, as he wandered in quick yet quiet examination even upon the terrace outside, "there is no one, and yet that ejaculation. It seemed so distinct and peculiar!—(a pause)—pshaw, it was the cat!—(another pause)—to be sure! I have been dreaming about the pioneer, and am half asleep now;—how stupid—luckily no one has been disturbed. Gracious, this night air is quite cool to the—limbs—aw! (yawning). Ha! what is that? Jove, how stupid I am. The slightest noise made by the breeze startles me.—Well, this is amusing."

Returning to his room with uncertain feelings, he awaited in indefinite expectation some further development, but after a varied reflection upon the singularity of his vision, as nothing further disturbed the deep silence, he commenced to pass the night in the humdrum manner of nature recuperating herself.

CHAPTER III.

NEIGHBOR LAURA.

One day, soon after his arrival, Charles's aunt, a maiden lady who had now reached the age of from twenty-nine to seventy, and who was the permanent resident of the country-house, proceeded to visit an old gentleman of the neighborhood and his daughter, a lively young lady who had lately arrived from the metropolis, and for whom in callow times Charles had ruffled his pin-feathers in tender pride as her especial playmate. The indefinite idea of a union between these two families from motives connected with a long friendship, had frequently passed through the minds of the elder members thereof, and as it is usual in these cases to keep the project with some secrecy from those most interested until the period when they think for themselves and marry whomsoever they please, it had not assumed a shape until Charles's late return from the old world, whither he went to finish his education, (by getting stoned by Arabs in ancient cities, or scouring deserts on the top of camels,) and until the recent emancipation of the young lady from a boarding-school, which came pretty near finishing her's. The aunt, and the young lady's father in particular, had already conversed frequently and with fervor upon the subject, the former taking a maiden aunt's interest in it; and as she had dropped the alarming observation that the family union could be accomplished at any rate by his marrying her in case the young people should not fancy each other, the latter had also become quite frantic in his zeal for the proposition. It being observed by the two, with some sentiments of chagrin, since the advent of the young people in the neighborhood, that the young lady was disposed to be universal and love everybody, while the young man seemed possessed of scarce enough of the divine afflatus to bestow upon himself—the spinster, after much study, had hit upon an ingenious plan of directing the young people towards each other, which was immediately agreed to by the other conspirator, as he had discovered that he hadn't the slightest power of originating one himself.

On reaching the mansion of the old gentleman, Charles, who had accompanied his aunt, having nothing in particular to say as usual, accepted the challenge of the young lady to a game of billiards, and the relatives being thus left alone, the following colloquy took place between them.

SPINSTER, *in a startling manner.* "The Misses White took riding lessons!"

LAURA'S PARENT. "Eh, did they, indeed?"

AUNT, *with severity.* "They had eruptions, and were disappointed in their expectations."

"God bless me. You don't say so. Did they have eruptions because they were disappointed, or was it *vice versa?*"

"Oh, lor, how abstracted I am becoming, to be sure, Mr. Wellwood. I was thinking of some dear, dear friends you are unacquainted with—aye—'twas but the revery of friendship! Forgive me!"

"Well, I will this time," said the old gentleman, with a suspicious air.

"How natural the young people look together," said the old maid, after a pause.

"Yes, it's very natural for 'em to be together just now. It reminds me of an occurrence like it, which—"

"Certainly! of course! And do you remember our last conversation, Mr. Wellwood?"

"Oh, yes, and we must press 'em," said the other, with sudden liveliness.

"But what if we should not succeed? Aye, what if fate should have decreed that the union of our families may never take place—at least in this way, although—"

"Fate is all right. (Heavens! She is commencing—

it reminds me of a man I once knew, precisely in a similar condition of peril, by energetic measures, thus and thus, he saved himself. I must keep it up!) Hooray! We must succeed. We'll manage them. Yes, you take one side and I—"

"Oh! I pray you do not get excited yet, Mr. Wellwood," said the old maid, somewhat pettishly. "Indeed, you must reserve your energies. Do not be indiscreet, Mr. Wellwood, and have confidence in me."

"Well, I won't," replied the other, in a brief manner, calming down.

Here, on a sudden, both were seized with a desire to talk to each other at once; the spinster being filled with the immediate execution of her project, and the old gentleman being reminded of an occurrence which he had heard of. However, as the latter was obliged, after a few determined minutes, to give up, on suddenly recollecting that the point of his narrative was slightly indelicate, the old maid proceeded to unfold her plan more at leisure, and reduced it finally to an immediate execution. By the time she had finished, the young people had concluded their game, and soon after she took occasion to walk up and down with the young lady in the conservatory.

"Laura, my child," finally said she, after a mysterious silence, "I am about to reveal a secret which doesn't belong to me, which—"

"You are certainly correct. If it doesn't belong to you, you have no right to keep it a moment."

"Yes, well, there has been a subject upon my mind of which I have long wished to divest it. It may not be becoming in me, and indeed I don't know whether it is exactly right—"

"But as it is on your mind, Adeline, I don't see who is to do it, unless you do," said the young lady, persuasively.

"Well, then, my dear, I will proceed. There are moments when we feel, as it were, that any slight demonstration of feeling, by acts of affection observed in our friends in reference to parties not yet aware that those demonstrations indicate this affection, as connected with such feelings, enables us at once, as it were, to discriminate with reference to these feelings which—"

"Certainly," said Laura.

"And I say discriminate, although accompanying our diagnosis of the case, there may be natural feelings of interested intimacy which we ourselves must experience, and from this very interest which thus arises out of that collateral relationship, we may be said to be, in a measure, both the physician and patient."

"I do not know precisely what you intend to illustrate, Adeline, but I can fully appreciate the delicate difficulty of such a position. What would the feelings of the physician in such a case be, for instance, if he lost his patient?"

"Yes, this is a serious matter, and although having an intimate relation with social existence, I wish to consider it here only as touching upon that more personal point which I referred to just now, to be sure, and being taken as connected with those demonstrations in any other matter referring to that point—"

("Gracious! These—that—those—the other!) By the way," said the young lady, mildly, "before we proceed any further, allow me to observe, Adeline, that whatever this problem of social existence may be to which you refer, it appears to be one of a very abstruse nature.

Would it not, therefore, be better to entertain a stricter economy in the employment of demonstratives? They are a very useful part of speech, no doubt, but quite confusing when immoderately partaken of."

"Well, then, I will come to it at once—yes, ahem! Have you not noticed the singular languishing air which has lately betrayed itself in my nephew Charles, my dear girl?"

"Yes. I never saw such laziness and indifference in my life."

"Oh, no, not indifference, but melancholy and languishment. He is consumed with a secret passion!"

"What?"

"A longing, lingering passion," continued the old maid, with great hesitation. "Yes—and you—and you its sacred object!"

"Oh dear—what did you say?"

"Yes, he probably would have betrayed his ardent passion ere this to you, but no doubt he feared that he might be taken in, so to say—excuse the phrase."

"Ha! ha! Gracious heavens!—but—"

"It has even got into his appetite. He can't eat or drink—think of it, my dearest girl—such is his passion for you! That is, with any ease."

"But he sleeps with facility, I can assure you. While I was talking with him the other night, he positively went to sleep."

"Ah! his passion sought refuge in the sweet visions of slumber. There all his maddening wishes seemed reality and—besides that, you are mistaken, he didn't go to sleep."

"Yes! and what is more, I think—indeed—he snored!"

"It was his melancholy choking his natural utterance."

"But such general indifference."

"Ah, there it is; he is piqued with yours."

"But there might be some slight demonstration!—Dear me!" said the young lady, musing, "once in the city just after he returned from Europe, I remember he seated himself by my side and said, 'Laura;' then having raised his eyes with an air of complaint he suddenly arose and walked off. Though the conversation was brief, his manner was certainly fervent!"

"Yes! yes! and now, my dearest girl—but let us go to the billiard-room. He must betray his passion. In your presence there must be moments when unguarded looks or words will reveal this preying, aye, consuming secret! Certainly!"

The placid object of this conversation had been making a most malignant run at billiards, the old gentleman's part of the game being in fact principally to trot around, spot the balls, and mark the game. In consequence of this, and from the irritating fact that he didn't know how to commence the conversation which he desired to hold with the young man, his feelings soon got into a high state of ferment.

"Bah!" said he, "I give up the game."

"Ha! ha!" said the young man, lazily.

"Hang me if I want him for a son-in-law," murmured the exasperated old gentleman.

"It is your shot," cried Charles finally.

"Ah! you missed, eh?" said the old gentleman, suddenly mollified, and forgetting altogether about the spinster's important project. With great deliberation he proceeded to execute an extraordinary scratch and immediately assumed a majestic look. Finding the expression of grandeur to be somewhat inconvenient however, he contracted himself to simpler dimensions, and proceeded in the natural tendency of his benevolence to inform his young neighbor what he might expect for dinner, if he stayed.

"See him!" said the aunt, in romantic vivacity, entering with Laura, "worshipping with secret, consuming passion, the cruel deity, the god of love—"

"Stuffed with olives, and swimming in his own gravy!" said the young man, at this point. "Yes! I'll come over to-morrow. If there is any thing I can adore, it is a fat little fellow in such a state."

("Gracious!" said the aunt, "a little fat fellow in such a state! Dear me, Mr. Wellwood has forgotten.) He says he's coming over to-morrow," continued she, quickly, in a louder tone. "What for? To be with you. See, see the hidden meaning of passion!"

"Heavens! ha! ha! what a disguise to assume for one's feelings. However, it certainly possesses the merit of being effective," said the lenient young lady.

"Do you know, I never languished so much in my life as I did just before I arrived here," continued the unconscious young man. "Time passes pretty well here, doesn't it? I was at Pau, last summer, and upon my word a half dozen of us didn't do any thing but get up in the morning and sit all day long upon the piazza wrangling about whose watches were right and whose were wrong. One has a little enthusiasm here."

"Your presence inspires him," said the aunt, desperately, in a whisper to Laura.

"And it is that very thing. I think it comes of

having a sharpened appetite. The taking of food always produces certain agreeable sensations which it is impossible wholly to annihilate, by Jove!"

"Ha! ha! Heavens! if my presence inspires him in this way, I wouldn't dare to let him have my hand to kiss," said the young lady to the aunt. "He would probably commence to eat it to show his devotion."

"Then these sleeping arrangements here are particularly agreeable."

"Mark—(the wretch. He is more unromantic at this moment than ever,") said his aunt, in a state of suppressed exasperation, and with a smile of mildness. "Mark, he refers to the pleasant visions of slumber of which you are the loved subject!—(Oh the wretch!")

"No dyspeptic dreams to disturb one's rest. By the way, the other night I—It was singular," continued he, with a serious air, passing his hand over his brow and musing, "I wonder—it was quite laughable, but I am almost sure—however—I won't say any thing now, I think—"

"Look at his distraction, Laura. Can you wish to have any thing more conclusive than that?" said the persevering aunt, in temporary triumph.

"By the way, whence came that old man and his daughter you have on the place, aunt?" asked the young man, still musing. "I saw them eating a divided apple under a tree, with a lonely pleasure which—"

"Gracious, what perversity! the pleasure of eating again!"

"The manner in which they enjoyed it certainly attracted me."

"Oh dear! this puts me in a rage," said the old

maid; "I never saw such persistent wrong-headedness in my life. It won't do to stay and dine here. He has become temporarily insane on the subject of food. It would be fatal."

Discomfited with her attempt, she broke off the interview abruptly, and drove off home with her nephew even before the completion of a narrative which the old gentleman had now commenced, and in which he endeavored to perform the arduous intellectual feat of beginning at the middle and telling it both ways.

CHAPTER IV.

RUDOLPH AND HIS PASSION.

Afar off stood the reverend mountains. The woods were waving nearer, and there were rolls of velvet in the afternoon air. As the ethereal breakers baptized the cheek of the idle Charles, they seemed to him to come down from those Indian years and green forests of the past, which the weird dream brought up to his memory. While seated, in this soft bewitchment, upon his terrace, a horse came up the way beneath the trees so swiftly that he seemed to swell up to the house like a blast of the breeze, in a brilliant equine manner, such as the prospect of oats always inspires in the noble creatures. There was a young lady upon him, a debonair capitalist in animation, immediately followed by a gentleman who, in consequence of the precarious state of affairs, appeared to be judiciously absorbed in revolving the best methods of keeping his seat.

"Laura, my child!" said Charles's mother, in quiet dignity.

The accompanying gentleman was engaged in catching his breath. Charles sauntered up to her horse and extended his courtesy, when a giffy of perturbation and turmoil whirled in his stagnant spirit, and as the mother folded her to her embrace, Laura blushed at his air in all the stammely color of health.

"I am glad to see you," said the fair forefigure of the scene.

"Do you see she says she is glad to see you?" immediately commenced the aunt, *sotto voce*. "Take a sentimental air and dignify this devoted passion."

"It is singular! She certainly looked at me at that moment in a piercing manner. It is a sudden infatuation! I wonder if it is my shape or my intellect?" reflected the young man, in idle vanity. "I conjecture the latter. To be sure, I haven't used it much lately, but its original dazzle thus appears unimpaired to her. It will pain, I think," continued he, after a pause, with spirit, and with a secret sentiment of pity for the young lady.

"Yes, do you know, I thought so before I left home?" said the latter, in great vivacity, as if quite struck with his unusual manner. ("Oh, it will be so pleasant to flirt with him, at any rate.")

("She is a delightful girl. It must be my intellect; but love never had a residence in my bosom, and never will. How can I return it? I might produce an intense esteem for her—a kind of wild and infatuated respect, perhaps. Somehow, it embarrasses me now!")

"Mark!" whispered the irrepressible spinster again,

"although she thought it would be damp, she braves it all to come and see you."

("I will protect myself with this subject of rainy weather. It will not be dry at any rate. Or shall I reveal that singular dream? How wild! but, pshaw, the idea of having been deluded from my couch by a vivid imagination and a tom-cat is rather laughable, and—) Laura, let me embrace—"

"Hold, rash man!" cried the convulsed aunt, on the *qui vive*, "it is too much!"

"Eh?" said he, feebly, "but do you know I thought I would take this opportunity of getting laughed at for once. I had such a singular dream the other night, that—"

There was a young girl, a dependent, seated near Charles's mother, engaged in sewing. As Charles uttered these words, she started quickly, and cast a rapid glance at the faces of the assemblage. With almost kaleidoscopic rapidity, however, her countenance immediately assumed its habitual expression.

"I was—" continued Charles.

"Will you wait, please? I have forgotten. Let me go disrobe myself," interrupted Laura.

"Go with her, Dinah," said the aunt.

The young lady proceeded to a chamber after the manner of a wet washerwoman, with her riding-habit held on high, the girl following behind her. It was very warm, and she was in a bright glow of pleasure with her thoughts and her health, as she reached the apartment. The hand of the silent young attendant trembled, as she assisted in arranging the new comer's toilet, from nothing more, perhaps, than the secret sympathy which exists, in spite of themselves, between young girls of their age. A hook refused to be unfastened, and became beset in the lace. The girl fumbled, and blushing at her own vain attempts, looked down.

"Oh, pshaw! stupid creature," said the lively young lady.

"The pleasure which your beauty gives me," said the waiting-girl, with sudden energy, "cannot be effaced by what you may say to me. The one is too pleasant to forget, while the other need not be remembered."

"Oh, dear! Eh! what?" said Laura, looking radiantly upon the young inferior.

The young girl blushed her reply in a deeper dye. The hook had become disengaged. Upon leaving the room together, the young lady, as if in a forgetful and abstract manner, fell upon her neck and kissed her quite violently, no doubt causing her the sweetest surprise.

"Where is your father, Laura?" asked Charles's mother, looking at her with pleasure, on her returning. —The young man's dream was withheld again.

"I left him at home, filled with unsatisfactory emotions, certainly. He was throwing things at the servants—would you believe it?—in consequence of my having checkmated him. So, as my neighbor came along I proposed to gallop off and see you. Really I never saw any one so unreasonable as papa is. Just before this, he had become very angry with me, because he could not give an appropriate answer to a conundrum which I proposed to him, and after several feeble efforts, expressed a malignant desire to wring the neck of my canary bird. Didn't he, Rudolph?"

This was the gentleman on horseback, who, having recovered his wonted powers of respiration, had dismounted from his horse and mounted to the wide and easy flight of steps leading up to the shaded terrace, saluting in a careless and almost sullen manner, the assemblage. He nodded an idle recognition of Laura's remark, and as he turned around, he bestowed upon the young girl who had returned with Laura and taken her seat again, in a very singular manner, and as rapid as it was singular, a queer, wild glance—of burning passion it may have been. The girl as quickly deprecated it by a dignified, tired look from her eyes, and turning her head away, pursued her work. It happened about this time that the spinster aunt, who was still revolving deep projects connected with the family alliance between Charles and Laura, took the enthusiastic idea into her head, in furtherance thereof, of calling the attention of the sullen gentleman to their manner towards each other, on observing his glances that way.

"What?" asked he, almost morosely, in reply to her question.

"Did you notice that look of love she gave then? It was almost terrible in its expressiveness."

"Did she? did she?" said the young man, quickly, in a thick whisper; "did you see it? heavens! I didn't know you were aware of this."

("Dear me, I didn't know that he was, or any one else, for that matter. It's very singular. But no doubt he has conjectured their love for each other, it's so natural, yes.) Why certainly—"

"And will you, will you approve of it, when I tell you that—"

"Approve of it? of course I—"

"I thank you, thank you," said the other warmly, shaking her hand.

("Eh?")

"And has she," continued he, glancing at the sewing girl "has she ever said any thing to you about it?"

"Eh? certainly. She told me no less than yesterday she thought so much love had never been bestowed upon her, that is, if it could really be so."

"Good heaven! why she never would have me think that—oh why, why should she conceal those feelings from me?"

("Dear me, but)—I don't see exactly why she should reveal them to you."

"To whom—to whom, I ask you, should she reveal that love, if not to me?"

("He shows extraordinary interest in this matter, certainly, but he is a little too ardent.) You are her friend, Mr. Warriston, I know, but I must say I should not approve of her making a confidant, upon this subject, of a gentleman. It isn't delicate."

("Good God! this cursed old prude thinks it isn't delicate for a woman to tell her love to its object, because he belongs to the other sex.) But she must—she must, I say. This very night, this very night tell her for me to meet me at the park gate. Even there to convince her, if she wished it, on the spot I would have a clergyman present and—"

("This is more extraordinary than ever! He seems not only to take it for granted that Charles is to marry her, but—such frantic interest in another man's marriage I never saw in my life before! He positively indicates that he would like to have the ceremony performed this very evening, and in the park!) But why in the open air?"

"Oh, let it be anywhere. I will confide in you.

Would she but consent, I'd have it done now, in this very place even."

("He is intoxicated.) No unseemly levity, sir!"

"Ma'am!"

"The odor of spirits is in fact very disagreeable to me."

"Well, ma'am, if either of us has been drinking them, it must be you, ma'am!"

"Sir! Be quiet, or you will be exposed. See, Miss Wellwood calls you, and perhaps she will now confide in you as you wished, ha! ha!"

("Hey! Oh, the devil! This is enough.) Ha! ha! You have been superintending brandy-peaches, ma'am, haven't you? (However, thank Satan, she didn't understand me!") continued the sullen fellow.

"Rudolph, here is a letter from a friend of Charles, Col. Norcomb," said Laura, opportunely approaching him. "He was decoyed in, the other evening, he says, to witness the revolt of the Water Nymphs at Niblo's, and contracted the rheumatism in consequence of the liquid nature of the piece; and he feels aggrieved at his stupid medical adviser, who for some unexplained reason caused his head to be shaved, although the lameness was confined entirely to his legs. He is coming up here soon. What is the matter?" continued she, with renewed liveliness. "Why are you so silent? I never saw such forlornness in my life. Pluck me a wilted rose, seek-sorrow, with your migniard hands, and then get you back into the cave of Trophonius. Come, lazy-bones, let us take a walk."

While the young lady tripped over the sward with that halo about her which should always encompass a bright womanly creature thus in the aurora of her days, the old maid was still sternly gazing at the young man Rudolph. The mother's eye dwelt with love and admiration upon the group. "And yet," she murmured, uneasily, "how indifferent is my boy's nature. Will he ever be any thing else! Could the union of their lives now take place, the wish and happiness of mine would be completed. Dear Laura, you have inherited from your mother the love which she captured from me in our bread-and-butter days."

CHAPTER V.

THE POSSIBILITIES OF HUMAN NATURE.—THE YOUNG LAWYER—NAT BONNEY.

There was in the neighboring town of Templeville an individual, somewhat ill-bestowed, both by nature and education, who kept the chief apothecary and variety shop thereof. For a long while his chances of success had been rather attenuated, and as his customers were of that class who prefer to do the cheating themselves when any operation of that kind is proposed in a bargain, it had been a source of great wonder and speculation how he could possibly continue in his business, until an ingenious and peripatetic philosopher of the town suggested that he stole his goods. In deep admiration, the entire community became his customers, and the other man who didn't steal his goods was forced to close his establishment. In consequence of this, he had got so far as to be spoken of among certain of the chapel-goers as their candidate for selectman, and was troubled generally with a sense of the grandeur of his growing position, and particularly with an irrepressible desire to excruciate himself and those who listened to him, by speaking in public assemblies, it being literally an unspeakable torture for him.

One afternoon, two or three days after Charles arrived in the family place, this individual was receiving the admiration of one or two others hanging around him at this moment in the hopes of getting a drink of rum in the back-store, when a young lawyer of the town came in to make an unimportant purchase.

"Sir," said the shopman, "you observed—"

"I asked you—Have you got any matches?"

"Yes, sir, we have lately purchased some illuminers of extraordinary and marvellous attraction. They are ingeniously arranged in quadrangular receptacles (consentaneous nods of approval among the admirers), and are of extraordinary and marvellous attraction, on the corruscating friction being applied. You will observe that they lie horizontally with variegated tips, by a delicate arrangement, in the quadrangular receptacles, on the exterior of which they—they have—the thing what you put 'em in."

"What?"

"In quadrangular receptacles—"

"Have you got any matches?"

"Yes. Here are some lucifers—"

"Well, why didn't you say so?"

"Sir, I have the label for authority. As religion is my safeguard, I forgive him," continued he, calmly, and in a low tone to his friends, "and I pity his ignorance."

"An illuminator of extraordinary and marvellous

attraction. They had better put you at once in a quadrangular receptacle too," said the young lawyer. At this remark one of the crowd of admirers was forced to laugh, being a man of humor, though seedy. The Individual gazed with such compressed exasperation and sternness upon this offender that he was compelled to get behind another man and stay there until the wrath of his patron had melted away in the oblivion of its cause.

"Will you speak to-night at the chapel?" said another of the admirers to the proprietor of the shop, feeling uneasy, and wishing to change the subject. "Sech bilins of the blood I had when you addressed 'em the other night. When you were relatin' your experience, and told 'em how many times some of them envious rich old families had lied about you and abused you, and what scoundrels they were otherways towards any one who wasn't rose quite so well as them. I felt as though I would come up and borrow twenty-five cents more of you, jest to get an opportunity to tell you how I liked it. Obadiah Baylon speaks sing'ler, but if any comparison is to be made between him and you, I thinks he speaks worse than you do. His head is sing'ler. I want him to convert the Irish, they are an ign'rant set. Do you know Irish Sal told me I was a nasty beast, and sing'ler to say, she took that occasion to say you was another."

"If you hadn't been a dirty coward, you'd have offered to fight her for it. It may have been true in your case, but you knew she was lyin' about me. This comes of havin' such fellers as you about!" said he, in the simplicity of his grief. (The crowd shrunk back. There was a pause. No rum under this bad humor, which promised to grow.) "Howsever I forgive you now. I know you owe me forty-five dollars, and I can make you pay 'em, but I don't want to have any difficulties with any one. It ain't Christian, and I must feel humble and religers. Ha! who's this," continued he, as an elderly man with a shuffling gait and in thread-bare apparel entered the shop. "It's that old State's-Prison bird who has pretended to be so humble and penitent since he got out. I like to keep these fellers under. It does me good, it makes me feel well," murmured he, either acknowledging that affable weakness of human nature which loves to triumph over a fallen being, or disposed to avenge himself for the affront of Irish Sal in this circuitous manner. "Besides that, the old woman at Punkin Place who has taken him in, will send him away soon enough, and it's good in the end for the shop!"

The expression upon the countenance of the new-comer was a curious mixture of the nobility which sorrow always gives, and the confusion of self-abasement. Noticing the conversation between the shopkeeper and the others, he had attempted with an humble, hesitating gesture, to draw the attention of the former to him.

"I wish to get some lavender," said he, irresolutely.

"Have you got the money?"

A faint blush came over the old man's face, and there was a slight movement of his temples. He replied, "Yes," with a confused laugh, and an affectation at clearing his throat by coughing.

"You see," continued he, suddenly, bowing to the young lawyer, who had lingered on the threshold near him looking idly up the street, "I thought I'd buy some. I want to surprise my daughter My daughter, sir, (straightening himself up pompously at the mention of her name,) is very fond of its odor." The young lawyer thought it was no doubt owing to the fact that man was originally constituted as a social being, and desirous of communicating knowledge, that the old man imparted to him this immensely useful piece of information, as he did not see any other reason just then for it. The stranger now attempted, in a confused manner, and by way of propitiation, a little friendly familiarity with the shopkeeper as he obtained from his hand a small vinaigrette of the delightful perfume. He soon bade him adieu, however, and passing by the young man, bowed to him with that airy politeness which belongs to poverty alone.

"Here, stop! where are you going?" cried the shopkeeper, with an ugly grin at his friends and a scowl at the old man. "What do you bring counterfeit money here for? I've heard of you. Here! bring back that lavender, and go about your business. I don't do that kind of business. Get out."

The other stopped timidly on the threshold of the door. The blood had flushed to the top of his forehead. His lip quivered for a moment, and attempting to smile, he stammered out some humble excuse, when the proprietor continued further, "Here, take your money, and leave. You needn't come here again!" The piece (which was black enough, to be sure, and seemed as if it had lain for a long while in some drawer) fell on the floor as he threw it, with a ring, and the old man was about to call attention to this indication of its genuineness, when he concluded to pick it up and to be the first to offer peace. Here the young lawyer in a low voice, which might have been a sepulchral imitation of some bandit chief with a voice as base as his calling, said to the shopkeeper, "Take the money and give him the lavender!"

The latter looked at the young lawyer in a somewhat surprised and crest-fallen manner, saying, "I was going to all the while. I jest wanted to—" (His admirers were backing towards the door, there being symptoms of trouble). Don't you see!" continued he, in a propitiatory confidence, "I jest wanted to—"

"And you, sir," continued the lawyer, in a lofty manner, turning to the old man, "would do well to take this individual's advice, and keep away from here entirely." The old man hesitated as to whether he should take the lavender or the advice, but he shortly took them both and walked off. And now the young lawyer appeared to be laboring under a fearful increase of internal emotion.

"Boo!" yelled he, suddenly, in startling propinquity to the countenance of the disturber of his feelings. The crowd of admirers in a body fled, panic-stricken, from the shop, post-haste after the constable.

"Oh dear! Really this is sing'ler," said the shopkeeper sorely alarmed, as the young lawyer began fumbling about his head.

"I think I will chastise you," said the latter, seeking once more a dignified and impartial air, and holding the offender by the ear at arm's length, in his abstraction.

"Allow me to explain, I beg," interposed the affable shopkeeper, in a slight delirium. "Oh! you hurt!"

"The eternal fitness of things," said the young lawyer, musing, "as more particularly applied to the quiet grandeur of the social fabric, has been in a measure disturbed. I must put him to bodily torture."

"Oh, dear! let me go."

"The glorious avenger of justice, Nemesis, the great Rhamnusia demands that anguish should be inflicted upon his person," continued the advocate, in rapt abstraction.

"Oh, dear! this is more alarming than ever; oh! He referred to rams. It's somethin' else. I'm not the party—not the party."

"I won't chastise you now. I'll thrash you tomorrow," said the young lawyer finally; "that is, if I haven't any engagements," concluded he, as he released the auricular organ of the confounded shopkeeper.

The mean man rushed in a frenetic manner to a basin, and clapped a wet towel upon the side of his head, while the advocate, with an unruffled demeanor, proceeded from the shop.

CHAPTER VI.

THE OLD MAN AND HIS DAUGHTER.

The aged individual who caused the difficulties into which the unhappy shopman was plunged, was a character who had come to the village three or four years before. Having expended his previous existence in deliriously working out an enigmatic problem—that of his worldly destination, in his old age he had jumped furiously at a conclusion, and found, after all, that he was destined for the State's-prison. He was tried and sentenced for the crime of forgery in New York, adding one more name to the degraded, sorrowful list of criminals in the great metropolis. After some time, spent in the prison, he became quite stupid and foolish. It was remembered, also, that even before his shiftless crime was discovered, he had secretly endeavored, from fright or penitence, to restore some of the money gotten by it, and in consideration of these facts, and of his age, the governor accorded him his mercy.

He went about again in a dull manner, and in his endeavors to obtain employment or a haven from suffering, finally came to this neighborhood. But here also honest people shunned him, and it must be confessed that the noble alacrity in this respect, of the citizens of the district, would have done honor to people in time of a plague. Had they been obliged to have had relations with him, for instance, it would not have been except through the medium of a pair of tongs. Although the negroes, with whom he and his young daughter lodged in an old house away from the village, were always kind to them, to be sure, they were poor enough themselves, and the unfortunate old man and his daughter may have even gone supperless to bed at times. Finally, through the representations of the young girl, who appeared to be quite energetic, Charles's aunt was induced to take them upon sufferance for a day or two, to labor at the Place, and afterwards held them more permanently, but still with the precarious feeling of unreliability. About the time that Charles and his mother arrived, however, the old man had become installed as light-artillery man to the cook and self-constituted gardener, and the young girl had actually worked herself up to the position of alleviator of the arduous occupation of the aunt herself—her chief duties consisting in listening to the conversation of that lady, and showing her appreciation of its circumlocutory style—an occupation, by the way, which promised to turn her head gray in a very short time. In consequence of this glad change in his affairs, the old man was rendered quite flighty, indulging in earnest speeches, to people who were quite uninterested, about the fine character of his daughter, and how they were going now to pay up all debts, and his affairs were going to be arranged, &c.; but alternating this state of mind, however, with fits of melancholy abstraction.

In his labors, it must be confessed, he did more damage than good, perhaps, but it was observable that his daughter generally was successful in correcting his mistakes. They were commencing, then, to live an easy life upon the premises, (perhaps for the first time in their lives,) though they were still looked upon with suspicion and coldness. His history had earned for them the reputation of untrustworthiness, and it seemed also that the girl, young as she was, was already beginning to discover in her manners and expression certain peculiar traits of mingled hypocrisy and boldness. Apparently talented by nature, she seemed disposed to hide her powers in a cunning way beneath an appearance of modesty; although, at times, the very energy of her character made her appear forward in spite of herself.

The old man was engaged, one bright morning, in arranging a bush in the grounds, accompanied by his daughter.

"It is a curious fatality," said Charles to his mother, happening to observe them at the moment from the parlor, "that such people as these are continually getting into our confidence. Do you remember the Italian refugee who taught me a new and inextinguishable accentuation of the French, and then ran away with my wardrobe, leaving a note explaining that he was going to drown himself, and wished to have his corpse appear respectable? It is a wonder that aunt was induced to foster these people; however, as she is treasurer of the Dorcas Society, this may be considered a special deposit, I suppose."

The mother looked up quietly, and her eye rested upon the young girl, who was pausing at the moment from her labors around a little tree. The sunshine struck through the foliage, and fell upon her face and hair, and a peculiar smile rested on her face, in which the observer thought she saw, young as the girl was, indications of a natural mixture of boldness and dissimulation.

"He has a quiet way," continued Charles, who was idly regarding the old man; "I think he might have made a good gentleman, but he is a very poor gardener. By Jove! he is actually pulling up that orange tree from its tub." He went out and accosted the destructive party. "Have a care, don't you see?" said he, sharply.

"I didn't intend—I—was thinking about something else," said the old man, humbly. A painful dream of the past seemed slowly fading away from his face. "Jane will do it, she knows. My daughter can do it better. She won't forget. But you are not going to turn us off, are you?" continued he, with a scared air, "it shall not happen again."

The young girl looked at Charles. She was still resting quietly upon the hoe, with the sunlight in her hair. The look this time indicated submission and curiosity.

"There is no harm done," said she, firmly, and with a smile of confidence.

"Why don't you get James to help you, my girl?" said he to her. (James was a lazy, good-for-nothing youth permanently attached to the mansion, who happened to be, at the time, lying in shady tranquillity upon the barn-floor, engaged in reading, with absorbed attention, that classical work, "The Pirate's own Book.")

"Oh, we can do it. Father likes to have me with him, when I have nothing to do in the house."

"What did he call you Jane for, my girl? I thought your name was Dinah." The old man had commenced to delve, in a great fluster, around another bush a few feet off.

"It isn't Dinah, it is Diana!" said the young girl, familiarly. "You know the goddess was called Jane too, after Janus, the two-faced god. So, father used to call me Jane when I was small, because, he said, whenever he looked into my face, he saw two faces, one looking towards the past, and one towards the future; which made him review the one and hope for the other."

"What—oh yes. So you are a two-faced girl, are you, Jane? Well, it is well to know one's own nature," continued he, carelessly.

She blushed and laughed shortly as she noticed his idea, but there was a quick, proud motion of her head. "And do you remember, sir, what the Romans did when they celebrated the feast of my godmother?" continued she, with earnest rapidity, and almost in confusion.

The store of customs at Roman feasts in Charles's memory was very nearly limited to the agreeable one they had of lying down to feed at them.

"Well, certainly, that is—yes."

"Don't you know, they suspended their prejudice and ill-will towards every one when they mentioned her name? I claim the right of an heiress," said she, laughing bitterly, and blushing together.

Charles felt a new emotion. He had an indefinite impression that she was defending herself and rebuking his slighting idea in quite a delicate manner. He was about to reply, when he suddenly discovered that he had no remark to make which was likely to be satisfactory to himself, and on further reflection he concluded he would betake himself to the house again. About an hour after this it rained in a very disagreeable manner, and the aunt being in the parlor, called to the girl to come to her for a moment. Charles, lying there upon a sofa, was refreshing himself by revelling in rancorous feelings, and silent indulgement of opprobrious criticism, against a poor, inoffensive author, merely because he happened to be popular.

Charles's Aunt. "Dinah, you know the table this way (gesture) in my chamber at the left-hand side of the door as you come out, about half-way across, standing up against that side (gesture) of the room in the middle space between the two windows next to the one nearest this side?"

Charles. "Make a chart! make a chart!"

Aunt, *severely* (on noting the young girl's smile.) "Run, girl, and fetch me my thimble. She doesn't know any thing. She does very well, that is to say, considering the unfortunate life which she has been leading; besides, you know one cannot expect any one to know one's inmost wishes at any moment; and, moreover, her character, of course, is not yet formed. However, those elements which have appeared to me thus far, I am sorry to say, are mostly faults."

Charles looked towards the girl, who was returning. As she walked along, her head appeared upturned towards the portrait of the old pioneer, which still hung upon the walls of Pompney Place, and yet her gaze was bent beneath and towards the aunt. The attitude, for the moment, seemed to him so like that of a struggling fascination, that he almost started up, and yet he laughed immediately at the ridiculousness of the idea. She soon retired, and the aunt, noticing Charles's continued gaze at the portrait, commenced the relation of a great many pleasing anecdotes concerning the descendant, Mr. Pompney, and his eccentricities; as how he used to experience a malignant joy and secret triumph in breaking his own windows, to induce people to believe that the ghosts of his ancestors did it; and how he used, at times, to take into his head other merry freaks, such as pretending to be taken very crazy and imbecile, and insisting upon being led around by his wife, whom, now and then regarding in an unsteady manner, he would accost with, "Hallo! I know you? I've seen you before!"—his wife, whom he had known, married and single, for forty years.

CHAPTER VII.

THE ESPECIAL CONFIDANT OF LAURA'S FATHER.

It was a fair blonde morning, and it seemed as though the soul of nature were visible, when in a pleasant office in the town Mr. Bonney sat before a table with his legs and the papers of his profession thereon, engaged in thought. This young gentleman knew as much law as was safe for him as a gentleman, and practised as much as was safe for his neighbors. He had arrived at that peculiar age of man when the occupation of love is his business, and the practice of his profession his relaxation, and was just then thinking of a young lady lately arrived in the neighborhood, who, he was under the impression, rather preferred him to her bonnet, although his acquaintance with her was as yet somewhat limited. The particular gnomes consecrated by sleep to keep his spirits in repair had also fulfilled so well their work of the last night, and his physical feelings were so buoyant, that he was disposed to cherish the notion on the whole, that the grand scheme of things had not received any detriment when he was taken into it. An ancient buggy attached to an eccentric team, consisting of one tall horse and a short one, came up to the door in a manner evidently intended by the quadrupeds as a sarcasm on the idea of locomotion.

"Good heavens! her parent!" exclaimed the youthful advocate in a suppressed manner, as the occupant came in.

"How are you, Nathaniel?" said the other, saluting him. "Broken your fast early, eh? I knew a man once, who was taking his breakfast one morning, and not knowing the exact time of the day, he—his name, by the way, was Timble—his mother was a Rooter; old Rooter, his grandfather, built a fine residence at Yonkers, which was unfortunately burned the day after it was finished—I knew him well—he rewarded a fireman for his gallantry in throwing his wife out of the window and thus—let me see—he was taking his—no—it was not he—it was—"

"Look here! I say now—excuse me a moment—just keep on in your narrative. I'll be back in half an hour or so," said the young lawyer, rising abruptly.

"Wait! Where are you going? I've got a little business I want to intrust to you," said the old gentleman, with a short stare, and suddenly reverting to the object of his visit. "A little negotiation which I have resolved upon making, and I am led to this step (mysteriously) by some matters which are (chuckling) of a highly delicate nature, but as I know of no person in whom I can confide more implicitly than in you, Nat, I have no hesitation in doing so. I want to purchase the Gosling farms, and I want to purchase them for (coming nearer and whispering with great importance in Nat's ear) for my daughter, eh! By the way, you must come over and see her. However, she is now so devoted to one, she is positively rude to all others in her indifference, Nathaniel. Yes, to her future husband, Nat! Our old friends have arrived at Pompney Place, you know, and this is a wedding present. The young man came especially to propose, and by heaven, he has done it!"

The young lawyer started at the communication of

this intelligence, and was about uttering an exclamation of overpowering lamentation thereat, when he suddenly checked himself, and converted it into one of salutation.

"Good—morning, how are you?"

"I am well. What is the matter? You are not unwell, are you?"

"Not at all," replied the unhappy lawyer, immediately, laughing at the exquisite joke of being thought unwell.

"Well then, I want you to negotiate this purchase for me. You know, if old Mudgeon knows I want it, he hates me so, he'll double the price immediately with the intention of doing the same thing again after I write to him on the subject. I'll tell you a story about him presently (the wretched lawyer looked nervously towards the door to see if it was open)—but I've come over to concoct a plan with you, to delude him into selling it at not over twice what it is worth, at any rate. We've got time, and we can succeed in this, Nathaniel. What a beautiful homestead it will make. What a happy couple they will be. Charles dotes upon her, and she loves him to distraction."

"She doesn't," roared the young lawyer, in sudden excitement. "I deny it and call for proofs."

"What! What the devil do you want proofs for? Don't I tell you she does, in the most devoted manner?" said the old gentleman, pettishly.

"Eh? Well, perhaps it is unnecessary," said the young lawyer, slowly; "but you see it was my legal mind, you know."

"Well—well then—now for old Mudgeon. You must commence by writing a letter to him. I have been thinking of some points. Sit down and write, and I will dictate them. Oh, we'll catch him. It's ingenious."

"Oh, dear, I've lost her before I've got her. I am a kind of premature widower," murmured the advocate, twining his fingers in his hair distractedly. "But no! not even Louis Napoleon or James Buchanan could win her from me, that is, if I had a little start. Devil take Mudgeon!"

The complacent old gentleman was walking up and down, and gazing at a fly to compose his thoughts. "John Mudgeon, dear sir," commenced he, "I hope your family is well, and you still continue in the same God's blessing as heretofore, with the exception, of course, of the lumbago, which we all know you can never recover from." (He's had it so long, he takes great pride in it, and gets his back up on it.) "A moneyed man from New York has just arrived in haste," continued he, in the execution of his wily project, to the young advocate, who was taking down his words in the most distracted manner, and evidently entirely engrossed with his own thoughts—"noting the extraordinary tendency of your lands on the Gosling farms to produce mustard—"

"I shall have a brain fever, if it is so," murmured the other, desperately.

"To produce mustard principally, (that is an idea which is not to be sneezed at, Nat,) desires through me to make proposals—"

("The thought of her marrying him in this sudden way!")

"To go into the business of manufacturing mustard thereon, say for table use, poultices, &c.—Please reply, &c."

("It will drive me to intoxication, I've no doubt of it!")

"That letter will, I think, give him the necessary roundabout emotion to commence with. Here, let me see how it reads," continued the old gentleman. "Why, what is all this! What the devil—what do you mean by this? '*Dear sir, a gentleman of the village, noticing the extraordinary tendency of your farm to produce brain-fevers, desires, through me, to make proposals to marry you and go into the manufacture of mustard poultices on the spot. Please reply, or I shall be driven to intoxication!*' Driven to intoxication! He is inebriated already! Alas! that one so young should be drunk so early in the morning as this. What's the meaning—Perhaps it is—They don't buy that coffee of Wagstaff's, do they, at your house?"

"Eh?" said the wobegone young lawyer, looking at the letter weakly. "You see, my thoughts have been scattered—sitting up with a sick friend—delirium, and all that—I tired myself out handing him toast to eat all night, and lying down on him during the intervals, to keep him in bed."

"Ha! ha! very good; by the way, that reminds me—I knew an elderly man once, who—"

"Hallo! I say," said the lawyer, rousing himself suddenly. "None of that, you know. Hadn't I better write this letter over again at once?"

"Certainly, of course, you attend to it—but do you know, I knew an elderly man once, who—"

"I say," continued Nat, in a lively manner, "give me the points again."

"This elderly man was in just such a predicament, he—"

"Of course I know what to write to him. I can do it during the day. Good gracious! it is time to go up to court. I've got that case—like Richard, scarce half made up and—"

"Certainly. You can ride up in my buggy, Nat.—Well, sir, that elderly man," the old gentleman was about to commence as they took their seats, when the eccentric conduct of the quadrupeds attached to the vehicle fermented, to so high a degree, his spiritual nature, as to render the immediate continuance of the narrative quite impossible. Having evidently come to a previous understanding, they began to amuse themselves at once by backing with great rapidity down the street, and after retrograding for some distance, varying their diversion with little violent runs forward, and sudden facetious stops at unexpected places, together with other brilliant manœuvres of a like equine nature, which, although they were such as were calculated to make a horse laugh, so to say, were, on the whole, improper at the time. Finally, they rushed off at the top of their speed towards their place of destination, and with such a wide difference of opinion with regard to the proper manner of trotting, that it certainly was quite remarkable, taking into consideration their recent unanimity.

Order, however, having been comparatively restored, the old gentleman recommenced the recital of his narrative with such energy and incontinence, that Nat rashly contemplated either throwing himself on his mercy or out of the wagon. Whenever he got into difficulties with regard to facts while torturing Nat with the elderly gentleman, he was accustomed, in the episodical manner of the man with the kettle-drums, to refer to the other and more soul-harrowing subject—his daughter's proposed union with the heir of Pompney Place. Suddenly, however, he raised the young advocate's spirits from the depths of despair to the heights of hope. He revealed to him that it was not quite fixed that the hated rival had already proposed, but it was only that he thought so! So vivacious were the young man's spirits rendered in consequence of this, that the hasty manner in which he made the usual courteous inquiry for the health of the judge who presided over the seat of justice, scared that learned Theban into the belief that he was really unwell.

CHAPTER VIII.

THE DULL YOUNG MAN'S IDEA OF WOMAN'S LOVE.

After dinner, during the sweet hour of twilight, the residents of Pompney Place, with a party from Laura's residence, consisting of two or three sweethearts from Saratoga, attended by some rapid young cladders, were loitering upon the shaven grass, amid the peacocks with their argus-eyed plumage, to inhale the fragrance of the roses already dew-besprent, to watch the shadows deepening o'er the durden, and to gossip upon the season at the watering-places. One of the bevy, following idly the bats as they wheeled in the air in pursuit of the flies, suddenly uttered an ill-suppressed exclamation, as if in answer to some serious thought that weighed down her mind, and bent her brow. Its unusual manner caused a slight movement of inquiry and alarm among the coxcombs who were smoking near by.

Lady, *with a laugh.* "Nothing, I assure you, worth revealing. But simply the shadowiness of the hour inspired me with an absurd revery, of which, of course, I was the mobled queen."

"Oh disclose it to us," said the party, in chorus, gathering around. "Let us have the romance which would contain such a jewel of a heroine."

"My romances are too warm to be frozen into words, but let me give you the predicament of this. Do you know, I thought myself reclining somewhere, with the dusk of melancholy around me, but one whom I loved was at my side, (movement among the gentlemen.) when a velvet bat came down as though to drink its fill from my lips. Suddenly it assumed the lofty stature and form of the evil genius of misery, floating indistinctly on sable pinions, and said in the tones of the concealed Jones in the play, 'The being whom thou lovest have I doomed to misery, if thou dost longer ask his affection. Choose, then, his misery or thine. Wilt thou give him up, or wilt thou doom him to damnation?' What did I reply to the horrid creature, come, guess?"

"You must have replied," said Charles, answering readily, "that you would see him damned (sensation among the bystanders) ere you gave him up, for that is woman's nature. Yes, she loves to be loved better than she loves the being she loves."

"How ungracious!" exclaimed a young lady, vivaciously. 'You do not know woman's nature. Why, I myself feel I could love disinterestedly enough to give up the object of my love, were it for his happiness, but I am quite sure, you know, (naïvely,) that my lover would think too much of me to let me do it."

After a while, the assemblage having retired to the parlor, they floated in the light fairy habiliments of summer, to low purling music in the mazy thread of the dance, and Charles, inspired with the scene, seemed as if he wished to make amends to himself for his opinion of woman's sweet selfishness. With a flush of pleasure on his brow, he devoted himself to the fair girls circling in the graceful rounds of the dance, which so surprisingly develops all that is genial or hopeful in female youth, and became once more the pleasant fellow he was, before he felt the satieties of idleness. But this was no more than a paroxysm. Indeed, even while gayly conciliating the beauty who had brought up the delicate problem of love with the honey of adulation in a secret alcove, she was forced to notice the flatness of his feelings traced upon his countenance.

"I knew it was all hollow," said she. "You are only agreeable when you are a hypocrite, sir. Go and immure yourself in a wine-cellar, and reflect upon the emptiness of the bottles as you drain them slowly, one after the other. But, seriously, you do not seem to be particularly brilliant in the haziness of common and vapid pleasures. Perhaps it is in the sunshine of sorrow, such splendid sunshine as that only, your nature can be seen. Indeed, you appear to be waiting in listless melancholy for some great bereavement. Grief will make you wise."

"Pshaw! I think of turning butcher and slaughtering lambs for excitement," replied he, laughing; "no, it is the—no—by the way, how strange!" continued he, in a wandering manner, but suddenly lighting up, as his eyes happened to rest upon the young girl Dinah, at the other end of the room, who was listening to the aunt in a dignified and apparently self-protecting manner.

"By Jove!" said the young man, suddenly, in a still lower and entirely indistinct tone, "that still attitude! Do you (abruptly to his wondering vis-à-vis) believe in witches?"

"Yes," said the beauty, "whether they are wandering in disembodied spirit, or are animating human tabernacles."

The old maid had spoken sharply to the young girl, having previously given some characteristic direction which she had failed to entirely comprehend. In fact, this young girl seemed destined to undergo with this lady the fate of the beauty in the tale, the trouble of whose existence was an old fairy bothering her continually with fearfully entangled skeins to unravel. However, when she was at liberty, she left the middle-aged fairy with a quick step, and threading her way outside of the dancers, retired from the apartment, while Charles, resuming his conversation with the heiress, indulged in many wicked remarks on various matters, being as desperate with regard to the feelings of others as he was to his own.

Shortly after the departure of the young dependent, the young gentleman, Rudolph, appearing somewhat exhausted by his quadrille enterprises, and fanning himself, wandered mechanically, or as if to take the air, towards the door at which she had departed. Looking around carefully at this point, with an observing regard, he quietly walked out. The girl was proceeding slowly upon the terrace in the shadow of the trees, and on observing him, she at first quickened her step, and then, stopping, leaned against the stone balustrade. The faint odors came up from the fields, and she turned her face from him to the west, and sought the breeze.

"Why do you treat me thus coldly, Diana?" said he, quickly, in a breathing, passionate whisper. "I can make you equal with them. I will take you away from them, if you will but trust in me, and even if your father—"

"Hush!" said the girl, starting quickly.

"Away from this cursed old woman, these miserable—" continued he.

She turned to escape. He followed her as she went from him, when—quick the scene changed again—for as he passed a by-passage-way, his pursuit was brought abruptly to an end by an unpleasant confrontation with a short individual bearing a salver in his hands. This was a young male retainer of the establishment, fated by his tutelary power to produce such collisions. In fact, as he was never found when he ought to be, he made up his deficiency by emerging constantly from unexpected places when he ought not to. The cook, a sinewy and malignant female, was envenomed with a satanic antipathy to this unfortunate young man, and had, in fact, administered corporeal punishment to him that morning. The result was, that even at this moment he was meditating in a vinegary manner upon human nature, and contemplating a general revenge. The young girl had already disappeared, and the gentleman was overcome with passion.

"Out of the way, you pirate," said he. The bosom of the injured Gluckinson swelled again with indignation. "It is not his calling me a pirate," said he to himself, "that I consider a title of honor and distinction, but it is his manner, and I must have satisfaction from somebody, and by heavens, destiny has made the right difference in our sizes. I'm the biggest, I'll follow him, and frighten him. Hollo! you. Hollo!" said he.

"Scoundrel!" said the young gentleman, suddenly turning.

"Eh? oh, don't! Oh dear!" said Mr. Gluckinson, in a feeble voice.

"Sottish mummer!" said the young gentleman.

"I shall be obliged to you for your orders," continued James, fatuously—"perhaps you will take a cream?"

"Get out, you rascal!" said the passionate young man, rushing at him in fury. "Sottish mummer!"

The unfortunate youth, dexterously retaining the waiter of creams upon a level, immediately fled to a distant apartment, and having shut himself securely therein, commenced to relieve himself of his excitement in a philosophical manner, by returning the opprobrious epithets of his enemy in a loud voice through the keyhole or in eating the creams.—The young man, in the mean time, had returned to the saloon. The flush of his countenance had given way to the habitual pallor.

CHAPTER IX.

TWO SYMPATHETIC NATURES.

As Nathaniel approached Squire Wellwood's dwelling on business, for the first time since the advent of the daughter of the house, he observed through the trees some ladies alighting at the door, and in the observatory, upon the top of the mansion, the young lady herself, like another Tanaquil, though merry, calling out to the visitors the state of the establishment within.

"Oh, heavens! There she is! Elevated as she is above the rest of her sex, (especially at the present moment,) who can help loving her? Goodness! she observes my form. That lovely eye—both of those lovely eyes bent upon me," said he, dodging behind a tree, "I feel as if I wanted to go home. This, then, is love! Oh, be still, my heart, and lie down! She is now observing my bearing. She averts her gaze a moment from me, but to revert in memory to the last time she saw me. She is lost in sweet musing," continued he, pursuing his ardent imagination, "now she turns pale —perhaps she falls senseless in the arms of a friend. Dear me!" continued he, after a few moments, as he sat down in a summer chair in the conservatory, which he had gained.

"Good morning," said a sweet, silvery voice. A pair of lustrous eyes were bent upon him. "Papa wished me to welcome you."

"Heavens! I say, you startled me a little, you know, Miss Wellwood!"

"Will you accompany me to the parlor? and papa

will soon meet you. You have dropped your papers, allow Samuel to collect them, Mr. Bonney!"

"Certainly! (While he's doing it, I'll try and collect myself!")

"And, Sam, bring a glass of wine for Mr. Bonney."

"Yes, marm."

"(Goodness! what is this? Fate, in the form of this domestic, has left us alone together. It is a specially dispensed hour. I'll seize the opportunity, and say something ardent to her at once. I must. I'll summon up courage, and express myself in an extraordinary manner.) Miss Wellwood, the momentous occasion has now come when the vehemence of my feelings urges me to ask you—to ask you—ah—how do you do?"

("The vehemence of his—) Oh, very well, indeed, thank you. Will you take this glass of wine, Mr. Bonney? You will feel refreshed by it, after your walk, you know."

"Ah, yes, I am refreshed, indeed, when I drink in the heavenly spirit of those—eh?—of that tumbler, you know." (By heavens, I will ask her to let me write to her, I can do that; they like letters, even if they shouldn't like the man who sends them.) Miss Wellwood, I seize this occasion to ask you if you would receive—that is, if I might send you a—"

"You will send me a—?"

"Yes, yes—that is—you know—I—"

"You will kindly—"

"Yes, yes—a theological work or two from the library, to amuse you, you know?"

"Oh, certainly, certainly, with pleasure! (Theological work? This is singular.")

"Oh, Miss Wellwood!" continued the young man,

in rash precipitancy, urged on by his reflections upon the state of affairs, " although this is the first time that I have had the felicity of having seen you on your own roof —I mean—under your own roof, to be sure—let me ask you—I know you are looking in another direction, and it is what makes me ask, is there, oh tell me, can I feel that there is any prospect here—such as would warrant my coming here frequently, you know ? "

(" A prospect, such as would warrant his coming here frequently ? What does he mean ? He is an infatuated enthusiast of nature !) Certainly, it is very fine, Mr. Bonney ; I was just contemplating it, and I felt as if I would like to be thus engaged forever ! "

(" Heavens ! what unexpected frankness ! She confesses she'd like to be engaged !) But not to me—not to me ! "

(" But not to him ; he does not like the view as it appears to him there.) Ah, it is on your side I find fault with it. The opening there is too great. Don't you think so ? "

(" Oh, the cursed inequality of our purses ! She has already been thinking of me, but objects to the opening on my side ! ")

" I think, on the whole, an abrupt slope would be better, don't you ? "

(" Heavens ! Can she be actually advising me to slope ! and in what singular language, too. My hopes are dashed down. I—I—")

" How are you, Nat ? " asked the old gentleman, bursting into the room at this moment. " The girls are on the piazza, engaged in cat's cradle, and run away, Laura. A letter from Mudg—eh ? I made her come down. Although she seemed to want to in this case, she generally has to force herself into being polite. But you must excuse her, her ardent attachment, you know, and all that. Well, Mudgeon has consented to treat—"

"No, he hasn't."

"What! the dev—"

"No. Presenting his respects to you, he says that it is useless to play that, or any other, game with him; that he contemplates donating the land to the Templeville Association of Reformed Inebriates on their signifying their intention of erecting an asylum thereon, and naming it after him."

"What! Is he going to stick a house full of drunken men, hooting and falling out of the windows all day long, in the midst of gentlemen's residences? I'd like to see him do it, hang him!"

"Wait, we'll find some flaw and scare the Inebriates off, and, being bothered, he'll be glad to sell to us."

"Yes, yes! It is righteous enough to scare him into it, isn't it, provided we pay him twice what it is worth?"

"That is a peculiar point," said Nat; "whether cheating a man into doing himself a favor is in strict accordance with a high moral standard or not, I can't precisely determine."

"Ha ha! it will serve him rightly. I once knew just such an occurrence, or something similar to it—that is, it was not exactly like it. It happened to a man living in—"

"Hold on! Wait a moment—"

"What is the matter?"

"I thought I heard the ladies coming down stairs, and I thought I would warn you to—"

"Of course! certainly. He was living, at the time, in Cayuga—he had a bald head, and five front teeth gone, and—"

"I must go. I think I had better pay my respects to your daughter, and go," continued the wretched Nat.

"Certainly, see her by all means before you go. Sam, call your mistress. Let me see. I believe I said there were five of this man's teeth gone—I was wrong, there were six, which time and hard biscuit had caused to succumb. Well, sir, he—"

The young lady, accompanied by her young friends, sailed graciously into the parlor.

"Look at her!" said the old gentleman, in a low tone to Nat, suddenly remembering his conspiracy with the spinster, and her language in reference to the matter. "Beneath this mask of vivacity, she is hiding a low-lived—I mean—love-lorn pensiveness."

Nat did not hear what he said. He had been practising a concentrated look of melancholy and affection with which he hoped to awaken a responsive thrill in the bosom of the young lady on her return. One of these, at this point, met the old gentleman's gaze.

"God bless me! What a distortion! What is the matter? Bilious?"

"Oh, no," said Nat, feebly, immediately reducing his expression to the elementary smile, and flirting his gaze like a Drummond light around upon the young lady.

("Dear me, his conduct is very singular! At this moment his looks are even idiotic,") said the latter.

("Ah, she murmurs. She is affected. Yes, she observes my sentiment. Oh, now let me confine myself to little quiet allusions in the conversation. I've been too precipitate."

The young ladies to whom Nat was introduced here commencing a sprightly altercation upon the gossip of the day, he rattled with them, though in found thought devising a beautiful and deep-laid turn.

"We students of legal lore are singular, ladies," said he, at a propitious moment. "We are enabled often to think of three or four things at once."

"Yes! and how many are you grasping now, Mr. Bonney?" asked the unsuspecting ladies.

"Ah!" said the wily counsellor, "can you consider the countless diversities of a perfect character. Thus many, though they be lost in its loveliness as the blessed stars are in the daylight, do I think of now, for I am thinking of—"

"A miserable scoundrel, that Mudgeon," said the old gentleman, who was meditating apart upon the intractable Mudgeon's message.

("Her looks confuse me. I don't dare to say it)—and—and do I think of now!" concluded the wavering young man.

("What eccentricity," reflected Laura. "Can that glass of wine have mounted to his head? His looks are singular, and his remarks are incomprehensible and)—Pardon me, Mr. Bonney, do you not find that this habit of entertaining so many ideas at once sometimes produces a confusion in their communication?"

"Eh?" said Nat, slowly. "Well, perhaps it does. (Any how," reflected he, consoling himself, "this failing is no worse than its opposite, that eminent characteristic of the female sex, of having a great power of communication, and no ideas to call for its use.")

"But I hope you will not consider that I shall entertain a less opinion of your profession on that account, Mr. Bonney," said Laura, laughing. "Indeed, as human beings—that is, the most of them, you know—they are entitled to our good will and respect."

"When does the ball of the Lancers take place?" lisped a young lady hanging on Laura's arm, and making eyes at Mr. Bonney. "Will the regiment dance in unison a new war-hornpipe expressly invented for the occasion by the drum-major? How curious it will be."

"Very good—very good," joined in the old gentleman, recovering his equanimity at this point; "that reminds me of a legend of what a band of intoxicated Mohawk warriors did once. You see," continued he, complacently following the party toward the piano, one of them having accepted Mr. Bonney's sudden proposition to execute the latest fantasia—"these warriors having come across a white man wheeling a barrel on a wheelbarrow in the forest—they—that is—I think it was a barrel—they—"

"Oh, I'm going. I must go to my office, ladies," said Nat with some symptoms of ferocity.

"Eh?" said the old gentleman, staring at him. "Well, I'll go too. You can go on Thomas, and I on Timothy. We'll go around by the Gosling farms—it is shady," continued he, resolving, like Shehrazade, to postpone his story for a short period.

Nat resignedly followed the old gentleman, for the sudden conviction that he had certainly made an alteration of some kind in his position with the young lady, made him feel as if he could cheerfully endure any amount of torture. In the easy moments of conversation as they went along in the leafy winding road, having forgotten the drunken warriors, the Squire proceeded to observe that the intensity of passion on the part of his daughter, shown towards Charles, was hereditary, and derived from the paternal side of the house, and that this mutual love was fortunate, as they had made up their minds on the match when they were babies, (he and Charles's father,) and farther, that he had often speculated upon the possibility that some other person might attempt to win the affection of his daughter, and that, upon such an hypothesis, the painful necessity had always occurred to him of removing such person from his earthly sphere of action by a lingering species of torture.

"I should consider it my duty to tie him before a slow fire. I would, by Heaven! What business would the sacrilegious wretch have to steal in and interrupt sacred arrangements?"

"But supposing she loved him, and didn't the other, I don't see how the arrangements would be sacred," said Nat. "On the contrary, I should say they would be damnable and—"

"Oh pshaw! It is not love that is the important element in these matters. It is very well, but the family arrangement is the thing. These marriages of inclination without the family arrangement are disastrous. Roast butterflies for dinner, and nothing else!"

CHAPTER X.

MASTER AND SERVANT.

At the breakfast table one morning, Charles expressed an unseemly irreverence for the memory of the venerable and world-honored Christopher, stating with an aggrieved air that if it had not been for the mischievous and overweening curiosity of that navigator, it would have been his lot, in all probability, to have been born in France or Russia, or some other country where, as conspirator, perhaps, he might now be enjoying himself and disturbing the government. All of which was very ingenious. Having indulged in a few other pleasantries of a like doubtful nature, the restless young man, (who, if he had been born a blacksmith, would have been happy enough,) with the dissatisfaction of idleness in his soul, sauntered away in melancholy stupidity to hear the noble laugh of nature in cheerful solitudes, and still green chancels amid the lofty forests.

Emerging from the civilized groves of his father's estate, he plunged into a thick forest of lofty pines, where scarce a single ray of sunlight penetrated the intertwined branches, and after pursuing a winding road, he came to a little gloomy apartment of thickening verdure where, seated upon a rustic seat made by a fallen tree, he listened for a long while to the songs of the chatterboxes in the neighboring thicket with a new, exalted sense of breathing freedom. His heart swelled within him as sweet nature caressed him, and smiled upon him, and pressing his own hand in lonely pleasure, he rose once more to pursue his way through the maze of verdure, breathing the fresh air and the delicious odors of the tangled wild, and struck with the low sound of the distant waterfall. Some way off in the thicket, as he walked along, a clear boyish voice, in a slow song, fell upon his ear above the tinkling water. The accents were bright, but there seemed a kind of sadness in them. He reflected that the song ought not to have been such. It made him nervous. Soon, however, it degenerated into a careless whistle. "He is coming this way. I'll put myself in ambush," said he, "and scare the little fellow as he comes up. It will make him brave," and he stooped amid the bushes. The rustle of the parting branches was soon heard near by, and he jumped out, like a lazy tiger from the jungle, upon the comer.

"Eh! what," said he, surprised himself. The girl Dinah stood in the attitude of defence before him, holding a basket firmly in front of her, which she had placed there instinctively. The blood was mantling her cheek. "I beg pardon," said he. She had now recovered herself, however, and bowed to him with a decorous obeisance.

"Where is the boy?" said he.

"What boy?" asked she.

"The boy who was whistling."

"It was only a tom-boy. It was I," said she, laughing.

"I recollect now, it seemed like your voice. Where have you been?"

"I have been to the house where I used to live. I thought I would gather some blackberries as I came back to present them to—to your mother."

She looked like the blooming child of the genius of some bygone summer, who had inherited her parent's old clothes, and her sylvan place of haunt in these leafy woods. She wore a dress of faded green silk, but it fitted neatly to her person, and fell in graceful folds.

"Will you have some of the blackberries?" asked she.

"No," replied he, after looking at her for a moment. His tone was low and gentle. "You are going home, are you not?" continued he, after a moment, with an indolent gesture. "Yes! Well, I was going the other way."

"Good-morning, sir," said she, respectfully. "There is a large path by the beech yonder, leading towards the lake. If you desire to go that way, it is easier."

"Stay a moment. What made you whistle?" asked he, having nothing better to say, and evidently wanting to say something.

She blushed a little, and laughed. "I was, like Cymon, sir, in the greenwood shade."

"Well, perhaps, it was better to whistle that song than to sing it in the way you did," said he. "It sounded to me very like a Methodist hymn."

"It's a love-song. I learned it of Judith," continued she, with a slight air of abstraction; "a colored girl we lived with. She has the religious nature which characterizes her race, and I suppose we both give it a camp-meeting air, without knowing it."

"Judith, a colored—a servant once—a—"

"Oh no. She is my friend. We do not know many people living here, besides those at your home, sir," and she drew herself up with a proud air and left the sentence unfinished.

A feeling of pity for the young girl, whose sorry circumstances had forced her to take a negro for an intimate (as girls must have intimates) took possession of him. Were her thoughts and desires restricted to a degree which such a companionship alone would indicate? From motives of curiosity, he continued the conversation.

"Well, you say," resumed he, "that she is your friend. Do you think she is capable of appreciating your friendship?"

"No. She treats me as her superior, because I am white—but"—she paused again, as if what she were about to say, might be perhaps uninteresting to her master. With a kind of coquettish carriage she started up to go, but still hesitated and lingered again. Upon the French principle of fraternity in the human family, she was no doubt thinking she would continue the conversation with him a little longer. She was holding the basket of berries against her frock with both hands, and underneath an air of sadness as she stood thus, there yet appeared in her manner a constitutional kind of firmness, as though poverty and misery could never change the serenity of her mind.

"Shall I hold the basket?" said Charles. Just then he asked himself if he would be inclined to Laura, were she as poor and inferior in station, for instance, as this girl. "It is all in position. There is no nature about it, of course, except that," said he. He sighed audibly. There was something disturbing his soul all the time. His dissatisfaction increased, and leaving her abruptly, he pursued a careless reflection as he wended his way in the wood by himself.

CHAPTER XI.

THE SOCIAL HOUR.

A LARGE party was gathered to dine that evening at the house. Among others, were two wits from New York, to give it an intellectual tone. They both appeared with a dull air, each evidently oppressed with the weight of his own reputation and overcome with a melancholy fear of the other. The company, especially the literary part of it, however, were in a constant state of pleasing expectation of a great encounter between these wretched beings, and Dr. Fuffles, the clergyman of the neighborhood, kept his eyes upon one of them in such a continued manner, as to engender in his mind an apprehension of bodily injury.

"It has been a fine day," said this unhappy creature, after a few moments, to the other wit.

"Yes, but rather too warm," said the latter, imbibing his soup noisily, with an undefined intention of protecting himself.

"Ha!" whispered Dr. Fuffles, to his next neighbor, Laura, "he already evinces satire. The encounter will commence presently."

"Oh, how I love Sir Walter Scott, dear Sir Walter!" said Charles's aunt, suddenly after a pause, to start the literary air.

"I detest him, ma'am. I detest his works. I can't bear to have them mentioned!" said Mr. Pithkin, a large gentleman seated at her side.

NATHANIEL. "Are there any particular works you have reference to, Mr. Pithkin?"

MR. PITHKIN. "Oh, no. I can mention no particular work, sir, no particular work. I detest them all so much I have never been able to read any of 'em."

"But Byron! Mr. Pithkin, oh!" said the aunt, turning in poetic abstraction to him,

> 'Know'st thou the land where the cypress and myrtle
> Are emblems of deeds that are done in their clime?"

PITHKIN, *promptly*. "No, ma'am."

At this point, the wit who had the biggest reputation for saying ill-natured things, having finished his fish, evinced suddenly a great internal excitement. Leaping high into the air, (that is, metaphorically,) with a frisky curvet and caracole, he came down in a rebounding swoop, and immediately thrust a fearful witticism at the second wit. This party of the second part was taken unawares. Feeling that something had passed through the moral centre of his intellectual universe, a convulsive and idiotic smile passed over his countenance. He said nothing just then, but, no doubt, had an intention of doing so after a moment or so. This assault caused a temporary hush in the conversation. In a moment, however, easy and more common-place ideas commenced their pleasant riot therein, and, indeed, kept agreeable possession thereof till the dessert —each one talking to his neighbor, as he ought to in successful dinner-parties, and no one listening, in a highly natural manner. At this point, however, Dr. Fuffles suddenly concluded to cough with such startling deliberation, that the attention of the entire company was called to him. Having finished, that morning, a sermon for the coming Sunday, which treated of some exquisite metaphysical subjects, he deliberately intended to give them a few pages in advance, at that time, and on the spot. Without swerving from his purpose, he instantly commenced, and the whole table listened, bowing their ears in respect for the man, or cowering with fear of the subject, while he called to the trembling mastery of the assembled minds those severe and commanding thoughts which, when they do come, seem to stalk forth, as it were, like majestic ghosts from the recondite shades of metaphysical speculation. And particularly did he commence to refresh himself by inviting from the dwelling-place of the unknown, through the chaste corridors of his idiosyncrasy, those noble tyrants of speculation, the conceptions of the cause, the absolute, and the infinite.

"The cause as such," said the attenuated gentleman, with an inspired air, and looking sternly at Mr. Pithkin, in order to collect himself, "exists only in relation to its effect—the effect being an effect of the cause. On the other hand, the absolute implies a possible existence eternally out of all relation, though it may paradoxically be said that it exists first by itself, and afterwards becomes a cause. But here we are checked by the mysterious elements of the infinite, which are contained in it, and I ask: How can the infinite become that which it was not from the first?"

"You have me there," said Mr. Pithkin, under the impression that the doctor directed his remarks towards him.

"If causation," continued the doctor, as if in rapt inspiration, "is a possible mode of existence, (this proposition the exercised Pithkin assented to with alacrity,) then that which exists without causing is not infinite; that which becomes a cause has passed beyond its former limits. But a limit is itself a relation, and to conceive a limit as such, is virtually to acknowledge the existence of a correlative on the other side of it." In this pleasant manner did a great metaphysical contest of thoughts take place, which resulted, as usual, in all the ideas being left dead upon the field.

"I don't know—I can't say," said Mr. Pithkin, feeling it absolutely necessary to say something in reply, "that is—if you should—do you know, (bursting,) it isn't peculiar to me, perhaps, but somehow or other I am generally at a loss to express myself when I haven't any thing to say."

"You say you can't express yourself," said Laura's father, eagerly jumping at the opportunity, as Pithkin paused, "you said you couldn't express yourself, I believe. Well, that reminds me of a man once, who—"

"But he didn't say so," exclaimed Nat, violently; "he didn't say he couldn't express himself."

"Well, perhaps he didn't," said the old gentleman, hanging on persistently, "but anyhow, it reminds me of a wealthy man once in New York, who never went out of his house but once in twenty years. It had cost him so much, he was obliged to stay continually in it, in order to make it pay. Well, that once, when he emerged from his domicile, finding himself expressed, as it were, across the threshold by the toe of his brother's boot, he turned for one startled moment, and said: ''Tis well! I now feel my end to be'—that, is, he said —I feel—dear me, let me see—I think he—"

"Heavens!" said Nat, "I say, the ladies are going to the parlor."

The ladies had risen and were immediately followed by Mr. Pithkin, Dr. Fuffles, (who accompanied his ancient dame, Charles's mother, with downcast eyes,) and one or two others. Pithkin, having been distracted between his desire to stay at the table, and to pay a slight homage to the maiden aunt—Bacchus pulling on one side, and Venus on the other—had resolved to go, having previously promised the old gentleman (in whose story he had exhibited extraordinary symptoms of being interested) that he would return as soon as the fair lady would permit him. But unfortunately, after the coffee, being filled with poetic desires, she commanded him to attend her on a walk in the wooded avenue. A fine air was being played by a young girl in the saloon.

"Mysterious odors," said the aunt, overcome with her poetic feelings and the fragrance of the summer night, as they walked along, "from heavenly depths are wafted in the evening air."

Pithkin murmured something about having taken cold, and being unable to smell any thing.

"In the vortex of human passions, Mr. Pithkin, we, wretched, gasping creatures, vainly grasp at the fragile waifs that are whirling in the fearful maelstrom," continued the poetic being.

"Ma'am?" said Pithkin. He eyed her suspiciously. He didn't know but what she intended to faint, or ask him to support her, or do something of that sort. However, as she confined herself to the poetic exaggerations of speech merely, until they reached a summer-house near the western wall of the park, he became reassured, and concluded it to be safe to comply with her request and sit down by her there. Night was closing down—the evening star was glistening in the west, and a little crescent piece of the moon was casting a small light over the trees. A faint sound of music from the house committed burglary on their attention.

"What Protean shapes," said the languishing lady,

reverting to the dinner-table, "does the human intelligence assume; now the bright, gay, gleaming, falchion of wit, now the ponderous, massive, battering-ram of reason."

"Yes," said Mr. Pithkin, "and I think wit is preferable to reason, but it is more difficult. Do you know, I am continually inventing smart sayings; but, somehow, they are not appropriate to the occasion."

At this moment a rustle was heard in the immediate vicinity behind the summer-house. In the gloomy shade of night, they saw the indistinct form of a stranger standing perfectly still, and looking severely at them.

"Oh dear—what is that—that strange"—exclaimed the maiden, timidly.

Pithkin was so much overcome with his own apprehensions at this apparition, that he had no leisure to attempt to dissipate hers. With a sacred care of personal interest, in fact, he was about to take refuge in flight to the house, when the singular cause of his fears suddenly disapeared.

"Ha! ha! stealing fruit," said Pithkin, with leonine boldness at this juncture. "He's leaped over the wall. He thought to intimidate us by looking severely at me —the poor devil—actually thought to intimidate us!"

"But did you remark his splendid nose, Mr. Pithkin? He has got the nose of a gentleman I once knew —Heaven, is it the—Pshaw—no—"

"You don't mean to say he's got somebody else's nose?"

"Yes! While, all around it, his other features seemed to be the gloomy home of dark and fearful passions, it seemed to me to have a noble, tranquil expression."

"Yes, like a small mountain in quiet grandeur. It is a wonder it wasn't sinister too, it had got into such bad company. It was rather laughable, his attempting to intimidate us, wasn't it? Ha! ha!"

"Oh dear!"

"Wha—what's the matter?"

"He's coming back."

"Gods of heaven! the proprietor of the nose?" exclaimed Pithkin. Through the trees in the dusk, he turned his dismayed vision, and beheld the singular stranger leaning up coolly against the iron railing of the park on the road, as though he lingered to finish some improper mission, which had brought him first within the park.

"Wha—what if he should attempt to knock us down and rob us? We are away from the house," said the panic-stricken Pithkin. "Oh, dear! He has been watching for us! Oh Lord! my legs refuse to do their duty. Shout for help! Help!" cried he, faintly.

"Never mind. Oh, dear! He's gone again. I'm so thankful. He has disappeared again."

"Eh? Lord bless me! So he has!"

"Oh, what a narrow escape!"

"Ha! Yes, a narrow escape he has had, indeed," continued the valorous Pithkin, with a frightful air. "As it is, I've a great mind to run after him, and catch the rascal."

"Oh, no! I know your ardent love of justice, Mr. Pithkin, but don't—don't expose yourself in its cause; I pray you don't, for my sake."

Pithkin concluded on the whole he wouldn't for his own, and further accepted with alacrity the proposition of the lady, to return at once to the house. They reached the saloon in safety, Pithkin now and then blenching slightly at indistinct objects on the path. On arriving at the house, he felt quite sorry that he hadn't chased the rascal, knocked him down, and brought him in, tied hand and foot. They found the dance in progress. The young lawyer, Nat, was seated in a window, with a ferocious expression on his countenance, and Charles was floating in a waltz with Laura, with a strange feeling in his head, the result of accumulated rotation, while the young lady herself with a bright, gay air was now and then glancing at the unhappy lawyer as she turned. "Think of his audacity and familiarity with me, as if he had known me fourteen years and a day," said she to herself. "I have danced with him five times already, and he wants to come and ask me again. I just wish he would do it."

Nat, while laboring under an intense desire to punch somebody's head, was entertaining the father of his hope, by listening in wretched desperation to another intricate anecdote, which the latter was proceeding to unfold at leisure.

"Oh, such a singular adventure," said the fair spinster, rushing up and relieving the distracted lawyer. "Oh, such an adventure; indeed, a narrow escape from the jeopardizing purposes—yes—of some lawless person. Do you know, in walking with Mr. Pithkin to breathe the refreshing air, we had reached the end of the park, when I cast my eyes about me and discovered, in the foliage near me, a sight which made my blood curdle—I saw a young man—"

"Singular effect which youth has upon the imaginative female," murmured Pithkin; and the fair enslaver continued to embellish the adventure. She had reached the point where she said "he had overskipped the wall with one bound, encroaching in his sky-rockety transilience upon the bright ray of the star which hung down lowest," when the inevitable parent of Laura was unfortunately struck with its resemblance to another occurrence he had once heard of—"It reminds me of two young miners in California," commenced he, precipitately, "surrounded in their lonely cabin with bears. One of them was so overcome with his fears that he temporarily lost his reason, and expressed it as his opinion that the only way that they could save themselves was to take their razors, and by a close shave they might do it. In the mean time the bears had got into the kitchen, and one of them was carrying off the cooking stove, another singular circumstance, when the courageous miner in a moment of great exasperation—in a moment—he—let me see—he—"

Mr. Pithkin had cast his eyes accidentally upon the portrait of the old pioneer. "Gods of heaven! what—see you not a resemblance?" he suddenly ejaculated—"Was it—"

The spinster interrupted him with pettish quickness, and taking him by the arm walked away, followed closely by Nat, who in desperation took this chance of evading the two miners. Charles still lingered in the reflecting position in which he had heard the occurrence related by his aunt.

"I don't want him for a son-in-law," said the old gentleman, looking at him after floundering a while. "He listens with such confounded attention he puts me out. I'll go find Nat again."

CHAPTER XII.

UNREST.

The ladies and gentlemen, the next morning, projected a drive to a secluded wood in the vicinity, called the Dark Woods, the depths of which were celebrated in the traditions of the neighborhood as having once constituted a favorite council-chamber of the aboriginal tribe which occupied this region. It was represented that one charmed and romantic spot, in particular, was still haunted by their spirits in solemn assemblage on still summer days, and that this Indian senate-house was still guarded with sacred jealousy by those ghostly people, from the intrusion of earthly feet. People who thought of going there were continually losing their way, or were prevented by other and more mysterious accidents and obstacles from accomplishing their object. Persistent mortals, in a few instances, had found their way thither; but even on these occasions they were immediately driven away by insects in the form of musquitoes, whose supernatural size and unearthly power led them at once to believe that their presence was considered, and thus resented, as an intrusion. The party then derived its principal interest from the fact of their making the essay to visit this place.

While they were awaiting, in groups, the disposition of the equipages, the aunt said to Dinah, "should Mr. Charles soon return, inform him of the picnic, girl. Perhaps he will come. Oh dear, by the way, does he know the road, I wonder, to be sure! It is very intricate. Let me see. First we went along the country road, and then I remember we passed a stage-coach, just beyond which, we turned off upon a branch road, leading down that way (gesture) from the same side of the main road which we were on—the stage-coach being on the other side—yes—yes—you give him the directions, Dinah. Oh what a romantic place it was," continued she, addressing a young exquisite. "I remarked to Mr. Pithkin, who was driving my buggy, it was such a relief to the artistic eye, that no more infants were to be seen making dirt pies as on the high road, and he replied, he thought so too, alluding further to the fact that they had thrown stones at us in a very disagreeable manner, you know, and with considerable force, indeed. While progressing through this romantic scene, and enjoying the exquisite emotions which it produced, we came to a small and dark-flowing rivulet, when a singular and dangerous obstacle met our vision, could you think it? Indeed, the sudden revolution which it caused in my feelings will never be obliterated from my fadeless memory. On the rustic bridge which crossed the stream amid the dark still scenery, there was standing a gigantic and solitary animal of the bull species in an apparently infuriated condition. At first he shook his horns violently, and accompanied those motions with low, sinister rumblings; but as we approached, however, a singular change came over him, indeed. He became suddenly quiet, and the occupation of staring at us in a dull, steady manner appeared at once to have absorbed all his faculties. I was about remarking to Mr. Pithkin that it was certainly singular, when turning very pale, he hastily exclaimed, 'Oh dear! he's shutting his eyes. He is going to make a rush.' Fortune favored us. We had just time to turn around when it took place. He chased us for over a quarter of a mile, with fearful snorts, and with his tail curled on high in a singular manner, like a corkscrew, for instance, and we were momentarily expecting to be dashed in pieces by the infuriated animal, until he suddenly disappeared. Mr. Pithkin said it was a narrow escape from a gloomy extinguishment. He was so overcome, that he ate up all the luncheon, and drank up all the wine, before his spirits were restored, and as that was the chief enjoyment he expected from our visit, we concluded to go back." (Sensation on the part of her listener. "Haw! by Jove, haw!")

The party, after an intricate winding, in which Nathaniel Bonney, who had been constituted the guide, led them off eleven times in a wrong direction, finally concluded to rest under the shade of some lofty trees near a milestone on an old deserted road, which ran along by the dark forest. Here it was recommended they should refresh themselves with luncheon, Laura having proposed, however, that their leader, whose enthusiasm respecting the discovery of the place, she remarked would make up for his want of knowledge respecting its locality, should occupy a previous half-hour in essaying the discovery of the romantic council-chamber, by penetrating the wood on foot. Nat, having a presentiment, suggested that they should eat the lunch first. In the ardor of the morning, he had forgotten his breakfast, and even now, in spite of love, experienced the cravings of hunger; but as Laura appeared to discountenance the proposition in a somewhat severe manner, he proceeded immediately to take the most expeditious method he knew of to find the place, by losing himself at once in the wood with a resigned air. In less than ten minutes after he had set out, he became entangled in such a wonderful and complicated maze of verdant tangled wilds, that even at this early stage of his search, the chances of ever extricating himself suggested themselves to his mind as exceedingly attenuated, and the farther he went the more confused he became.

After half an hour had elapsed, he at last encountered a cow-path, which led in an extraordinary and bewildering manner nowhere—that is, he was astonished to discover that by following its tortuous course, he was continually arriving at the same singular spot. The pangs of appetite were now beginning to manifest themselves in an unpleasant way, and he endeavored, as he continued desperately to career in the charmed circle, to fill up by dint of intellectual enjoyment the void which began to make itself felt in the flesh. Amusing speculations, for instance, upon the power of the human organization to exist without food, suggested themselves to his mind, and he recalled with an indefinite feeling of satisfaction at this point, several notable shipwrecks on desert coasts, in which that power had been assisted in an extraordinary manner, by the judicious use of buttons and berries.

Before he had reached this mysterious spot, he had endeavored to convey intelligence of his situation to his party or arrest the attention of any one within hearing, as simple holloing did not appear to do it, by organizing an ingenious system of sounds, calculated by their peculiarity to attract observation; such, for instance, as groaning in one direction, snorting up another, sneezing up another, &c. But all was silent, with the exception of the sounds of nature, and time was rapidly wearing away. He sat down under a blackberry bush, and under the influence of his appetite commenced deliberately to dine. He had reached the dessert, which consisted, as usual at that season of the year, of blackberries, when he heard voices. His party had instituted a search for him? No. The voices were low and strange, and came he knew not from where. Was he near the charmed spot in which the ghostly Indians were holding their noonday council? There seemed to be a dull cadenced interlocution of voices, which he fancied to be the distant argumentation of the chiefs, while he thought he could hear the steady murmur of approval from the ghostly crew. Perhaps the latter, however, was nothing more than the sound of the blue-bottles buzzing in the shade. By and by stillness reigned. Gracious, what was that? In the gauzy distance under the trees he saw two heads gliding along at first in Indian file, and then in silent divergence. He had barely time to conceal, from instinctive motives, his somewhat excited being in the thicket which formed the sides of the little hall through which the path ran, when a tall, lithe young man of extraordinary, wonderful beauty, yet half-attired in torn and earth-stained linen, passed by him, brushing his way through the thicket. On his countenance were marked the lines of melancholy and dissipation, but in his eyes, though beneath a still and fixed gaze, the fire of a wildness was burning with a deep lustre.

"Come, oh come to me from your grave! These woods are ours!" muttered he, as he passed the astonished Nat, who crouched impulsively. On his hand, which he held, in a mechanical manner, to his bare breast, was a wound, and upon his breast also, by his hand, another bleeding wound, as if freshly made in passing the thick branches of the way in which he came. "Oh, can you come no more? Yes, yes. In her dear love you live. With her dear love shall I be saved!"

Nat, in his confusion, allowed him to disappear in the thick wood, and the noise of his receding he had hardly noticed, or it had died away ere he had recovered from his astonishment at this singular interruption of the still hour. Curiosity, however, soon took its place in his bosom, and he commenced to pursue rapidly the direction which the mysterious stranger had taken. "Some extraordinary loafers loafing extraordinarily! This one looks like an escaped bedlamite. I will find out, if I can catch him." But, unfortunately, he became once more entangled again in a series of most extraordinary and inextricable labyrinths of thorns and branches.

It was late in the evening when he emerged mournfully upon the road in his drawers, and he felt, at least, a firm conviction that whatever supernatural power reigned in that gloomy thicket, it was exorbitantly jealous of the approach of human beings.

On observing that the absence of the young lawyer was seriously prolonged, the ladies, at the suggestion of Laura, joined together in commanding a search by the rest of the gentlemen, who immediately obeyed. They all succeeded in coming in, to be sure, within two or three days, in a straggling manner, representing themselves to have been pretty busy during that period in thrashing about in the wilderness. There was one exception, however—the exquisite from New York, who had not been educated to such matters. He was never heard of. Some time afterwards, indeed, it was represented that he was seen in the metropolis in a state of great disgust whenever the romantic wilds of the country were mentioned; but the rumor, as a fact, was not considered reliable. The result of this forest visit, then, was that the ladies rode home alone.

Charles did not return from his solitary ride until after noon, for he had purposely avoided the picnic. As he walked up on the terrace and towards the saloon, he heard the bronze clock with its angels ticking upon the mantel-piece. A low, gentle song from female lips, was also marking, with its measured beats, the flying time. He stole rapidly to a window, and, concealed by the curtain, looked within. The song had stopped, and its maker, the young girl Diana, was idling about in the airy room with indecisive steps. By and by, she sank down into the cushions of a sofa with the graceful, yet awkward jump which girls who are not done growing, are likely to make. Here, after a few apparent moments of meditation and abstraction, he saw her take from her bosom a worn and common-looking miniature, and at that moment he was struck by the singular look which quickly passed over her countenance. The locket, by some eccentric law of association, had, perhaps, brought up in her mind for the moment the instinctive appreciation of her own unhappy condition, accompanied, probably, with the usual inimical bitterness which natures, no matter how young, when steeped in poverty or degradation, feel towards the laws of society, which, they think, first cause that poverty or degradation, and then punish it. However, it seemed so peculiar, that it brought out in the young man's mind, for the instant, the romantic fancy that some ancestor of her's, hundreds of years ago, had suffered so much as to bequeath to his posterity an unfailing liability to those lines of anguish.

She looked again at the locket, however, with apparently about as much interest as one would who was estimating its value, and, although the reflection may have been wrong which he was induced to make, in the vacancy of the moment upon this action, and upon the mechanical manner in which she conveyed it to her lips, he, nevertheless, would have derived no other impression from the whole, than that her nature was one of those which are undemonstrative in their tendencies, even had he observed the tear which dropped and glistened upon the locket, as she placed it again in her bosom. Casting his eyes fortuitously upon the broad mirror above the mantel-piece, he observed the eyes of the image of the girl resting directly upon him in an unconcerned glance. This immediately induced him to reflect that she had been aware of his propinquity all the while, and, with that sentimental artifice to which young girls are naturally prone, had thus affected a delicate show of private emotion in his concealed presence for the sake of creating a favorable impression.

Although somewhat disconcerted with the thought that he had been discovered in an equivocal position, he was still pleased with the consciousness which these rapid reflections and the contemplation of the position of their object afforded him—that his mind was beginning once more to search in its old natural way of simple philosophical interest, for the springs of human action. The girl rose and gave him a profound bow as he entered the window, and he was forced to notice immediately its peculiar grace. Whatever was inherently betrayed in it, it seemed further to be characterized both by the grace of childhood, and the dignity of womanhood, as if it were an indication that the soul within, in its transition from one of these epochs to the other, was retaining the good of the past, while it usurped that of the future.

"You were singing," said Charles, as the girl hesitated to leave the room; "can you play the piano and accompany your voice?"

"No! when I sing, I usually accompany myself with a broomstick," said she, with a laugh.

"You scorn accomplishments, do you?" said Charles, forgetting her antecedents.

"Oh, no! If I had known how to play the piano well, I would not have answered you as I did."

Her true position struck him here, and he asked himself what she would have been, had she been brought up with all the advantages of the higher classes of society. Without doubt, like all the rest of her sex moving therein, she would have not only entertained a supercilious contempt for the plodding duties of domestic life, but, like the rest of them, she would have put off the uses of her intellectual abilities too, and, falling into the aristocratic female's habit, (which has become a fixed system of flattering the understanding of the other sex, by carefully avoiding the use of her own,) would have soon reached the much-desired position of plaything. Women forget that those are men undeserving of the name, who are under the necessity of listening to such a concession.

"As you really don't know any thing about these accomplishments, you were certainly wise enough in affecting humility," continued he jocosely.

"The wise way of affecting humility is to acknowledge deficiency in something which we are rather notorious for possessing, isn't it?"

"Then you mean to say you are a master of music already! another St. Cecilia?"

"Oh, no! I was only showing that, while I have the vice of affecting humility, I have not even the usual wisdom which accompanies it."

"But you know how to dance well?" The graceful way in which she sat still had discovered that to him.

"No; but oh, sir, I am so delighted to see the dance!" said the girl, in vivacious forgetfulness.

"Your education has been neg—" said Charles, "I beg your pardon; I didn't mean to—" He reflected that he had again forgotten entirely her position and antecedents in talking with her.

"Oh, sir," said she, interrupting his thought ere it was half expressed, "you have done me honor in thinking I might worthily bear these accomplishments, while you forget they were debarred from me."

At this point, the clatter of the horses' hoofs and the roll of the carriages were heard—the party were coming up the avenue on their return. The mother noticed that Charles had already returned from his visit to Dr. Fuffles, and Laura, with a soft air, found fault with him for not having come to the greenwood.

CHAPTER XIII.

CHARACTERISTICS.

Some time after the party had left, the house was again enlivened by the arrival of two friends, a Southern gentleman and his wife, accompanied by seven colored servants, who, by the way, were continually quarrelling upon the proper partition of their duties. If two, for instance, were engaged in lifting a trunk, one of them, feeling aggrieved at the manner in which the other managed his end, would deposit his, and relieve his feelings at once by kicking him. However much they thus contended with each other upon the particular offices to which destiny had elected them, upon the execution of the same there was an evident unanimity, and they all were harmoniously agreed to maintain the dignity of labor in a practical way, by as little familiarity with it as possible.

Colonel Norcomb was a gentleman of leisure, not likely to be particularly addicted to stupendous ambitions of a worldly nature, and his contemplation of the future had reference chiefly to the hope that his own name and the virtues of his wife would be handed down to posterity. At present, however, his wife was his child, and all his thoughts were wrapped up in her being. He bought horses for her, he travelled with her, and he carried around the dark retinue for her, (with the sinister hope they would take an opportunity to run away, however.) In the natural tendency of this affection as his chief occupation, he had lately been seized with a ridiculous desire to exploit certain brilliant refinements thereon, suggested to him by some wretched but ingenious French novels he had been reading, in which, for instance, extraneous flirtations were recommended to the married individual, as productive of opportunities for an exquisite reconciliation with himself, or information given with strict injunctions of secrecy to friends, of the jealousy of one's wife or husband, as leading, ultimately, to the pleasant possibility of believing it one's self.

As for the smiling wife, her time was principally occupied in laughing at him, in shielding with her gentle disposition the lazy darkies from punishment, and in taking violent fancies to young girls. In reference to the latter, she had not been in the house ten minutes before she began to inquire for one, and her husband, having duly considered the facilities which the establishment afforded, immediately brought in the maiden aunt. The young lady, however, in a weak voice, quickly ordered her to be taken away again, and her affection fell finally on the girl Dinah, as there was no more proper recipient thereof in the house. The girl stood her martyrdom with unflinching firmness, and, notwithstanding she was violently kissed forty times a day, freely forgave all the assaults which were made upon her.

Charles's mother and the colonel's wife having gone out to drive one day, (the latter insisting, as usual, upon taking the object of her immediate affection with her,) her husband cast about him, in an idle manner, for something to do.

" Where did you say that girl came from ?" said he, turning to the maiden aunt, as they stood together in the library; "my wife thinks, at present, that she is perfection, and I can predict, from its violence, that her fancy will last for two days more, at the very least."

"It is a most singular history," observed the aunt, as they sat down together on a sofa. "Two or three years ago, her father came to this town, after wandering about the world in an apparently idle, shiftless, and finally criminal manner, having even been incarcerated for forgery in the State's Prison. The misfortunes and misery which appear to pursue the human destiny on various occasions, followed him wherever he went. They clung to him here, and by their ravages his being is entirely broken down, would you think, and in his endeavors to obtain employment he has invariably failed in a singular manner. Some time after he arrived, instead of saving what little money he had, he indulged in the romance, would you think, of causing the remains of his wife to be brought to this town from the place where she had died in their wandering To be sure, it was an honorable enough act, considered in the abstract, and showed his affection, but not at all advisable at the time, considering his circumstances, would you think it? Well, however, you should have seen the funeral. That very day I happened, would you believe it—to be driving along near the church, taking the air, which I consider highly necessary to our existence as healthful human beings, or unhealthful, for that matter, indeed, when I observed a small procession coming towards me. Behind a hearse walked this old man and his daughter, dressed in neat but well-worn apparel, and after them a colored man and his wife and daughter, but not another soul, would you believe it? People naturally shunned them, and besides that, you know, human beings are hateful, and I hate 'em—that is, some of them."

At this episodical utterance of feeling, the maiden aunt stopped, and blew her nose in a pettish manner, while the Southerner was unusually silent.

"In spite of their wicked tendencies, and their degradation," continued the aunt, resuming her narrative, with a severe air, "I then resolved I would assist them at the very first opportunity, but I forgot it, although I had occasion to remember it several times; the human mind being eccentric, indeed, in its mysterious workings."

"I know it is," said the colonel; "but it is pretty regular in matters of this kind."

"Yes; well, they lived along in some way or another for a long while, until, in answer to the young girl, who asked me quite often, though not persistently, to give them a place, I consented, would you believe it? they appear to be disposed to pay their debts with the money they earn, and are of quite a saving nature; but still, you know, they belong to that class of people which we find so often in the world, whose finer instincts, if they ever had any, have been extinguished by their poverty and shiftlessness, to be sure. Whether their apparent gratitude to me is temporary, or perhaps entirely hypocritical, is a question which remains, of course, yet to be proven by my experience with them. The old man is stupid and silent in attending to his labors, but the girl is quite smart and cheerful; though, I must say, I fear she is as unreliable as her father. It was only the other day that she betrayed tendencies of her nature in such a way to me, as led me to believe, indeed—I fear they are not to be relied upon—not at all; but I think I did rightly, nevertheless. They cannot indulge in their vicious propensities to any great extent in the position which they occupy here, you know, colonel, and, at any rate, they can be dismissed at any moment, as I then said in reference to the point," continued she, with tremendous energy, though commencing to wander slightly, "you know how difficult it is for the human intellect, as it were, in reference to its duties, you know, towards the human heart, indeed, in the various ramifications of the social net-work—I may say, will lead to that very thing, and—to be sure, I was conversing with my sister this very morning upon the propriety of dismissing them, you know, and although my sister related some occurrences, you know, in which she thought, you know, she had observed cunning and dissimulation, you know, on the part of this young girl, you know—('No! I don't,' said the colonel, briefly) she still thought the cause she mentioned was not at all sufficient, even not considering it in the light of humanity, to justify such a step, inasmuch as there was no harm to be pointed at and—"

She might have died on the spot from a hemorrhage of words had not the Southerner here astounded her by suddenly seizing her hand, and putting it to his lips with a passionate gesture of excessive devotion.

"Oh, dear! what is this?" said she, starting from her position, and withdrawing her hand with the lightning-like rapidity which a mud-turtle evinces in causing his head to disappear into his interior.

"I love you!" said the fervent colonel.

("Gracious heavens! another! and a married man. Oh, horrible! This it is—to be too fascinating!")

("She is old enough to be my great grandmother,

and it is safe to say so, and besides that, I really love her for what she has done.) I love you!" repeated the ardent Southerner, in pursuance of his new theory.

"Ah, that fatal avowal! Heavens! he is young, but he is married, and it is of no use," said the maiden aunt, both with vehemence and irritation.

"How are you now?" asked the colonel, enthusiastically.

"Sir, that was an assumption, you know, of a privilege which should belong only to those—who—" continued, feebly, the lady.

"Eh? can't a man express his love for an old friend of his family? I love and venerate you!" said the excited colonel, punching the startled female in the ribs, to restore her to easiness.

"Sir!" said the lady, episodically, "I well know the mysterious feelings of sympathy to which you allude, and which too often, alas! exist in the bosom in spite of ourselves, and I know, too, how irrepressible they are—but you musn't do that again. (I wouldn't allow any person to do that, even if he were a single man!")

"Oh, I didn't mean to be impolite. In the South it is a common token of friendship and admiration, you know," continued the gallant colonel, immediately bestowing upon her another ardent look.

("Dear me, this must not continue a moment longer! He a married man and I single, and his wife —ah fate! let me not be the unwilling cause of estrangement between two happy hearts!) Rouse, sir! rouse yourself! Think of one to whom you are already affianced! (Poor girl! I pity her.) Fly, sir, fly from my fatal influence. Leave the house at once, and keep the fatal secret ever locked in your unhappy bosom. Go, go, unhappy young man, and absence may dissipate it! At least, go now!"

"Eh? Well I will. I think I had better take a walk, hadn't I? You needn't say any thing about it, eh? (Maybe I was too enthusiastic, but she is a good old soul, and I really love her for what she did,") reflected the colonel, as he left the apartment.

"Oh heavens! he has gone! Ah! little do my female friends know the sad havoc which I thus unwittingly make, in spite of my own feeble, powerless will, among the poor hearts of those beings of the other sex who are cast in my fatal path. One more. Alas! shall I—shall I—reveal this terrible secret to him—to him—who has the best right to this frame—(frame! that poetic word which he has used himself in referring to the casket of all his hopes.) No—no—my Pithkin, I will warn you by signs, but I will spare you the cruel revelation!"

While thus fixing her firm resolve to withhold the secret from the innocent Pithkin, and devising various plans for harrowing up his soul, by conveying to him the idea that there was something terrible in store for him, without letting him know what it was, she was interrupted by the arrival of her sister and Mrs. Norcomb, accompanied by the girl Dinah. Charles, who had observed them from his window, assisted them to alight, and accompanied them to the saloon. On the ride, the girl Dinah, in venturing to recount some scenes of her life in reply to the questions of the ladies, had become an object of thought to Charles's mother. She had, of course, naturally avoided that part of the history of her family which referred to the degradation and crime of her father, but she showed great tact in going further and dwelling upon certain of his merits, and in showing herself glad that an opportunity had been given her to tell them how good a father he had been, how he had loved her mother, &c. She had a certain right, of course, to dwell upon these points, and mitigate the darkness of his offence against society with the light of his virtues, but the mother thought she saw in her face no other indications of her nature than of that astuteness which had taught her the policy of praise of a father falling from the lips of a child.

As the conversation turned upon matters respecting a world from which the girl had been excluded by poverty, she became once more an humble and silent listener, but again when it appealed directly to nature, she seemed to forget herself, and boldly mingled her voice with those of the ladies. Both of them noticed with what dexterity she used the bright power of satire on this occasion, and as satire is a kind of open hypocrisy, the mother immediately took it as another indication of the artfulness which was either inherent in her, or had become a second nature by the education of her childhood. She remembered that it was with the same unpleasant conclusion that she had before this noticed the little ingenious replies of a complimentary nature, the flattering turn of general thought to personal application, which this girl was often accustomed to make, and while sentiments of repugnance filled her as she saw this insidious shrewdness so unnaturally engrafted in a being of such tender years, these sentiments were changed into pity as she reflected she was still old enough to make this tendency ineradicable.

In spite of these thoughts, and polished woman as

she was, instructing by her intellect, and warming with her heart the educated circles in which she moved, she listened, on this occasion, in unconscious deference to the girl, for she caught her now and then expressing truths which might have done honor to a philosopher, if not exactly in the language of a poet. An almost arrogant air seemed to rest on the young girl's face, as if the pleased regards of admiration which Charles's mother at times unconsciously bestowed upon her had made her forget her hypocrisy, and betray a further fault of her nature—a seeming disposition to take improper advantage of any concessions which might be made to her. Thus the mother noticed that as they drove up to the terrace, the girl uttered some truthful enough remark in such a careless manner, that it seemed almost patronizing. As Charles assisted them out, too, the girl, who came last, held out her hand also in the usual prerogatived manner of females, as if ordering the young man to take it and assist her out. There was a slight delay on his part, but he quickly assisted her to alight as he had the others. It was here that the girl seemed suddenly to remember that she had forgotten herself. Whether it was the involuntary aspiration of an innocent nature or not, the seeming confidence vanished from her countenance as quick as lightning. She hung her head, and her face became scarlet.

CHAPTER XIV.

MR. PITHKIN AT THE BALL.—AN INCIDENT.—AN ADVENTURE ALSO OF NATHANIEL BONNEY THEREAT.

THE ball of the Lancers took place, assembling together from the neighborhood a sodality of pleasure-seekers. Among others, the ladies from Pompney Place (with the exception of the disinclined Mrs. Norcomb) came to grace the scene, accompanied by Charles and the colonel. As they reached the scene of pleasure, carriages were arriving and departing—servants engaged in loyal altercation—ever and anon the hum of the promenaders within, swelling and dying away—graceful forms in the light habiliments of summer reclining at the windows—low laughter in the gardens—the beautiful everywhere tinged with American character.

It was at the conclusion of the first quadrille in which the chaste aunt participated, that her partner, Mr. Pithkin, excited by the dance in which she had pulled him severely about, prematurely sought the refreshment-room, leaving her to perform with the young advocate Nathaniel, the fancy dance which was next announced, and which was rendered exceedingly fancy by their execution of it. The prospective enjoyment of the evening by Mr. Pithkin had been marred at the outset by a fatal singularity in the deportment of his nephew, present on the occasion. He was further astonished at finding him, also, in the refreshment-room.

"What are you doing here, sir?" asked he, sternly. There was no one else there. The waiters, especially imported from New York, headed by the second cook, had rushed frantically across the street to the main kitchen in answer to a breathless announcement from the chief cook, that all were needed in boning the turkeys. "Let that punch alone. As it is poured out I will take it. I sent for you to come here from college that you might make an impression on Miss Wellwood—a good match —500,000 in U. S. 6's, and delightful to the relatives of both parties, especially to me, and here you are with your—take your hands out of your breeches! What is this! you smell horribly of cigars."

"Yes, I was stoking one before I came in," replied the fragrant academician.

"Stoking one! What language! By Heaven, you will worry your poor old uncle to premature gray hairs or baldness. Leave this apartment. Here! let that glass alone. Go up stairs. Remove your hands from your pantaloons, and join in the festivities." The youth obeyed the stern mandate, and his uncle, a prey to disagreeable reflections, having swallowed the punch in abstraction and followed him, was observed by the maiden aunt as he entered the ball-room again. A dark look passed over her face. She had kept the secret until then, and should she now destroy the peace of mind of that innocent creature, in the midst of such a scene of pleasure by requesting a few moments of private conversation with him behind a curtain? "No, no, he must not even know him!" Her card was filled up for three or four dances ahead. "How unanimous they all are! What wild, striving creatures are men, and yet they are pleasant things to have about! Look not dissatisfied, my Pithkin, if I do dance with them, the privilege of taking me down to supper will restore you!" Mr. Pithkin was not only dissatisfied, he was becoming exasperated. A cotillion had been called, and his nephew had become entangled in the sets. In one, the ladies on forming the basket figure, were astonished at finding five gentlemen, instead of four, enclosed within their chain of hands.

"It don't work at all," reflected Mr. Pithkin. "He seems to create no sensation upon the floor, except that of unmitigated disgust. There he goes with his hands in his breeches again. Hands out of your breeches!" roared he, in a suppressed manner to himself. "Gracious! this is more than I expected. I will go below. Perhaps the punch may refresh me."

On returning Mr. Pithkin observed, with astonishment, that the object of his disappointment, this time, had got into a prominent place in the orchestral balcony, among the musicians. He had wandered into the secret passage leading thereto, and appearing suddenly in their midst, had confused the minds of two trumpets and a clarionet, and thus disturbed the harmony of the piece that was being executed. The drummer, who wouldn't have been confused if a cannon had been fired at him, besides keeping admirable time, was finding opportunities to relieve his exasperated feelings by making short dabs at the intruder with his stick.

"Come down out of that! What are you doing up there?" roared Mr. Pithkin again, in a suppressed manner to himself. "Gracious! this is growing more unsatisfactory than ever. His conduct has twice forced me to go below, and deprived me already of three dances. I cannot dance with such feelings. I must go again. A glass of punch may restore me;" and again Mr. Pithkin sought the supper-room. It was no longer deserted. Three waiters and the chief cook had returned.

"What do you want here?" said the latter, as Mr. Pithkin opened the door.

"Oh, nothing! nothing!" said Mr. Pithkin, leaving slowly, apparently having made a mistake.

("Eh! it is the extra man they were to send me to open the oysters," said the cook, "he's come at last. However, the later they are opened, the better.) You ought to have come earlier. There is a good many of them," continued he to Mr. Pithkin.

"Three hundred, at least!" said the latter, whose mind reverted to the dancers above.

"Three hundred! With those that are here, and those outside, there will be two thousand, at least."

"What a number!" said Mr. Pithkin.

"Yes; but if they were all opened with a good knife, they wouldn't take up so much room as they do now."

This was the most curious and impracticable idea that Mr. Pithkin had ever heard—a proposition to reduce crowds in ball-rooms by opening each of the guests with a knife.

"And the quicker you take off your coat and go to work, the better. We are pressed for time. Open the large, fat ones first."

Mr. Pithkin fled abruptly from the room. The man actually wanted him to execute his insane proposition, and commence with the largest and fattest of the guests.

"I have made a mistake," said the chief cook, as Mr. Pithkin left with precipitation, "this is not the man. This one is apparently drunk, and they wouldn't send one here drunk."

On entering the ball-room once more, Mr. Pithkin stumbled against his nephew, who had evidently just resolved to go below again. "Get out!" said he, with renewed choler. "What are you doing here, rascal? Go back and join in the conversation. Don't you see Miss Wellwood is observing you? Go and accompany her to her seat. Ask her to dance or do something. Ask her if she wouldn't like to sit down and—take your hands out of your rascally breeches!"

"Look at that young man. He worries me—look at him!" exclaimed he, in great irritation to Nat, who had accosted him; "he told me, the other day, if I would present him with a meerschaum pipe to smoke over it, he would follow Dr. Fuffles's excellent advice and study metaphysics at the college where he was. So I sent him the pipe, and Dr. Fuffles the metaphysical works of a profound German philosopher, in the original language."

"What, does John read German?" asked Nat.

"Oh, no; not very well; but as the chief merit of the work lay in its unintelligibility, we wanted to make it more so to him. But the rascal didn't touch it. He succeeded in coloring his pipe, but no color of metaphysics as yet tinges his thoughts. You will excuse my loquacity to-night. But the fact of it is, that I have always been remarkable for that when I am inclined to talk. A great difference between me and my brother in that respect, Bonney; I was always like my mother, very loquacious, but Obad resembled my father. He hadn't any teeth, (lost 'em by accident,) and couldn't.—Would you like to walk out on the balcony and take the air, madam?" continued he, as Nat left him, turning to a dowager seated alone on the wall near him;

his feelings of courtesy beginning to flow with eccentric ardor. The lady, hinting that she didn't know him, promptly declined.

"Eh! you don't think I will be guilty of any impropriety, do you? I must do something," continued he in soliloquy. "I mustn't go near my friend of Pompney Place now. She has a noble mind, but insane ideas. In the excitement of the moment I might be involved in some ambiguous expressions leading to a committal, perhaps. These young ladies are very interesting. I don't know 'em, but I will engage in adventure. The poet has eloquently observed that the proper study of mankind is man—the study of woman is instructive, too. It is philosophical, even if it is a weakness. There are so many rascals disgracing virtue by assuming it, so many scoundrels assuming a dignified propriety of demeanor nowadays to cover up their crimes, that it is absolutely necessary for me to throw off my natural dignity sometimes to avoid suspecting myself to be one."

"Look at that form, Julia!" said one of the young girls, in an audible whisper to her friend, as Mr. Pithkin approached, in an affable manner.

"Eh? Do you like my form? Do you know now, if there was any way I could part with it, I'd make it a present to you!" said the latter, in a temporary burst of generosity.

"And those legs; but he must be used to them now," said the other, "nature having given them to him in earliest infancy."

"Certainly," said Mr. Pithkin, still smiling upon them affably. "It must have been at an early period of my career, as I can't exactly recollect the time when

I was without 'em! Gracious! my pleasant study is already interrupted. Here she comes after me," continued he, as Charles's aunt came over to accost him, on the arm of a gentleman, for supper was now announced, and the time had arrived for Mr. Pithkin to take her down to the banquet-room.

On entering the room, his feelings at the conduct of his nephew John reached their climax. He immediately observed, with mingled sentiments of horror and disgust, in a mirror at a distant end of the room, the conspicuous image of his nephew placidly engaged behind a screen in the singular occupation of opening oysters. That individual, having been caught by the chief cook as he was about helping himself to some punch a few moments before, had been induced by him to believe, on a theory which he did not precisely comprehend, that this singular duty of the evening had devolved upon him especially, and being of a benevolent nature, and remembering that he might eat as many of them as he pleased at leisure, he had entered with ardor into the discharge thereof.

"Drop that knife!" shrieked Mr. Pithkin internally, on observing this horrible reflection. "Gracious, it is all over now. Everybody sees him. Miss Wellwood has seen him. It is all over. His career is finished here!"

Mr. Pithkin took no pleasure in the supper. He partook freely of the punch, indeed, but it produced no immediate relief; and even when seated with the spinster upon the balcony of the garden after a dance or two was over, he still felt gloomy. "Goodness! how dark it is," said his fair friend; "the firmament is as black as a canopy of raspberry jam!" Pithkin secretly

applauded the boldness of the metaphor, and just then the orchestra struck up a singular composition, so wild in its genius that it distracted his gloom by its singularity. "I am very fond of music," said he; "in my college days I played the clarionet in the band for three years, though it is a most remarkable circumstance, I actually never liked music until I left off playing." The spinster uttered a sigh, and turned her languishing gaze upon him. "It seems as though the band, guided by some mysterious presence," said she, "had seized their instruments to execute in melodious frenzy these wild, delicious cadences, each feeling independent of the other, and searching the infinite in distinct paths of harmony." "I think they are intoxicated," replied Mr. Pithkin.

"How many—many sounds and visions are there in nature, which seem to tell us of another and a higher existence!" murmured his friend.

"Yes, and, by the way, particularly cats. There is something wild about them, and something unearthly about their yells, even when they are making love, which has always struck me! Haven't you noticed it?" asked Mr. Pithkin.

The spinster had cast her eyes upon the garden beneath. The moon had gone down. The night was obscure. The lowest audible sigh to the winds, and ever and anon distant muttering, might be heard in the horizon. A dull, repeated flash of lightning lit up the gardens away from the lustre shed from the lamps, when she observed a person amid the foliage, pushing a female with a rude blow from him, while she seemed to be endeavoring to persuade him away. She then saw the female rest upon the ground, and cover her face with her hands and then both disappear quickly. There was a certain wildness withal in this scene of violence which overcame the observer. And do not the wild spirits of sorrow and crime thus grotesquely love to mingle their work in earthly scenes of happiness! The spinster uttered a suppressed scream.

"Heavens! It is he; on such nights he comes," said she, with a romantic look at Mr. Pithkin, who asked her to halloo again, having arrived at that state in which he felt inclined to do it himself.

"Thus seated with you have I seen the pioneer! This time he comes with his murderess suing for forgiveness. Aye, know you not, it is said that on nights of earthly festivity and mirth they love to appear, either together, engaged in altercation, or one in terrible loneliness? Those who witness their quarrels, it is said, will subsequently be unhappy because they are married. Those who see one of them alone, will be unhappy because they are not. And this—this determines me. I shall be married at any rate."

"But you saw only one of 'em before, when we were walking together at the Place," said Mr. Pithkin, with sudden cunning.

"Oh, pshaw! no. It wasn't the pioneer at all. Some strayer purloining fruit; and besides that, I can't help it, if it was. Some influence mysterious and solemn, commencing from the moment just passed, whispers in my bosom that I shall be married."

Pithkin remembered, with a secret chuckle, that it wouldn't be to him at any rate, as, if he had ever seen them, he had seen but one. His spirits rose to such a high degree that he immediately joined once more in the festivities, gradually relapsing, however, through that stage of excitement in which he prophesied happiness to everybody to singing his own misfortunes, and finally to falling down in a singular manner. It rained severely when he was carried home on a shutter by a few friends. His nephew John had the advantage over him, as it was dry weather when he was carried home.

It was about half an hour before the occurrence in the gardens, which had been witnessed by the spinster, that the young advocate, Nathaniel, having been slighted by Laura, who, after dancing with him nine times, positively forbade any further attempts in that direction, rushed madly into the open air to cool his excited being. He had straggled, in his distraction, to a secluded part of the park amid an overpowering smell of lilacs and utter darkness, when he ran into a box-tree. At that moment a lady from the opposite direction, with rapid steps ran into it on the other side, and then the two encountered each other in a very unpleasant manner. "Heavens!" said the lady. "Oh, sir, take me under your care for a moment. I am pursued!" Nat had hardly time to recover from his stupefaction at this event, when a gentleman came up with some haste, stumbling along the path, laughing and muttering, "Confound the darkness! I think one of them went this way. If I catch her, I'll refer her to my wife for my irreproachable character. It's very exciting! I think it is the exercise. Gracious! halloo!—a man!"

"What do you want here, unauthorized intruder?" said Nat. The lady was concealed by the box-tree.

"Hush! a little adventure, you know. Did you see a lady come this way? She took it into her head to run away from me, you know! Ha! ha!"

"Ha! ha! certainly."

"Certainly what?"

"Of course she ran away from you."

"I hope you will consider my meeting you as of no consequence?"

"I'm not surprised at that."

"Why not?"

"Oh, nothing; you might as well surrender the articles you have on your person to me, and leave."

"What articles?"

"Why, the spoons from the refreshment-room, to be sure. (By George, I can't get him to go!")

"Heavens! a lady! Excuse me; I didn't know you were accompanied," said the stranger, peering into the darkness behind Nat. "Ha! ha! stolen tête-à-tête. Eh?"

"Sir!" said Nat, resenting the insinuation with great ferocity.

"Oh never mind," said the unknown. "We don't know each other. I am Don Giovanni! I thought you might have seen my fair refugee. I am going."

"Stay!" said Nat, in sudden weakness. "She sought an interview—eh—how do you do these things, Don Giovanni? What shall I say to her?"

"Say, eh? (I never thought of that)—say—why, tell her that the brightness of her eyes illumines the terrible darkness of the night, or words to that effect."

"The brightness of your eyes illumines the terrible darkness or words to that effect," said the excited Nat, stepping back to whisper to the lady.

"Oh dear, I shall die," murmured the latter.

"Don't," said Nat; "I shall take it as a personal

favor if you wouldn't. I say," continued he, struck with another idea, in faint hesitation to the stranger, who was about going away, " she might have a husband, eh, and you know he might—"

" Oh, don't mind the rascal.—If you meet him, tell him he is a rascal or something of that kind. He is one of course, or else he'd be here with his wife.—Yes, tell him he is a rascal," said the stranger, raising his voice in emphatic vivacity.

" Well, I will. Oh, devil take it! Yes!" said Nat, violently.

At this point, however, any person who had been able to see through the night, would probably have witnessed one of the most singular phenomena that could occur amid the various eccentricities of human conduct. This consisted in these three persons suddenly exploding from a position of comparative quiet, and flying frantically from one another in all directions of the darkness.

" Oh, it is my husband, Col. Norcomb! Let me fly!" whispered the lady.

" What—Good God!—the fire-eating Southerner Laura was to introduce me to," said Nat, in a cold perspiration. He dabbed his forehead for a startled moment with his handkerchief, and then fled.

" Whew! Peppermint!" said the Southerner. " That terrible scent. It is that individual who was paying such attention to Miss Wellwood, and by heaven, that is she. His conversation was illusory! Thank Heaven, I am not yet discovered! I fly!"

The colonel retreated with as great precipitation toward the distant ball-room as the pitchy darkness would allow. His wife fled in an opposite direction, and Nathaniel's frantic course partook of the nature of an insane sky-rocket's path. In one of the delirious angles which he had formed to escape discovery, he ran into the fence, in another he bounded off and struck a tree, from thence he precipitated himself into an arbor, and finally crossing the orbit of the lady who was traversing the circular path leading towards the back gate, this erratic comet came again in collision with the fair planet.

"Oh dear, how it lightens! I am so thankful it is you, sir. Ha! ha! We have escaped. I trust you will not reveal your secret to my husband. It is the result of a foolish frolic on my part. Will you please accompany me to my carriage near the bank, in the unfrequented street yonder?"

"Eh, if it rests with me to inform your respected husband of the singular occurrences of this evening, I am quite sure he will remain in a state of unenlightenment with regard to them," said Nat; "and, dear me, allow me to add you are still comparatively insecure from discovery Gracious! it is beginning to rain, too. Come under the shelter of this lightning-proof pine, madam, while I run to my residence for an umbrella. Oh, dear, I remember it was stolen during the last spell of dry weather. Our only chance is that some burglar who is careful of his health, has broken into my apartments during my absence, and inadvertently left one there. Stay! A novel idea! I'll borrow one!"

In a moment or two after this, an old and respected citizen of the place, who had come with two umbrellas to take his daughters home, was ascending the grand flight of steps outside of the banquet-house, holding one tight down over his head, and the other under his arm, when he heard the following declaration made to him in the darkness outside of the umbrella. "Sir, I seize this opportunity of divulging to you the profound sentiments of esteem and respect which I have always entertained for you. Lend me your umbrella!" This expression of regard and abrupt demand, was immediately followed by the lightning-like disappearance of the umbrella, which was jerked from under his arm by some unknown person, who vanished at once into the darkness, before his victim could turn around. The quiet flow of the old gentleman's current of thoughts was so disturbed by this remarkable occurrence, that he was fain to sit down feebly on a wet seat with the other umbrella, and stare for a while idiotically into the chasm of darkness which the ravisher of his property had reft in his disappearance.

Nat reached the lady with his acquisition just as the bottom of a small cloud dropt out. On the way to the carriage, which they soon reached, the lady was revolving the explicit manner in which she intended to vindicate herself, after tormenting her husband respecting the occurrence. How she had discovered the girl Dinah about to go away secretly from the house; how, on her telling her she was going to take a little walk, the sudden desire had entered her own mind of taking the girl and driving to town; how she had ordered James to harness a team and be discreet; how they had arrived at the garden; how Dinah became separated from her on their being chased by some unknown person. On arriving at the carriage, she saw that the girl Dinah had reached it in safety before her. Gluckinson was engaged in holding the horses, who were as frightened as he was with the lightning; and the girl, with wet clothes and pallid face, was giving him directions, in a low, yet firm voice. She laughed at the singular adventure as she recognized Mrs. Norcomb, and they soon drove off together, after Nat had been properly thanked by the lady, and enjoined to secrecy.

Thus almost in every earthly scene is there a strange mixture of sorrow and joy, of laughter and tears!

CHAPTER XV.

A CONVERSATION.

CHARLES's mother and Mrs. Norcomb, accompanied by the colonel, having driven to town, Charles was proceeding to the library to read, when he observed the young dependent, Diana, coming from a pleasant window at the end of the hall, in which she had been lingering for a moment. The warm radiance of the clear sunny day, such as might be found in climes by the Ionian or Ægean main, was softened by the breeze stealing into the corridor. The window looked out upon a still green glade, where the cattle were grazing with slow advancing pace, and in the distance, amid the trees, might be seen the spire of the church rising in pious pride. With the thought of serenity and purity thus prompted, what heart should not feel, on such a day, the enchanting hope and foreshadowed glow of a future happy existence?

"Stay!" said he, "wait a moment."

"I have some duties to perform, sir," said she, with perhaps a well-assumed look of earnestness.

"Important duties?"

"Important to me, because they are mine," said she, promptly.

"Well, then, stay!" said he, feigning a stern air of command unnatural to him. "You must consider it your duty to be respectful of my commands also, as I am master here."

"Certainly!" said the girl obediently. A sly look passed over her face.

"What are you thinking of?" asked Charles, noticing the look with some slight confusion.

"I was thinking, if fate let me select a master, I would choose one who had first shown he was master of himself," replied she, in mock bitterness at his feigned air of command.

"Eh? The members of every household should know their positions, shouldn't they?" continued he, fighting against the idea that he was conversing with an old friend.

"Yes; but when a master thinks it necessary to command, he ought to reflect that it may be only because he is master that he has the right," replied she, in defiant banter.

"But the kind master of a household will not always command, my girl; he can advise and reprove as a friend, for instance, and yet be master!" said he, the severity of his manner gradually disappearing.

"Ought not he to forget, then, that he is master? No—no—it is not so. He may forget it when he commands," added she, quickly, and with serious firmness; "but when his words fall in other tones, I think he should always remember it."

Could she be entertaining a suspicion unworthy of his honor?

"It leads the inferior to take advantage of his kindness," continued she, showing that she was innocent of his construction, and farther, that she was, perhaps, chastising her own inclination.

"As to reproof, it is never a good thing for the giver, do you think so?" continued she, after a pause, as if for the purpose of pursuing her advantage again; "we hate him if he is correct, because he has discovered a fault of ours; and if he isn't correct, we think him foolish!"

"But it isn't what the recipient of his reproof thinks of him at all," said Charles, suddenly forgetting himself, and becoming warmly interested in the subject, abstractly considered. "It is simply whether he succeeds or not. If he succeeds, he knows he has conferred a benefit; and if he doesn't, why—he doesn't, that is all!" concluded he, slightly at a loss on this point.

"And even then he has the gratification of knowing he has tried to do good, you know!" said the girl.

"Yes," replied Charles, with renewed feeling, "and very often, instead of its being a fault which is known by the one we reprove, it is one which, for the first time, we discover to him."

"And then, if he is not a worthless being," added Dinah, with apparent earnestness, "he must feel a kindness has been done him, yes."

Charles began to feel generously pleased. He saw that poverty and misery had evidently given to this girl one advantage: she had already learned to read human nature with facility, as though Providence had kindly given her this weapon for self-defence at starting in her journey through the world. Still, he further reflected, whatever vices she may have also learned in the rugged school, she was enabled to conceal by means of the same power, perhaps. He was about to resume the conversation again, in great interest, when he observed the girl gazing at him earnestly. • At the moment there appeared to him a sadness, with something even akin to a supernatural expression in the look.

"Oh, pshaw! an absurd fancy! I am stupid," said he quickly to himself. She had risen to go.

"Where did you live before you came here, Dinah? Sit down a moment," continued he.

"In New York, sir," she replied.

"You were very poor, were you not? You have been to school, I see!"

"Oh, no, sir; never. But my father taught school when he was a young man, and when I was growing up, he taught me as much as he could."

"What did he do in the city? How did you live?"

"Some time before we came here, he used to—used to—he was employed to sweep the avenues. For a long while he was unable to obtain work, and he used sometimes to drive his care away, by going to the political meetings they held in the wards. After a while, becoming familiar there, and some of those who had the power, discovering that he could write addresses and notices better than they, they accepted his assistance, and gave him this place on being successful. By-and-bye he was dismissed, as the alderman who helped him had been sent to prison for burglary, and then—"

"Well, what—?"

"My mother died," said she, pressing her closed hand upon her knee. "Don't you think it ridiculous that such men should have political power?"

"You say your mother died?" asked Charles; an

unpleasant thought had struck him. The manner in which she passed over that emotional event in her narrative may have naturally been a vehement concealment. From its very perfection, perhaps it was, that it seemed to him the indifference of heartlessness.

"Yes!" continued the young girl, rapidly smoothing her dress over her knee with both hands; "but perhaps it is judicious to let them have it, inasmuch as the only use they make of it is to send themselves to the States-Prison."

"And the trick of brazenness! Can she be affecting to forget her father's crime too? But in one so young! Can it be true that she is—") He observed that she was looking at him and blushing deeply, and even now when she started again quickly and with something like a shudder, this too seemed to him to be irritation at the disadvantage of her parent's crime rather than shame.

"Stay a moment," said he, in a low tone under the impulse of this thought. "You feel angry that you are living in a glass house, don't you?"

The girl seemed to observe in a moment the change in his manner, but she wore a faltering look, as though she knew it was the result of a prejudice which she could not help.

"But would not shame, rather than anger," continued he, "be more befitting to the child of him who committed this folly—of—"

"Oh! breathe not a word against my father," said she suddenly, with her nostrils dilated, and standing erect. "A father's name is sacred to his child, and may God bless those who shall so speak of mine to me!"

There was a defiance in her voice, but sorrow too, and they both struck the young man.

At this moment his mother, who had just returned from her drive, came into the corridor from a door near by, and looked with some evidence of surprise at the two standing there in a species of tableau. She accosted Charles with a familiar maternal embrace, and smiled also upon Diana, but the smile curled her lip in a singular way. The girl bowed decorously, and left the mother and son together.

CHAPTER XVI.

OBADIAH BAYLON.

The young man, Rudolph, sat in his stone house at the close of day in company with his overseer, an individual physically remarkable for having a curious weakness in his legs, and an irrepressible lock of hair which had stuck up since infancy on the top of his head.

The bailiff had come on business, but observing the young man engaged in a kind of melodramatic scene composed of passionate starts and indistinct soliloquies, he had simply contented himself during the past half hour with enacting the part of a Greek chorus, by sitting down and quietly deprecating the whole thing to himself. At last he cachinnated feebly.

"What are you laughing at, fool?" said the young man, suddenly turning.

"I want—I want to attend to business."

"I suppose you want to go off and pray somewhere with the rest of your brethren."

"I am older than you," said the bailiff. He had really a tendency toward religion, and felt hurt.

"Take your accounts off—I won't attend to them. I am tired and sick of my follies, and the imbecility of my way of living," said the young man confusedly. "Stay, wait a moment, Baylon—I want to speak to you about—I know you are inclined to dissuade me altogether from her, for some reason or other—but poor as the girl is, Obadiah, she has now inspired me with a new feeling—a feeling that I have never felt before—I am not ashamed to confess it—I can't help it—I even have felt like—"

The hitherto impatient chorus appeared to be a little interested and surprised at this point. "What! ha! ha!" interrupted he, "you don't intend to—"

"What is her family to me?" continued the young man. "What if the old man was a knave? I have no relations to pursue me, and I don't care for the world—"

"The girl's comeliness has driven him crazy! Well, this is the most stupid thing I ever saw!" reflected the other, looking at his own countenance in the glass. "I've got to handle her in a delicate manner, anyhow, in the midst of my plans. She knows me too well. She has a sharp eye for the singular in human natur'. As soon as I have any improper ideas, she seems to know it, and I've got to be really virtuous when I am about her, or she'll drive me from her presence. Some pattern saint watches over her, I guess! who won't allow any one else wicked near her."

"What is all this sottish mummery?" asked the young man, starting up peevishly.

"It is a good thing for you, if you deceive yourself into the belief you're serious, it will make your fancy more pleasant—" said the bailiff with a suggestive wink to the clock, being inclined to play with the infatuation of the young man, in his tendency towards humor.

"You scoundrel, your eccentric frankness is considered your peculiar sanctifying grace among your religious brethren—It is your hypocrisy—you are constantly suggesting evil to me. You've done it ever since I was a boy. I'll expose you in the chapel, or make such remarks as that again, and I'll knock your head off," continued the young man, who didn't seem to relish the other's insinuations just at that moment.

"You may, if you will," replied the bailiff, cringing, yet murmuring something in his humorous instinct about having it knocked off himself, or at least having it done at his own expense to save him the trouble. "But have I not in this matter assisted you without your knowing it?" continued he, sullenly. "Did I not accost the girl again yesterday? "I went to see her father. He at least knows what a friend I can be."

"You did—Baylon—and what—what did she say —Obadiah?"

"She said—she said—" replied the other, unable to invent a lie in time—"she said—"

"What did she say, fool?" asked again the passionate young man.

"She said," continued the bailiff, rubbing his restless top-knot in great difficulty, "that she appreciated your love—it was so gentlemanly—yes, she said that being a poor girl she relied upon the—upon the goddesses who watch over young and inexperienced females, and she said she wished—"

"You lie, scoundrel!" said the young man. The bailiff had perhaps been drinking a little, and was inclined to be poetic. "If you say I lie, I do, I suppose," replied he immediately, with a heart-rending deference of opinion, and muttering something in a sullen tone about being born in New Jersey, and being unable to help it anyhow.

"Leave the room!" roared the young man.

"Certainly," said the bailiff, leaving the apartment, slightly discomfited with his failure. He uttered internally an oath. "Let him talk to me in that way, I don't mind him. I can manage his affairs without him, I guess! (with a sinister look of mingled humor and wickedness.) He's downright infatuated with the girl! Let me see—if I wish to succeed in my plans, I'll have to drive her from that place, at any rate. Her honesty will be in my way as long as she is there, but I've got to be friendly too, he! he!" concluded he, feeling of his top-knot. "Now for chapel. They think I'm really religious there, because I ain't such a hypocrite in my language, as they know they are themselves, he! he! That is, some of them," added he, in a kind of superstitious fear of real virtue.

CHAPTER XVII.

A MORNING HOUR.

Charles was awakened at the dawn, by the low responsive twittering of the birds in the trees. A delicious fragrance was wafted into his chamber, and the brightness of the day was coming. Invited from his bed, a bath of pure water brought a glow to his person, and he resolved upon a morning walk. There was no one stirring in the house, and he emerged therefrom into the avenues of the park. Turning into a secluded walk, however, he discovered young Dinah there, up earlier than he, gathering a flower or two, and with her a little sickly dog. In spite of the calls of his mistress, the infirm animal fled precipitously at the young man's approach, to without stone's throw, and wheeling kept up an incessant series of feeble barks, while regarding the enemy with an idiotic stare from his rheumy eyes. The natural blush of modesty passed over the girl's fresh morning countenance. A faint red tinge was in the east.

"You are up early," said Charles, "before Aurora."

"Oh, no! See the dew she has poured upon the flowers!"

"Who taught you the offices of the goddess?" asked Charles.

"Father!"

"Do you like to read poetry?" said he, while taking a seat on a bench near by.

"Yes, sir," said she, and she also sat down at the other end, with a look of confidence.

"Perhaps you are romantic enough to write a little."

"I am too healthful, I think. If I were dying of consumption, I would," replied she, smiling.

"Do you think it necessary to know you are going to die, in order to write true poetry?"

"Oh, no, sir. Only, in this case, my writings would have at least one recommendation—they would be dying accents, you know."

"But there is some philosophy in your remark. The penning up of one's feelings may connect the two, may make a good poet of a man, and give him the consumption at the same time, may it not?" suggested Charles, in curiosity. "I suppose you have heard of Keats, he died of consumption and too much poetry."

"I thought it was criticism. That is what I would hate, if I were a simple poet," continued she, vivaciously, struck with an idea; "but if I had any hidden meanings, I would like criticism, because the more they criticise, the more the ends of the concealed relations of your thoughts will be shown to make necessarily the face you have given, and no other."

"Yes, it is so. Do you think I would make a good poet now?" asked Charles, confidentially.

"If—if you tried, I don't think you would make any thing bad, sir. Still that is it. You won't try."

"But I don't think I would make a good poet, even if I tried. My emotions have a constitutional way of getting into my thoughts, and producing a disgust," continued he, quite careless of his idea.

"Your emotions get into your thoughts and produce a disgust? Oh, I think you would make a successful poet, sir! The more unintelligible poetry is, nowadays, the more people like it!" continued she, in a murmur.

"I mean, rather," said Charles, correcting himself in a lively manner, "that I have no emotions, or at least that they are not strong enough to make me think. I have tried to discover an enthusiasm," continued he, in a kind of self-felicitating soliloquy. "I've tried to rejoice in my future. Even the business of life possesses for me no incentive to action!"

"Then why do you not occupy yourself with some subject which has no relation to the business of life, sir?" said Dinah, logically.

"But there is no subject, no subject within reach of my faculties even, which would excite me!"

"Perhaps that is the difficulty. It would no doubt be highly exciting to employ them upon some subject which is placed beyond their reach," said Dinah, with continued sprightliness.

"What one, for instance?"

"Oh, any one requiring commonplace or ordinary ideas!" said she, coolly.

"Such, for instance, as the study of the character of a young person—let me see—about fifteen!" said Charles, immediately, much pleased with his own retort.

"Do you consider the contemplation of one's own future the most interesting of studies?" asked she, permitting him to remain victorious.

"Yes, of course. The very constitution of human nature is founded upon a selfish principle, and every man is the first object of his own solicitude!" continued the young man.

"Well, as to that—as he is fitter to take care of himself than of any other person, it is right that he should be so constituted," said the girl, after a moment, with cogency.

"But a man fundamentally considers himself and his happiness as of more importance than that of all the world besides, though his fellow-beings don't think so by any means. Thus is every one fundamentally the enemy of the rest of his race," continued he, disposed to ventilate to this natural philosopher his ideas on this unsatisfactory subject.

"I don't believe it," said she, flatly. "How can it be otherwise than that men were at least originally constituted to rejoice in the prosperity and grieve at the misfortunes of each other!" continued she, glancing around the earth and sky.

"No, it is the other way," said Charles, facetiously. "They were constituted to smile at the misfortunes and weep at the prosperity of each other! Do you know," continued he, in his piquant view of human nature and with seriousness, "that all this sympathy of ours is only an exquisite trick of the imagination; that it is only when it cheats us into feeling their misfortunes as our own, that we feel for others? But particularly the possibility that we can sometimes feel a pang at the prosperity of others, shows how naturally contemptible we are!"

"But if man has a natural power which corrects these tendencies, I don't see how he is naturally contemptible," said the young reasoner.

"But this power of the imagination is an unfortunate one, which is not strengthened by use. The more it is used the less it becomes!"

"Well, the less it becomes the stronger becomes the simple habit of doing good, you know. When we commence to do good from principle, instead of impulse, and that is better, isn't it?" said the girl, after thinking awhile, and combating bravely for the human race.

Charles was struck with her brightness, but he felt her trueness to humanity still more. Her words, taken in connection with her youth, must have been the result of a native honor. How could it be otherwise, unless she was endowed with an almost unheard-of hypocrisy. Whatever faults she had then, if she had any at all, were not inherent, but only the result of her education in misery. He was beginning to take an interest in something once more. It would be pleasant, nay, in the honor of his nature, he even began to feel it was his duty to assist her in extricating herself from the consequences of her father's folly. He would banish the inequality of their positions, in offering her this assistance, (a willingness, by the way, which he might very well experience, as he evidently couldn't help it;) and, to produce the necessary confidence in her bosom, he would make her consider his kindness, even as an offering of friendship. The gratitude of such a bright nature would be a sufficient reward. But how if he were mistaken, how if she were endowed with such a cunning as to be amusing herself and making fun of him in this very matter?

The girl without doubt saw the general tendency of his thoughts, for she immediately added, as if for the purpose of strengthening their favorable bias, "It is this continued distrust of human nature which is the horror. People are considered guilty beings because they are human. It is about as profound a principle as that by which they are considered wicked because they are poor." There was a bitterness in her tone, but her voice immediately faltered. Why? Was it the remembrance that she could not rely even upon the fallacy of either of these principles, in the struggle against social prejudice which her young intelligence saw before her, or was it a temporary conscience of her own wickedness, which her youth might have naturally produced?

"You have shown that I should not distrust people because they are human!" said Charles, "and if it be reasonable, to—to—distrust the education of poverty and misery, do we not still know that it is within the power of the very human sympathy, which I would have denied, to correct that education?"

The liveliness of his manner produced no reply from her. She had bent her head towards the ground, and her countenance was hidden. When she looked up he thought he saw, amidst the evidences of other emotions, a look of dissatisfaction, which seemed almost a scorn of him. Perhaps, in spite of her antecedents, she may have been impatient because he suspected her at all.

"I begin to think it is because you are too unselfish, that you are unhappy, sir," said she, after a moment, with a changed air. "As it is the imagination which creates so much sensibility, why do you not repress it, or at least turn it away from the misery of others, to the world of romance? Commence to chase phantoms into shadowy solitudes!" continued she, earnestly, as if endeavoring to rescue him from his disagreeable state of existence with this lively yet potent direction.

"I would do so," replied the young master, disposed

to laugh at her compliment to his sensibility and his imagination, "but I might get scared. I would if you would go along with me. Two would dare to go further into the shadowy solitudes than one!"

"We might go so far as never to find the way back again," said Dinah, with equal liveliness, continuing the absurdity. "Then what would become of us?"

"Why, we should be together, wouldn't we?" asked Charles, in a soft way.

They had risen and come towards the house together, along the fragrant paths of roses, the rheumy dog following at an interval of five or six feet, in an uncertain state. The sun had now risen, and the groves were vocal with daylight's songs.

CHAPTER XVIII.

AT THE CHURCH.

It was a warm Sunday morning when the gentry of the neighboring district assembled in the ancient wayside church to listen to Dr. Fuffles. No breath of air disturbed the drooping foliage which overhung, in the green fulness of the season, the sacred mounds around the house of promise, and the translucent waves of heat trembled above the landscape. The lazy horses of the farmers, standing in the long sheds, or attached to the shaded railings on the road, stamped irregularly and whisked their tails in irritated incessance at the serene malignity of the flies; while, now and then, one with ears reversed and a short squeal, took a dental vengeance upon the shining integument of his satiric neighbor, for some sparkling personality in their silent conversation.

The assembled flock sit within the walls in somnolent files, manufacturing miniature gales with their fans of palm. The blood creeps slowly in their veins, and the lazy thoughts stick in their minds. Above in the gallery the little Sunday-school boys and girls blink in hushed awe at the pastor.

The young advocate Nat unbuttons his white vest, overcome with the warmth. A new and overpowering odor of mingled wintergreen and peppermint, dropped coxcombically upon its lining, reaches the sense of the gallant Colonel's wife, seated in the pew in front. Her spouse, who had caught a smell-less cold at the ball, has just innocently commenced to blow his nose. "Put up that terrible handkerchief directly," whispers she impetuously to him. The aggrieved spouse obeys, and sits in dumb wonderment at the singular command. The young girl Dinah, dressed in neat attire, and sitting in one of the retired Pompney pews, rises to give her seat by her gray-haired father, to another old man with infirm gait, about to walk inquiringly up the aisle. A weak voluntary is swelling from the organ, sounding like a feeble tuning of the instrument, and now at last the sermon commences. Morpheus himself, looking in at the door, gives one gasp and falls in invisible sleep upon the porch. The Doctor, in the course of his admirable discourse, exhibited many feats of mental posturing, which certainly should have attracted a lively attention. But, owing to their soothing regularity of succession perhaps, the audience manifested their sensations in the quiet manner rather of opening their mouths to express their wonder, and shutting their eyes to indicate their delight. When, at one point in the course of his argumentation, he had got by some mysterious process into reasoning violently in a circle, which he couldn't get out of, every man was asleep in the church but one, and he was a tinker who had been intoxicated over Saturday night. It had the singular effect upon him of keeping him painfully wide-awake. The Doctor having changed his ground eleven times, and begged the question six, closed his discourse in some such manner as the following, which he had adopted from an old divine, and which he was then convinced was the perfection of style in human language. "Though I oftentimes see not those things that I believe, then, my hearers, yet I must still believe those things that I see. Thus do I believe that there are many whose peculiar ambition it is to be ambitiously peculiar. If they may not do as well as they would, they would not do as well as they may. Now such worldlings would purchase reputation by the sale of desert, but the wise, my hearers, the wise purchase desert even at the hazard of reputation. These poor worms, then, have great reason to be ashamed of their pride, but no reason to be proud of their shame; for while they wish to be stored in their wants, they may be said to be decidedly wanting in their store," etc., etc. The result of this admirable and awakening discourse was, that the admiring audience immediately awoke.

And now another eccentric series of reedy fanfares, called a symphony, emanate from the vertical pipes, at the frenzied touch of the impassioned genius. The boy who blows the bellows blenches, or his mind is wandering in other scenes. The wind rushes fitfully through the cacophonous cylinders, exasperating Timotheus and putting him out. The young advocate Nathaniel, with one or two others, has risen to circulate the mendicant plate, for an extraordinary charity; and towards the completion of his pious tour, he speculates hurriedly upon the propriety of placing four cigars in the box, having left all his small change at home. Finally the doxology is sung with quavering voices, and the assembly moves slowly towards the doors, with hushed murmurs of gratification.

Under a still elm away from the church, was the grave of the mother of Diana. There was a plain tablet, and the usual simple domestic epic. As they came out, the father and daughter both looked that way. A thought of the past may have flashed upon the young girl's mind. One of the future may have struck the old man. As they walked towards the grave, the young man Rudolph reached them. "Do you wish still to avoid me?" asked he, of the girl, with a moody laugh, and aside from the father. "One would think I was a pestilence! Think you not I saw the glances of pretended idleness of your master, as you call him!" The girl said nothing, nor appeared hardly to notice the external world, as she walked along, and the young man turned to join Charles, Laura, and Nat, standing around a monument to admire its architecture.

"My uncle's tomb; raised by my only relative to himself," said he. "He did his best to show me the shortest way to where he has gone himself!"

"Yes," cried Nat, "and he left you his property, I suppose, for the sole purpose of expediting your passage thereto!"

"He was a fool, anyhow," continued Rudolph, in his unexpectedly pleasant manner, "and if he had lived, he would have driven me to be a knave, because I wouldn't be one too."

"What said the preacher this morning, Rudolph," cried Laura indignantly, as she moved away towards the portico. "The irascible part of a man's nature was given to him to assert his dignity, by repelling injuries, not doing them. Fie! and to the memory of your dead uncle."

"I beg your pardon, Miss Wellwood, but what do I care for what he said? Have not we all our own ideas?" continued he, to the young men. "While he asserts the falsities of religion, I prefer to speak the truth in my own way."

"But he who makes the truth offensive, Rudolph, encourages error," said Charles.

"I tell you," reiterated Rudolph, with a certain increase of gall, "that I will utter truths in my own way, even if I have to curse them out of my mouth."

"It strikes me," said Charles, "you had better bray them."

"You are a miserable knave!" cried Rudolph, with a sudden burst.

"Heavens! Sunday morning—you retract," said Nat, immediately to Charles, "and of course Warriston will. You say so, I believe, (to Rudolph,) of course, it is quite natural, yes—I—!"

The latter not only saw not the propriety of retracting, but was further breathing the word "mummer" through his teeth. Charles, turning towards him at the unexpected power of his repartees, suddenly dropped his hand as quickly as he had raised it. He moved away toward his aunt and the carriage, saying, carelessly, "Well, well, good morning!" and left the young man overwhelmed in the confusion of his anger.

Nathaniel, having at this point rejoined Laura in the portico, enjoyed the pleasure of being introduced to the Colonel and Mrs. Norcomb, with whom she was conversing. Had she noticed it, the young lady would have been much surprised at the singular manner in which they all three looked at the ceiling at the moment.

"Oh, it was Miss Wellwood there, there is no doubt about it!" thought the Colonel; "I muffled my voice. I don't think she recognized me, but he has. Several times I caught him looking piercingly at me in the church. Yes, I must warn him, I must warn him to be discreet."

"After all, how Frederick would scold me," reflected Mrs. Norcomb. "Oh, I wouldn't have him find it out."

"His wife hasn't mixed me up in it, if she has told him. But gracious! she may thoughtlessly," said the third of this self-communing trio, while the salutations of the day were being passed. A second curious phenomenon immediately took place. The three commenced to tug at each other's habiliments for a short moment, in a furtive but exceedingly energetic manner, and this triangular singularity, of which Nat was the distracted hypothenuse, was immediately followed by another, which consisted of a violent interchange of winks and frowning.

"Oh, the deuce! she has divulged," said Nat, suddenly observing the Colonel. He hurriedly reviewed his speculations upon the latent insanity of the Southern character.

"I knew it was she there with you!" whispered the Colonel to him, and looking towards Laura, who had at this moment walked away with Mrs. Norcomb towards the carriages. At this announcement, Nat was about to tuck up his wristbands in rash desperation, when the Colonel added hastily, "Never mind, you say nothing about it and I won't."

"What?" asked the astounded advocate.

"You want to be secret. Her relations, I know, wouldn't like it," said the Colonel, complacently; "but rest assured I won't say any thing about it."

"Eh, I think I will go. Good morning," said the bewildered Nat.

"I like to see people enjoying themselves," continued the Colonel, in parting confidence, walking along with him, "and in this little affair I had no business to have seen it at all. I know you have really fallen in love with her. I saw it at once, and these stolen meetings are pleasant. Any time you wish me to draw off the attention of the people about, so that you can have her all to yourself, I will do it with pleasure, eh?"

Nat had heard of Parisian morality, and also of some of the doctrines of the natural affinity school, but in his varied speculations, he had never anticipated such a startling possibility of depravity as this. The idea of a husband affably proposing to exert himself in blinding the attention of the community from the misdeeds of his wife, was simply unparalleled in the annals of viciousness.

"But there is one thing, you won't say any thing about my being there, eh? My wife doesn't know it, and I wouldn't like to have her," continued the Colonel.

("The depraved wretch! His wife at least is innocent.) Allow me to observe, sir," said Nat, sternly, "that it was entirely by mistake that I happened to meet her there."

"Oh, never mind, I assure you I shall be discreet," said the Colonel, stopping.

"(Heavens!)—but I now free myself from the whole matter, sir! It was entirely accidental, entirely accidental," continued the excited Nat, "and I should have immediately left her with you!"

"What?"

"It may be hard work for her, but her love should be bestowed upon you alone. It is your duty alone to foster it, and I now call upon you to foster it."

"Hey?"

"For the sake of society, at least, if not for your own."

("He's been suddenly sun-struck! What an absurd, ridiculous vagary! His head is weak!) Your head is weak, my friend. Here, just lean on me and step into the shade for a moment."

("He thinks I am a fool for refusing his rascally propositions! My duty calls upon me to defy him, and by heavens, I will on the spot.) Wretch! misguided being! You carry pistols. Are they loaded?" said Nat.

"No."

"Then lend me one and follow me!" continued Nat, in his distraction. "Back of the church, and at thirty paces. You will be handy to the graveyard!"

"What! Wait! It is Sunday! (What the deuce

has got into him! Is he infuriated because I discovered him there?) I say, don't you see it is Sunday?"

"Gracious! so it is. I forgot. Yes, the sacredness of the hour must divest me of a consideration of this matter, and go, sir; but perhaps to-morrow, to-morrow, sir, you may hear of my just indignation! I shall be cooler, at any rate!" Here he bolted off distractedly, towards the village.

"Heavens! what is it?" continued he, as he walked along, leaving the Southerner regarding him in amazement. "There is something in this terrible weather which makes people singularly dry. I was really thirsting after his blood, and just now Warriston—Deuce, I forgot to hand her into the carriage, or even to bow to her. Oh, dear! In such insidious ways as this does villainy visit itself upon innocent parties."

CHAPTER XIX.

A DIVERSIFIED VISIT OF OBADIAH TO POMPNEY.

On the following Wednesday, Obadiah Baylon made his appearance at the Place, with an apology from Mr. Warriston, who had been influenced by something or somebody, to send a letter of extenuation to Charles directly, although he probably gnashed his teeth while writing it. The latter received the missive, and read it, but beyond that, he took no notice of it whatever, and turning away from the ambassador with an impassive countenance, left him to meditate upon the unexpected drifts in sublunary matters.

"This young man's stomach evidently rebels against me! A man without politeness or bowels! Of course he don't know what a companion I am, as he is a man of wealth now, and I am only one who is going to be. But I can be instructive while sober, and whenever I am drunk I must be amusing."

While making this humorous reflection, and replacing more firmly upon his head his hat, which the topknot had been gradually moving off towards the back part, he observed his friend Dinah's father, wending his way hastily from the park to the stable. He commenced to follow, when, near the stable, a dog of the bull species, with a very broad muzzle, thought it his duty to set him. Just as the creeping animal had reached his calves, and was contemplating with sniffs which one he would attack first, the faint, suppressed shriek of the prospective victim called the attention of the old man; and benevolence in his mouth, extricated him from a very fine set of teeth in the dog's. "He is an animal without beauty, but evidently in health," said Baylon. "Teeth inserted at the shortest notice. Tie him up and lend me that hoe, and I'll beat him over the head."

"Do you want to see me, Obadiah?" asked the old man.

"Yes, I thought you might want to come to chapel. You are getting comfortably fixed here now, and you ought to come over and hear the preaching."

"Well, I will—I would like to," said the old man, confusedly. "We intend to pay you what is owing to you, pretty soon. You mustn't think you won't get it, Obadiah."

"Oh, never mind that; haven't I alway been your

friend? I want you to feel that way—and by the way, you must make Dinah feel so too. What a prejudice she has against me! But it is only temporary, I know. Well, good-bye. I see you don't want to be disturbed now. Come over to chapel and be more friendly, and make your daughter my friend. She'll know she's wrong in thinking hard of me!—They are entirely too comfortable here. If I want to go on in these parts, I must certainly have 'em out of this. The girl'll get power of her own, if she's left here. It's her nature. Yes, I will seek an interview with the lady mistress of this household," soliloquized he, as he walked with uncertain step towards the parlor, in which Charles's mother was sitting. His knees were the abodes of a constitutional weakness, and bent inward to a deep extent, as though they had been originally jointed the wrong way. Although, on his request being granted, he approached the lady with the timidity which such a nature would have in presence of her's, he was pleased to observe that she became so much interested in the conversation as to permit him to continue it, even after he had stated to her the pleasant peacemaking object of his visit, and to listen with much attention, as he was gradually led to refer to other matters. It may have been simply his singular humoristic manner which rendered the remarks of the inferior acceptable to the lady, but ever so little of the poison of prejudice is a powerful sweetener.

The conversation lasted some time, and Obadiah left with the conviction that the devil ramifies his business extensively on very little capital. As he walked off on the sward, his revery was interrupted for a moment by a slight episode on the part of Colonel Norcomb, who happened to be preparing his gun for a sylvan errand, and feeling indefinitely that there was something wicked about, was disposed to try the efficacy of his instrument upon the overseer. "Don't!" said the latter, laughing at the humor of the thing, but with a frantic gesticulation.

"Well, I won't kill you now!" said the Colonel, still drawing his aim upon him.

"Don't! It might go off before I do, sir. Tell him not to," said the bailiff, uneasily, to the youth, James Gluckinson, who appeared to be joining him at this point in a stealthy way, for some purpose or other. His equanimity being restored, he now wended his way slowly out of sight of the house, and so profound was his revery into which he fell once more, that he scarcely noticed the youth at his side, accompanying him in mysterious silence.

"She has licked me again," said the latter, finally, in a mournful whisper. The breezes took up the whisper, and bore it off to the home of the smaller echoes.

"Eh, what?—Yes!—yes!" said Obadiah.

"Oh, dear! Mr. Obadiah, she bullies me all the time. I can't stand it!" (Another silence.) She's very strong! I'll have to run away! I told 'em at the house, and they laughed, and Misses Adeline said, 'Why, what can exasperate the cook so against him? perhaps it is because he has not proposed to her!' (A pause.) She wanted to put me in the water-butt the other day. No one takes my part except Dinah. Dear Miss Dinah. How I do adore her, and she does me now, I know. First she pitied me, and now she loves me," continued he, with a melancholy chuckle.

"What is that? What were you saying—Dinah—what?" said Baylon, suddenly arousing.

"Dear Mr. Obadiah, the cook licked me to-day. She nearly strangled me. Please tell me what to do. Nobody'll help me, but you, who are a Christying, will."

"Resort to blessed religion, James," said Baylon, with a secret laugh, as he mocked the honest language of some of his brethren of the chapel. "There—there only can be found consolation for the troubles which hedge us about in this worldly career, of any kind, James. Above all, bear a contrite spirit."

"I do. She's stronger than I am, and I have to. Durn her!"

"No, no, swear not. Be ever humble in this earthly sphere. Better even than anger, to invite this woman to beat you, James."

"Oh, there is no need for etiquette. She doesn't mind it. But please, you'll help me. 'Tis something I've been thinking of, and it'll stop her m'lignince!"

"Yes, yes, well—go on," said Baylon, abstractedly, who had relapsed after his humor, into his revery again.

("Perhaps he won't hit back, and I can do it without lettin' him into it. No, it ain't safe.) Mr. Obadiah, the next time you come over, I want you to let me—you won't be angry—it'll scare her. I'll just punch your head, or knock it against the wall," said Gluckinson, softly.

"Eh, knock no one's head. Let me see, the girl is—Ever have a contrite spirit and humble," continued the absorbed Baylon, echoing his humor.

"It's better if I drew blood; I'd seem more ferogious. But if you say so, I won't. I'll just threaten to do it. I'll take up a bottle, and pretend to throw it, eh, is it agreed?"

"Yes—yes—well—James,—I am thinking of matters."

"Well, you remember—it's agreed now. You mustn't go to confusing me, by saying any thing harsh."

Baylon quite engrossed with his own thoughts, still nodded upon general principles, and from fear that the agreement might be revoked in some way, Gluckinson at once artfully turned the conversation upon pirates. Finally, as he was about leaving, having awakened the overseer's attention by some singular ideas which he put forth in deference to him, upon the compatibility of that romantic profession with a devotional nature, he enthusiastically concluded to continue with him through the wood, especially as the cook was in the rear; and commenced to regale him with the thrilling story of a pleasing and accomplished Corsair, who in the terrible fulfilment of his stormy yet fascinating career, cut the throats of a whole ship's company which he had captured, save one, whom he reserved for the experimental purpose of skinning alive, having invented a new method in some studious moments, which for novelty and exquisite torture, he flattered himself had never before been equalled. The denouement was, that this person turned out to be guilty of the meanest kind of ingratitude; for having accosted the Captain one morning on deck, with "Good morning; it is damp weather," he immediately spitted him with a long sword, as he was about replying "Yes, I think we will have rain," and leaving the instrument sticking in his abdomen, walked forward to converse further with the busy sailors on the weather, and other interesting subjects. This narrative pleased Obadiah very much; but still, he said he felt sorry the hero was killed.

CHAPTER XX.

IN THE WOOD.

DIANA, returning from a visit to the negroes living by the lake, kept her pace through the midwood. The kindled grace of health still glowing on her cheek, thus slighted the wooing coolness of the shade; but her languid foot in returning elasticity, acknowledged its gratefulness. As she pursued her springing steps like the forest doe, amid the changing scene, a pensiveness stole upon her face. Perhaps there was a young heart singing its silent praise to Him who made the solemn aisles; a bright mind bowed in philosophic contemplation of the varied beauty of His work. The growing sound of a waterfall waked her being from its revery, and charmed her steps by the dewy softness of its murmur, towards its incessant flood. At the gnarled foot of an elm, around whose trunk the graceful woodbine wrought its embrace, the young girl casting upon the dark velvet grass her summer hat, seated herself in pleasant, negligent rest. In such places as these, a species of fine wordless reasoning is apt to be inspired in the bosom of the melancholy wanderer, finding a temporary rest from the persecution of misfortune, or in the bosom of those more unhappy beings who are flying from the consciousness of their own vice.

In the simple ecstacy of an hour with nature, they are made to feel that God is good, even when He seems to reward the virtuous with suffering, or punish the guilty with success.

The girl rose with a vivacious air. She saw the black flood rolling lazily over the low-resounding rocks just above, with now and then an idle dash of foam; while in front of her, and beneath the slow eddies circling on the bosom of the widening basin, the rays refracted from the white pebbles of the bottom, met her sight. She unhooked her dress, which parted over her bosom, and falling in loose folds on either side, fluttered gently as an occasional breath of air strayed from the deep recesses of the grove. Upon a leafy branch, overhanging the opposite side of the musical stream, a squirrel had placed himself, and was expressing his astonishment and gratification at the gentle presence of the new comer, by numberless affable frisks of his caudal bush, and a merry twinkle of his black eye. The trout darted to and fro in their liquid home, now and then adding a dimple to the surface, as they jumped with a snapping sound at the dancing fly, or the unfortunate long-legs, sprawling on the winding current. Besides these sounds, some few slighter touches of harmonious eloquence from nature might be heard, such as the fall of a twig, the rustle of a leaf, or the alighting of a vigorous grasshopper. It was now the dead hour of noon, and the birds had ceased their songs and retired to concealment within the thicket. Unclasping the buckle of her shoes and removing her stockings, the young girl placed her feet in the refreshing stream.

A kind of being, known to the imagination of the classic age, when depicted upon the canvas or eclogic page, are represented as men with short, crooked horns sprouting from their heads, and the more decided in bad character, with the feet and legs of goats. They were the retainers of the drunken god, and in his mad orgies, the latter were especially conspicuous for their riotous obliquities. The superstitious peasant of the golden ages offered to these sylvan monsters his first fruits; while the girl of his love, as she passed in the grove at the twilight hour, asked protection of heaven against them. While Dinah bent over the rushing stream of the "Indian maiden's fountain" in the sequestered depths, lingering in girlish delight as it parted around her legs, two of these beings, who might have come down from classic ages through Indian scenes and forests to the present time, lay secreted in a thicket near by, and within passionate view. One was an old and malignant satyr,—the other a faun, possessing a youthful face, the lines of which indicate a good heart within. As they lay concealed, the elder monster whispered to the younger, that this lonely being, simple as she was in her mortality, was the associated favorite of more than one goddess; that while Cytherea had fastened around her waist the zone conferring radiant beauty, Diana had thrown about her the halo of virtue, and Minerva had given her the kiss of immortal wit; and that he didn't like to meet her.

"I guess I won't say any thing to her now," said he, "and we won't disturb her. I'm afraid of the gods."

As they walked away in quiet, he began to converse with the faun upon other subjects, and commenced particularly to inquire with reference to his own reputation among those with whom his companion dwelled. "Do they ever say any thing of me over your way?"

"Yes," said the young and truthful faun, "I heard 'em the other day!—they said you were one of the biggest scoundrels that ever lived."

"Well, well, that will do," replied he, quickly changing the subject to other and more agreeable matters, and now falling into an evil revery.

On the way the younger, who went foremost, held a bough innocently to let his companion come through the thicket unmolested, but relinquishing it too soon, knocked him against a tree with great violence, and caused him, in the manner of the poet Horace, to damn the man's great-grandfather who planted it.

CHAPTER XXI.

NAT AND THE SOUTHERNERS.

Mrs. Norcomb made up her mind to divulge her escapade to the Colonel.

"Do you know, Fred, I've been very foolish," said she, as they were retiring one night.

"More than usual?" asked the Colonel, blandly.

"Oh, no; but I allude to it, because it is a case in which it has not been the result of my usual confidence in you. It was all by myself. I went alone to the ball the other night."

"What? Eh?" said the Colonel, quite astonished. "I didn't see you. I didn't—"

"I know it. I wanted to surprise you. I took

Dinah, and we drove in together. It was late when we arrived, and—and I didn't succeed in getting into the ball-room, for—for—as I was crossing the park to reach the ladies' dressing-room, a person who imagined he knew us, approached us, and—"

"Oh, the deuce!"

"I didn't know him. I couldn't see him. I think, however, he was shorter by a head than you, at least. As he immediately commenced to pursue, I ran back to the carriage."

"Oh dear, enough, I forgive you. You escaped, and I forgive you," said the Colonel, hastily at this point.

"I knew you would—"

"Yes, yes, certainly. (If my wife was running away from a man, under the very same circumstances under which I was chasing a woman, and there was any impropriety in the circumstances, it is my duty to forgive her at the very least!")

"But I want to tell you all about it, you who are so watchful for me—such a faithful husband to me always—"

"Oh, never mind, never mind!" said the Colonel, wincing slightly. "It is enough, I forgive you! (Gracious, a suspicion suddenly comes over me!")

"I encountered Mr. Bonney, the young lawyer—"

("Oh the devil! It was. It accounts for his insanity. In my mad career, I was chasing my own wife. What if she should find it out, after what I said! Confound the French novels!")

"The wretch," continued the wife, with a slight smile, "the wretch who caused my fright, (That's me!

There is no doubt about it, it was a wretched idea!) came along stumbling in the dark—"

"Yes, and the scoundrel attempted to speak to you—the impudent rascal ventured to say something," said the Colonel, with a violent gesture. ("I must appear heated!")

"Yes, although he was careful enough to conceal his identity. After some few minutes' parley, being probably intimidated and frightened, you know, ha! ha! by the superior presence of the young lawyer, he went away—not without advising the young man, however, to knock my husband down if he should meet him. Think of it—to knock you down! I believe, too, he said something even about gallantry, demanding that he should offer to kiss my hand at least, which for the time apparently made a deep impression upon the young man, as he—"

"He didn't, did he? (Calhoun! What a retribution for my impropriety! I advised him to do this very thing, and to knock myself down, if I should interfere!)

"Oh no, he carried me safely to the carriage, where I found Dinah, who had been separated from me."

"Ah, I like him. I must see him immediately, and thank him, (and warn him, by Calhoun!) Sue, we don't know this miserable individual. Perhaps on this occasion only, Susan, he went so far as to forget himself, by way of experiment you know, may be. At any rate we can't find him out just now, and say nothing about it at present, eh?"

"Well I don't know, but I am so glad I have told you, and now I feel happy, Fred—don't you?" said the young lady with a smile.

"Oh yes, yes! After all, it may have been rather the result of circumstances than any thing else, eh, don't you think so, the result of circumstances? However, I'll go immediately, and see if the young lawyer knew the unprincipled wretch. If I find him, I don't know whether I shall kill him or not. (At any rate, I might safely promise her to be present on the occasion of my dissolution.")

The Colonel went to town the very next morning, and thus the young lawyer Nathaniel was soon pleasantly relieved of a stern duty, which he had been revolving the performance of, in consequence of his brief intercourse with the Colonel, and which he had resolved should consist in the erection of a stage in front of his office, the calling of a public meeting thereat, and his denouncing to the citizens from his elevated position, in unmeasured terms, the unworthy character of the Southerner sojourning in their midst; and further, as the latter conjured him not to let his wife know that he was the derelict individual, and as soon thereafter, the wife conjured him not to let her husband know she knew it was he, he promised them both, and thus became the intimate friend of both, and confiding to them in return the secret of his love, sought much after their society for consolation.

Coming up one morning, for instance, to the Place, with sporting intentions, and seeking the Southerner's apartments, he discovered symptoms of suppressed exasperation upon the countenance of the latter.

"Sue is always wanting to wait upon me, and fatiguing herself with my wants. I saw you coming up with your gun, and I thought I'd better be putting on my boots, when she insisted on getting them for me, instead of sending for those rascally niggers; and now she has gone to see after my gun. She is always watching for opportunities of this kind, to wear herself out." (Kicking one of his slippers into the air in a rage.)

"Do you know what I'd do now, if I had a wife who would commit such an enormity? I wouldn't put 'em on after she brought 'em. I'd hunt in my slippers."

"These boots must have cost a great deal of nightly vigil to the ingenious individual who made 'em. They are too small in seven places, and too large in four. It's my wife's idea, instead of permitting me to buy my habiliments at regularly accredited places, she insists upon my going into dark alleys, and other obscure places, to patronize attenuated tailors and bootmakers who happen to have a large family of small daughters. I have my revenge, however; I go there furtively on other occasions, and kick 'em. My hair will want cutting pretty soon, and I've no doubt she'll find some individual who will propose to do it with a hatchet—"

"His family being at dinner with the shears!"

"Yes—There's my wife down there now, with that girl Dinah! Not a solitary nigger glads the scene. I rather think they've gone off to enjoy the rum of some abolitionist about here, exhorting them to fly. It is quite probable he will not succeed, but I still have hopes," continued he with a cheerful air. "I begin to feel better. Do you know, Nathaniel, that that young girl Dinah there, is a good girl. There is many a sermon to human nature, in the actions of girls of her age; and besides that, every word she utters appears to have been dipped previously in common sense.

My wife loves her, and so do I as far as my wife will let me. She is a good girl. There isn't any one about here that can compare with her. No, not one."

"Look here, I've no objection to your making that statement on the spur of the moment here, but do you mean to assert that Miss Wellwood is not the most remarkable specimen of spirit, education, common sense, and brilliancy of complexion who ever lived, or who ever is going to—do you mean—"

SOUTHERNER, (maliciously). "Why, Laura is a very good girl, but do you—do you think she—is much—do you think that—"

NAT. "By Jove! this is unexpected and infuriating. Have you got your pistols with you? I propose that we stand off at ten paces, and try a shot at one another."

SOUTHERNER. "With all my heart."

NAT. "On the whole I conclude I won't; but—"

SOUTHERNER. "Oh do. It will put you out of misery!"

"Whenever I mention her name, Colonel, I feel a vacuum here," said Nat, laying his hand upon his forehead, but quickly changing it to his bosom. "The raging fires of my hope are e'en now almost consumed, and I feel I shall be obliged to carry about inside of me, for the rest of my wearied existence, the gloomy crater of an extinct volcano."

"An awful load!"

"It is singular; the more I show my devotion to her, the more coldly she treats me. The other day on leaving her residence, when I asked her if there was any thing I could do for her in the village, she said, 'Yes, stay there!' To be sure, she said she was coming over herself; still, on the whole, it was unsatisfactory."

"Why, Nat, what a fool you are! You must affect indifference for her. You must rouse her pride! It is the chief spur to women's feelings, the vain creatures!"

"I can't. How shall I do it? She makes me blind. She blinds my understanding with her wit, and my eyes with her beauty."

"How? Sit down with your back to her for instance. Laugh when she says any thing serious, and look solemn when she attempts any thing facetious. Put your hands under your coat tails—if it were only winter now, and there was a fire, you might lift them up. There is nothing so fearful to woman as indifference, it is worse than hate. Do you take snuff? Take snuff, but refrain from sneezing; it will argue superiority."

"Great heaven! lift up my coat tails, it's brutal."

"It's philosophical. I've tried it. Just think of it."

"Think! I have been really so much occupied with my emotions, I haven't had time to think, and yet I feel I could talk in an inspired way to her now,—in the language of poetry."

"Don't you do it. Confine yourself to prose; you might scare her."

"Ah, that beaming eye, brighter than all others!" commenced Nat.

"You don't mean to say that she has got one eye brighter than the other? I never noticed that."

"Oh, the maddening sparkles of her beaming eyes," said Nat, reiterating his thought in a different form.

"Well, to use a maritime expression, in a modified manner, bless her eyes, I say. Let us go a hunting."

The two hunting dogs who usually accompanied Nat and the Colonel, were eating their breakfast out of a common dish. One of them, the lean one with a broad face, had just walked away with the principal bone of the meal, slily abstracted from the platter, in a moment of unguardedness on the part of the other and fatter one, who, having raised his head with a snuffle of astonishment, was now gazing at him, with intense disgust visibly expressed upon his countenance.

"She is a goddess," continued Nat, as they walked towards the stables, in ecstatic rhapsody upon the object of his emotions, "although there is no goddess who has her mortal beauty;" and thereupon he raised his gun, and fired into the old oak under which they were passing, partly as a salute in honor of his love, and partly to clean out the instrument of sylvan warfare. An ancient owl, who had been sound asleep in the tree, slowly digesting the last chicken he had eaten, fell at his feet. If the aged bird had had time, he would probably have not been less astonished than Nat was, at this unexpected occurrence. As it was he had given up digesting earthly chickens, on the instant, and his spirit had immediately flown to roost in some venerable tree in celestial fields.

CHAPTER XXII.

THE FATES SIMPER.

It was a still July night, when Charles, who had prolonged his visit to the residence of Dr. Fuffles until past midnight, started beneath the moon towards his home. The intellectual excitement caused by the conversation with his friend and pastor, still possessed him, as he walked along gazing at the tranquil landscape, or the chaste planet as she ever and anon entered a cloud and quickly emerged again.

The clergyman loved the son almost as much as he had once loved the mother, and his naturally sentimental temperament had discovered itself in this conversation, tinging his thoughts with romance. Charles, excited with the glowing images brought from the pastor's stores of poetic literature, resolved to deviate from the road to his residence, and passing circuitously by the lake, view its scenery in the pleasant silence of the midnight hour. The last subject of the conversation recurring, the young man as he pursued his way, thought rather with the pulses of his heart than his intellect, of the sweet lingering hours of Puritan love in early New England; of the blooming lips of laughter, and eloquent cheeks, which graced the clergyman's female ancestry. The life of gilded youths generally damages, by rude over-use, that delicate machine which is placed in the human bosom to manufacture feeling for its possessor. In its ill-used condition, it generally produces disquiet instead of happiness. Charles felt more sorrow, because these women were in the dust, for instance, than pleasure at the recital of their loves.

The narrow by-road which he had taken, as it neared the lake, passed through a forest, whose precincts the light of the moon could not penetrate, save at intervals in the cleft thus made by the road, which wound along like a spotted snake, now in shade and now in silver light. Not a sound fell upon the young man's ear as he passed along this leafy corridor. Emerging therefrom, he beheld far in the distance in front of him, a lofty mountain, which, looming above the smaller ones around, and encircled at the summit by a white cloud of fog, looked, to his fancy, as if it might be a female giant sitting up in her night-cap, with her family nestled around her, to await the return of her friend and partner—some intoxicated mountain absent upon a debauch. Nearer by, the road ran down by the lake, whose surface here and there might be seen through the trees, reflecting in deathly stillness the pale light of the planet. A distant cock started from slumber, and probably laboring under the hallucination that the morning was breaking, might be faintly heard upon the other side of the water, crowing his premature welcome to the god of day. Charles stopped on the leafy margin, and leaning against the rocks which the night dew had not dampened, mused upon the still scene, in a revery characterized by exquisite melancholy.

He was at last about continuing his walk away from the subdued splendor, and towards his couch, when the dull regular sound of the row-locks of a boat, and the easy plash of oars suddenly fell upon his ear, proceeding on the facile echo of the night's stillness, along the water from the distant side of the lake. Soon, while gazing in the direction to which the sound attracted his attention, he dimly discovered emerging from the haziness, upon the silver shining surface, and rounding a small wooded island, which seemed a part of the mainland, a little black object, whose course was directed nearly towards the point at which he was standing. His curiosity was aroused, although he naturally conjectured that it was the boat of some nocturnal fisherman, returning from a favorite stake, haunted by the pouts, and loaded with the finny spoil. The tiny vessel slowly approaching in its oblique path, however, his conjecture was modified, as he indistinctly observed its occupants to be a man and a woman, rowing along in silence. Who were they? Some farmer and his wife or daughter, who had been to visit a neighbor on the opposite side of the lake, and were returning at this belated hour to their homes. They turned their boat as they neared the lateral shore, towards a little gulf of the lake, covered with water-lilies, around which the road ran ere it diverged, and Charles soon heard the crunching noise of its bottom upon the pebbles, as it landed on the side the farthest from him. Here instead of disappearing upon the road, which was overhung at a short distance with foliage, they stopped in the space cleared by its proximity to the lake, and commenced to walk up and down together, in a singular, loving manner. The fog still gathering over the water, conjoined with the distance, prevented a distinct distinguishment of this pair; but the young man was enabled to observe from their motions, that their feelings seemed the vivacious and mettlesome product of romantic and enthusiastic natures. Hanging upon the arm of the other while they walked, the female bent around often, as if to look in his eyes in a tender confiding way, or perhaps in a quick impassioned kiss placed upon his cheek, to show the earnest token of her affection for him, while he, on his part, seemed to display a kind of affable haughtiness in his gait, as though he were proud for the moment at having her upon his arm.

This sprightly softness, this romanesque sensibility, between two beings at such an hour, and such a place, though singular, would perhaps have seemed easily referable to a natural yet sentimental cause, had not another incident in their eccentric communion suddenly startled the silent observer. The low conversation which was taking place between them in the purring tone of affection, had been too indistinct to be remarkable, until it was suddenly broken by a loud and bitter laugh on the part of the male. It was the same voice he had invented in his considerable dream of the pioneer, and which had been echoed to an excited imagination, in the silent hall of his residence thereafter. He stepped forward in the earnest rummage of this affair. A singular scene of wrangling seemed suddenly to have commenced between these two beings, or rather of bitterness on the part of the male; for the girl stood apparently bowed in silence to the reproaches of the male, which were attended by wild gestures. His singular speech fell thus in sudden excitement from his lips, as if called forth by some old subject of strife between them, which had been mentioned once more. In the impulsive conviction that wrong might perhaps be done between them, Charles did not refrain from crying aloud an alarm of warning to these beings, whether they were supernatural or not. His halloo was mingled and annihilated by the wild echoes of a dozen hills, as though it were mocked by fiends guarding the interview, yet it appeared not to have failed to startle the actors, for they ran quickly along the road, and as they reached the leafy bower, the female turned to listen.

Who was this listening being? In that peculiar attitude he had further proof that his dream was not a thought-born unreality, for it seemed the same as that of the pioneer's sweetheart, as he saw her in the dim chamber. Were the legends true, and did the spirits of those beings thus live over again their earthly existence of loving and quarrelling? But it was here that the young man was overcome with extraordinary feelings of astonishment from another cause; for in the midst of these fancies, the previous motions of the female seemed growing familiar, the remembrance struck him, that he had once before observed this attitude, as the attitude of an earthly being, and he thought he now saw through the temporary thinness of the fog, moving, as it gathered, the pale features and peculiarly falling hair of that being, of the girl Dinah, the resident of his own mansion! For the moment, the investiture of this young creature with other than human attributes, aye, even to the thrilling convertibility of her living, breathing presence with the shadowy identity of the princess of the past, seemed not the slight and passing work of fancy, but of the faculty which deals with reality. Yet in the midst of his confusion, impelled by the simple conviction of his senses, he rushed along the road bordering the lake, to the spot where the singular scene had occurred. He reached it to find no one there, although the noise of some one retreating through the groves, seemed borne faintly to his ear.

At last, with the firm supremacy of his commoner sense, with the conviction that it was the girl Dinah in all her humanity, and that she would, without doubt, seek the mansion, he determined to reach it before her, and by accosting her, clear up the mystery. It would have taken him perhaps an hour to accomplish the distance from the lake to the mansion at an ordinary pace, but animated by the impulses of a tinged curiosity, he reached, in a much shorter time, the nearest gate of the park, which was one in its rear wall, glowing with the warmth produced by his rapid pace. The fog, though moonlit, had become so thick that the outlines of the house were not distinguishable, and even the most adjacent shrubbery of the pear and other fruit trees, whose long branches overhung the avenue upon which he entered, was concealed in the silver sheen. Under the lessening influence of his expectation, which now seemed hardly valid, he pursued upon the earthy unresounding avenue, the familiar way from the postern towards the mansion, and reason indeed was determining his footsteps to his chamber, when he stopped again, for a soft and flying pace seemed suddenly passing him in the deep fog. He even thought he heard her rapid breathing, he even imagined he felt the touch of a floating robe. Ere the flash of his indecision ended, one of the dogs of the place jumped upon him in joyful meeting, and with heightened noise, scampered off in the fog and over the bushes, to return again as quickly to him. Yet this last cozening and trickery of his imagination, if it were such, was stronger than the deductions of reason, and with a hasty command to the dog, he commenced a reinvigorated ransacking. It was again without success in the silence and the fog, and after a few penultimate moments at the door of the main hall, of confusion of thought, in which self-ridicule at a proposition to rush into the girl's chamber was conspicuous, he at last retired to his couch with the reflection, that even apart from the romantic singularity of the scene, producing solid wonder, the further gratification of his curiosity was quite pardonable. As master of the house, at least, he had a right to investigate this midnight adventure of a servant, by subtle or open inquiry.

CHAPTER XXIII.

RELIGIOUS PENANCE.—A SCENE OF PASSION.

Mr. Bonney was walking along the road at evening towards Squire Wellwood's mansion, secretly practising the taking of snuff, and causing the air to resound with explosions, when his attention was called to an individual approaching him, who appeared to be selecting with great deliberation, the diameters of the mud puddles as his line of march. Nat was astounded. He at first supposed it was an escaped lunatic; secondly, a person tight; thirdly, a person whose boots were tight; and fourthly, he saw, to his amazement, it was the learned clergyman, Dr. Fuffles. In accordance with the High Church doctrine of penance, the Doctor had lately proposed to himself to chastise his heart at judicious intervals, with a severe application of the virtue of humility, assisting the punishment by a consonant neglect of person. He had on this occasion persistently refused to have his face washed all day. His hair was now quite dishevelled, and his countenance was much spotted with mud.

"Mr. Bonney," said he, in calm continuance of his pious purpose as he came up, "let virtue still triumph over a pitiful sinner. Let me acknowledge to you that I am vicious, that I am a man of crimes. Nathaniel, I have committed murder!"

"Good God! when?" said the startled Nat, jumping back a foot or two, not knowing but that it was a freak of insanity, and he might be contemplating another.

"That is, in my heart—in my thoughts. What makes me unfailingly wish for a fire-arm, when cats disturb me in my studies, for instance, but this murderous rage in my heart? What made me wish once, under the same circumstances, to throw a child out of the window? I meant to convey to you the fact that I too am filled with all the vices to which man is liable. Every one, I know, thinks me a good man. You, for instance, think me virtuous; but let me ask you, why has not a man with such a perception as yours, long ere this observed my failings—"

"I have, Doctor. I did some time ago," said Nat.

"I ask you—why have you not observed that I am but a poor miserable creature of appetite and passions? Why are not the mean tendencies of my nature easily discoverable to you?—"

"They have been—some of 'em have been quite transparent," said the affable Nat, desirous of showing a cheerful consonance with his eccentric pastor.

"Young man," said the Doctor, with sudden severity, "you've interrupted me twice, in the most unwarrantable manner. Now let me ask you, and I will do it with candor and coolness, young man, what do you mean by it?"

"Why, you did it yourself," said Nat. "But perhaps you are mistaken, Doctor, in your proposition. I think you meant to say that we are all prone merely to vices, and included yourself in the general arraignment. You had better take a pinch of snuff."

"Yes, it was so," said the Doctor, somewhat mollified, and recollecting the chastisement still due to his nature, as he took the snuff. "You are right, young man. Yes, we are all prone to vices; and I meant to say that I did not arrogate to myself any immunity from some of them; but it was rather to a terrible pride, the worst pride of all, I meant to refer—a pride of intellect. Unwise friends allude in fondness to my talents and genius; they speak of me as distinguished. Nat, I am not a man of genius. I obstinately say it. Let the world continue persistently and infatuatedly, to assert the contrary. I know it and confess it—I am not a man of genius."

"That is the point," said Nat. "Now do you know I have always thought so?"

"Let them call my mind great, and point with admiration to its energies; who so well qualified to judge of it as I am? I know my intellectual deficiencies, and I assert to you that I have them."

"I see, I see, you are intellectually rather than morally deficient. It is your head that is weak, and not your heart. Yes!"

"Young man, I am astonished and grieved. I knew

your father when he was a boy. I was in the house when you were vaccinated. You have grown since then, under my spiritual guidance, to an expanded manhood, and the result is you don't know any thing at all, and what is more, you are inclined to be vicious. Good-night. I grieve for the state of your bosom."

"Well, good-bye, Doctor; I was going to visit Miss Wellwood."

"Eh? You will find her at the Place with Mr. Warrison. I saw them enter the Park gate. Good-bye, young man, I grieve for you."

"Ha! still better; even in the presence of the hated rival," reflected Nat, recurring to his snuff vigorously as he walked along; "That is, he would be a hated rival if I had my own way about it. But nature has mysteriously developed in my bosom, a devilish disagreeable liking for him, which I somehow cannot get rid of."

Numerous and almost daily meetings were now brought about between Charles and Laura, naturally effected by their adjacence, and more particuarly by the growing desires of either to bask in the sunshine of the other's smiles. Charles was carried away by Laura's sweet regard of the wants of his moral nature, her devotion to him, by the simple power of being loved by her, in fact.

"My love for this dear girl," thought he, "would perhaps have slumbered forever unawakened in my bosom, had I not first known that she loved me. A woman who is a woman, and who loves a man, need never despair. If she only perseveres, she can win him to her, had she to bring him out of hate. Unless she truly loves him she will fail indeed; for one half of the power of her love consists in the fact that its absence is unmistakable to the object of it. Really, I wish she didn't feel so ardently her attachment to me. I sometimes feel indeed I have no right to such deep affection." Laura also, while seated by his side upon the terrace this evening, was wrapped in soft musing. Her mind reverted to the absurd attention of the young advocate Nat. "He never could love me with one half the wonderful devotion Charlie has already shown. At any rate, I cannot be so diffusive now. Heavens! there he is. What strange behavior. What does he mean by those singular stops?"

The young advocate might be seen upon the avenue approaching the house, with his hat cocked upon one side of his head. At intervals of ten or twelve feet he stopped, and projecting his leg, executed short and incomplete pirouettes, with a pleasant negligent air of deliberate regardlessness of appearance. Laura bowed to him in some wonderment, as he approached the terrace, under which he stopped and drawing himself up, held his breath in a very uncomfortable manner, and looked sternly for a moment at the parties seated above.

"Ha! they regard me. She already calls his attention to my scornful bearing."

"What is the matter with him?" said Laura, to Charles; "he looks like a fool."

"Oh, nothing," said Charles, somewhat puzzled himself.

Nat put his eyes upon the unhappy woman, and walked majestically upon the terrace.

"Good evening, Mr. Bonney," said they both together.

"I reply, good evening—I say, good evening to you," said that individual, pompously, looking toward Charles.

"But what is—this is singular," ejaculated the young lady.

"Ha! ever the idle question of the young and inexperienced female," said the young lawyer.

"Eh, what?" asked Charles, with a little severity, "what did you say?"

"Oh, nothing," replied the other gentleman, with a sudden change of manner. "Good evening, good evening; a little abstraction. (I was bordering on the impolite. He noticed it. I'd better stick to the supercilious.")

"Oh, well, collect yourself, Mr. Bonney," said Charles.

"Have you heard the melancholy news?" asked Laura, reverting to a subject of her conversation with Charles. "Julia Colgate has lost her grandmother, Mr. Bonney."

"Ha! ha!" exclaimed that individual.

"Dear me, I assure you, sir, this matter should not be treated trivially. We have not grandmothers to lose every day of our lives, sir."

("That is intended as a joke, no doubt. Playful allusion to the limited number of grandmothers provided for us by nature. Now is the time to look devilish solemn, but I can't, it is too funny. Ah, this affects her. I wonder if it is safe to try the snuff-box now. I think I could do it without sneezing.")

"And now, Julia, with her husband, is going to leave Mrs. Colgate, and live at the West," continued

Laura. "What must be a mother's feelings at parting with her only child!"

"Never having been a mother, it is impossible for me to say, ha! ha!" replied Nat, disposed to be witty.

"It is proposed among our neighbors, to have a picnic at the lake to-morrow, Mr. Bonney," said Charles, somewhat puzzled by the young man's conduct, and inclined to refer it to a slight intoxication.

"Oh, yes: and do come, Mr. Bonney," cried Laura, with ill-concealed warmth. "We shall have such fun. The more the merrier."

"Hurrah! Of course. By all means. Oh, yes!" exclaimed Nat, with equal ardor, sending to oblivion the sage advice of his friend the Southerner, in the delirium of ecstasy which this proposition excited in his being, and had he not been interrupted by an extraordinary occurrence, which a few moments after took place in the house, it is quite probable he might have dismounted his conversational organ, upon the subject of the proposed pleasure party, ere his fervor was assuaged.

The young man Rudolph, who had sought an opportunity to accompany Laura to this mansion, for the purpose solely of meeting the lowly being who was now wielding, perhaps involuntarily, such a power over his feelings, failed not, in the cunning of his desires, to watch the moment of careless conversation, when he might loiter away from the ostensible objects of his visit, to seek the real centre of his ill-balanced thoughts. The necessities of Dinah's position in the house soon gave him an opportunity. Were the scene which ensued between these ill-assorted beings to be described by Beethoven or Mozart, the masters would employ the grand crash of the orchestral instruments. Could the darkness have been lit up with melo-dramatic fire, it would have seemed as if there were, as usual, a splendid demon with fierce eyes there, ready to fly away with a weak-minded girl. However, in this case, it was the demon who was weak in his violence, and the young girl who was strong in her quiet. Whatever he may have said in the commencement, as he caught her in the dark hall—she may not have regarded, but she soon heard him breathe her name, in tones in which the mad infirmity of a fitful temper seemed mingled with the wild idolatry of an unrefined soul. By the dull light of the night, the flash of passionate unholy love was discovered in his eyes, and a fierce wanness was spread upon his face. The demon of unlawful passion, thus taking possession of this earthly tabernacle, looked out of the windows and shook the weakly frame. The young man knew not what he did, or cared not if he knew.

He lingered on Dinah's lips till she got fairly tired. She laughed at the absurdity of his wild conduct, and had good sense enough not to create a disturbance by resisting him, and to wait patiently until his madness should exhaust itself. These moments were no doubt two or three centuries to the poor besotted drunkard of love. His moral nature was staggering with it. His spiritual constitution couldn't stand so much.

The spirits who were watching the interview saw him draw himself away, blushing like a peony, and saw the grace which passion had given him, leaving him standing for a moment, much in the position of a sheepish boy, detected in purloining sweetmeats. His constitution was one weakened by excesses. The blood fled in moral and physical eccentricity from his vitality, and he fell like a log, fainted away upon the stone floor. When he came to, Dinah held his head, brushing back his hair, and Nat, who had first arrived, was standing by in a most extraordinary state of weak excitement. The explanation by the girl, and the harmless issue of the accident, finally installed it in the minds of those assembled as somewhat ridiculous; but in addition to this result, Charles in a moment divined its real antecedent, and further the cause of the meeting upon the lake and of the unusual rage which accompanied the betrayal of feeling towards him, on the part of Warriston at the church! His reason, with a flash, projected not only the relations between the latter and the girl, but also between the reckless young man and himself, and while it led him to pass by the illusion of his hearing at the interview on the lake, as an exaggeration of this young man's voice, easily made by his own romancing fancy under the analogous influence of the hour and the scene, he laughed shortly in the rapid progress of his reflections, as he returned with the others to the parlor. "How now—does he think that I am as base as he would be, and have—ha! ha! But he cannot dare to be other than honorable towards her—even simply considering her as a member of our household, and yet their inherent and social disparity. It is laughable."

The emotion was effaced for the moment, as his memory reverted to the remarkable scene in the misty moonlight, of which he had been an involuntary witness, and notwithstanding his reasoning, a feeling with regard to the young girl still rose in his bosom, romantic, though perhaps absurd in its nature. Yet while he laughed again at his own foolishness, he resolved to seek in some manner from the girl herself, an explication of these occurrences in which she was apparently involved, for her youth, her seeming tendencies towards loftiness, tenderly suggested to his mind that she should have some friend and protector, in her relations at least with this young man, Warriston, and if not against him, against the evil power of her own circumstances. Yes, the degrading thought that she contemplated an illegitimate alliance with this young man, he spurned at once from his mind as an indignity to her character—as an impossibility; for some power made him feel, that upon entering this luxurious but horrible condition, if she were thus tempted to escape from the limits of poverty and misery, the possession of that fair face, of that singular nature, would wither and die with the first simoon breath she drew there. And further, notwithstanding the appearance of passion upon her part, in the interviews which he had beheld between them, he could not but feel that no fire of sympathy was glowing in her bosom, for his unequivalent neighbor, even were their relations honorable. Though well-educated and possessed of certain powers of attraction when he chose to exert them, and bearing about him especially that pleasing air of independence which wealth generally bestows, Warriston possessed no inherent attributes which could wake her soul in the ravishing harmony of sexual love. But while thus reasoning and taking for granted, of course, that she wielded the power in the relations, whatever they were, which existed between the two, no consideration was offered to his judgment in opposition to the conclusion that she was deceiving his ill-conditioned neighbor, in her ambition to extricate herself and her father from the miseries of their poverty and degradation. The inconsonance of this method of her ambition with the finer parts of her nature, and the innocence of youth, overwhelmed, curiously enough, in his mind, the honorable character of the aim. In his desire, as a student of human nature alone, to dissipate from his consideration this indication of a failing in her character, which was often conjectured by others, and as often gainsaid by him in his silent finalities respecting her, he wished that Rudolph's had been such a character as would have inspired a true sentiment of love in her heart, or he would willingly have believed still that some mystery connected with her was calling for his own interposition in her favor. The girl explained the occurrence before Rudolph attempted to, and Charles, who was the only one who knew the artifice she was employing, remarked the natural address with which she successfully used the machinery of headaches, swoons, assistance, and characteristics to dissipate its suspicable difficulty.

As the others left, Warriston lingered, apparently to thank her.

"Why were you so violent?" said she, in a low tone of anger to him. The flashing look she had seen in Charles's eyes, may have impelled its utterance. "You might have asked me in a decorous way, and saved your agitation," she added, with a satirical laugh. "It might have been avoided by the reflection that I would have permitted you."

"My love produces nothing but bitterness," replied the young man.

CHAPTER XXIV.

THE PICNIC.

At the particular request of Mrs. Norcomb, the girl Dinah accompanied the ladies, although Charles's mother had shewn considerable disposition for her companionship, by intimating a wish that she should stay at home with her.

The servants had proceeded ahead, and the party having assembled at the Place, started off in great merriment on the road towards the lake, the ladies mostly in carriages, and the gentlemen on horseback. It fell to the lot of Nathaniel to be mounted on the long-bodied horse Thomas, belonging to his favorite's parent. This horse was built very much in the style of the Spanish galleons of old, very high up at both ends, and very low down in the middle. Though ill-favored in personal appearance, he had been blessed with a bright understanding and a strong will, so that whenever he was led to understand, for instance, through the medium of his sensations that there was a horse-fly on his rump, no earthly power could prevent his stopping to bite off the same. Or if he heard a buzzing conspiracy in the air near his rear, to break it up, by kicking violently at it, in its inception. Nearing old Aunt Sallie Tyler's on the road, Nat expressed his fears that the animal would certainly come in pieces, if he continued his disjointed attempts at loose prancing much longer. An old man, the spouse of the ancient Sallie, standing on the road, as he witnessed these performances, was giving utterance to short yells of laughter, accompanied with convulsive grasps at his back, and rheumatic cries of "oh!" Soon Thomas, catching sight of a ruffian desperado in the shape of a monster horse-fly, lying in ambush on the leaf of a tree ahead, backed abruptly into the side of Mr. Pithkin's buggy. In consequence of this oblique excursion, Mr. Pithkin was precipitated heavily from the vehicle, and his fair companion, Miss Adeline, fell on top of him, administering to him a severe blow upon the nose with her fist, which she had clenched in terror as she fell. Amid the confusion, Mr. Pithkin rose from the ruins with a gibbous eye, a sanguinolent nose, and with feelings and pantaloons badly lacerated, but still in a stately and rectilinear manner.

Order being restored, Charles and Laura among the rest, galloped ahead, and Nat and the Colonel after them. Nat's attention was now wholly engrossed by the pleasant conversation, which he observed was being held by Charles and Laura. Their countenances were lit up with pleasure, and it was quite evident the subject of their tête-à-tête, was one which was deeply interesting to both. Nat was silent. He watched the beauty as she bent over toward Charles, and viewed her various gestures with inexpressible feelings of love and jealousy. The Colonel, who had a great love for animals, and had been surveying the magnificent creature which Charles bestrode, finally broke out in rapture. "Fine neck she has, hasn't she?"

"Neck! no painter in his dreams of grace ever saw such a neck. I can't bear to look at it. It is too beautiful. By Jove! Colonel, she must be mine."

"Yours? It is no use. Charlie has her on trial now. He is going to take her, he says—"

"But he can't win her. Providence made her for me. You know it. He can't win her, I tell you."

"Win her? He don't intend to. He says he is going to purchase her."

"How dare he talk in that way of a creature he should respect for herself alone?"

"Look here! Nat, I didn't know you were so enthusiastic as all that when you take a fancy, you are a good fellow."

"Enthusiastic, Colonel? Why," continued Nat, impressively, pleased at the opportunity of expressing his love for Laura, "I adore the very ground she walks on!"

"Good! I like that. They say her bottom is uncommonly fine."

"Bottom! Good God! who said that?"

"But she is vicious, (mysteriously.) Look at that bad habit of snorting she has. It is an indication that she is vicious."

"Ha! ha! (hysterically.) Look here, Colonel! It is not usual for me to contradict any one, much less you, in any criticism which may be based on truth, but I am damned if she snorts!"

"Well, you needn't be so dogmatic about it. Your fancy has beclouded your observation, Nat. But it is indeed reasonable after all. She is certainly a beautiful creature in every point. Those legs of hers are the neatest I ever saw."

"By Jove! he is insane or drunk, but responsible. Colonel Norcomb, sir, this is a little too much. This is unbearable, sir, and superinduces fire-arms. Such a remark as that is not to be borne from any one, not even from one whom I have respected up to this moment as

I have you. Oh, Heaven! to think of talking of having seen her—"

"Ha! ha! Is there any thing improper in looking at a mare's legs? There they are. Look at them yourself."

"What? I have made a slight mistake. I thought you alluded—when—oh, dear! (Thus am I fated to be supinated.)"

On reaching the lake, James Gluckinson was despatched to a neighboring potato-field, to procure bait, from the fact of his having become thoroughly acquainted, by many minute personal researches, with the secret hiding-places therein, of that desirable tribe of vermicular beings designated as *lob;* and the Colonel sent his retainers to assist him, remarking, however, that their indolence was of so serious and chronic a nature, that most of the worms would probably escape into the bowels of the earth before they could succeed in capturing them. After a lengthy period, the youth returned and reported the colored individuals as engaged in a general fight, and explained his own delay by stating that on his way back from the preserve of worms, he was obliged to disrobe himself entirely, in consequence of some of the more riotous, which he had inclosed in a pepper-box in his pocket, having escaped therefrom into the interior of his pantaloons, about which they had commenced to crawl in a very disagreeable manner.

While the parties floated around in their fragile barks upon the lake, or seated upon the shaded rocks in quiet covert, awaited the expected bite, Charles, deserted at the moment by Laura, lay idly reclined upon the verdant turf, gazing at the huge shadows as they chased each other, like shapeless monsters in play, upon the side of the mountain. Although his look was thus averted to the passing griffins, he still could easily see the girl Dinah, as she strayed cheerfully in the silent labor of assisting the domestics to spread the lunch. Though she was thus engaged in the commonplace scene, and thus distant as she appeared from him socially, he still felt an irresistible desire to watch her motions, while he pursued a reflection of some interest and singularity. Here was a young girl, whose character and person were half-formed at best, but as far as they were developed had been unfolding, since earliest childhood, under the chilling influences of misery and poverty, and yet she was exercising an infatuating influence, simply by her personal charms, over one young man, brought up in the midst of the satieties of refined life, while in the mind of another, the quality of her intellectual, and perhaps also her moral being in a measure, had already produced an irresistible sympathy towards her. The apparently besotted infatuation of the young proprietor, Rudolph, for the physical beauty of the girl, (for he seemed to worship her with a sensuous religion,) may thus have had a reasonable, although a wicked cause. His aunt's benevolence in receiving the girl and her father into her household, was perhaps delicately natural in the opportunity which it gave them of forgetting their degradation. But the bestowal of his own sympathy seemed absurd in its irresistibility. He recalled quickly, however, the particular reasons for it. He had seen from the traits of character which had been at times displayed to him in his conversations with her, that the instincts of this girl were all fitted for a much higher sphere than the one which poverty and the criminal follies of her parent made them move in. He saw that she had already received such an education, too, that she would fill creditably some higher position than this station, of the dependant of a household; and he had resolved to execute the very easy matter of assisting her to rise from her lowly condition, when once assured that she possessed none of those evil traits, to which her bitter experience had rendered her so liable, and which would make this contemplated assistance on his part not only foolish, but criminal. However, the first step in the discovery of those traits, if there were any, he had felt, was to cause her to experience a certain equality with him, which would sooner or later induce her to relax that natural guard of reticence, which she possessed, and which was indicative of them. After the long idleness and vacancy of his intellectual nature which he had been experiencing, he felt that his soul had been led particularly to assert its natural bent once more, in the study of this girl's character. There was just enough undemonstrativeness in it to make it interesting to him, and to really make it a study. 'Mid the peculiar extrinsicalities attached to it, her age, her humble position, her bitter experience, and the degradation of her father's crime, made that interest melancholy enough to tinge the whole with a color of romance. Thus in the benevolence of his heart, he had resolved to put aside the social difference of condition, and assist a young and tender soul with his sympathy and confidence, in its struggles to free itself from a condition to which it was evidently inherently unfitted. And now after all, even when observing the servants speak with an apparent air of superiority to this strange girl, and feeling, too, as they perhaps did, that she was not of their kind, that there could be nothing in common between the position of an old and faithful domestic and her degraded condition, her nature seemed to him constructed upon different principles from those of the common herd, there appeared a superior power in her individuality, which was indefinable, almost mysterious, and which thus, perhaps, completely commanded his.

The repast was now ready. The straying ladies and gentlemen returned from their sail in the tented boats, or from their equipoised perch upon the sunless rocks. And amid the sound of chicken-bones and gushing wine, gay voices might be heard, pleasantly excited by the cool enjoyment of the hour. Dinah, at first, walked about the gods and goddesses as cup-bearer, like another Hebe, wearing a variegated garment, and upon her bosom a nosegay of beautiful flowers; but Laura soon made her sit down by her side, between her and Mrs. Norcomb; at which Charles gave a nod of approbation to her, and she secretly blushed acknowledgment to him and to the young lady.

As soon as the repast was concluded, and while they amused themselves with cards, and songs with the guitar, as it was yet too warm for the dance, Nat proposed to give an exhibition of his equestrian skill, in a short shaded space. In return for the self-sacrificing manner in which this unfortunate advocate had rowed the ladies about the lake, had baited their hooks, or now and then extricated them from the bellies of the too voracious fishes, Laura had occupied a great deal of her time in unnecessarily referring to the accident of the morning, and had nearly driven him distracted by showing the unpleasant interest she took in his horsemanship. To be sure, she made him sit down by her at the repast, and poured him a glass of wine to drink, but it was not until all appetite had been dislodged from his being by the mental hunger and thirst which her pertinacious allusions had created in his bosom, to vindicate himself in her view by some distinguished act of equestrian daring with the same difficult being, which she had several times observed he was unable to manage. Fired with this idea, he caused the concinnous Thomas to be led up from the distant shade, and mounted with a subdued excitement, which bore the appearance of coolness. The heated Thomas, on his way towards the inviting sheet of water before him, had revolved the agreeable idea of an ablution in the same; and in consequence thereof, the unfortunate advocate, had been on his back for about an electrical space of time, when the enthusiastic animal darted with the speed of slow lightning to the pond, and made directly for the middle thereof. In vain Nat tugged at the bridle, and cried "whoa;" nothing was soon seen of the horse's person but his head, and nothing of Nat's but his, surmounted by a white hat, and these two objects thus presented upon the plane of the lake, the supernatural phenomenon of a phantom equine head being chased perpetually at an ungaining distance, in a serpentine course, by a man's with a melancholy expression, and in a white hat. Finally, as they were nearing the shore, amid the adjurations of the assembled crowd to "hold on," and some rather energetic commands of rescue, on the part of Miss Wellwood to the domestics, the white hat suddenly disappeared with the head in it. Its owner had been dis-

lodged from his seat by a sudden and violent change of mind on the part of the horse, with regard to direction. When he came up, he was in the vicinity of a log, which was half-submerged, near an inaccessible part of the shore. There, after being occupied some minutes in a frantic endeavor to work along the tree, by means of his legs, which might plainly be seen, bent with the refraction of the reflected rays, and in violent motion, he was finally rescued by the grasp of the gallant Gluckinson. As the wet condition of his nankeen pantaloons rendered his presence unbeseeming for the while, he was led immediately by the same benevolent individual to concealment in the bushes, where, with the same dignity with which an embowered old bird awaits on the nest the arrival of a posterity, he waited until his habiliments should dry. During this somewhat prolonged interval, his mind was occupied by the artless conversation of the innocent James, who took this opportunity of stating to him, in a dark and ambiguous manner, his predilection for a piratical career, and of alluding with mysterious and gloomy looks to the fact that it was the destiny of his life to war against an unsparing foe, who now wore a culinary shape. All of which, Nat being unable to grasp the exact meaning of, and perhaps being somewhat irritated at the slow progress of the drying process, he endeavored to relieve the tedium of both, by pitching into the unfortunate youth at judicious intervals, either knocking his head against a tree or drumming on it for a short period. While he was receiving from Dinah's hand an iced lemonade, sent by one of the ladies, whose name he was endeavoring in vain to discover, and was retaining her, to persuade her that the divulgement of the initials at least would be no betrayal of confidence, a game of "hide and seek" had been proposed, and was being put into execution. When she returned, the party had scattered in the pleasant breeze, to concealment among the rocks and bushes, excepting Mrs. Norcomb, lingering as the seeker, who told her to hide also. She ran down, and stooped in real pleasure and fun, between two noble rocks which stood at some distance by the water's side, when Charles, emerging from the bushes above on the other side, with a hasty "Hist!" slid down to where she had secreted herself. There was hardly room for two, and she told him it wasn't fair, and he must go.

"It is too late."

"No, I will go," said she, in a quick whisper, and she was about going round still farther on the shore, when a third party confronted her. It was Rudolph.

"You thought to escape me!" (He was pale with emotion.)

"What?" said she.

"I well know with whom you have been," sneered he. "I have seen his looks, and your cursed blushes, all along."

With quick woman's art, she smiled upon him, but his absurd jealousy blinded him. "'Tis for him you reserve your favors, is it?" continued he.

"Leave my presence, sir," said she, sharply. She seemed to feel the dishonor to her self-respect, or perhaps she was acute enough to use decisive measures at this point, and perhaps more on his account than her own. The look of command which she assumed had its effect upon him, and he was really about to walk away in confusion and silence, when Charles unfortunately appeared, attracted by the peculiar tones of the conversation. The fury of Rudolph all returned at his coming.

"You seek to play your miserable hypocrisy in more favorable quarters, do you?" said he, to Dinah, in a low tone.

"What is this, Dinah?" asked Charles, who did not exactly understand the state of affairs.

"You would honor your sex, and disgrace its opposite, by a more comprehensive artifice, would you?" continued the young man.

"One moment, Rudolph; allow me to suggest that such language is improper to be used to this young girl," said Charles, quickly.

"You would escape from the degradation," continued Rudolph, not regarding Charles at all, "which your father's miserable crimes have brought on you, in a more brilliant way, would you?—"

"You forget your own honor," said Dinah, "and my right as a woman."

"You do not hear her," said Charles, who thought he was perhaps overcome with wine. "Let me join with her in reminding you of your extraordinary inconsideration."

"You can take yourself away from me," continued Rudolph, still addressing Dinah, in the drunkenness of his jealousy.

"What!" exclaimed Charles, indignantly. "If it were not—but—let us not mar the pleasures of our moments here. Remember yourself," continued he, pulling him by the coat.

"And this mouther can go with you!" continued the young man.

"Do you dare—" cried Charles, suddenly—"One word more, sir. You consider yourself a gentleman. So am I. I consider it the duty of a gentleman, at least, to protect the members of his household. What I have solicited in vain, I must now compel. Leave this spot, sir."

"You are a miserable shuffler, and sottish mummer!" cried Rudolph. "It is as her paramour you would protect her!"

Charles forgot himself, and took him by the throat; but he quickly relaxed his grasp, for his anger was gone, and there was nothing in his bosom but shame of human nature. Just then, a clear voice from the cliff above, rang out "I spy;" and its owner, Mrs. Norcomb, turned and sought the goal rapidly.

The passions of the young man Rudolph were strong, but his frame was weak. He rose with a scowl and an oath. "You know I am unequal to you in strength, and would take advantage of the inequality. You have struck me, sir, but you shall give me satisfaction in another way."

"If you think to engage me in a duel, you are mistaken. I neither believe in that nor would I fight one with you if I did. You have been justly punished for your insulting meanness to one who is not only a woman but is inferior to you in station." The idea of a duel being mentioned to him, again touched his gall. "The miserable scoundrel!" said he, in a ludicrous rage, as Rudolph went slowly away. "Let him learn to curb his anger, and then—"

"Hush!" said Dinah, sorrowfully, as she followed him. "What sincerity is there in recommending a virtue which you do not practise yourself?"

"Certainly," said Charles, with a laugh, "instead of being angry with him, I ought to pity the poor fellow, from the simple fact that while he has been unable to conquer his own temper, he has been further exasperated by the sight of my moderation!"

This contretemps was unseen by any one save the actors, although the sudden absence of Rudolph exacted some inquiry, but well knowing his sullen and eccentric nature, it soon ceased. In the mean time, the game continued in great glee. Laura endeavoring to find a suitable concealment, stumbled upon Nat, and with a slight shriek discovered him standing up against a tree, with an immense jack-knife, reversed and upraised in a dagger-like position, carving industriously the letters *Lau*—thereon. The old maid had got into a cave among a lot of toads, and while Mr. Pithkin was leading her out, reminded him again of the sacred promise which he had made to her on the way to the lake. Endeavoring to impress upon his mind in a dark and mysterious manner that destiny had thrown a being (who, she gave him to understand, was Col. Norcomb) in fatal antagonism to him, she had succeeded simply in raising the idea in his mind that the Southerner didn't like him, and had been talking in a derogatory manner about him. With a reservation in reference to the case of the son of the South's attempting to revile him or depreciate his virtues to his face, he had promised to hold no intercourse with him during the picnic. "If he gives me any of his sauce, however," said Mr. Pithkin, "I'll have to call him names back. Human nature can't stand it!"

The festivity lasted until the set of the sun, and returning to Charles's house, by invitation of the aunt, it was prolonged until late at night. Before retiring, Charles sought an opportunity to ask Dinah to meet him on the morrow, and appointed a place, for the late occurrence was a pleasant revelation of her high antagonism to her own circumstances, and the moments he now expended in the contemplation of her character ceased to shoot back, like retreating Parthians as they fled, arrows of distrust of her character.

CHAPTER XXV.

OBADIAH AND THE GIRL.

THE cook of Pompney Place had gone to chapel, having tyrannically ordered the unfortunate Gluckinson to sit up until she returned. The young retainer had already read two thrilling stories about pirates, had taken one nap, and with idiotic gaze was drawing straws in the candle, when the girl Dinah looked into the kitchen. The chief emotion of fear being temporarily removed from the bosom of Gluckinson, by the absence of its cause, had given ample room therein, at this time, for the play of those of an amatory nature. It was not a matter of surprise, therefore, that on Dinah's entering into a cheerful conversation with him, and pleasing him with her attention, his remarks in reply to her, which first glowed with the tinge of esteem, were soon imperceptibly heightened to the warm color of personal affection. His admiration for her, in fact, soon became so inconvenient to himself, that he was forced to disclose his passion on the spot, and call her in ardent terms his "sweet holly-hock," accompanying the dulcet epithet, with a pantomime expressive of his desire to ornament his bosom with her.

"Tell me about that pirate with long hair, and Medora!" said the young girl.

"Oh, b'mine! b'mine!" continued the infatuated youth.

"Come tell me James, did you like Medora?"

"How much money do you expect to have. It little matters. What has love to do with bank-bills. That's what I heard Mr. Charles say to Misses Wellwood. Oh, you ought to have seen 'em! They were seated in the parlor. Suddenly, she was about to make a remark, but didn't, and then he said somethin' in reply, and then she said somethin', and then he made another remark, which hurt my feelings. He told me to 'Get out.'"

"He didn't mean to be harsh, James. He is kind and good."

"I know it. He isn't as good as you are.—Say, wilt? Wilt?" continued the youth.

"Stay, I hear some one coming in the path."

"Oh, dear! It's the cook. I see her. Won't you open the door please. She'll grab me. Oh my! Obadiah's coming too, and another man. Ha! fate. Now's the time," continued he, with a sudden change of manner. "Aha! strike!" muttered he, gritting his teeth, and giving other evidences of sudden ferocity. "She has stopped to look at the soap. Fate is jerking her back for a moment so I can get started. What do you want here?" said he, with an irreducible mixture of a scowl and a wink, as Baylon and his friend entered.

"Eh, I want a chair, James," said Baylon.

"What! you want a chair! I'll chair you!"

"Eh?" said Baylon.

"Do you affront me?" continued Gluckinson, fiercely, "I want to know if you came here to pick a quarrel with me? I want to know it? You're pious, and have been my friend; but no man makes an ass of me, whether he comes from a prayer-meeting with women or not!"

"You forget yourself," said Baylon, in some astonishment.

"Do you twit me? Mind your business. I care not for any man's piety or bluster. I will kick any man down stairs here, who can't behave like a gentleman." At this point, Baylon's friend looked at the fell-minded youth. "Ha! This is your friend is it? You brought bullies here to back you, did you? (*sotto voce:* I'll quarrel with him a little; you protect me.) Who are you looking at, sir?"

"What? Who is this?" asked the friend of Baylon.

"Let him alone, I think he has been drinking," replied Baylon.

"Let me alone! You say that. You bring your bullies here do you. If any man in this room, be he a bully or not, doesn't confine his language properly, I'll throw this tea-pot at his head! I mention no names, I quarrel with no one, I say, but I won't be bullied by any person or persons. Away from this house, I have knocked people on the head before this."

"Oh, dear, what has got into him?" said the cook, "and may be he's got a pistil!"

"Ha! let no one come near me," continued Gluckinson, with renewed vigor. "I say, if matters come to worse, it will be useless to attempt to hold me. No bully shall attempt to hold me!"

"Let the drunken fool go out," proposed the friend.

"What do you mean?" inquired the puzzled Baylon of the young man.

"What is that to you?" continued Gluckinson. "If any man makes himself my enemy, I don't care a straw whether I tell him his father's a bitch or not. You come here to attack a man, in the sacred precincts of his own kitchen, do you? Very well! Very well! No blackguard can succeed in scaring me."

"This is a nice humor. What do you mean by this foolery?" repeated Baylon, rubbing his top-knot in irritation, as he had been particularly desirous of appearing with a borrowed dignity in presence of the girl.

"Eh! what! foolery! Don't you remember?—"

"Fool, what do you mean by addressing this gentleman here in this manner?"

("He calls me a fool! It is a hint for me to draw off.) Oh, you say he is a gentleman, do you? Very well. Let it be, then. I'll say no more now. If he conducts himself properly, I'll consent to say nothing more on the subject. But you can both remember, that no blackguards, pious ones or any others, had better attempt to intimidate me, either in this room or anywhere else. I protect my rights. I am the child of fate, and when I hear her alarum—(the bell, here rung)—I have got to carry hot water up stairs. Do you understand, cook? You see me. Hooray!" concluded he, looking at her with an insane scowl.

"Oh, he's taken mad!" said the cook, who, unlike Governor Pickens, was not born insensible to fear.

"What's the meaning? Oh, I am much obliged to you, Mr. Obadiah, and you Mr. Sucker, (Mr. Sucker was an attentive coachman of one of the neighbors), for coming over with me. It is so delightful to feel religious, especially since they have let the men and women sit together in the chapel—but what is the matter with him, Miss Dinah? Oh, dear! has he got a pistil?" continued she, under the exaggerations of conscience, and under the influence of a suspicion, also, rushing into a closet and holding a bottle up to the light, "I am so glad he's gone away!"

Lingering at the singular demonstrations of aggression on the part of the truculent Gluckinson, Dinah had rested near the door, which she was about leaving.

"Good evening, Miss Dinah!" said the overseer Baylon, with a cringing bow to her. "I spoke to you once, and you didn't answer me."

A look of scorn and contempt passed over her face.

"I thought I would stop in as came along, and perhaps I might see your father."

The girl consented to a few moments of private conversation, which he now humbly begged to have with her.

Mr. Sucker was desirous of showing in a peculiar manner, to his friend the cook, that he didn't include her of course, in the statement which he had made in meeting, that he felt himself safe for salvation, and didn't care a tinker's anathema, who else wasn't, and he seated himself with her, in a distant corner of the spacious kitchen, leaving Dinah with the overseer. As the latter continued to converse with the girl in a low tone, she was so much his superior at least, that it seemed like the damned son of Circe, and a Lady who was her own Sabrina. There was an appearance certainly, of her clearly understanding what he secretly meant, and of convincing him of her knowledge, of that which he though the could conceal; for he seemed disposed more than once to slink away. Indeed, in spite of himself, the presence of this young girl seemed always to exercise a tormenting power over the fellow, in lifting him, temporarily at least, from his vulgar and wicked habits of thought, and kindling in his bosom some ludicrously exasperating aspirations after principles, which he felt he was not made to attain. The glory with which his mind was thus informed, was tantalizing to him: the momentary awakening from his besottedness, was but into a horrid dream of virtue.

At the close of the conversation, every thing was quiet in the kitchen. The cook and her friend had walked out into the garden, and only the slight hum of a young fly might be heard, as she spurned the nets of a spider upon the ceiling. With a proud look of conscious superiority, the girl told him plainly, she knew what a false traitor he was in heart. "Why do you attempt to deceive me? You think you have power over us, but I can thwart you!"

The man acknowledged her power in a submissive posture, and with a cringing smile, seemed anxious to win her favor. "Why are you vexed? Why do you frown? Have—" The smile upon her countenance drove away that upon his, as a good angel drives away a fallen one; and he fled into the night like the false enchanter, his wand snatched from his grasp and reversed, with backward mutters.

CHAPTER XXVI.

A VISION.

Towards twilight, Charles betook himself with some secrecy, to the place of assignation with the young girl in whom he was taking such a singular intellectual interest. As he rode along, having mounted his horse for an appropriate concealment, he felt that an oppressive gloom, had lowered over his feelings, occasioned perhaps by the breathless state of the atmosphere. The sun had gone down in cloudless splendor, conflagrating the pure ether of the west, and a late dusk of purple was now darkening in unusual stillness over the scene. Passing along by a farm-yard, in which the milky mothers were awaiting with distended udders the coming of the cow-boy, he observed that they now and then gazed in boding silence into the heavens, or, with a deep breath expelled slowly from their nostrils, stopped the chewing of the cud in unison as it were, to observe the scene with rueful gaze. One or two heifers were engaged in a belligerent shock of horns; and a young and vigorous bull with a wild eye, was rushing about eccentrically, as though a demoniac spirit had temporarily taken possession of his muscles, particularly those of his tail.

Seated upon a fallen tree in an adjacent forest, with the shadows of the wood around him, the light crackling of the branches first aroused the young man from the revery into which he had fallen, and apprised him of one, who now stood by his side. "I have come to meet you," said she, quietly. So soft had been those little foot-falls, that Charles exclaimed in surprise, "Why, Hebe! how did you come?"

"In a chariot drawn by peacocks," said she, with a laugh.

"I have asked you to come and meet me thus alone, Dinah—because, you know—"

"You want to be secret for my sake." She did not add, that there was perhaps still in his mind, unknown to him, the lingering thought, that his interest in her might turn out to be illy taken.

"But it is going to rain, and I can't stay long." There was a restlessness in her manner, and she looked around, as if some one might be coming in the wood.

They sat down together on the fallen tree. In the distance through the glade, might be seen the tall cliffs, overhanging the rivulet, and forming the side of the gorge through which it run, and at one particular spot a platform-rock on high, celebrated as the place of solitary communion with their Maker, of the race now passed away. The sound of the brook fell on the ear, and that was about all to disturb the silence. Under the simple influence of nature, the girl seemed suddenly to forget the presence of the young man, and listen to voices which he did not hear. Thus there was a pause, even at the outset of their conversation; for he unconsciously awaited the breaking of her revery. Such was the sympathy of being between them, that this took place as a natural part of their intercourse. The horse moved irregularly amid the bushes, around the tree to which he was tied.

"What is that?" said the girl, rousing from her thoughts. "Did you come on your horse?—and I walked all the way here to meet you. I wouldn't have come, unless you had commanded me. It isn't right."

The two were like two young men together, whose friendship was warm for each other.

"Have you done wrong simply because I commanded you?"

"No, I want to be guilty of impropriety. It is romantic. I don't like to walk in the paths to which society has restricted me. Yes, I suppose every one is so," concluded she, with a sigh and an indescribable gesture.

"When I was a little boy, I used to steal lumps of sugar. They were a great deal sweeter than those they gave me."

"Yes, I remember once mother gave me a chapter or two of the Bible to learn, and I did not wish to, but telling me one day, that it was not best to learn too much of the Scriptures at one time, I immediately went to a secret place, and committed the whole of St. Luke to memory, in a fit of opposition. It's for liberty—for liberty—"

Charles noticed her eager way—"What would you do now?" said he, "if you could do as you should please, in the wide range of the universe?"

"Let me see—I'd—I'd torture good people, so I could have the pleasure of being forgiven by them" said she, with a smile at the affectation.

"I believe that is what refined tyrants desire when they flay martyrs. It is; Isn't it? That is a hidden luxury. I suppose forgiving would be flat to you."

"You know we like to see that in others, better than to practice it ourselves. But I've never had an opportunity. However, I suppose if I ever had one, I might do it, just a little and by degrees. I would be very angry at first, though. But the hardest is, to forgive those who injure the ones you love. I cannot—cannot—Yes, I will too," said she, changing in the most sudden and decided manner. "No, I won't either!"

"How can you tell! You don't know what you'll do. You don't know yourself."

"I know that! I know that! What do I care about knowing myself. I want to study some one else."

"Well, you can study me, if you desire."

"You are very kind. You wish to offer me a splendid classic to read, do you not?"

"Certainly, I have no doubt now, but that you would find new beauties in me, to the end of your existence."

The girl smiled. Perhaps it indicated that she knew already, by intuition of human nature, more of his beauties and his faults, than he did himself.

"But why do you not care about knowing yourself, Dinah? Do you not like your own thoughts and feelings?"

"Oh, no! Let me not think of myself. No, not now!" exclaimed she, earnestly, and apparently ere she was aware.

She might indeed be referring to the condition in which she was placed, by her father's degradation and crime, but there appeared to him for the moment, some thing slightly deeper in her manner.

It was here that he was induced to allude in an indefinite way, to the inclination which had been growing within him, to ask for her confidence and friendship. There was no necessity for his guardedness, for she seemed fully aware, that the benevolence which chiefly characterized his intentions, was lofty and honorable, and was such as should stir her to a passionate expression of gratitude. That heart which appeared to be beating fuller and stronger at the moment, that vigor which lent energy to her words, indicated to him, that his benevolence would assuredly be rightly repaid by its young, yet appreciative recipient. Indeed, at the moment, although her intelligence may have told her that it was perhaps but an ephemeral weed, which he had carelessly permitted to spring up in his bosom, possessing none of the fibres of a lasting and hardy plant, she did not restrain her nature from graciously shedding upon it a few apparently sincere tears.

In the ensuing conversation, which soon returned to the channels of pleasant badinage, and which confirmed the intellectual as well as moral interest which he was taking in the girl, he concluded it inexpedient, did not wish, or perhaps saw not the opportunity, to refer to her relations with young Warriston; and in the real pleasure which the interview afforded him, he would fain have prolonged it to a greater extent, had not Dinah suddenly aroused as if from a dream—had not the restlessness of manner which was noticeable on her coming, and which may have been the simple warning of prudence, possessed her again after a short period.

The evening air was still, the sky was quite dark, and as she now looked into the wood and along the pathway, she rose quickly and said, "I must go, sir. It will rain before we get back."

"Oh, no! not to-night. Not until towards morning."

"But I don't want to stay here any longer. How foolish for you to come all this way into a dark wood, to talk to one—to one—who cannot—" She laughed with apparent acrimony; and the young man thought she was ridiculing him, as if she were his superior in arrangement of such plots. "But I will go."

"Stay, you must," said Charles. "Don't go yet. I'll take you near to the house on my horse."

"If you were going to fly up, away up into the heavens with him, I might be induced to get on."

"I command you to stay."

"What did you say, sir?" said she, smiling and pretending not to have understood him, as she ran down the dark glade, ere he knew it. A sudden waft of wind coming through the trees, here swept over the young man, and sped across the fields beyond, to die away in the distance with mournful sound. Its swell and fall seemed as if a trembling chord had been touched in mistake, by the grand old harper, ere he commenced to strike up his symphony of the storm. As the young girl ran, he rose, but lingered, for he felt he ought to let her go, and yet it was against his will. She turned and bowed to him two or three times in a laughing manner, as she walked courteously backwards from his presence, and at a bend in the opening disappeared from his gaze. "Well, I will let her go, she is ever prudent. It is best for her to be at home, and I must take my quadruped. But the next time I'll come on foot as she did!" continued he, as he rode along the still road which he had reached. "It will not rain for two or three hours yet—there is not a cloud in the heavens, though it is dark enough and warm enough, whew!" Plunged in reflections upon the singular character of their object, he sauntered, perhaps for a full hour's space, in an irregular career, and finally with his horse's head towards the distant village, while the frequent sighing warnings of the air were lost upon him in his abstraction. Reaching the main road, his prudence was at last aroused as a dull muttering fell on his ear, and turning towards his home, he spurred his horse to a brisker pace. In the glimmering of the sky he observed that the threatening clouds were slowly rolling up from the horizon to conflict in the mid heavens, and the wind was now commencing to sway the moaning trees and sweep briskly over the fields. The horse increased his trot in the darkness, now and then shying at the dark boughs bowing in the gloom, or stopping to show his paws in fear to the coming demons of the storm, as they lit up the gathering clouds with electric fire. At last, as the young man was nearing the old church, a living chain leaped out of a dark, dull cloud above the trees forward, at which he was gazing in apprehensive speculation, into the sea of lighter gloom around, rattling with a deafening crash its links to the ground in the distance, and the rain came rushing down in torrents. The horse bellowed almost in his high-mettled poltroonery, and the disordered young man with difficulty kept his seat, as again with a nearer sound of thunder the lightning illumined the steeple of the church. The supernatural fighting of the hour seemed directly over the church, and the sacred spire looked as though it were a quiet finger of scorn pointed at the demons in battle above. Charles, seeking shelter in a place safe from the lightning, rode his steed up the marble steps and between the pillars of the consecrated portico. There as with frequent peals of thunder the livid sheets or chains of lightning, lit up the darkness, he retained the bridle of his horse, and occupied the lingering in patting his neck, in whispering loving words of encouragement into his ear, or in contrasting the warring discordance of the hour with the radiant satin sun-scenes of peace he had so often seen spread over the place. While the contending demons fought with new noises in the air, he imagined he saw the grinning angry faces and undefined forms of the monsters about the church. A drunken whoop struck in his ear amid the sound of the ceaseless rain and the fitful thunder. What was it? He was startled from his position of subdued wonder. Again, and here amidst this trouble, that singular voice which he had heard in his dream, and on the misty lake, once more was firmly projected into reality by the wild eccentricity of his imagination. He trembled with physical fear, for it was again and as clearly repeated. It was now uttered in a mingled tone of mockery and exultation, and it seemed to come not from the air, but from amid the lonely graves in the churchyard. A bright flash of lightning suddenly revealed the tombs and monuments in death-white reflection, and amid them a brief and consectary sight struck his vision at the distant part of the churchyard. Over one of the graves bent a being, scratching feebly at the top of the mound like a half-starved vampire. His long hair was dishevelled by the rain and the wind; and his countenance, dripping with water, was turned up towards the sky. On that face by the flash Charles saw an unnatural look, and the fierce wildness of wicked passions. He raised his voice, and dragged his chicken-hearted drawback with a clatter down the steps to tie him to the iron fence. Amid the rushing of the rain he heard a feeble cry. Again a quick flash lit up the scene, and he saw that the object of his intense curiosity had disappeared behind the tombs or the church! He ran quickly towards the place; but the storm was raging with greater fury, the heavens blazed but to dazzle, and the rain, swept forward by the rushing blast, struck his face and distracted his motions with blindness. Wonder when tinged with a feeling of the supernatural is as confusing as fear, in the pursuit of discovery. The excitation of curiosity, the interest of pride, the intoxication of enthusiasm, are subdued by even a slight connection perceived between a fact attested by the senses and a superhuman power. Was it the imagination that, amid the grandeur of the hour and at the dim suggestive sight of the old pioneer's tomb, had thrown out not only the gibbering voice but even the apparition of the ghostly hero? That the creative power should so overwork itself, is but a rare possibility and connected with a disordered state of the body, which the young man's health belied; and thus he now stumbled about in this wild nightmare's nest with the feeling that the singular being he had seen might be for all he knew in funereal proximity to him, or might be more happily dropping downward through the welkin of hell, or riding away in the air by the side of his paramour at the head of a host of witches. He saw him not nor heard him again in his prolonged and confused search; and though he might conjecture, for such a scene, many natural avenues of appearance and disappearance easy to be traversed by earthly feet, he returned amid the driving rain towards his horse in an excited bewilderment, which proceeded from the very correctness of his reasoning. The animal was rearing at the lightning, and had already broken the bridle in his terror at being left alone; and the young man, remembering the holiness of the temple's precincts, led him away to the sheds. As soon as a lighter gloom pervaded the heavens and a renewed search was unrewarded, he ventured on his way home, with a mind filled with varied speculations at the singular scene of which he had been a witness. Were there such things in the grand system of nature as the visitation of supernatural beings to the human senses? Was it the pioneer emerged from his grave in his doomed wandering to meet his pale mistress, and disclosed in the very act of smoothing in wild apprehension of discovery the mound he had disturbed? While Charles would fain laugh at what he deemed a childish absurdity, he was still forced to acknowledge the overwhelming power of the sense of solemnity which possessed him, in reflecting upon the convicted fact that this mystery, whatever it was, was connected with humanity in his view, through the young girl Dinah. Thus even in the interview immediately antecedent to this apparition had he accumulatively felt that her restlessness of manner was indicative of some powerful warning which she seemed to obey even in the high honor and purity of her nature. Was it fear for her fate, was it the pity of a sympathetic nature, which thus possessed him? Even if it were such, it was more interesting to him in its delicacy than the fanciful theory with which it was consonant but not necessarily postulative, that the pioneer still roamed, and that this young creature with all her warm and breathing humanity, was a being of another existence eking out a spell-bound span in earthly fooling.

On his return to the mansion all was dark and silent; and, observing in the unrequiting particularity of his survey that no light was visible in Dinah's room, he retired to his room overwhelmed with the growing perplexity.

CHAPTER XXVII.

THE DENIAL OF CONFIDENCE.

THE next morning, which was a bright sunny one, with a refreshing air after the last night's storm, Charles took an early opportunity to converse with Dinah's father, as he was engaged in his light and cheerful labor, amid the shaded bushes of the park. In answer to many questions, which he put to the old man in a guarded manner, respecting his former and his present life, for the purpose of evolving something which might bear upon the character of the young girl, it seemed evident, that whatever may have been the relations in which she was now engaged, they were wholly concealed from the parent also. His history of his former existence, was much the same as that which Dinah, and he himself, had given upon former occasions. When he neared the crime of which he had been guilty, and of which he was now certainly repentant, the young man spared the blushes of the wrinkled face, by a speedy diversion of his thoughts, and felt as he observed this broken-down old man, that the daughter could indeed have concealed her affairs from him with as much naturalness as a father would from a child of tender years. The old man upon this occasion appeared to rejoice in the particular fact that they had paid some of their debts, and as usual in the general one, that Dinah was a brave child, in whom he was to rely in his old age.

After breakfast, the mother and aunt drove to the post-office, and while the domestics were variously engaged, the wished opportunity of approaching the girl herself, without fear of interruption or misconstruction, was presented to Charles. It was with heightened interest that he sought this interview, and more particularly as he entered her presence, a certain conversation with his mother happened to strike his memory, in which she had advanced the fancy, that in the midst of the lovely looks of the young inmate of their house, in spite of the natural indications of that soft voice, and of that mild and gentle eye, she thought she could see, at times, the dull appearance of treacherous cunning. But that very softness of her presence seemed to disarm him at once of any theories which would have made his conversation stern, and there appeared only at the moment, in the graciousness of her nature, something which seemed of a higher existence, one more spiritual than wickedness would dwell with.

"Dinah, you are very young," commenced he, kindly, but he looked at her steadily, "and perhaps in spite of that quick perception of human nature which you possess, may still fall into circumstances hereafter, in which you will regret that you have not offered to learn the rules of life you need, from some older and more experienced friend. It is this secretiveness that I would censure. Your conversation led me to believe that nature has given to you powers which, if exerted in the right direction, will not only secure happiness to you, but even bestow it upon others, who may come in contact with you hereafter, however humble destiny may make your social position. Although your actions cannot have any other personal interest to me, still I would, as one who strives to do good when he sees his efforts may be successful, warn you that, unconsciously to yourself even, there may be transmitted to you certain hereditary faults—" He paused. The young girl blushed to a deep carnation, and turned from her still and listening position. "I mean not," continued the young man, gently, "to unnecessarily allude to the misfortunes which you could not help, and for which you ought not to suffer," (the girl's eyes glittered gratefully,) "but does it not seem to you beneficial to yourself to repose confidence in an older and more experienced—friend, as I willingly have constituted myself to you, in one who has solicited it for your own welfare as I have? And have I not the right, as master of this house, Dinah, to protect its inmates from the irregularities or improprieties of those who are paid to serve them?"

The young girl started quickly at the last words of the young man, but as quickly repressed the movement. She looked him steadily in the face. There was no apparent preparation for a denial, which might have been successful; no affected astonishment, nor was this look a pretended look of inquiry. She even said, coolly, "I know it is wrong for a servant to be away from the house of her master so late at night as I was, but had I not sanction ever to transcend this rule?" continued she, in a kind of sharp way, as if she were right, "to meet one who loves me, and should love those whom I—serve?" A smile took its place upon her countenance, as though simply under the sentimental insinuation which she had made, she felt safe in her secret, and could afford to flaunt it before his advertence.

The young man asked himself what he was trying to prove. To corroborate a theory of the supernatural, founded upon an airy sound, which might easily have been an exaggeration of his fancy. The repeated recurrence of the voice of his dream, was the only chain of inexplicable wonder in the occurrences which he had in his mind. She was now naturally referring to his neighbor Warriston, but then to think of her falling upon his neck and kissing him under a moonlit heaven! "And do you desire, Dinah, to keep secret from me the name of this being whom you thus met?" asked he, still with an indefinite feeling.

She was aware of his knowledge of her relations with Rudolph,-and as she gazed in his face, whilst he indulged in these reflections, a faint brightening was perceptible upon her countenance, which might have indicated that there had been some slight apprehensions of which she was now relieved. "Of whom were you thinking just now, so—so bitterly?" said she, quickly.

"I thought you were too sensible a girl, Dinah, to meet such a character as my eccentric neighbor, by moonlight in such a way!"

"Why, does he not love me, sir; and would he not protect me?" In spite of her efforts, there was a certain dreariness and increasing agitation appearing in her manner. The young man was about to proceed, when he observed that she had burst into tears. This was the first time since he had commenced to take notice of her character, that she had betrayed any evidence of weakness of feeling, or at least of any inability to master her emotions when she chose. She repressed her tears, however, almost as quickly as they had burst forth.

"But, Dinah," continued he, "I will state to you frankly, the reason which has impelled me to be thus inquisitive. I thought I heard a voice, Dinah, on the night of your meeting with our friend at the lake, which seemed different from his, different from the possible human voice, I was going to say, for it was a voice I had heard before, but that of the unreal creature of a dream." He stopped, for the girl immediately looked at him in curiosity, and then corroborated in a low, respectful way, the reasoning which had before passed in his mind, and which brought up to him the absurdity of holding her responsible to account for the vagaries of his brain. "But, Dinah," continued he, disinclined for this reason to recount his dream, though there was still a natural or artfully assumed look of inquiry upon her face, "I would not have thought to question you from this shadowy fact alone, had I not heard that voice in my waking hours, on other and apparently inexplicable occasions. Pshaw! it was no less than last night, amid the thunder and rain which followed our interview, that I took refuge in the old church, from the storm. While there, I heard that voice again, and in unmistakable clearness; nay, even saw the being who uttered it, standing over a grave in the churchyard, with his face upraised to heaven, and he, I am sure, was wholly unlike our neighbor, Rudolph. You may rest assured, Dinah, if he had not disappeared with as much successful melodrame as he stood fooling my senses, I might have then been able to satisfy my curiosity, and saved this discovery of its inquisitiveness to you. What is this? Who is it? Am I the dupe of my own fancy?" continued he, in a mixture of soliloquy and inquiry. "Have I not a right to ask you if—if—" He looked steadily at the girl, while he stopped, ridiculing himself. A mingled look of astonishment and confusion was visible upon her face, as he proceeded to relate the particulars of his adventure at the church. Her astonishment may have been natural, for her confusion seemed a part of it, and the look of appeal which soon followed it, the overwhelming beseeching look of tender desire that he should have confidence in her, caused him to conclude at once that she at least knew nothing of this latter occurrence, and was also justly dissuading him from farther inquiry into her actions of the night on the lake, as a matter of honor at least to Warriston.—("It is so. In this look and in those tears which she but just now shed, she gently denies me her confidence, and rightly too. In my ridiculous inquisitiveness, and with my absurd fancies, I have been led to ask her to betray a delicate secret, to which I have not the slightest right.")

"I well know that you have the right to question me about being on the lake," said she, "but when I first ask you tó—to—"

"Say no more, Dinah. I will not ask you to reveal any thing to me which I have not a right to demand, Dinah. I feel that you will always respect the rights of those whom it is your duty to serve, in your conduct, and that you will not conceal from them any thing which they should stand cognizant of."

At these words, the girl was violently agitated, as if from an internal reproach; but she concealed her emotion from him, by pulling up the work with which she was engaged, and plying her needle with affected attention. He soon left her with a kind, gentle smile, and pursued in solitude his own reflections, which were however, at best, but unsatisfactory.

CHAPTER XXVIII.

MATHEMATICS.—EVANGELICAL SATYRS.

NAT BONNEY commenced to review his mathematics. He did not carry off the prize in this estimable branch of education in his academic days, but on the contrary, had been quite remarkable for the difficulty with which he got across the Pons Asinorum, involving a fight with his tutor, and tears on the part of his aged parents. In fact, he philosophically proposed to plunge into this study once more, with the hope that the distracting emotions of his bosom would be temporarily overwhelmed, and perhaps ultimately annihilated by the continuous feeling of disgust which it would unfailingly produce. On beholding the ancient and dog-eared Euclid before him once more, he remembered with agitation the fervent wishes which he was accustomed to breathe in his youth, that its venerable author might appear once more upon earth, to afford him an opportunity of taking vengeance on his person. Great was his astonishment to find that by the lapse of years his antipathy to a contemplation of those great and fundamental truths had been converted into a delightful appreciation thereof. He laid it to the fact that, amid the necessities of his profession, his intellect thus craved at times the food of truth. What interest there was to him now in the idea of a straight line—a thing which might be possessed of any amount of length, but was totally deprived of the other dimensions. What a singular thing it was—surpassed only in its singularity by the severe idea of a point which was simply nothing at all occupying a position, reminding him forcibly of the statesmen of his country. He shut his book, and left his office to take a walk in the gloaming.

"The idea of the human intellect bending from this dignified study to become the servile slave of the emotions which the female character excites. Ha! awful muse, let my mind be ever wrapt in these chastening thoughts.—By heaven! it is intolerable. She hardly spoke to me at the picnic. How can I excite her sympathies? I might go and hire a horse, and run his head against a tree within sight of her mansion, and fall off insensible. I should be taken up stairs into the front chamber by four farm-hands, and by my bedside she would listen to delirious murmurings of my incoherent passion, mingled with feeble moanings, say in reference to the pains in my legs, and my desire to pay for my lodgings while there. And then as I convalesced, oh, rapturous thought, she would sit by my bedside, and minister to me with her angel hand, gruel and buttered toast. My happiness would be so much the more complete from the fact I am fond of the latter. At last with the vigils of sympathetic pity, she would become debilitated and unwell, and if until this moment her being was not swimming in the great sea of love, she would unfailingly commence to strike out here. The minute a woman suffers for a man, she must love him,—is an axiom in the mathematics of the heart!" While indulging in this ecstatic romance, as he turned a corner into a leafy avenue, he stumbled against another human being, who, like himself, was buried in reflections. Nat's gaze was astronomically turned, and Rudolph was engaged in the geological occupation of perusing the stones of the pavement. They came together with such a rude force that it caused their heads to resound with a hollow sound. "I say," said Nat, "go back and do that over again, you know."

"Oh, well! it is an accident; which way are you going?" said the other young man, sullenly.

"I? Oh, I am just out for a little walk of ten or twelve miles after tea. I've been sitting, and I want to stretch my legs to that extent."

"If you have no objections, I will go with you a little way. You were not a witness of the occurrence which took place between myself and the individual who resides at Pompney Place, and considers himself the Pluto of this hell about here. The coward struck me, and then refused to give me satisfaction. Curse him! I hate him, and the very air he breathes, and his family too, for that matter, and I don't care who knows it. I'll have my revenge. I detest the sottish mummer and—curse him. I—I hate him," roared the furious young man. His manner was perhaps disagreeable, but the fine flow of his ideas was quite noticeable.

"I don't. On the contrary I like him. To be sure I am like you, I don't want to, but I've got to," said Nat, with a resigned air. ("In the curious arrangements of affinity, I suppose it is because Laura loves him.")

"I detest him. He is a knave!" said the other, pursuing his tender train of reflections.

"I can't go as far as that with you, and it strikes me, on the whole, that your prejudices are of the most damnable order. It is better to confine yourself simply to calling him a fool. (When my agitation becomes excessive, I shall be obliged to go that far myself.) Or, remembering that Pompney Place is his residence, you may proceed at opportune moments, to decry its beauties or—"

"Oh pshaw! good-night. I'm going. Here comes that old proser Fuffles. Three-quarters of his conversation with me are expended in rebuking me for that terrible sin—of hating his friend Charles as he calls him. I can't endure him. My overseer wants to go to New York, and I think I will go with him, and get out of this infernal region for a while."

"Oh, please see that he gets into no danger, will you? Wrap him up well at night, and prevent his taking cold. Take care of that beloved member of society," said Nat, in sudden enthusiasm, "and see that he doesn't eat too much, for my sake."

"Eh, what for?"

"Well, I don't know, exactly. D'ye see, I've often thought it might afford me pleasure to put such a man as that out of existence myself, you know."

The young man left, Nat finally proposing as the requisite relief to his feelings, that he should exhibit tobacco juice, through the medium of the eye, to the constitution of any canine animal belonging to the disturber of his repose. Nat soon joined the learned Doctor, and turning back, accompanied him towards the village. Their conversation was of a much more agreeable character, although the Doctor introduced, and persistently stuck to the harmony of Charles's and Laura's characters, as the subject of his remarks. However, as Nat, with much energy, immediately revived his mathematical enthusiasm in order to overwhelm the emotions which were thus stirred again in his bosom, some slight confusion of thought was caused at first, but finally a compromise was made in the union of the two subjects which was quite successful, and entertained them both for a considerable length of time. For instance, the Doctor would say, Nat having referred to some property of numbers, "And the same wonderful principle may also be applied with unfailing success to the problems of social existence. Thus in the union of Charles and Laura, you will see how immediately their power in society and life will be increased by it manifold."

"Yes, I see," Nat would say, appreciatively. "You take Laura as number one, for instance, and placing Charles as a cipher along side of her, they immediately become ten together. Yes, I see."

"Well, perhaps it is too far to carry the application to particulars," replies the Doctor, slowly. "However, in the main, I observe you have my idea."

Continuing, in this manner, a harmonious interchange of ideas, and enjoying the refreshing night-air, they took the wide avenues at hazard. In a schoolhouse upon one of these, a public meeting was being held, and from its interior a concert of groans and grunts might be heard emanating at stated intervals. Hearing shrill ejaculations of pain as if from a female in torture, Nat proposed that they should enter, and the Doctor, although demurring at first from a decided yet delicate feeling of intrusion, finally overcame his scruples, and accompanied him to a back seat. Several people were upon their knees between the benches, in different parts of the room, uttering indistinct cries, and one large man was beating violently with his clenched fist the seat in front of which he kneeled. Others were seated, and while gazing intently at the desk in front of them, relieved now and then the feelings which the scene inspired, by uttering short suppressed yelps, or by convulsively tossing their arms in the air. Near the desk was a female, who had evidently experienced religion, sitting on a three-legged stool, like the Delphian oracle, with her hair standing on end, her eyes sticking out, sparkling shines of perspiration on her countenance, and apparent shivers running over her whole body; while a crowd of priestly men, among them the overseer Obadiah Baylon, conspicuous from his top-knot, were busy about her in calling attention to the inspired articulations which she was uttering in loud howls and cries. The Doctor was inclined to flee abruptly from the place, but Nat restrained him. Near them on a back seat in the other aisle, Nat saw the white collar of the girl Dinah, and the long hair of her father, almost as white, and further ahead he observed his friend the apothecary, evidently in a great state of internal excitement. He was just then much occupied in inventing a new method of expressing his religious fervor, as he was aweary of his efforts with language, and had been some time revolving the efficacy of walking out into the middle of the floor and falling headlong into the pit of some one's stomach, proposing, in order to give prominence to the affair, to select the organ of Obadiah Baylon for that purpose. The inspired female, having at length exhausted herself, the men ejected her from the railings with considerable force, and a worthy brother, Tarbox by name, took the stand. Rolling his eyes around the room, he suddenly caught sight of the uneasy Doctor in the retired seat. "Avaunt, Beelzebub!" said he, "There he sits—there sitteth the false prophet of Satan," continued he, pointing a very dirty finger at the object of his objurgation. Here all the people looked around, and the Doctor and his friend were immediately placed in an unenviable state of notoriety.

"I say, Doctor, he is alluding to you," whispered Nat.

"There sits the false prophet of Satan," continued the brother, "who donneth the garb of celestial origin, and belloweth forth lies to the Episcopalian Pharisees, for the blessed truth in his pinnacled temple."

"Nat," said the Doctor, "as this house is not consecrated, it would not take much to induce me to chastise this man immediately, Nathaniel."

"Why does he defile us with his gloves," continued the inquiring Tarbox; "why does he defile us with his broadcloth, and his tuckers, and pinafores, head-ornaments, rings—"

It is impossible to state in what manner, under the growing excitement of the moment, the object of this harangue would have answered the various inquiries put therein, had they not been brought abruptly to an unfinished conclusion by a worthy brother, who, having an eye to the morality of the congregation, shrieked out excitedly at this point, "Brother Tarbox, your wife has gone home, and brother Williams has gone off with her!" The unhappy Tarbox bolted frantically for the door at this announcement, and his place was immediately taken by another and apparently modest brother, who commenced his address by complacently stating that he was "but an humble laborer in this vineyard."

Unfortunately he had an enemy in a back seat, who, instigated by the promptings of his hatred, immediately cried out "Louder."

"My brethren," reiterated the brother, raising his voice, "I am an humble laborer in this vineyard, but—"

"A little louder, if you please, brother," said the malignant creature in the back seat.

The unfortunate speaker immediately tried to comply with the suggestion, and stated again, in deafening tones, that he was but an humble laborer.

"Will our brother speak a little louder?" once more asked the relentless foe.

"My brethren, I say I am but an humble laborer in this vineyard," yelled the infuriated brother. "Do you hear that, you d—ned scoundrel?"

Nathaniel and the Doctor left the house in the midst of the confusion which followed, and the latter, falling down the front steps in the darkness, felt inclined to think the abraded condition of his shins was especially sent as a punishment to him for intruding his presence upon this gathering.

CHAPTER XXIX.

A CHANGE IN GLUCKINSON.—THE FATHER AND DAUGHTER TOGETHER.

It was one of those still summer afternoons so common in our country, at the pleasant hour when the overhanging foliage is no longer sought as a shelter from the heat, but the shadows commence to be long and wide from the descending sun, and the lustre of the heavens is softened to the eye, that Charles's aunt and mother took a drive in the phaeton.

"Really, I do not know what is the matter with James," said the former, as they stood on the steps of the terrace viewing the pleasant scene, while William was making a flourishing circuit on the walk with the ponies. "When I requested him just now to tell William to put in the ponies, he scowled frightfully at me, and in concealed mutters, which seemed to be a violent defiance of me, I thought I heard him say something about murder, would you believe it? At one time, it seemed as if I overheard him express a desire to assassinate me with a razor. I was so frightened, I ran away from him. And William tells me, that when he came to the stable just afterwards, he continued his singular conduct, and proposed to cut his throat if he didn't behave himself, and the throats of all the horses. But he says when he dared him to personal combat for it, he ran out of the stable. The maids tell me too, that for the past few days he goes muttering about the house, breaking out every now and then into a swaggering blustering, and attempting to domineer over them with vaporings and threats of violence. Dear me, I don't know what is the matter with him. I fear his mind is affected. Indeed, I do. He is threatening every body in the house. If it were only occasionally, I should consider it the result of intoxication. Dear me, I wish I hadn't permitted Dinah and her father to go to town this afternoon. However, they were so indifferent about going, there was no pleasure in refusing them. Talking about pleasure, William, you must certainly prevent that strange cat, in some way, from prowling about our residence. I can't endure it. He makes most horrible noises, and besides that, he disturbs the equanimity of the cats at home. My little pet came in the other day with her face all scratched up by this monster. You must shoo him away."

"Yes, marm," said William.

"Mrs. Norcomb insisted yesterday on giving a present of money to Dinah," proceeded the spinster, continuing to retail the events of the household to her sister-in-law as they drove along. "She said it was in honor of her birthday, could you believe it, which occurred last May, would you think? Now, it is usual to receive presents on one's birthday, isn't it? And I think if any thing was done, Mrs. Norcomb ought to have waited until next May, and then received a small sum from Dinah. But alas!" continued she, with a mysterious manner, "who knows what terrible overpowering information may be divulged to her ere that day arrives, and perhaps on that anniversary she may recall to memory, with regret, the day she was born! No! No! (with heroic firmness, in a low, indistinct manner,) I will not divulge it to her, and I am sure he wo'nt."

"What do you refer to, Adeline?" said her sister-in-law, who was engaged in viewing the scenery. "I didn't quite understand you?"

"Oh, nothing, nothing," replied the maiden aunt, gloomily. "But a passing thought. Cheer me up, Delia. My weak unhappy bosom," continued she, taking hold of her stays, "needs support.—The girl came and asked my permission to take the money. As I knew she would, whether I permitted her or not, I allowed her. The amount rendered her quite delirious for the moment. Her eyes sparkled, and she ran off to her father."

"The poverty in which she has lived made it appear large to her."

"Yes, indeed. Money appears, indeed, to be as great a necessity with the lower classes as with us. When I was paying off the farm-hands the other day, there was an unnatural brilliance and a longing in her eyes as she saw the money, and I caught her in her room soon after, counting over anxiously some small change she had in an old worn-out purse. I fear she is bad," continued the old maid, whose bosom was commencing to rankle against Dinah, as she suddenly remembered that the girl had exhibited merriment at the unfortunate accident which befell her and Mr. Pithkin on the day of the picnic. "Things not within her reach, at least, are safe. Do you think I had better dismiss her and her father?"

"Oh, no! No! Perhaps we may be doing them injustice to suspect them now."

"The old man is quite stupid and infirm. I don't think he will attempt any more evil himself. He has turned himself to religion, and is fond of going to the chapel."

An inclination to silence here took possession of the occupants of the vehicle. The hour of twilight, and the place occupied by the old church and its yard, were approaching. One or two of the more enthusiastic beetles were abroad, winding their little barbarous horns, to celebrate the event of the dying day; and the pendant bat in his home in the belfry, commenced to flutter his leathern pinions and peep feebly into the welkin, as he felt the tyrannic seal of light melting away from his sleepy being. Hope loves best to whisper her promises at the hour when the shades of darkness comes over nature or the soul, and the tender religious thought stole upon the minds of the pensive women, as the dusk came on.

As they drove down the cross-road, running through fragrant fields, and by the side of the churchyard, in order to pass home by the highway, the chirrup of the retiring birds might be heard in the trees, the lowing of the cows in the distance returning from the pastures, the bark of the house-dog, or the cheerful song of the farm-boy. A dog of mixed ancestry, who had been sitting on the road, outside of the churchyard looking wistfully in, or now and then pricking up his ears at the distant sound of his kind, rose from his sitting posture and wagged his tail modestly as the familiar vehicle approached. Within the churchyard, at the back part, where the graves of the poorer class were placed, the ladies observed the girl Dinah and her father, who had evidently stopped there on their return from the village, to visit the grave of the wife and mother. The girl, in a stooping posture, was smoothing the grass growing thereon, while the old man was wiping in a brisk manner the dust and dirt from the headstone, and clearing out, in a flurry, the letters with his handkerchief.

At the sound of the carriage, they immediately rested, and recognizing it, bowed respectfully and came forward as the aunt stopped and called them. The girl reached them first, and with a smile bade them good evening. She cast a hesitating upraised glance at Charles's mother, while she patted the dog's head who had commenced to gambol about her.

"You must not stay out so late, Dinah," said the aunt; "you will be wanted at home, and it will be dark before you get there."

"We were just going as you came up," said Dinah, "indeed—"

"It is some ways," said Charles's mother. "Your father appears tired. Let him get on the seat with William, Adeline, and Dinah can sit with us." The girl blushed suddenly at this, but was afraid to refuse.

The arrangements being made, William gave a cabalistic order to the ponies, who immediately whisked their tails in unison, and off the vehicle rolled once more, the dog barking and frisking about it in great joy. In this manner they soon reached home, nothing having occurred to mar the pleasantness of the return, except some little uneasiness on the part of the aunt, which caused her to push Dinah into her sister-in-law, in a very disagreeable manner, most of the way.

CHAPTER XXX.

DINAH IN HER BOWER.

The young girl sat at the window of the room in the afternoon, carelessly regarding the long view without. The air was not sultry, but the wind was warm which came in at the windows. She had removed her stockings and shoes, and her naked feet rested gracefully on the cool oaken floor, their whiteness contrasting in a dazzling way with its sombre hue. Outside, in the court near the stables, a dog and pigeon, emblematic of peace, were eating from the same dish, while a second canine individual of an excessively indolent temperament, recumbent beneath the spreading elm, was blinking in pleasant idleness, and speculating in soft distraction, upon the propriety of joining in the festivities. The young girl placed her hand upon the high top of her chair, and turned to lay her cheek upon her arm. A large thick lock fell around her neck, and ended in perplexity on her shoulder. The dress which she wore was bright and large flowered, and notwithstanding its old grandmother style with full sleeves banded to the wrists, bore an air of exquisite summer freshness. What thoughts passed in her revery? Was she not a young creature full of human hopes and fears? Perhaps she thought of the relations of blood, and her father's life and extinguished hopes, of his happiness, and the pious duty of a child. Perhaps of the Southerner's generosity. Perhaps, as a shadow of sorrow came over her brow, she thought of her mistress, whom she would like to love, or of the malignance of the overseer, Baylon. The breeze laden with perfume, played with the frippery of her stomacher, and now as her mind turned towards another being beneath the same roof with her, a languor seemed to have taken possession of her frame, and she appeared as one whose whole system was agitated with a feeling entirely novel to it. What indefinite ecstasy was this which shook her frame? Her eyelashes drooped involuntarily. Was it the sacred inauguration of the first love of the woman, in one whose girlhood was slowly fading in the brighter effulgence of the coming period? A blush colored her cheeks, for perhaps, while she felt this earthly rapture which swelled her palpitating heart, and caused the tremor of her being, there was mingled with the woman's glory the maiden's shame, or perhaps she felt it was such as made the superior beings whom she knew to be watching over her laugh at the mortality of her nature.

CHAPTER XXXI.

A MIDNIGHT OCCURRENCE.

Charles retired to repose, tired with the long ride upon which he had accompanied Laura, and the conversational efforts which her beauty and spirit had excited him to make thereupon. He knew not how many unconscious hours had passed in the depths of slumber, when he awoke with a start, but it was still one of the dead hours of the night. His sleep had refreshed him, and he commenced to recall the vivid scene of the wild and laughing girl, the spirited horses with wide-spread nostrils, and the varied scenery. Now the long-fenced field with the farm-house near by, now a rustic bridge crossing a shaded rivulet, shut out from the setting sun by a dark mountain, from amidst the forested coverts of which the hoarse-roaring water dashed over its rocky channel; and now a narrow, gloomy road, running through a sombre grove of lofty trees. He thought over again of the sparkling manner thrown out against those tranquil scenes as they rushed along, and turned on his side to laugh once more, in the irresistible way in which poppied people do, at some lively remark uttered by the fair equestrian he had accompanied. It seemed to awake a confused echo in the broad halls. "I must not laugh so loud the next time. If I arouse the house, I shall have to get up and retail the theme of my merriment to them before they are satisfied, which evidently wouldn't do —which evidently wouldn't do," soliloquized he, throwing his legs along the bed carelessly, "considering my present pleasant position." The night air was cool, and he buried his head in the pillow, and shut out from his other ear with the counterpane, the sound of the silence. Towards sleep again in a dreamy way, he thought he heard a curious disturbance in the interior of the feathers, producing a deadened noise to his applied ear, as though there was a charmed spot a long way distant in the downy depths, where a few tiny spiritual beings were engaged in walking about, and conversing irregularly. He raised his head when the imagined noise struck in a full reality upon his ear, coming through the opened windows of his bedchamber, and seemingly from those of apartments below. He sat up erect in the bed; for again, in this dead hour of the night, that unnatural voice which he had heard in his dream, in the mist, and in the grave-yard, once more concerned him. It was not now the meek idiotic inquiry, weakly fashioned by the thickened tongue of a babbling sot, nor a simple reproach, nor a whoop, but the violent irrepressible malediction of some thwarted being, dangerous in his anger. The sound of a short scuffle was borne to the young man's ear, quickly followed by a half-suppressed exclamation of a second being in entreaty.

He had jumped upon the floor, and stood paralyzed by the fearful sounds, for fearful they seemed to him, when a sharp cry of terror or anguish went out into the air, almost simultaneously with the dull explosion of a fire-arm. The humanity of this last sound, (not to speak satirically,) brought him to his senses, and dissipated his fear of the supernatural, and half-attired, he rushed down stairs into the hall below. There he observed Col. Norcomb advancing from the other end with considerable rapidity and with a light in his hand, and near the library door, the senseless form of the unhappy Gluckinson with a gun lying by his side. Through the opened door, it was observable that the library was dimly illuminated, and as he reached it, he saw standing therein in front of him, in the attitude as it first struck him, of a witch suddenly discovered in her nocturnal work of wickedness, and then of a criminal convicted in the commission of the crime, the girl Dinah. The oaken cabinet, containing the documents of the estate and other articles of value, was wide open. Some of the papers lay strewn upon the carpet amidst the shivered fragments of the lamp's globe, the light, still burning, having been apparently tipped from its position on the centre table and replaced by some quick hand. Relieving his mind at once of doubts, with regard to the condition of the faithful domestic, Gluckinson, whom he happily discovered was unharmed, and already beginning to revive from a fainted state, the true nature of the midnight occurrence, and of the character of the girl was presented to him in these unmistakable indications of an attempt at robbery. They had been foolishly harboring in their house an unscrupulous girl, the daughter of a broken-down criminal, perhaps the young accomplice of others, and cunning enough to deceive them, until her evil inclinations and plans were now exposed in this fortunate detection.

This neighborhood, like most other romantic country places, had its local superstitions, to which the vivacious minds of the more imaginative referred every event which was uncommon enough to be without the ordinary routine of their daily lives, and to the sustainment of which, also, the more staid of the inhabitants, perhaps, had lent the activity of their local pride. Thus the belief in the visitations of the old pioneer, had become a sensitive fixture in the neighborhood. He himself had fallen into the thoughtless habit and referred, indefinitely to be sure, those events which had lately passed within his ken, and which had borne a slight appearance of mystery, to a supernatural agency; a mystery he now saw could easily be dissipated without calling in the aid of the restless walkings of the old pioneer, or of any other unearthly power. The girl, probably, had some idle dissipated lover from among the enemies of society, who had been secreted in the neighborhood for some time, and whom she had finally conjoined as an accomplice in this predatory attempt upon the mansion. It was he and not Rudolph, whom she met at night in the mist. It was he without doubt, who, seeking in his nightly tramp shelter in the church, and surprised there, may have played for a prudent or a humorous purpose, an easy prank with the superstitious fancies of the neighborhood. Yet, in the midst of these reflections, Charles remembered that the face which he saw in that solemn place, and the hour of thunder, bore almost a ghastly expression of sorrow and misery, and that there was a wildness of despair in those motions, which seemed real. Above all, that voice. It was indissolubly superplaced in his memory's stores, upon one which was no reality but the furniture of a weird dream. Why such a connection? And further, this girl possessed a bright, active intelligence. She well knew the power which she possessed over the young man Warriston, and that the road to comfort was much easier through his possessions, than through robbery. But here was the fact that she had been caught in the flagrant act. That was certain. His hurried reflections were unsatisfactory, yet the theory which they evolved, rested in his mind as not only possible, but the most probable.

"Sit down in the chair," said he to her, with some sternness. The whole household had been aroused with one or two exceptions; the father of the girl among the number, who was afterwards discovered really and soundly reposing his aged limbs, tired with the labors of the day. The lights which the different members thereof had brought with them, lit up the library brightly, and the girl's face appeared as pale as marble. "There is nothing gone," muttered she, in a low voice, as if she were already trying to defend herself. A quick examination was made, and nothing could be discovered by those acquainted with the contents of the scrutoire to be missing. The depository of money in daily use was untouched. Only the papers, in fact, appeared to have been disturbed, and particularly those which bore reference to the estate. The folded patent of the original grant from King George to the old pioneer of the lands of the neighborhood, was lying in broken fragments upon the floor, torn at the aged crease across its middle, and near by it the deed of Colonel Pompney, by which these lands had passed out of the hands of his race, also disordered and torn, but still legible. A thrill ran through his blood, as the young man noticed this singular disturbance of these documents thus morally related, and he turned to glance, in sudden and absorbed interest, at the countenance of this young girl who had thus once more become connected with the old pioneer and the traditions of the past. He was about to obey the irresistible desire of the moment, and demand from her lips an account of the occurrence, real or feigned, when he observed blood trickling down her arm. "What is this?" said he, in astonishment. She rose to walk towards him, and staggered in faintness. Her paleness had increased to a deadly pallor, and the peculiar look which comes over the relaxed muscles of the face so much like a smile, appeared on her countenance. Mrs. Norcomb, and one of the domestics, rushed forward and caught her ere she fell, and as the latter sustained her in an agitated manner against his person, a wound which she had perhaps purposely endeavored to conceal, was discovered upon her arm; not caused by a gun-shot, but one which a knife or some sharp instrument would make. The blood had trickled down from her arm upon her dress and the carpet, and she was now weak from its flow, or the idea of it. Her dress, too, had evidently been put on in great haste, and it seemed as if she had been suddenly aroused from her bed, and that a struggle had taken place in the book place. All this bore the marks of an antagonism, on her part, to some one who had also been engaged in the midnight act, and yet whose late presence she would fain conceal.

She was now reduced to such a condition, although the wound was apparently not dangerous, that humanity demanded, no matter how guilty she may have been, that she should be removed to her apartment, and Charles concluded to forego his intention of sifting the affair by examining her upon the spot. All was confusion and distraction, and amidst it she was allowed to retire to her room and remain in quiet until morning. After a while, order being in a measure restored in the excited household, and an incoherent statement being obtained from the half-restored Gluckinson, in which it was apparent that he had shot off his gun in the hall to alarm the house, and then fainted away from fright, Charles visited his mother's apartment, and the two in a prolonged conversation discussed this unusual occurrence with varied theories. As a conclusion to their consideration of it, and the subsequent examination of the girl, they resolved, even if it were not necessary in the discharge of their duty to themselves and society, it would certainly be beneficial to the girl herself, if she were at once subjected to a judicial examination. At first, they both felt a great repugnance to such a course, from the notoriety which attached to such matters, and from a real humane unwillingness to appear against the girl. The theory of robbery on the part of the girl, was stronger in the mind of the mother than that of Charles, although it was even to her a source of perplexed reasoning, why she should have undertaken it, when she had appeared to have been conscious of a power within herself to accomplish her ends in a higher, more legitimate, though perhaps, still unscrupulous manner. As to Charles himself, in his confusion the girl's statement, which tended to exculpate herself, bore a general air of truthfulness to him at first; and for the time, it made him sick to see that agitated young being, with sorrow and trouble, and apparent honor in her face, no matter how consequential that suspicion may have been, subjected to the suspicion of having been engaged in a base violation of the laws of society.

Her exposition was briefly as follows: that she imagined she heard some one approaching the house in the park; that she rose and saw from her window a strange figure gliding stealthily along the terrace; that she was proceeding in her determination to alarm William and James, sleeping in the porter's room, when, passing the library, she saw this person therein, and before the cabinet with the table lamp-lighted; that, in the difficulty of his flight which ensued upon her appearance, the lamp was overturned, which she sprang to restore, and it was at this time that she received the wound. More minute and unimportant particulars she hesitated not to give, and any inclination on her part to avoid them was as easily referable to a modest repugnance of dwelling upon her own bravery, as to any thing else.

Suffice it to say, that to all others, save the mother and Charles, the relation carried satisfactory conviction with it; but while the mother gainsaid it, she hardly knew why, Charles had, besides a confirmatory tremor and agitation in the manner of the young girl in her recital, a distinct reason for disbelieving it. Simply its incompatibility with the evidence of his own senses. The peculiarity and unmistakability of the voice of the person who had attempted this midnight robbery, indicated a groundwork of deceit in her statement. That voice he had heard emanating from the lips of a person, whether supernatural or not, whom he had seen in company with the girl on terms of apparent intimacy. He had seen that person more distinctly in the graveyard, which now proved to him, with the aid of this last occurrence, that he was not mistaken in thinking that the other actor in the wrangling scene could not be Rudolph, his love-sick but unromantic neighbor; and with this deduction of hypocrisy in reference to that case, and however mysterious may have been the connection of this voice with his vivid imagination in the dream of the one which once belonged to the old pioneer, and however singular the rude handling solely of the papers which bore reference to the possessions of the pioneer and his posterity, the young man felt sure at least, that her statement was untrue. One point he happened to think in all this confliction of speculation had not been clear; and, irritated by his baffled desire to clear up the matter, and vindicate the girl in his mind, he suddenly asked her, with a mingled air of triumphant hope, and hesitating fear of making her discredit her own statement, displaying all the while a rather paradoxical reliance on her honor, "if she knew who this person was with whom she had come in contact?" It was at this moment alone, during the whole of the conversation, that she seemed thoroughly decided in her manner, and even an appearance of anger appeared on her face, as she denied the questioner's air with firm words. She suddenly paused, however, perhaps as if she remembered that her father had once committed as great an offence as that which this attempt indicated. Rejecting, then, the ridiculous fancies of the supernatural which had been raised in his mind, and otherwise taking a comprehensive view of the subject, the education and probable tendencies of the girl, together with erroneousness in his ideas of her relations with the young man Rudolph, among other particulars, he finally rested for the time upon the conclusion that the girl had contemplated this robbery conjoined with an accomplice; that, during the act, they had commenced to quarrel, as he had seen them before; and that, being alarmed, the accomplice had fled without the booty. But here another singular fact presented itself to his mind in opposition. The dogs, who were quite fierce and usually on the alert at night, had not prevented the approach of this stranger to the house, or apparently even noticed it; for it was not until the explosion of the gun, fired under the influence of human fears, that they were aroused. The mother proposed clearing the girl in the eyes of the world from any suspicion, and then dismissing her from the household on some honorable pretext, with a sum of money. She argued that, even if the girl were innocent, the occurrence would be noised abroad in the neighborhood; that, in addition to the already unenviable reputation which she and her father bore, such was the nature of the community in which they lived, that an imputation from this occurrence would rest upon them, which could after all be best cleared away by a formal examination; that, as there was no probability of her being retained in custody, but on the contrary might be discharged according to her own statements, with some honor, they had better submit her to this formal examination. She then referred to the inference which was undoubtedly to be drawn from this, and other events connected with the girl, that she was unreliable.

"What other events?" asked Charles, although he immediately thought of occurrences which certainly were worthy of suspicion, but which he knew his mother to be unacquainted with.

The mother colored slightly, and after a moment of apparent confusion, said she meant to refer to the girl's character, as evinced in her general manners and habits of thought and action.

Charles, taking a blind pleasure in defending the girl, even in spite of his own convictions of her deceit, at first denounced the proposition almost as an act of cruelty and meanness; but he afterwards saw that his mother was right, if Dinah was to be dismissed, and that, although she was not particularly disposed towards the girl, sentiments of pity had, perhaps, actuated her in proposing this step. "At any rate," thought he, "she cannot be harmed by it, and if she is really unreliable, we shall feel a clearer right to dismiss her thereafter."

As to the assistance which Charles might have derived from the unhappy Gluckinson in his speculations, it was not until several days after the occurrence that he could procure from him any statement of particulars sufficiently lucid to be considered as authority. The youth soon revived, indeed, from his fainted condition in the hall, but his mind was in an extraordinary state. On recovering, he seized the empty gun, and pointed it violently towards a door which led from the hall into a passage-way down-stairs. This new alarm of his bewilderment immediately communicating to five of the Colonel's colored retainers and the butler, they hustled back of him, and hurrying him towards the door with many struggles, bolstered him up thereat in his spirited act of defence. Turning slowly, he at first brought the weapon to bear on the Colonel, who was fain to make an instinctive motion indicative of his desire to have the weapon lowered, and then he pointed it in intense excitement at the extinguished lamp hanging in the hall. Finally an indefinite direction appeared to have been given to his alarmed fancy, and for some time afterwards, as he imagined foes in divers directions, the crowd might be seen rushing convulsively about the hall from one spot to another, pushing him violently towards the different doors and windows, out of which he pointed his gun in a frantic manner at various objects. The confusion, however, being in a measure quieted, and the excited domestics being brought to a temporary stand-still, Charles endeavored to question him. But, as before stated, nothing could be obtained from him beyond the fact that he had rushed into the hall and fired off his gun. In the alarm of the occurrence, he had been temporarily bereft of his wits, and it was not until a week or two afterwards that he wholly recovered, being a part of that time in a wandering state, during which he manifested his hallucination in a harmless manner, by writing short letters to his friends, containing mixed ideas upon his illness, or in arranging sticks, stones, and sprigs in the form of a flower-bed upon the floor, in which he sat triumphantly, and from which he frequently selected straws, and kindly offered them to those who came to visit him; accompanying his gifts with such remarks as "There's rosemary for you!" "There's gilliflower!" and alluding now and then to the fact of his name being Thomas, and his being in a chilled condition! From all of which, it was gathered that he had been a student of the immortal Shakspeare, and that his disordered ambition was now running upon those characters who had been represented by the great master as having been in a condition similar to his own. He was finally restored to sanity, however, by the constant application of a powerful reactionary agent in the shape of disgust, produced in his mind by the aunt's compelling him to swallow at stated intervals gruel made by his enemy the cook, which was exceedingly unpleasant from the small feathers discernible therein, and which often stuck in his throat in a disagreeable manner, and bore the appearance of having been made of that particular kind of meal which had been devoted to the leisurely access of the fowls. It appeared, however, from the statement which he made as soon as his mind was restored to lucidity, that he had been lying in bed that evening, speculating upon the manner in which he was gradually subjugating the cook. For several nights past, he had been endeavoring to put into execution a brilliant thought which had occurred to him, of achieving success at once and in a decisive manner; but his constitutional fears of darkness had somewhat retarded his progress. His project consisted in approaching the door of the cook's chamber at a distant end of the house, in the still watches of the night, and groaning suppressedly thereat, upon which, as she would probably be induced to open the door to inquire into the cause, he intended to punch her violently with the but-end of an old gun which he had in his room, accompanying the measure by a brief statement in unearthly accents that he was a supernatural being, come to punish her for her misdeeds towards the innocent Gluckinson, whom he watched over.

On this night, which was the sixth, having been unable to get beyond the threshold of his door for the first three, he had advanced as far as the library in the execution of his wily project, when he heard a noise therein, and saw some one arresting the lamp from its fall, which scared him so that he went off in a fainting fit with a loud cry, and the gun immediately went off too. The consequence was that the household was aroused, and he was found by them as aforesaid in his frightened condition. The report was also the cause of another singular effect, as yet unmentioned, which it had produced upon Charles's aunt. On retiring that evening, having blown out her light, and in accordance with a careful temperament placed it in the middle of the wash-basin for security against conflagration, she sooner or later commenced to dream; and on this occasion, as the last thing she thought of was the basin, and the perpetual sub-stratum of her thoughts was Pithkin, her dreams were composed of various changes on the possible unions which might be made of these two subjects. At first, she dreamed Pithkin, in a fit of jealousy, tried to drown himself in the basin, by holding his head therein in an infatuated moment, and that, failing in his attempt, he kicked it in a disappointed manner into the air. Then he was represented to her mind as a statue placed in Madison square, in the great metropolis, holding out majestically, in his right hand, a wash-basin, in which were five blocks of houses, piled one on top of the other, and sustained at the base by two bulls standing in the basin in a caryatid manner.

Three thousand girls, belonging to the principal school of the city, marching by in solemn procession, each fired off at the basin, as they passed, a large-sized bottle of blue ink, and finally the lady bringing up the rear, elderly, but still beautiful, gave it a violent kick with her foot, (her leg growing suddenly to an enormous length,) and it flew into a thousand atoms. At the same time, her back-bone cracked with a loud crepitation, and the aunt was awakened by the report. She had just time to observe, in the dimness, the candlestick strike the ceiling violently, and the basin fall on the floor in two large fragments, when she concluded to faint away. Gluckinson, who was now lying in a similar condition below, had put a bullet directly through the centre of the bowl. The aunt lay comfortably in that state until somebody reached her apartment, and revived her, and off and on, until morning, was lying in fitful conditions, more or less comatose.

CHAPTER XXXII.

NAT IS INFORMED OF THE OCCURRENCE.

The young lawyer, Mr. Bonney, sat in his office the next morning after the occurrence at the Place, writhing in the anguish of poetical composition. He had proposed to write an ode to Miss Wellwood, on her having refused to dance with him, and had reduced himself to a state of semi-intoxication for that purpose. A little boy walked up the avenue of rose-bushes, and was about to cross the threshold, when he observed the semi-possessed advocate's agitated movements, and thought it advisable, with the admirable sagacity of youths of his age, to await at the door.

"Go away!" said Nat, "I'm out."

"I've got a letter for you," said the boy, immediately pulling out of his pocket four tops, two sausages, and a pet frog, in order to produce the epistle.

"Well, put it down, and run home and tell your mother she wants you," said Nat, relapsing into his meditation, and gazing distractedly through the youth into the vacancy behind. A person looking at nothing presents much the same appearance as a man who has suddenly perceived symptoms of cholera in his system, and the good little boy, much affected, asked him if he should run for the doctor.

And light of my soul—
And light of my soul, these heaven-born thrills—'

The devil finish the verses. He is a poet, and knows how. Stay, boy, give me a rhyme to 'thrills.' I'm confused."

"Pills!" said the boy, promptly.

"By Jove! it is singular. This tender boy has opened a new channel of thought. I'll begin again. It is a sublime idea, and must be in blank verse:

'The groaning Gods of eld, sick with ambrosial surfeit,
Medicin'd their giant frames with swallowed planets.'

It's good, but how to apply it to her refusing to dance with me, must at present be left to destiny. D—n it, there is more labor in this than I thought there was. Hollo, boy, what do you want here? Go away!"

"Give me a cent, will you?"

"There are two for you. Go and buy food for worms with 'em at the confectioners. Hold on! wait! The letter is poisoned. Medici, what a nasty-looking epistle. What is this? '*For a Square Gnat*,' written up in one corner, and '*Bonney*' all over the face. The rectangular gnat, without doubt, got scared at the Bonney, which is another formidable insect, and flew up into the corner. '*Deer Sire, sins the whoful events apende larste heave-Ning—*' '*Ning!*' Let me see, what language is '*Ning*' in? '*I hev suffrd with phever, and also I suffer with attacks from eggs, and I think I shell be obligged to suckum! I et won plate of Sucket-Hash and—*' Now, my friend," said Nat, unable to restrain himself, and addressing the small boy, "in confidence, tell me who is he, and excuse the temporary ebullition of profanity, what the devil does he mean by suffering with attacks from eggs, and being obliged to suck 'em? Why, he hasn't signed his name. Who is he? Where did it come from?"

"I don't know," said the boy. "A nigger man

gave it to me, and told me if I gave it to you, you'd give me a cent." Here he darted off to the candy woman's, leaving Nat to continue his perusal of this entertaining epistle, of which he was unable to make any thing definite, the writer having filled the remainder with analogous stuff, about some attempts which had been made on his life since a certain occurrence, by a person who, from all appearances, must have been the cook of the establishment in which he resided, as the said essays at his destruction were evidently made through the medium of his food. However, his curiosity was so much aroused, that he thought it advisable to comply with a request of the writer contained in the note, to meet him at the hour of eleven, which was approaching, within the precincts of a certain shady grove in the outskirts of the town, where he would in person disclose farther particulars respecting the infamous affair. At his approach to this sequestered spot, he discovered Mr. Pithkin there, evidently in a state of expectancy similar to his own, the necessities of which demanded the arrival of another and more mysterious party, for that worthy citizen immediately, and with much alacrity, dodged behind a tree to avoid the advocate's observation. After some time passed by the two in entirely ignoring each other's presence, and continually passing from one bush to another in a secret and silent manner, or eyeing one another from a distance, Nat came away quite dissatisfied, as the third party did not approach, and he was more unable to solve the curious document than ever. Having returned to his office and bestowed much unavailing reflection upon this singular matter, he finally shut the windows of his office, and placing himself in an arm-chair, shut the windows of his soul also, and stopped reflecting altogether, believing, with the famous French philosopher, the process of thinking as a general thing to be unhealthy, and to be indulged in sparingly. An hour or two after this the little boy approached again with a second letter.

"Go away. You can't blackmail me. You've mistaken your man, I tell you," said Nat, rousing from his nap with great presence of mind. "Begone, dull—boy!" The little boy freely left the letter this time without remuneration. Money was no longer of any consequence to him. He was gorged, and all he wanted now was a place of retirement and sequestration for a short span from the cares of life.

This letter, it seems, had been taken from the person of a colored gentleman, inebriated at a neighboring publican's, as the latter, according to his humane custom in summer, was carefully placing him in his ice-house, to be kept from spoiling with the heat. It was written by Colonel Norcomb, and from its contents Nat was enabled to judge that the other was a mark of friendship from the retainer Gluckinson. The Colonel gave an account of the occurrence at the Place, stating, among other matters, that Gluckinson had been temporarily bereaved of his wits by the affair, and that his insanity had commenced to show itself in that exceedingly prevalent form of a desire to write letters when he hadn't any thing to communicate. He alluded to the probability that Charles would confer with him during the day, in reference to the occurrence, and proceeded to inform him that the coming Thursday had been set for his departure to Saratoga with his wife and Charles's mother, and that he intended to visit the neighborhood of New York before his return, in order to meet a friend from South Carolina, who having been convicted of circulating the Bible as an incendiary document among his slaves, and the choice having been accorded to him of being hung, or of reading the letters and speeches of Henry A. Wise, had fled to the North. The letter concluded with an allusion to Miss Wellwood, in which the Colonel expressed his deprecation of her conduct towards the young advocate, in language which Nat generously concluded the writer had probably been led to believe was the height of impassioned philippic, from a faithful perusal of the Charleston Mercury since infancy. "By Jove! it is a little too strong," exclaimed he. "I never saw such blackguard stuff in my life—'black-hearted malignity of conduct—atrocious sentiment of pestiferous antipathy.' However, it is all in the ardor of his friendship for me."

Although the Southerner apologized for the idle contents of the letter, by stating that it was for the purpose of giving his rascally niggers something to do, and, while curiously enough, there seemed to be a paradoxical air therein of suspicion of the young girl Dinah, it was evidently written with an honest desire to protect her as much as possible in her troubles, and failed not to have its weight with the well-disposed young advocate.

CHAPTER XXXIII.

A JUDICIAL EXAMINATION.

The town of Templeville is a town rotten with talent. There may be other towns like it, but few; as there are not great men enough in the world to make up many such places. There is one more, of course. On the other end of the diameter running from this place through the centre of the earth, another has been wisely placed, in order to keep this great globe well-balanced, as it bowls around the azure circus. The inhabitants actually stagger under the weight of genius which Providence has ordained they shall carry, as the simple aborigines did in Pizarro's time, who used to go about, laboring enthusiastically under a weight of golden ornaments which they never knew the value of. Everybody there is possessed of an immense fund of unnecessary information respecting somebody else, and expecting daily to find out something more; and the militia of society there keep their reputations in such a state of lustrous brightness, that when they brandish this shield in the faces of the wicked they do battle with, it is enough to put the latter's eyes out, and make them fall.

It having been stated that a servant had been arrested at Pompney Place for the triple crime of theft, arson, and attempt at murder, and that there would be a preliminary examination of the would-be assassin before the newly elected justice of the peace, Judge Pithkin, there was a tremendous rush to the court at the time appointed. It was not that there was any lack of litigation and court business in this neighborhood, for there was hardly a day in which some individual did not charge his neighbor with harboring an intolerable bull, who kept goring his peaceful ox; but criminal trials were comparatively rare in the district, owing to the fact, that when a crime was committed, the police suspected everybody, and rarely apprehended the criminal from the inefficiency caused by their distraction. The predecessor of the new justice had died of joy just after, and in consequence of being elevated to fill the place, and the inhabitants, by an overwhelming vote, had immediately requested Mr. Pithkin to take his place, perhaps with the expectancy that the same order of events would be repeated. From the instinctive desire to behold a human being in distress, the citizens commenced to throng to the court-room, to which the constable was disposed to deny them admittance, without doubt from the same motive.

"What are you about, Taylor?" said the justice, on arriving and noticing the struggle. "Let 'em in, constable, let my friends in! Let 'em all in! Place chairs up near the bench even! Let them be near me! I do not feel proud at all, gentlemen!"

"But I thought I was not to let any damned rascals in, unless they belonged to the profession!" said the constable, who was a feeble and modest man, and who had been led to use this bad language simply from the excitement of his position.

The young girl, Dinah, recovered from her wound, and other persons immediately interested were present, and the judge took his seat, looking around affably. "Open the court," said he, after a hushing murmur went around the audience.

The constable blushing deeply, looked under the benches in a hesitating manner, as if seeking for some prying instrument necessary for the operation, and then in an inaudible manner, swelling in gradual assurance, exclaimed, "Oh yes! Oh yes! I do now proclaim this court to be open, accordin' to law, by order of the justice of the 4th district, Devolvement Pithkin. Oh yes!"

"Taylor," said the justice, bending his gaze upon him, "the form is imperfect."

"By order of the justice of the district, Honorable D. Pithkin," iterated the constable.

"Who is counsel for the prisoner?" asked the judge, in a satisfied manner.

"I never thought of that," said the prisoner. The many eyes bent upon her confused her somewhat. "I didn't think—I didn't think it necessary to have one!"

"Never mind—never mind that—" said Charles, quickly, in a whisper. "Confound this folly of mine. I have spoken with Mr. Bonney, Dinah, and have told him all about the occurrence. It will only be a few minutes, and you will be cleared."

"I shall serve in that capacity, if your Honor pleases," said Nat.

"Very well! Very well!" said the judge, quickly. "As the court is as yet somewhat imperfectly acquainted with its duty, owing to its recent elevation, it has requested the assistance of a legal friend, Mr. Bildad Knox, in the questions it shall put in the course of the examination. Do you waive the slight irregularity, Mr. Bonney?"

"I waive!" said Nat.

This announcement immediately produced a sensation among the more uninformed of the spectators, who expected to witness some operation on the part of the young lawyer, akin to the impressive ceremony which is usually performed with the American flag, when the general comes down before the militia.

"And—there he is! Mr. Bildad Knox will please take a seat adjacent to the court!" said the judge, with a smile of condescension, as an elderly individual, remarkable for having in his possession a very large forehead and a very small trunk, entered the court-room, slammed the proffered chair violently on the floor twice, and then sat down in it, in an important manner. His forehead, by the way, he carried in the usual place, and his trunk under his arm, having evidently borne in mind, in relation to the latter, on starting out that morning from his office, the advice of the aged elephant to his only son, on starting out into the world, and taken it with him. However, both articles looked as if they had nothing in them; and the former, singular as it may appear, looked as if it were not his.

"It is somewhat remarkable," said the judge, with the preconcerted intention of producing an impression at the outset, "that things have gone on worse in this neighborhood, since I've got into office, than they were ever known to before. This prisoner is charged," continued he, after a moment, amid suppressed excitement, and reading furtively from a paper which he had prepared, and hidden behind his hat, "with wilfully and feloniously having entered the house, commonly known in these parts as Pompney Place, on the night of the 16th, and then and there, with bayonets, sabres, cutlasses—with cimeters, sticks, bludgeons and cudgels, —with swords, broadswords and rapiers, (great sensation among the audience,) poniards, stilettos and battle-axes, claymores, poleaxes, bowie-knives, tomahawks, catapults, battering-rams, and—"

"Wait a moment!" said Nat. "I suggest to the court, that its course of proceeding, though somewhat novel, is perfectly allowable, I suppose, but still may somewhat encumber the examination with which it is now engaged."

"The court won't be interrupted," said the authoritative individual, conscious of his power, and infected with courage by the catalogue of tremendous instruments of warfare which he was recapitulating.

"I suggest to the court," said Mr. Bildad Knox, "that the prosecuting witness be immediately examined, afterwards the other witnesses, and then the accused sent to jail."

The evidence of the prosecuting witness, who was Charles, was thereupon immediately taken, and was certainly remarkable. As prosecuting evidence, its chief merit must have laid decidedly in that which he didn't say, for the facts of the case which he stated were all in favor of the prisoner. As Mr. Pithkin was a human being, he felt disappointed. He remembered that she laughed at him, when he was unavoidably pitched out of a conveyance. Besides the weight of this reflection, he felt that if the accused were committed, the importance of his position would be heightened in the eyes of the community. However, the judge immediately rose superior to the man. The consciousness of his stern position as a dispenser of justice triumphed over his prejudices. Other witnesses, the servants of the house, were examined, who knew nothing at all about the matter, the judge being particular to take notes of their evidence above the others; and then the reservoir of witnesses being exhausted, a short pause ensued, during which, the judge commenced to revolve a plan of examining everybody in the audience as to what they knew about the matter, in order to prolong the excitement. Soon after, Colonel Norcomb, who had been disinclined to appear as a witness, it not being necessary at all, drove up to the door with Charles's aunt, and Charles, being anxious that his own favorable testimony should be corroborated by the Colonel's, persuaded him to appear. As they entered the court-room, the countenance of the judge was singularly affected, and as he fixed his eyes upon the Southerner, his feelings appeared to have been suddenly estranged from his kind.

"Name?" said he, gruffly. The dignity of the judge, as well as the affability of the man, appeared to be strangely deserting him. However, although he was slightly acquainted with the witness in society, it was not to be expected that he should know him on the bench. The Colonel gave his name.

"No other name? No *alias?*" continued Mr. Pithkin, looking at the witness severely.

"Eh! what?" asked the astounded Colonel.

The court whispered to Mr. Bildad Knox.

"Certainly, certainly," said the latter, looking at the court approvingly after a moment; "the statute expressly provides that no idiot or criminal shall be received as a witness in any court of this State! There appears to be some just doubt in the mind of the court," continued he, looking around, "whether this individual can be sworn as a witness, before he has been examined as to his mental and moral capacity to testify!"

"Do you mean to apply that infernal statute to me?" asked the Colonel, whose blood was beginning to boil.

"The court will not say you are either of these," replied Judge Pithkin, calmly, and putting himself in an affable position; "but being imperfectly acquainted with your idiosyncracies and also your antecedents, from the fact that you have been until recently a stranger to this community, how does the court know you are not? You may be both."

"The statute doesn't preclude idiots from becoming judges, at any rate!" said the Colonel, relieving his feelings slightly. At these audacious words, the court appeared to be moved internally, but by a superhuman effort regained its composure.

"Sit down and hold your tongue!" said he, after thinking a moment, with great presence of mind.

"I have the honor and lassitude to do as you say," said the Colonel, who was disposed to yield, as he was tired of standing, and felt that he had crushed the judge enough in his last remark.

"He certainly has a cunning look," said Mr. Bildad Knox, turning to the judge, on noticing the smile of the Colonel. "Do you know the nature of an oath, man?" continued he, addressing the latter.

"Oh, never mind," said the judge, "let him pass; you may swear him."

The Colonel was put on the stand, and commenced his evidence by stating, in a romantic manner, that "truth was stranger than fiction,—that—"

"Hold, wait!" said the judge; "a man who believes truth to be stranger than fiction is certainly not reliable as a witness. He can't go on." And here another trouble ensued, which lasted some time. However, the Colonel was finally allowed to give his testimony uninterrupted, and the examination closed therewith. Mr. Bildad Knox then proceeded to address the audience in a speech, of which the first half was entirely unintelligible, and the last half simply improper to be put forth under any circumstances; the former being a summary of the evidence, and the latter the usual vituperation of somebody, with which advocates invariably think it necessary to wind up with, the lawyer in this case having selected Babington Macaulay, the great historian, as the object of his obloquy. Nat replied in a speech full of felicities, by such comparisons as likening the judge's character to the sun—that there might be spots in it, but they did not interfere with its brilliancy, and it was a source of wonder how they got there; that Americans knew the price of liberty, because they knew the price of every thing; that with a mysterious and sacred mutuality, by their very existence they conferred an everlasting and inexpensive dignity upon each other; that the noblest death he knew of was to be killed by the fall of a liberty-pole—a patriot's death; and wound up by blackguarding Mr. Bildad Knox in a manner which entirely surpassed that individual's effort in billingsgate, and excited the audience to the highest pitch, from the fact that its object was present, and personal vengeance might be expected to be taken by him at any moment. The judge then delivered his decision amidst an intense hush, and proceeded to observe that the prisoner must be committed, and the witnesses put under bonds to appear at the next general term of oyer and terminer in the December following, with the exception of the witness Norcomb, whom he should order to be incarcerated until that period, as his testimony was too valuable to permit of his being let out on bail; but Mr. Bildad Knox whispering to him simply that he couldn't do it, he observed that on the whole the prisoner must be discharged. That he didn't know which was the most detrimental to the proper administration of the laws and a judicious execution of justice, to believe that the occurrence took place in all the particulars as evolved from the witnesses, if it did not, or to disbelieve it, if it did. That to withhold the belief of the court in this occurrence, if the court had witnessed it itself, might truly be said to be difficult; but that to give the assent of the court because it was witnessed by other individuals, would call for too heavy an endorsement of the character of some of them, (looking at the Southerner,) a responsibility which the court was unwilling to assume. That the court was not obliged to give any reason for any thing it did, but that it was willing to state, among other matters, that as the witnesses who saw the accused in the library, evidently didn't know what she was there for, and as the number of those who didn't see her there greatly preponderated over those who did, the court would order an entry to be made discharging the prisoner.

And so Dinah was discharged, Nat having decided beforehand that Charles should refrain from making any allusion to his fancies, and that the girl might hold her peace during the examination.

CHAPTER XXXIV.

THE OLD MAN IN TROUBLE.

On the day succeeding the examination of Dinah, the justice, Pithkin, who was suffering from the reaction of that excitement, and was regretting that he had not been able to imprison a half dozen of people, the prisoner, one or two witnesses, and both lawyers for contempt, aroused from his torpid revery as he walked slowly along one of the avenues of the village, on hearing the exciting sound of merriment and laughter from grown as well as childish voices. He looked up and observed in the distance an old man in a state unbecoming gray hairs. His relaxed muscles hardly sustained his staggering form, while the lines of his face bore the well-known indications that another intellect was on fire. And yet the fury was unable wholly to extinguish the marks of sorrow, if not of other intelligence, still perceptible there, beneath the idiotic grin and excited glare of drunkenness. The old man here stopped suddenly and seemed to address the hushed crowd, which had gathered around. His incoherent accents produced another roar of laughter, one of the boys turning a somersault to express his delight, and then the procession moved on again after the aged being in profound gratification, as he now and then varied his eccentric course by obliquely encountering a tree-box, or executing a serpentine manœuvre.

He had performed, with great difficulty, the feat of extricating his handkerchief from his pocket, and was engaged in instinctive essays to free his forehead from the dew distilled thereon by the physical torment of his nature, when his eye struck a little, chubby, rosy-cheeked, dirty-faced boy, whose little soul, while it could not comprehend the scene, had been asserting its joyous nature in infantile shouting and hurrahs with the rest. The old man waved his handkerchief towards the little cherub as a token of approach, and by the wildness of the manner struck such terror into the infant that he was immediately reduced to an excessively pituitous condition. He then issued an excited order to the assembled crowd to all go to the devil, when the liquor doing its climacteric work, threw him heavily over to the ground. An old man drunk is the sublimity of earthly misery or human frenzy. His head struck with force the pavement, his coat was torn by an adjacent tree-box, and his aged breast was exposed to the gaze of the assemblage.

A young girl had been approaching the crowd from the opposite direction. As quick as thought she reached the unhappy fallen being. She threw over him her mantle, and then stood in front, her fragile form almost fiercely erected to shield his exposed form from the improper gaze of the now rapidly gathering crowd. It was the girl Dinah, who had sought and thus found her father, wandered from his home. There was not a demand for respect in her face, but it seemed almost a command to honor her parent, as she stood there at the moment in an attitude of defence, with her full eyes bent upon the crowd. With the trembling tenderness of filial piety she turned to raise him from the ground, and a man stepped out of the crowd to assist her.

"So the old fellow is drunk again, is he?" said a villager to another, by way of recognition of matters.

"Drunk again!" reiterated the other; "the same drunk he has been engaged in ever since he got out of prison, I guess."

"Drunk! he is sober, you mean," interposed the apothecary, with a grin. "He ain't used to being sober, and that's what makes him act so."

"I pity him!" said another. "His daughter's being tried, and his own degradation has made him get drunk to drown his trouble. He always seemed fitted to be something besides that which he is."

The mob of boys had become quiet, and although there was ample ludicrous cause in the flaccid, uncertain manner in which the old man rose from the ground, an honest hush succeeded. In all the purity of nature's sympathy, one or two of the small boys had begun to cry, they knew not why hardly, on looking into Dinah's face, as she took one hand of her father to guide his erring footsteps; and the most riotous, and the ringleader, in fact, of the youths, was actually engaged in belaboring another for having hooted after the old man.

"Let me take your place! I will take your place! I can hold him up better!" said another of the villagers to Dinah, stepping forward kindly.

"Away!" here burst forth the justice, Pithkin, to the crowd, accompanying his command with a majestic gesture. "I order you to disperse. Go off." His voice was a little husky; something for the moment struck to the depth of his obtuse yet honest intelligence, as he saw their actions and faces in the scene, which told him that neither of these beings were to blame, and that both were suffering a degradation which perhaps they didn't merit. The consideration that the old man had atoned for his remorseful error by a long incarceration, and that the girl had committed no positive crime, probably raised this feeling of sympathy, under the excitement of which he would have even gone so far as to designate the assemblage as an assorted set of rascals, if it had not been composed of his neighbors. A look of gratitude fell upon his face from Dinah's eyes as she saw his order being gradually obeyed, especially by the boys, to whom the scene at best was a sorry sight.

(" She behaved very badly towards me when I got knocked out of the wagon, but perhaps she laughed in joy at seeing that I was safe and spared to the community.) Clear out ! " reiterated he to the diminishing crowd of boys.

" I guess your father is not in the habit of doing this thing, is he ? " said one of the villagers to Dinah. The apothecary here slunk away.

" Oh no, sir," said the girl, quickly, " and—forgive him."

" Certainly, of course. It's all a mistake, I know. It always is," cried Pithkin, in a temporary burst of enthusiasm. " He hasn't done any harm. You like me, don't you ? Where can you take him, let me see ? "

" I want to be taken to the graveyard," said the old man, in a low incoherent voice, beginning to revive. " Put me up in the steeple. I can go to bed in the bell. When Jane rises from her grave to go to heaven, I'll grasp her clothes, and she'll take me along with her ! " The old fellow's white hair was much disordered and fell over his eyes. Dinah decently brushed down the thin locks one side over his sunken temples, and commenced to arrange his cravat. She had composed his coat together as well as she could.

"I don't want him taken to my house. Hang me, if he shall be taken into my house. What do I want drunken men in my house for," continued Mr. Pithkin; "however, as it is just round the corner, you can take him in there. You like me, don't you? Let him remain there. You think I'm a friend, don't you? A good sleep will do him good, and I think when you can reduce it to a quiet, gentlemanly drunk in apartments, it is not so worthy of censure after all. It disturbs no one, and has the merit about it of affording gratification to at least one human being."

"She's a good girl! she's a good girl!" continued the thick-tongued old man, with a wild eye and feeble smile, as he tried to place his trembling hand upon his daughter's head and knocked her hat awkwardly aside. "What do they want to throw blame on her for?"

"It struck me as rather foolish," said Pithkin, replying in a natural manner to the old man's question. "However, nothing will come of it if you keep shady, and don't do it again."

"I will knock you down!" said the old man with sudden ferocity, as the maddening thought of oppression and persecution of one he loved floated across his disordered brain.

"Eh!" cried Pithkin, jumping forward a little in a lively manner. "Here's the gate; bring him right in here. Carry him up stairs and put him to bed, and say nothing about it."

The girl, in a few short words, acknowledged her gratitude to Pithkin and the neighbors who had assisted the steps of the old man, and she was finally left alone in the chamber to sit by the side of her sleeping father, and to commune in the quiet of the room with her own thoughts, as they passed rapidly and in some disorder through her mind.

"She has a beautiful eye," said one of the villagers. "Her face looked as honest and beautiful as the days are long, God bless it!"

"However, you can't tell," said another; "you don't know any thing about these people who have once lost honor, you know."

"Pshaw! if everybody was honest," said Pithkin, "who was beautiful, and every one a rascal who was ugly, they'd have you both in jail in less than ten minutes. You can't tell from looks. An investigation of character, founded on nothing but a thorough knowledge of facts, is the legal and the only proper way. I don't allow my mind to judge in any other manner, and I won't!"

When he returned in an hour or two to his house he found the girl and her father, who had not become quite sober, and was still confused and stupid, about to leave the gate. She hesitated for a moment, and then asked him, amidst an iteration of thanks, if he would endeavor to palliate the occurrence as much as he could to her mistress and Charles, when he should meet them.

"Certainly, my girl," replied he. "I'll do it if I remember it; but I can't be expected to remember all of these things, of course not; and hang me if I will!"

CHAPTER XXXV.

THE DEPARTURE OF THE MOTHER AND THE SOUTHERNERS.

The morning having arrived on which Charles's mother, accompanied by Colonel Norcomb and his wife, intended to depart for a short sojourn at the watering-place, they took leave of Charles and his aunt, who promised to join them in a few days with Laura Wellwood.

Among other remarks, in a conversation with her sister-in-law, the mother said: "I think it is better, perhaps, to dismiss them quietly with a sum of money, as these late events have shown quite conclusively that they are really unreliable, and perhaps dangerous! I have appreciated fully the kindness of your nature, Adeline, in taking them into the household, but I have feared all the while that their modesty, at least of the girl, was but the cunning of an unscrupulous nature, desirous of attaining a position to serve the bad purposes which were being formed in her mind. As young as she is, she evidently has learned how to feign a respect which she doesn't really feel, in order to gain favor; and that very humble consideration of her own and her father's position, which ought to be the indication of gratitude, is, after all, but an empty display, made for the artful purpose of exciting our compassion to a still further and undeserved extent. It was not at all improper on your part to exercise your charity in this unusual way, dear sister, as you wished not only to relieve them of their necessities, but to contribute your mite to the welfare of society, in elevating their moral character. But this case only shows, Adeline, how impossible it is to transcend with satisfaction the common rules which have been laid down by society, with regard to a proper system of beneficence and charity towards the erring. The sinful, who are suffering for the necessities of life, have certainly a demand upon us for relief; but it is hazardous and uncertain to exercise our benevolence in a greater degree by endeavoring to mitigate the moral penalty which the social sense of justice has affixed to their crimes. Even when their heartfelt repentance appeals to the sensibilities of society for a restoration of their former rights, it is of doubtful propriety; for in rendering the social pardon easy of obtainment, we but tempt the guilty to a renewal of his guilt. Indeed, the rarity of the instances in which such a course has succeeded, and the frequency of those in which it has failed from the conduct of the criminal himself, would seem to show that the social sense should be a strict rule for the individual. To be sure, in this unfortunate instance, the unhappy old man has reached an age and a state of mind when the commission of further crime may seem to him fruitless; and the bitter recollection of the past, of the apples of Sodom that he has gathered, that were ashes to his lips, may be accompanied by a sincere repentance. But does not this case show how crime, withering and dying in the nature of the criminal himself, may have already dropped an ineradicable seed of bad example in the being of others within his influence?"

"How often and how naturally are we accustomed to look for an excess of openness in youth? But in this young girl a secretive disposition shows that her tendencies towards an unscrupulous life are already nursed and sheltered by her in their dark growth, from the withering effect of the moral sunshine without. I had not thought that Providence would have given to any one such a clear perception, such a nice judgment, as the girl appears to possess, without the hinge to turn them to bear upon her own career; for certainly she knows not the weakness of the career she is upon, and the bright faculties which she seems to possess are but instruments of self-injury to her."

The aunt was silent. She acknowledged the potency, the kindness, even, of her sister's reasoning, and shared the unpleasant melancholy which this stern yet well-meant consideration of erring youth naturally produced. An account of the father's intoxication in the village had reached them, and added its disagreeable weight to the propriety of discarding the wanderers from virtue, and even the kind suggestion of the mother to accompany their dismissal for charity-sake, with a sum of money, seemed at the moment injudicious.

As the group stood on the steps of the terrace, awaiting the arrival of the carriages, the girl approached from the side of the house, and with a hesitating bow, which might equally have characterized a timid sycophant approaching a powerful being, or a truthful child seeking for good-will, presented to the mother as a token of remembrance on her leaving, a nosegay of flowers. The stern, bitter look of mingled regret and censure, which her reflections had produced on the latter's brow, faded away, and gave place to a softened, melancholy expression; and, indeed, in the quick suffusion of her countenance at the time, something else beyond a melancholy might have been recognized—a momentary uneasiness, as it were, and dissatisfaction with herself. She thanked her, however, with a sedate answer, and soon dismissing the subject, turned away to attend to some other matter. The girl noticed her returning coldness. The earnest, furtive look for approbation quickly faltered into an appearance of stifled hope, and she stole away as soon as Mrs. Norcomb had spoken to her some kind parting words. Could the mother have followed her lonely steps to her apartment, she would have observed the young creature upon her knees by the bedside. Were those the words of some witch, fated to undergo a life of human hopes and fears, the success of which should be her purgation, begging relief from the demons who tormented her with half-disclosing her supernatural relations to mortal ken, or were they the outpourings of a pure and truthful heart, acknowledging to her friend and Maker the weaknesses and temptations of an earthly nature, and begging for charity for all, and for guidance in the path of goodness?

At the depôt the party awaited the arrival of the train in the sitting-room, and were enlivened by the presence of the young lawyer, Mr. Bonney. The overseer Baylon, too, who was loitering about the depôt, saluted them with an air of great deference, and approached to inform them of the continued health of their neighbor Rudolph, whom he had left in New York.

In the course of a short conversation which Charles's mother permitted him to engage in with her, he alluded to the late occurrence at her mansion, of which he had just heard, as a proof of the sincerity of his remarks with regard to the girl Dinah and her father. Indeed, the antagonism of Dinah was productive of unusual acerbity in him, and he was even led to overstep the bounds of prudence, and go so far as to attempt to assail, in an ambiguous manner, the chastity of the girl; having in his mind, without doubt, her relations with his master, whose name he was fortunate enough not to mention. But he almost overturned his machinated fabric of various insinuations by this error. The lady dismissed him suddenly from her presence with an indignant reprehension; for with all the faults which she had seen in the girl's character, the remembrance of her face, her words, all her actions, gainsaid the insinuation without thought.

In the mean time Colonel Norcomb, in a pleasant conversation with Nat, had endeavored to impress upon his mind the belief that Charles had commenced to be actuated by feelings of the darkest jealousy towards him.

"Gracious! you haven't been imprudent, and divulged it to him, have you?" said Nat, who had enjoined the strictest kind of secrecy in this matter. "I never saw such a singular case as mine. I can't defy my rival, because it would reveal my passion, and it would be insanity to reveal my passion, because she loves him, and she will continue to love him as long as I don't defy him! At any rate, he might confide it to the old gentleman, who would immediately confide his daughter to a nunnery before he hears of the exact state of affairs; or, perhaps, taking advantage of my sunburnt and distracted condition, have me spirited off to the South as an able-bodied but weak-minded nigger."

"Oh, no, I haven't said any thing," replied the Colonel, who had thought to encourage Nat with this innocent fabrication; "but in the various interviews you have had with Miss Wellwood, your manner, you know, and hers, may have—"

"I don't see how he can derive any poignance from that. It appears to me that if she has displayed any feeling towards me, it has been simply an afflictive desire to drive me distracted on her part; and if any reciprocity has been observed on mine, it has been the immediate gratification thereof. I am conscious she loves me, Colonel, but how any one could ever discover that from her manner towards me, is more than I can imagine!"

"Very true," said the Southerner, in sympathetic condolence at the singular state of affairs in which Nat was involved.

"But you must keep it a profound secret, Colonel. I have been rash at times, yet some power watches over me, which prevents her discovering my passion. There is, no doubt, some providence in it!"

The Southerner, having promised him, here stepped aside in the fulfilment of a pious duty of his nature. Obadiah had stooped upon the shaded platform with his legs bent sidewise, in inquisitive examination of the direction of one of the trunks which had been placed thereon, when the Colonel, observing his position, and unable to resist the impulses of his antipathy, kicked him with such violence, that the victim made a brief but rapid excursion into the air, and finally buried his topknot to a considerable depth in the sand beneath. The Colonel, having thus relieved his feelings, immediately renewed in placid serenity his walk with Nat, and engaged in pleasant conversation until the return of Charles and the ladies, who had driven down the street for a short purchase.

"He kicked me!" said the aggrieved Obadiah to Nat, after the train had left. "He knows I am non-resistant!"

"Are you? It is gratifying to know that, as I intend to kick you also," replied the young lawyer who, having been infected with a general admiration of the Southerner's actions, on this occasion displayed the same in the flattering form of imitation by administering another sincere kick to the now thoroughly astonished recipient of the first. The disgusted overseer walked off, but finally recovered his spirits and chuckled, "I got all the money he gave the gal, anyhow! Three per cent. a minute! So the proud lady is my ally, is she?"

CHAPTER XXXVI.

LAURA AND THE AUNT.

Laura and her father, visiting their friend and pastor on the way, were making gentle progress towards Pompney Place to dine, a few days after the departure of Charles's mother to the watering-place. It was a wet day, and the water of a dull storm, prolonged through the morning, stood in puddles on the road. The foliage of the trees and the fowls hung in a sloppy manner, and the subdued Timothy and Thomas endeavored in vain to lift their melancholy tails.

"And she told 'em that she wouldn't marry him!" said Laura's parent. This was the thrilling point of a long and intricate narrative, connected with the younger days of the pastor and Charles's mother, and he had arrived at it with much difficulty and danger to his equanimity. However, as it inculcated a moral, he persisted, although other persons "whom he once knew" presented their tales to him in a very distracting manner. "Yes, she told her parents that," reiterated he, surrounding the fact with gloom.

"I say, she told her parents that!" continued he, in desperation at seeing no excitement.

"You said that before," cried Laura. "Of course she did, she didn't love him. At least she loved another!"

"D—n it! This is the result of hours of careful training!" said the old gentleman, hitting the darkey in front in an exasperated manner, who immediately communicated the shock to Timothy and Thomas. "She always was a proud, wilful girl, and her conduct on that occasion drove Fuffles into metaphysics, and by that means her parents into an early grave. They were obliged to listen to 'em."

"Why, Charles's grandparents were both over seventy when they died. But you meant," continued she, putting her arms around his neck, "they were so happy because their child married the man she loved, that they arrived at that age much sooner than they otherwise would have done."

"No, I didn't, either. However, let us dismiss the gloomy subject from our minds. Here we are at the gate. That infernal Mudgeon! I wish Nat was here. I have got the greatest story to tell him when I see him."

Charles and his aunt received them on the wet terrace, and a few drops spattering on their bare heads, they all trotted into the hall together.

The aunt had received a letter from her sister, and Laura one from Mrs. Norcomb. The aunt's was filled with love on the part of the mother, and many allusions to her darling Laura, which brought the blood of affection to the listening girl's heart, and suggested to her mind a long train of thoughts as good as kisses. Mrs. Norcomb's letter alluded in one point to Dinah, and asked Laura still to countenance the girl for her sake, even if there were imputations resting upon her character. Laura in a short soliloquy had discovered to herself that she would have helped Dinah for her own inclination's sake, and she had resolved on this visit to say a good word for her to the aunt, who, since the occurrence, had expressed sentiments of distrust and hints of dismissal.

"Col. Norcomb sends his love to you," observed the young lady, as she folded up the letter.

"And even absence fails to dissipate that fatal infatuation!" murmured the spinster. "Thus still he lingers in wretched, unrighteous hope!"

Laura soon found out that the aunt was more prejudiced against the two dependants, than ever; although curious enough, while she drew a complete character for the girl as she seemed to see it, and referred in terms of pity and poetry to her ambition, cunning, and unscrupulousness, she still seemed now and then to discover that there was another and pleasanter character for her concealed in her bosom and apparently from herself, which was the real product of her own eccentric heart and mind. When her sister was not thinking and feeling in her, unknown to herself, she showed her own kind nature. However, the young lady herself felt, while combating the charges which the aunt in her possessed condition brought against the young girl, that there was something wrong in the late affair, which justly subjected the latter to suspicion.

The aunt continued to answer Laura's inquiries, and stated that the girl had been disposed since her trial to seek the solitude of her room. She communicated the fact that she had burst in upon her on one occasion, and observed her concealing by her side a piece of work upon which she was engaged at the window. Upon discovering it to be a piece of embroidery in the form of slippers, she questioned her with regard to them, and was informed by her, after some hesitation, and in a confident way, that they were for Mr. Pithkin.

"In my surprise and astonishment, would you believe it, at the answer, I was about to precipitate myself upon her and take a speedy vengeance, such was the violent shock given to my feelings in considering the possibility of her having sinister intentions, when she frankly explained to me that the judge had kindly sheltered her father at the time he was overcome with wine, would you believe it, from the rude gaze of the populace, and that she desired to send him some mark of her gratitude, which certainly discovers that she has a high sense of obligation at the very least, although many faults are visible in her actions, of course. She asked me if she might present him with these slippers, and, of course, I not only answered affirmatively, but even became so much interested as to prescribe the form of note, you know, which she should address to him to accompany them, would you believe it; and although I did not at first notice her demurring to the idea, would you believe it, ('I would,' said Laura, hurriedly,) of dispatching any note at all, and her suggestion that she should simply send her father with them, you know, and ask him if he would accept them, you know, I afterwards was compelled to take into consideration her singular perversity of character, when she thought it was a little too much to put into the note these words, 'the tokens of a deep-felt appreciation of the grandeur and might of your intellect as well as the kindness of your heart,' and laughed at the idea, would you believe it, although she subsequently consented, and not only inserted them, but also by an ingenious arrangement, would you believe it, made such delicate allusions to me at my suggestion, would you think, that I should have been lost in admiration if I hadn't discovered that, under a feeling of poverty, she had made the slippers out of the cloth of an old coat which she had cleaned up, and—"

The discourse of the spinster was something in the nature of a waterspout, of tremendous power of suction from the ocean of her thoughts, but of rather thin magnitude, and easily destroyed by a simple shot of interruption. Squire Wellwood, after wandering somewhere with Charles, had entered the room. "You said a coat *which* she had cleaned," remarked he, with great quickness; "that reminds me of a singular incident, being one *which* happened to a friend of mine—" The spinster was so thoroughly overpowered by this remarkable connection of thought, that she immediately forgot her own narrative, and asked, with a thrill of interest in the hero, "Was he married?"

"That is the point! He broke both legs trying to get married, and—"

"But I am glad Dinah was discharged, are you

not, Adeline?" said Laura, working to favor the girl. "Even if she has been guilty, it seems hard that she should be crushed out of a wish for honesty just as she commences life."

"Yes, Nat was smart," said the old gentleman, replying affably, as he now felt himself able to proceed at leisure with his narrative. "He is an able barrister."

Laura was sorry that Dinah had not been cleared altogether from any imputation. Besides that, somebody had lately been overwhelming her with the most terrible specimens of doggerel at the rate of about two sonnets a day, and she was inclined to believe that it was the young advocate who was thus taxing her fortitude as a human being. "No, he isn't," said she.

"He is," said the old gentleman.

"No, I deny it," said she, warmly.

"Aha!" said the old maid to herself suddenly. She had made a discovery.

"I say he is," continued the old gentleman.

"No, he isn't."

"This is filial gratitude," said the parent, slightly exasperated. "I say he is," roared he.

"Well, perhaps he may be," replied Laura.

"But I think you ought not to depreciate the poor fellow now, Laura," continued the spinster. "Think of his being wounded the way he has been!"

"Wounded! Gracious heaven, when?" cried the young lady, in sudden excitement, "oh where—when did it—"

("I am sure now.) I mean in his feelings," replied the aunt complacently. "Do you know he told me he felt quite severely cut up on your having refused to dance with him, and—"

"He told you so, did he? And pray what right has the gentleman to call in question my manner towards him?"

("Goodness, Charles has been too lax. He has been too secure and inattentive. The ruse has been entirely too successful with him. Yes, I'll change it. I'll rouse his pride. It is the only spur to men's indifference, the vain creatures!")

At this point, a domestic bawled out in a deafening manner that festal joy laughed in the mantling goblet, and that the banquet awaited their presence. Charles now coming in, in a slow and sedate manner, accompanied Laura to the table, and soon, between the ceaseless flow of the aunt's talk, ever contingent to the hour, and the ceaseless efforts of Laura's parent to make his go in the same manner, the young people were easily driven to the verge of distraction.

CHAPTER XXXVII.

A TACIT CONFESSION OF COMPLICITY.

A few days after Charles's mother departed, Obadiah Baylon visited Pompney Place, coming to gratify his malice against Dinah, as likely enough his hate was aroused to such an extent, because she had revealed to him a contemptuous estimate of his character, and scorned his antagonism which seemed both natural and purposed. While proceeding upon the avenue to the house, he laughed enough to shake his unconfirmed knee-pans, when he reflected that he had an unconscious slave in the mistress of that estate, with thousands at her disposal, the proud lady educated in refinement and luxury.

He first encountered the retainer Gluckinson, who proceeded to thrill him with his exaggerated romance, and dwelt particularly upon the latest form of his hallucination, in which he had imagined himself a fire-engine. "And when there was a fire," said he, "the cries of my distress might be heard all over the house, they were so piercing." Before he left, Baylon proposed to further his plans by wedging into the mind of the innocent youth several pleasant insinuations with reference to Dinah, the least of which were, that she would steal and was not virtuous, and the most exciting that she hated him, and was really the secret cause of the cook's canker towards him. A short contest took place between the ire of the youth and his native desire to forgive the girl, but finally Baylon was gratified to hear his formal announcement, that however much he had hitherto liked her, he should feel it incumbent upon him thereafter to hoot at her, and make faces at her father upon every convenient occasion.

Baylon had requested a meeting with Charles, intimating that he wished to confer with him upon the difficulty which had taken place between him and his master. The young man was still agitated with contending emotions with regard to Dinah, and anxious to free her from the suspicions which the renewed memory of slighter events connected with her and her father did not strengthen, and with further interest he resolved to see this man, Baylon, as he reflected that the latter was somewhat intimately acquainted with them in New York, and knew enough of their history, perhaps, to assist him materially in judging of their characters; although he was well aware that he would have to take into consideration the evil tendencies which belonged to the nature of the man himself.

Obadiah was ingenious enough, however, in the short but interesting interview, to conceal his antipathy, and succeeded in strengthening the unhappy opinion which Charles had been gradually forming of the girl's character. At first endeavoring to produce the impression that she was intending to take Rudolph as a paramour, he afterwards adopted, with easy alacrity and a pleased manner, the idea which Charles had not refrained from putting forth, that the person who had attempted to rob the house, was, in all probability, the girl's lover as well as accomplice, and by mixing up the two, confounded such an ugly though harmonized theory of her conduct, that Charles was forced from feeling to exclaim against the possibility of it—"With that face it can never be!" But the interest which he took in the matter had to be satisfied, and it now assumed the form of a determination to do justice in the case. He sent for the girl whom he had scarcely once accosted since the trial, and who in fact had seemed desirous of keeping in quiet and solitude since that event. She noticed with a start the presence of Baylon as she entered the library. While on the other hand, the look of scorn which she gave him, and then quickly concealed in the confusion and distraction of her manner which followed, seemed to want not its usual ludicrous effect upon him.

After a few words of preliminary coldness, in which he endeavored to convey to her an idea of his duty and his continued suspicion, and to hide his sympathy, Charles commenced once more to question her in reference to the late occurrence. Having again asked her with an indefinite expectation, if she knew the person whom she drove out of the library by her alarm, and warned her to tell the truth, he was surprised to notice an increasing confusion in her manner, as if her young mind, though bright, was after all inexperienced enough to be overwhelmed by a renewal of the examination; and he observed further, that she did not even desire the absence of Baylon, who was thus constituted a witness to the interview, indicating a desperation of distraction with regard to the consequences of disclosure. She commenced to murmur as if about to make a thorough confession, and there was such increasing agitation in her manner, that pity took its place in his bosom, and the old thought came to him again, which fancifully held her to be one whom some evil genius possessed, and whose evil commands she had to obey, in spite of a better nature.

But all this quickly changed. She had started up with some energy and looked at Baylon, and as she paused, a bitter smile, if not a sad one, passed over her face. The knowledge of his hate and his inferiority, perhaps had roused her, and with her consciousness of Charles's prejudices, made her feel that her confession would be a foolish act, and at least a triumph to him in its injurious consequences to her. She refused with an obstinate silence, which was but a characteristic acknowledgment, to answer any further questions which were put to her; and the idea of pity soon wore away in Charles's bosom, as the conviction of her confessed complicity in this matter, of her hypocrisy, ingratitude, and depravity came over him. He now asked her in the manner of accusation, whether she had not been deceiving him and his mother since she had been in the household, and abusing the care and consideration which had been shown her, with an idea of playing a part out of keeping with her modest position. She gave confession to all his accusations by her silence, and as she thus stood apparently convicted of guilt, Charles saw no penitence in her passive manner and bowed head, but the stubbornness of a hardened nature. Her trembling and pallor seemed that of fear, and her compressed lips the signs of disappointment of evil; and although young, and just entering life as she was, his disgust overcame his sympathy, for she seemed to have been aware, and to have tried to make use of that very idea.

A full conviction of her depraved character had come over him, and as he ordered her to leave him, it was still further strengthened by that which seemed to him the very hardihood of desperation. No matter how much she had been sullenly overcome by Charles's indications of his estimate of her character, she seemed determined that it should not be a matter of triumph for Obadiah; for she threw such a threatening look of mingled anger and contempt at the latter, as she withdrew, that his top-knot stood up straight, and he seemed more knock-kneed than ever, in the excessive perturbation which ensued therefrom in his nature.

CHAPTER XXXVIII.

THE WOUNDED HEART.

Nat galloped up the carriage-way on the afternoon of the next day to pay his neighborly respects to Charles's aunt, and while giving directions from the terrace with regard to his mare as he had concluded to stop and dine, commenced a pleasant conversation with the lady seated in a window of the sitting-room.

"How is the health of Justice Pithkin," said she, presently. "Oh, tell me—tell me—ah, what horrible presentiment now seizes me—is he—is he well?"

"The last time I saw him he was suffering from severe pains, and was in an inflammatory state."

"Ah," gasped the aunt, sinking on the sofa—"Help me, for I am aweary!"

"Here, Dinah!" cried out Nat to the girl at the far end of the terrace, "tell William just to give Kitty some water. Eh, what, you feel faint, Miss Adeline? Certainly, you can fetch a smelling-bottle for Miss Adeline, Dinah, and a bucket of Indian meal with some oats in it, and let her be rinsed off, Dinah."

"Oh, I feel somewhat better, Mr. Bonney," murmured the spinster in a weak voice, as Nat suddenly recollected that the judge's pain had not been very severe, and that the inflammatory state of the patient arose merely from exasperation at being unable to tell at any moment in what part of his system it was, as it appeared to be a rheumatism with a roving disposition. "Otherwise he was in fine spirits. We were talking about love, and he gave it as his opinion that a human being should never reveal his affection to his wife before marriage."

"Thus proofs of his devotion accumulate!" murmured the aunt.

"I left him, as he wished to study the complaint, which he had in his hands at the moment."

"Heavens! did he have it in his hands?"

"Yes, he had been sitting upon it just before, you know."

"Oh dear!"

"Eh, you understand me, I meant a suit, you know —a legal paper."

The girl brought the smelling-bottle, and then went away again. She had attired herself in an old yellow silk dress, which seemed to fit the cool temperature of the day, and had made herself as neat as possible as if this were a kind of holiday for her and her desperation. Charles met her as she was returning, and asked her to stop for a moment, while he took a seat upon the shaded terrace. He had come up from the park with a book containing a letter from his mother, and it was evident that he had not so much expended his time in reading the work perhaps, as in continuing his reflections concerning the girl, to whom the letter referred. He had certainly lost all confidence in her, and singular indeed was the effect which his disappointment had upon his manner towards her. He seemed to take a delight in severity, and what was disgust or pity yesterday, had become almost an unnatural anger to-day. With his feelings withered by mistrust born of her obstinate silence, his antipathy to the girl no longer rested upon the proven facts of her unscrupulousness displayed in the evident intention of assisting in the robbery of her benefactors, but he seemed rather to take pains to entertain a still baser view of her character, and to feel her presence under the same roof with his mother as a womanly dishonor; just as boys, irritated by the poisonous bite of an insect, like to dig at the wound. According to Obadiah, she had quietly received the apologies which Warriston had offered her, and had taken him back with many kind words, and if any relation existed between them, it was for money to share in dishonor with her real lover. He requested her to sit down upon the settee, and she immediately obeyed him.

He then told her plainly that he had finally determined to send her away from the household, and he thought he would now announce it to her in order to give her time to make her necessary preparations for leaving. He then alluded to her youth, to the folly of her degradation, and expressed the usual hope that she would meet with some one who would have a good influence over her. Visions of retaining her in the household, of discovering her associations, and of endeavoring to exert such an influence had come over him heretofore, but the possibility of her receiving with secret ridicule such an effect of her hypocrisy upon him, now filled him with the gall of utter carelessness for her welfare. As such thoughts as these had passed through his mind, he had asked himself more than once how it was possible that one who hardly seemed old enough to be the author or recipient of love or passion should have already reached the horror of their depravation. He alluded directly to her relations with his neighbor Rudolph, "whose locket you wore in your bosom." She started up overwhelmed with confusion. "The—" commenced she vehemently, but immediately changed her sentence, "Mr. Warriston has paid me attentions which must be unnoticed by me, and they should be by others. If they are sincere, I can only pity him," continued she, bitterly; "if they are not, let me leave it to others to despise him."

("Yes, it was her lover's locket, and she is now making a show of earnest horror respecting Warriston.) You may do your best with your power over him," continued he, for he had got tired of her hypocrisy. "I will not interfere with you, or with any other of your plans. You may rest assured I shall keep your revelations private, although it is my duty even for your sake to warn him."

"Allow me sincerely to pity you," said the girl, proudly.

Nat, from whom the aunt had excused herself ere dinner, after wandering on the avenue below the terrace looking at the roses, here approached Charles with a lively salutation.

"Stay," said Charles to the girl, for she was about to leave, and he drifted into the very melancholy possibility of human nature for which he had struck Warriston. In spite of his announcement to her that he would prejudice no one against her, he finally put forth in presence of the young lawyer as well as to her face, the idea which he really entertained of her relations with Rudolph. It was couched in the peculiar satiric form which young men sometimes make use of in their masculine conversation with regard to women they do not respect. The insinuation seemed to fall upon the girl's ears, as she stood there in trembling and fear, like hot lead.

"Oh, what an indignity!" cried she, throwing up her head, and with heaving bosom.

"I say, Charles," said Nat, astounded at this deviation from one usually so courteous, and pained to vehemence by the stricken air of the girl. "Do not forget your respect for yourself, even if you may have none for her."

"Bah! let us change the subject," exclaimed Charles. "It is true. Great God, it is true!" said he, in secret.

The girl had fled from his presence to the house as if overwhelmed with the consciousness of dishonor from one to whom she was longing, and would have died to show her heart to.

On her way to her room, which she was seeking with rapid steps, she was confronted by Gluckinson, who, filled with a consciousness of his wrongs, proposed to convey to her upon the spot, in a brief and fervent manner, his idea of her meanness towards him, as referred to by Baylon.

"I despise you! Obadiah said you as good told the cook that I said that she said—but never mind, I despise you, and have scorn and contempt for you, and shall so continue, although I always thought you were my friend. It's my duty."

"What! James! and you too!" said the girl.

"I can't help it. Baylon told me to do it," said the innocent faun.

"Don't you believe him, James," replied the girl. "He is a bad and wicked man."

"I can't help that. For what you did, you may be considered a mean—"

"James, look at me!" said the girl, as though

taking pains to erase the prejudice from the youth's feeble mind for the sake of his peace rather than hers. "I would not harm you for the world, and I want you to let me be your friend. If we are only kind to one another we will be happy, James."

The innocent-hearted youth had looked into the superiority of her face. He stood still for a moment, and then holding out his hand began to cry. This evidence of his honest friendship seemed to make the girl once more exult in human nature, and she put her arm around his neck and kissed him for the sake of the race perhaps. Her act of nature immediately inspired the youth with terrible feelings of belligerence towards various parties known and unknown, and for the first time in his life, probably, he felt real feelings of valor.

"I want to hit somebody! I'll hit everybody—Durn 'em!—As to that ere Baylon, I'll spatter his nose over his face the next time I catch him! He is a scoundrel, and I'll knock him upon the head with a stick."

"Hush! hush!" said Dinah. "You will be my friend without that, won't you, James?"

CHAPTER XXXIX.

THE DISMISSAL.

The next morning, before noon, his aunt having been driven to town by James, Charles called Dinah into the library, in accordance with his fixed determination to dismiss her and her father from the Place.

It was, indeed, disagreeable for him, for notwithstanding the indifference which the conviction of the girl's unworthy character produced in his bosom, her youthful appearance, and a certain constitutional sadness of her face, the descended result, perhaps, of the suffering of her parents through a long life of shiftlessness, still appealed to his pity. This he speedily repressed, however, for in his present state of mind even pity seemed to be the effect of a kind of idiosyncratic deceit, which belonged to the unfortunate natures of these people. Although he was still unable to fix his mind in the belief that the girl would betray the honor of her sex, for some unknown power of feeling seemed always to rudely repel the thought as it sought passage through the chamber of his judgment, he had, nevertheless, been fully convinced of her deliberate attempt to betray the interests of those to whom she should have been grateful, to some outcast of society who thus evidently had a strong hold upon her; and this was enough to justify his indignant refusal to his own inclination, which asked the retention of the girl under the roof of those with whom such baseness should not come in contact.

The girl's father, through all the past difficulties into which he had been plunged with his child, preserved a stupid kind of silence; although, in spite of the oblivion of second childhood, now fast gathering over his spirit, he would have been able to have communicated the secret connected with the late actions of his daughter if he had known it, or was not under the careful surveillance of her obstinacy. She certainly had not been able to conceal from him up to this moment the bitter results of her accusatory silence; but in reference to their coming departure from the Place, she now went so far in her desire to conceal its character from him, as to beg from Charles a command that he be kept in ignorance of it, and alluded with some appearance of sorrow, whether natural or artful, to her desire to keep his old age from grief. Charles respected her filial love, even if it were but appearance. He saw that the old man seemed to have had enough of trouble in his stronger years to produce purification, and he readily granted her desire.

She had evidently prepared the mind of the old man for the change, as he waited with a cheerful air outside of the house, while she stepped in to see her master, and receive from his hand her final quittance. The dog, which she some time before had picked up on the road in the critical sickness of distemper, and built up into a sprightly friend, drew the exhilarating conclusion from the little bundles which she and her father brought with them from their rooms, that an excursion of unusual prolongation was on foot; and no doubt visions of canine dissipation in the way of pleasant scampers through the woods or along the highways, and of rencounters with foreign dogs whom he could venture to growl at, being under protection, floated across his limited mind. The old man by a short command repressed the ardor of the animal's agility, and then seated himself upon the iron settee and awaited the coming of his daughter from the house.

The girl bore about her, as she entered the room for the last time, a certain air of submission and resignation, as if to what even a frank confession could not, perhaps, have helped; and if there was the pride of stubborn desperation in her manner, it was visible only in the exaltation of her natural grace into dignity. Charles was reflecting upon the unfailing correctness with which society places its seal upon the character, when she entered; but her appearance warped so far the decisions which he had been brought to by his natural antipathy to depravity, that the first glance he cast at her conveyed once more the unconsciously expressed hope for her own sake that she might now voluntarily make a frank avowal of her evil inclinations.

But the indefinite intentions which floated in his mind of causing her to be placed in the charge of some society of reformation or under other good influences, were now wholly dissipated by her persistent silence. She no doubt divined his thoughts, and may have been rejecting them in secret scorn, and perhaps ridicule. At any rate, whatever emotions she experienced were now concealed under a manner which bore the appearance of carelessness at the result of the interview, and a restless, feverish desire to abbreviate it. However, she made to him a respectful bow, which he barely noticed, as it was at the critical moment of his emotion at the proven want of principle in her youthful nature.. Here had she been—but he would not reiterate then the condemning facts connected with her unfortunate stay in the house and neighborhood. He had seen enough to know that the interest which she had excited in him she no doubt had laughed in her sleeve at, and had intended to make use of as soon as she or her accomplice saw fit. His conviction was now firm that the sooner he discharged her from the household, the better it would be for society and individuals.

As she had friends in those with whom she was leagued, neither she nor her father would suffer from physical wants, wherever they might wander; and furthermore, he intended to blindly give her a sum of money without considering the use she might put it to.

It was not unmitigated anger, perhaps, which now possessed him; but that natural courteousness of demeanor and pleasant smile, which would have indicated in the olden time that he belonged to the right-worshipful order of knights and armigers of the heart, were now gone from him, and the absence of his grand air clearly indicated that he entertained no pleasant feeling towards her, and that his desire for her speedy dismissal from the Place was earnest. Indeed, as he held out some bills towards her, he was induced, by the violence of his irritation, to intimate without hesitation his disgust at her depravation, his own leniency with regard to it in consideration of her youth and sex, and his desire that she should not think of returning thither again.

At this outburst of a mixture of numerous emotions, from which that of pity was certainly absent, the manner of the girl changed. Besides the restless indications of coming gladness at the opportunity of leaving the room, a loftier impatience, a noble weariness of the persecution to which her human destiny subjected her, seemed to be manifested in her countenance. She laughed in a dull way, and as she held out her hand mechanically to take the money from his, she stood for a moment thereafter in the same position, as if lost in temporary confusion. She turned, however, from him, for she saw the interview was over, and almost ran as she left the apartment.

There was not a person of the household to be seen outside; and indeed, for the past few days, the domestics had generally appeared to shun her. Her father and she then took up their bundles, which were small, as they had few habiliments, and their other worldly possessions had been left in care of the negro to whom they were now going. The dog gave a bark, and gambolled around them. Dinah took her father's hand; and thus arranged, the three friends started away, and gradually disappeared amid the trees surrounding the noble old mansion. God looked down in pride upon his three creatures as they pursued their way, and sanctified the pure joy of the old man and the humble follower, and the secret tears of the child.

CHAPTER XL.

UNEXPECTED INCIDENTS.

The young man felt restless. An uneasy feeling not only pervaded his bosom, but it seemed to have an influence over his intellect. The old feeling of satiety or of distrust which he had so often experienced, now came back to him in fuller force than ever, because the agent by which it had been temporarily dislodged from his being was now a proved piece of hypocrisy. How that one so young, one so bright, should be such, he laid to the faulty arrangement of society, for he scouted the idea that she could be so by nature, whenever he recollected her face or manner. The events connected with this girl which his memory dwelt upon, seemed to him to have taken possession of that faculty as chief matters of consideration; and, indeed, with her youthful countenance and figure his imagination made easy pictures of the virtuous possibilities of human nature, and singular enough to him was the utter refusal of the latter faculty to harmonize with the former, and attach to his consideration of this girl any vice, or even any characteristic which was not in its nature honorable and virtuous. But memory carries the day when such an extraordinary conflict takes place between the two faculties of the mind, although she is in fault, and has treasured up weak facts and slighted strong pointers to the truth.

Impelled by the desire to seek an oracle, Charles sought again the depths of the woods, and wandering on in abstraction, for the breezes were stirring enough to render his physical exertions unheeded by him, he soon reached, by ascending paths through rising groves, the platform rock overhanging a deep gorge in the mountains looking down even upon the tops of some of the pines growing on the ragged sides, where it was said the devotional Indian, in times gone by, was wont to stand at the hour of the setting sun in communion with his Maker. Away beneath this dizzy height a brook brawled loudly, but the clamor became a murmur ere it ascended thus high. The crumbs of some pleasure party from the neighborhood who had lately sought this place, or maybe of some hunter resting from his venation to share his lunch with his dog, still were strewed about, and on the trees were cut in rude or fanciful letters, rude or fanciful verses, commemorative of the visit of some individual, the fact of whose presence had, in his own idea, conferred additional interest on the locality. The footpath by which Charles had ascended proceeded on the other side, and gradually wound down the precipice with now and then abrupt turns or breaks, to where a rustic bridge crossed the river. A part of this rude structure might be seen with danger from the rock through the branches and foliage, and now and then the black flood with its white foaming borders as it sped along. But above, the loftiest growth of trees almost shut out the heavens, and thus in this twilight of the embowered noon-day Charles reclined himself at length, and holding his head upon a bent arm pursued a train of reflections. He had not been in this philosophical position but a short period of time, when he was aroused by the noise of some one approaching along the dark avenue of the wooded table by which he came. The young man Rudolph appeared, brushing with irregular steps and heated frame, and broke into the open space whose floor was the rock.

"Thank God! I have met you! You laid your hands upon me," cried he, quickly, "and dishonored the rightful demands which I repeatedly made upon you to give me satisfaction." The latter word appeared to trip slightly on his tongue as "Sa'sfaction," and Charles immediately concluded that his applications to his flask had been in an inverse ratio to the successes of the hunting tour, which the gun in his possession indicated he had been engaged in.

As soon as the deception of the young girl had been made apparent to him, he had felt, in reflecting upon his relations with this antipathetic young man and those of the girl with him, that he himself had been in a measure wrong, and the young man right. In the irritation which the fact of the girl's unworthiness produced in his mind, he remembered that the very meanness which he had intended to punish in this young man, he had committed himself; and while he had been half inclined to pardon himself for it, he had wholly resolved, on Rudolph's return, to change his course towards him, by offering an ample apology. Although his neighbor was scarcely in a condition to appreciate his intentions at this time, he nevertheless was about to utter a deprecation of his own past conduct, in which to a certain degree his disappointment in the girl's character had mixed up in spite of himself a natural want of respect for it, when the apology cleaved to his mouth and broke in two, as if it had been struck by the angry power of some unseen and jealous being ere it was all uttered. In the confusion of thought he felt a comparison between Warriston and the young girl, and the superiority of her character, in spite of its faults, over his. They had both maligned her by throwing an accusing insult in her young face, and he was now about adding to his own meanness an agreeable understanding with this depraved young man in reference to her past career, by a careless satiric prediction with regard to her future. The reaction of feeling was as great towards Warriston as it was towards himself, and while he felt a self-shame, his former disgust for his neighbor returned.

"I've followed you. I saw you come up here, and I'm going to have s'faction," said the latter at this point. Amid the ridiculous indications of his inebriation, there suddenly appeared something of a sullen coolness, of the stupid determination which looks for the reparation of wounded honor by blood rather than apology.

"Pshaw! Go away. I don't desire to have any relations with you at all," said Charles, in careless anger, as he took hold of a limb and rested against it. He saw the other wildly raise his gun. He succeeded in diverting its aim from his own breast by a speedy spring and grasp, when it was discharged. The chief weapon which he had conceived he would have to contend with was the tongue of his antagonist.

"Villain!" gasped the astonished young man, "would you commit murder?" In his surprise and the consciousness of his escape, he stood rooted for a moment with the barrel of the gun retained in his grasp. The would-be assassin for honor jerked the weapon away in the continuation of his fury, and staggered backwards, as Charles easily relinquished it. The continued surprise of the latter, however, was now dissipated, for he sprang forwards towards his antagonist. Yet it was not in anger, but with the instinct which, it is to be hoped, is more deeply implanted in human nature. Warriston had fallen backwards with a shriek upon the edge of the dizzy height; in his effort to recover himself, the gun was thrown violently into the air. It fell against a projecting ledge forty feet below, the stock parted from the barrel and lodged in the thick branches of a tree, and the latter continued its jumping, ringing career to the very bottom of the cliff. But the fortune of the drunken man had not yet deserted its owner. The cliff, at the point where he fell, grew in projection as it descended for some way. At a short distance below, a clump of young firs were growing in brave and hardy vigor from a fissure therein, and outside of these the thick trunk of a majestic tree passed from below and shot into the air above the platform, while projecting its branches irregularly into the cliff's side. He rolled down the rough pyramidal face, and struck against one of the young trees. With the blind quickness of self-preservation—for that instinct was sobered into energy—he grasped a bough and swung himself around with a violent shock against the rocks, which still shelved out in the descent for some way beneath. Finding a small footing to rest his feet, he clung to the rough side like a storm-beaten bird, and in dizzy terror. Had he then, in his drunkenness, relaxed his grasp, no impediment, successfully powerful, would have been offered to a crushed and mangled body speeding and bounding until it reached the rocks of the brook-side below. His arms were bent to bring the centre of his body's gravity over the rock, and with muscles trembling with their rigidity, and appalled face pressed against the cliff, he uttered a cry of agonized desire for help.

"Put your teeth through your lip ere you let go!" cried Charles. With a momentary survey—for moments were precious—he swung himself from the platform by a vigorous branch of the old tree. It bent down towards the trunk and came in rustling contact with others, but his reliance in its green hardihood was well-placed. It bravely bore his weight, and his feet found a resting-place upon a stronger and almost immovable bough, which he had observed from above projected towards the temporary eyrie of his neighbor. Along this he moved not with a squirrel's carelessness, and guarding his equilibrium by a manual reliance on the branches above. It was a ticklish affair, but he could not pause. Suffice it to say he saved him with a swaying risk. "Rockaby baby upon the tree top!" With the strong grasp of health, he drew him into his leafy fort by the collar, and with an irritated laugh asked him if he should not drop him.

"The next time you wish to commit murder, try it on the highway, and not in such an unsuitable place as this;—in some spot where you can roll on the ground in your rage, if you do not succeed, without danger to yourself."

"You have saved my life," said the other, with a refreshing air of interested gossipry.

"Pshaw! if you had rolled over again, it would have been to fall against that limb down there, only about a foot or two lower. It is in case you had not concluded to stop there, I should have been tried for murder, perhaps."

At this remark, Rudolph turned his confused and bewildered vision down beneath the branch upon which they were standing, and quickly grasped more firmly the bough which he held. Away beneath, the trunk of the tree in branchless solitude shot up for a space of fifty feet, and with a diameter of corresponding dimension.

"Happy, happy pair!" said Charles. "I don't know how to get out of this myself;" and he looked around again to comprehend the ludicrous position in which they were placed, up an apparently inaccessible tree, engaged in soft converse.

"Ah! I see. There's a wide ledge and more branches, and we can get out upon that path. Why, the very cows are accustomed to go up and down this place!"

They did finally reach the ledge and path, though not without much difficulty and many shortcomings of courage on the part of the rescued individual, whose nerves were quite unstrung by his late adventure. By the time they had reached the bridge, scarcely a trace of his drunkenness was left, save perhaps an inflamed vision, and he there attempted in confused, ill-muttered exculpation to state to Charles that his intention was to force him to make an apology or grant a place of meeting; that his anger being aroused by his sneering manner, he knew not what he did, and he loved the girl, and—she drove him wild.

"Bah! take your girl! What means your folly in mixing me up with her! You are going one way and I will go another—I wish to be left alone. You owe me nothing, and need never allude to this occasion in any way, for you may rest assured I will not."

The unfortunate-tempered young man now knew enough to leave, but before he went he turned around and surprised Charles by acknowledging to him frankly, yet in a hurried way, his consciousness of the wrong he had done the girl, which at the picnic had provoked the insult.

CHAPTER XLI.

THE NEGRO COTTAGE.

At a considerable distance away from Pompney Place, and at the entrance of some still, dark woods where the trees commenced wholly to overhang the winding road, stood an old house which had never been painted and which was black enough to appear criminal; yet, from the air of neatness about, it seemed after all but the useful monument of somebody's honest poverty. Here lived the negroes, who being of no consequence to anybody, and in a measure proscribed on account of their color from familiar intercourse with the villagers, had perhaps received the friendship of the girl Dinah and her father with even a dash of homage. Aged oaks and firs grew around this melancholy abode, and oft in the stillness of the night the cries of the owl might be heard in them or the neighboring woods, dully celebrating his horrid sacrifices, or lamenting the hour when he told of Proserpine's eating the pomegranates in the gardens of hell.

At sunset, underneath a spreading tree on a little piece of greensward growing between the road and the front of the house, the young girl stood in a still attitude, with her sedate face turned towards the departing god of day. Her clear, undazzled gaze was bent full into his yet brilliant splendors, and the purple was in her hair like that of Nisus of old. There was a natural occultness and silent reserve in this young girl, and though that which nature had given her to rely upon may never have been told to herself, the expression of her countenance now gave tokens of the inspiration within.

Apart, on a small bench at the foot of the spreading tree, sat her aged father. His head was bowed in pious resignation to the troubles which the filial love of his child could no longer conceal from him. The mother of the negro family sat knitting on her flag-seated chair at the door, and awaiting the arrival of her son and daughter from their lowly service in the village. The cricket under the door-stone and the katy-did in the tree, were singing their unmeasured songs, and the dog stretched at length was watching with pouncing intentions the periodical jumps upon the grass of the ball of yarn, caused by the old lady's vigorous prosecution of her work.

The sublimity of the sun had quite disappeared from the heavens leaving its beauty, when the girl turned from her motionless, abstract position, and sought with dreamy steps the side of her parent upon the bench. There, in the silent sympathy of a common cause, the two no doubt thought of their loneliness in the world and estrangement from their race, and the stern necessities of the sterling poverty which had been awarded them. With a brighter and more hopeful air, the child soon came to dream of the pleasures of the imagination which had to fill the place of real ones in her young heart, for with a brave sigh of encouragement to herself, she began to utter the pleasant humor of her fancy and cheer her father with its idle conceits. Thus she crossed the desultory, shambling, saltatory waves of the restless sea; and then she thought of the East and the old countries, with their holiday divertisements of rigadoons, sarabands, and boleros, and the light thrum of the tambourine marking the time for the dancers. The father felt the return for the education which he had struggled through all his shiftlessness and degradation to give his child, and while she continued to throw the sunbeams of her fancy upon his spirit, secretly lifted his heart in praise to God for this gift to his declining days.

Soon they raised their united voices in vespers, and as the final noise of the sacred psaltery died away upon the air, the shades of night had gathered around the humble dwelling, and the father and child walked away from the cool breeze into the house. There they planned together their future, and studied to husband their scanty store.

CHAPTER XLII.

HEYDAY IN THE BLOOD.

Charles and Laura were seated together in the parlor of Pompney. They had been following each other about the house all the morning in a most singular way, and such was the remarkable infatuation with which they continued to stick together, and the unusual and eccentric energy with which they had endeavored to convey to each other their sentiments of affection, that it was quite evident they had both been lately stricken with a motive power quite new to their bosoms, and by some extraordinary coincidence of a similar nature in each. A certain ferocious and paradoxical consciousness of the magnitude of the labor in which they were engaged, and a subtle determination to triumph, quite unnatural to the simple ardor of reciprocated love, had suddenly appeared in the manner of each, while such was the devotedness of both to their own hallucinations that neither had observed these indications in the other. There was thus the wild glare of a temporary frenzy visible in the eyes of both, indicating an insane desire to occupy every moment until consummation in conveying exaggerated sentiments of the most inflammable nature to each other; while from the same cause, without doubt, most of the remarks which had been made, had been followed either by confused explanations to that effect, or by frequent attempts on the part of the utterer to withdraw for a short period from the other's presence, to meditate upon the exact effect which they had produced, and to prepare others of a similar nature.

But the most remarkable part of the matter was, that this fever suddenly passed off, leaving as a sole result the singular and apparently unrelated conclusion on the part of the young lady that the advocate, Nat Bonney, was a fool, and upon the part of Charles, in a secret circumlocution, that his aunt was another.

During the progress of the soft delirium, and at a moment when Charles was about to take the hand of the unresisting girl seated by his side upon a sofa, a scuffling noise of feet was heard on the marble floor of the hall outside, and the singularly inopportune Gluckinson rushed violently into the room, and passing the astonished pair under the influence of a resistless momentum, described part of an ellipsis around the centre-table, and brought up directly opposite them with a confused countenance and other symptoms of panic.

"What do you want here, sir?" asked Charles, naturally irritated at this unromantic interruption.

"Nothin', sir; I couldn't help it. He came over here, and—and he chased me in here," cried the youth, in an afflicted manner.

"Leave the room!"

"I'm afraid. He'll lick me," continued he, moving slightly in an undecided way. "Won't you please tell him to go away? He told lies about Miss Dinah."

"What?" asked the young master. A cloud passed over his brow. "There is no one there.

How dare you come in here without being called! Leave the room, sir!"

It is natural to suppose that it would only be under extraordinary provocation that the overseer, Obadiah, should have taken up a propensity of the cook.

He had called in at the kitchen a short time previously, for the purpose of leaving a note from the ardent Sucker to that female, and had replied to the affable inquiry with regard to his own health, that he was laboring under such a cold that he was almost unable to hear, and appealed frequently to a yellow pocket handkerchief to testify thereto. The youth Gluckinson, present in the kitchen, upon hearing this statement glided immediately from the apartment to a secret place on the path sufficiently distant from the cook.

"Now's the time! I'll blackguard him now. He says he's got such a cold he can't hear!"

He awaited the egress of the object of his new antipathy. Soon the overseer came by in the path.

"Scoundrel!" cried the inflamed youth, jumping out and commencing to follow him. "Villain! Snottish bummer! Miserable burgher!"

The overseer still kept his course, eyeing the youth. He was content with being very much astonished. Suddenly a perceptible increase was noticeable in the malignance of the young retainer.

"Davis!" bawled he in the overseer's ear. "Jeff!"

It was too much for human nature, even as low as Baylon's was, to endure. He turned for speedy vengeance, and chased the unfortunate youth even into the bosom of his family.

"Leave the room, sir!" said Charles.

CHAPTER XLIII.

THE POWER OF SYMPATHY.

There was something now in Charles's mind since his interest in the girl Dinah had become a memory as it were, which told him that a wrong had been done even to his feelings of charity in dismissing her in disgrace from the household, and still more deeply, a thought began to press forcibly upon him that he had thus broken an influence which nature had qualified him to be the agent of, in the rescue of her youthful nature from the degradation, to which all other of her associations, past, and present, were hurrying her. He remembered that between his intellect and hers there was that rare sympathy which is best illustrated by the simple statement, that they hardly had to talk to each other in holding their bright conversations; and still beyond this he felt a tie, which he scarcely knew the nature of himself, but which manifested itself in a longing to experience the triumphant pride of having saved her from misery.

He had visited the watering-place and returned with his mother, whose happy feelings may be imagined on receiving, on her arrival at home, information of the more determined attachment which her son had lately begun to manifest for Miss Wellwood.

It was a warm, pleasant day in which the young man had paid a long visit to his friend Dr. Fuffles, whose society he had now commenced to frequent more than ever. Among other topics, he had mentioned in the light of a question of social duty rather than a personal want, those ideas which had lately struck him in reference to the outcasts, as he had to term them, the girl and her father; and although the Doctor could not answer his questions in full satisfaction, as perhaps a part of their animus was concealed from the young man himself, he still offered to him the agreeable suggestion that he should again interest himself in the condition of the people, with a due regard, however, for the just, unwritten commandments of society, which demand that the first step in the purgation of the criminal shall be an heartfelt acknowledgment of the justice of his dishonor; and this intellectual condition the Doctor affixed to his advice, from a knowledge of a heart's weakness, which would shield suffering humanity, more especially old age or tender youth, even from the consequence of its own deliberate misdeeds. Charles then alluded to the course which his mother had advised with regard to these people, as being founded in a proper mixture of this wise sense of social justice, and this pity of humanity. The Doctor blushed, of course, as he always did, when the mother's name was mentioned, but in addition to this usual indication of emotion, a shade of uneasiness also passed over his face. The subject soon passed from their minds, however, and the conversation turning upon other subjects more interesting to the two, Charles finally rose and pursued his way homeward.

"Laura," soliloquized he, as he trudged along, "Laura seems to feel thus; and this fellow Warriston's confession of the wrong he did Dinah, was it sincere or a subterfuge? She permits him to see her as usual! But even if it be so, how—how unworthy she is of sympathy, and yet there is something which makes me think my nature is right! Let me see, it is now a month since I caught a passing sight of her in the village. No doubt she has avoided my presence. I think I did wrong, though not in turning her away from the house. No, certainly not. Even if she be honorable, she is smart and cunning enough to obtain money from him with all her innocent looks. I am glad of it. It is a just requital. But she is degraded enough without that, Heaven knows!"

He raised his head, and observed under the noble trees in front of the church, which was situated at some distance from the parsonage, a female standing with a basket beside her, as if to rest from the heat, and labor of carrying it. It was the object of his thoughts, Diana.

"Gracious! it is she. I am glad. She has brought that basket all the way from town, and is going home. It is pretty light, I imagine. Why should I desire to shun her coming? I hardly dare approach her," said he, confused with some new feelings which this unexpected meeting curiously developed within him.

He continued his pace mechanically, almost forcedly, for he saw that she had noticed his approach. She had taken up her basket and turned her footsteps in the way in which she had come, with the evident purpose of avoiding him. "She's going that way," ejaculated he, excitedly. "I'll follow her."

The girl suddenly directed her course obliquely to the railing of the churchyard and looked in for a moment, and then came back with regular and firm steps towards her late master.

"No, she isn't," continued he, more excited than ever. "I'll pretend to be lost in thought, and not see her. I cannot speak to her. I dare not. What is this extraordinary power which she has over my will? I'm afraid of her."

The two kept approaching each other, and soon from proximity she caught his eye. She blushed, but her step was haughty, her form was erected in a proud manner, and her clear, full gaze was bent undisturbedly upon him. Once more the lines of her grave young face made their indelible impression for his memory, as she pushed aside with one hand the brim of her hat, and bowed to him with that charming grace which her changing years could not rob from her form and motions. This common courtesy he succeeded in returning with confusion, but his tongue cleaved to his mouth and refused to utter a word as she passed quietly by. He hurriedly kept his pace without thinking to turn around until he reached the commencement of the churchyard. There leaning against the iron pillar at the end of the fence, he turned and saw her with bent head still pursuing her solitary way at some distance.

"The beautiful creature!" exclaimed he, as soon as he had recovered from his confusion. "She cares not to regard me, or perhaps she—she knows she must not. She is more sensible than I." He walked into the churchyard with errant steps, as she turned in a bend of the road, and soon he pushed his way homeward filled with sweet feelings, yet in restless agitation, for they semed to renew the reproachful warfare with greater vigor against what was the sense of his duty.

CHAPTER XLIV.

A BENEVOLENT VISIT.

"This is some of my daughter's fine business she takes it into her head to worry her old father's life out with. I don't know where they live, and I don't care," said Squire Wellwood, sulkily, while walking slowly down a cross-road towards the still neighborhood of the lake, having left Sam with Timothy to await him on the highway. "What the devil does she want me to go alone for? Perhaps to relieve me of the trouble of the charity, by giving them an opportunity of knocking me down and robbing me, before I have time to make the proposition. The idea of attempting to aid people who have already been tried and found disgusting, and on foot too, before dinner! It is a climax to the idea of taking a criminal into the bosom of one's family, because he is too old to do any thing, and consequently may be considered safe. The most extraordinary benevolence I ever heard of! I'd like to be intriguing somewhere. Now I've consummated this affair of Charles and Lolly, I want another intrigue. As Nat said, if I can succeed in making one match a month, I shall probably exercise more power than any other man living, and it excites me. He said, in the way of mischief, but his theory was wrong. Goodness! I never thought of it before. (His daughter had alluded in a conversation with him respecting Dinah, to her relations with Rudolph, and he was struck with a new idea.) I'll do it!"

Discovering with some difficulty the house of the

negroes to which his mission sent him, the Squire knocked at the door with his stick. Upon inquiry of the old colored lady for the girl and her father, he was apprised that the former was absent, but that the latter sat in the back room, and was awaiting her arrival from town, to which she had gone with some ironing executed for a villager. The old man, whose chief pleasure now consisted in seeking the consolations which the Scriptures promise to the aged and the young—the honest and the criminal—raised his eyes from his Bible as the Squire entered. He had been thinking of the troubles of his life, and his memory resting last upon the examination of his daughter for the robbery, he was fearful and timid of the world. He shrank back then in his chair, as Laura's father quietly approached to accost him.

"I've come to attend to you," said the latter, commencing at once the divulgement of his praiseworthy intentions.

"Yes! Yes! I know it. I have expected it!" muttered the old man, as his head sank upon his breast. ("It is I they want now.) Thank God, it is I who now suffer the infliction, and not my darling!"

"Hey?" said the Squire.

"Do your duty, sir!" continued the old man, with an air of sternness, in his despair.

"D—n it! I am going to. That's what I came for," said the testy Squire.

"How is it, when we would no longer intrude our presence upon others, we should still be persecuted and hunted in our poor solitude?"

("This is singular. He seems to be enraged at the idea of assistance being offered to him.")

"I will offer no resistance, though it is a bitter thing in my old age. You need not put on the handcuffs, for I am an old man, and will submit in resignation to my fate."

("There is something eccentric about the old gentleman. He gives me the absurd idea, that if he was a younger man he would not submit to be made an object of charity, until he was knocked down and pinioned. He certainly don't remind me of any man I ever knew before!) I want to see your daughter. If she is coming pretty soon, I will wait for her."

"Oh, don't! she might not bear your presence. We are unfortunate, but we are innocent, sir. Let me break it to her when you are not here. Go away for to-day. I will not attempt to escape. You can lock me in the chamber above. It's strong and secure!"

"Ha! ha! (Oh pshaw! I knew this mission was absurd. His sense of honor is high, but eccentric. He prefers to steal rather than receive money as a present!")

"You may laugh, sir, at the poor request of an old man. Yes, a long life of continued contact with confirmed criminals, has rendered you callous and suspicious of all."

"Eh? What!—"

"Take me to your house. But if an entry has not already been made for me, I will not go. You have no right to take me anywhere!"

("He wants me to take him to my house, and he won't enter it, unless I have a special entry made for him to go in by!) Ha! ha! ha! Oh, pshaw!"

"Heavens! The ghastly laugh of heartless malignity. While his form is pampered even to obesity, with the sighs of the wretched, the villain by experience if not by nature, is stamped upon his brow."

"D—n it! I say, you are an old gentleman, but I can't stand that, you know. Ha! ha!—oh, the devil!"

"Wretched man. Would you add profanity to the other miserable demonstrations of your character?"

"Oh! I am not going to stand that, and I won't!" said the excited Squire, dancing towards a window in a great rage, and commencing to throw books about.

He had been slapping the doors with his cane for some time, when the young girl Dinah entered, and soon restored both him and her old father, who had been witnessing these performances with the attentive gaze of fear, if not of admiration,—to equanimity and a pleased state of mind, by reconciling their misunderstanding. Her sober yet pleased looks, and the appreciative interest which she manifested in his conversation, soon led the worthy parent of Laura to specify the proposition of charity which he had to make, after several appropriate allusions to men "he once knew," and the girl thanked him and his daughter, whose name seemed blessed by her internally as she spoke it. She said, with a look of cheerful confidence, that they were not in want, and she would refuse then to take the money; the worthy Squire, after wrestling with his regret at this for a short moment, threw himself with all his mental vigor into the intrigue he had been contemplating, by conveying to her the startling information on the spot, that she was to be married on the following Wednesday to his neighbor Warriston, he himself seeing that the young man should be properly intoxicated if he manifested refractory symptoms, and proceeded to congratulate her upon the fine establishment she would come in possession of.

"I know you do not love him, and there is considerable difference in your ages, but—"

The young girl saw his earnest drift amidst his eccentricity, and said quietly, "Oh, sir, such a proposition is not worthy the violation you are doing your own honor to unfold it!"

"Eh?" said the ardent Squire. "This is a new place. It is just in such complicated places as this, I expected the difficulties would arise. Perhaps I was a little too fast." His eyes gleamed after a moment, and he issued a very eccentric command to the girl. "Kiss me!" said he. Although she did not immediately comply with his request, probably on account of its suddenness, he became more interested in her than ever, and proceeded in consequence to divulge to her at once, all those matters which had been of a pleasant nature to himself for the last two months, with the praiseworthy intention of producing the same effect upon her spirits. Only one matter to which he alluded seemed to agitate the girl in any other way than that of courteous attention. As the worthy Squire alluded in triumph to the coming marriage of his daughter with Charles, the girl bowed her head quickly, and concealed her countenance for a moment. She then proceeded to listen to the parent, who having alluded in a chuckling manner to the fact that there had been no rivals about, was peremptorily reminded of some eccentric member of the human family, who, impelled by motives of jealousy at the marriage of his love to his rival, stole secretly into a barn at some distance from the house in which the nuptials were proceeding, and hanging the house cat out of the loft window by the hind legs, so that she would barely touch the ground, malignantly awaited the consequences. In about fifteen minutes, being attracted by the cries of one of their kind, the number of cats who had gathered about the suspended animal from different parts of the neighborhood exceeded three hundred of various sorts and sizes, and their yells, as they fought in mistaken fury, and the impossibility of quelling the riot, succeeded for a length of time, which must have been exceedingly gratifying to the malignant rival, in confusing and breaking up the party within.

The fur flew fast and thick, and only eleven cats came from the scene of conflict. The rest were left dead on the field of battle. As Dinah laughed heartily at this funny anecdote, the old gentleman was more attracted to her than ever, and, saying that he would call again, left for the exasperated Sam and Timothy.

CHAPTER XLV.

A BRIEF VISIT TO THE NEGRO COTTAGE.

An irresistible longing to see this young girl now took undisputed possession of Charles. He had reflected that she looked poverty-stricken when he saw her. She wore the same muslin dress which he remembered she had two months before when an inmate of the household, and though it was neat and smoothly ironed, he could see it was old and faded. While thinking of her, it seemed as though she stood before him in the same attitude as at the churchyard, with her face turned towards him. "Yes," said he, as if looking at a picture, "she appears careworn, and underneath that proud look she seems to ask me for my help against poverty and temptation. She says that she is not yet lost, and that I can save her." He wandered away to the road from the park where he had been standing in pensive mood, careless whither he strayed. Insensibly his steps were bent in the direction of her house by the lake as he walked along. "Pshaw! Am I not foolish? Money indeed will be more acceptable to her than a renewal of my lecturing or bestowal of confidence, and let Laura assist her. Are there such singular, unscrupulous natures, possessing the power of winning honest people's sympathy in spite of their judgment? Shall I not assist some low-lived rascal whom she loves, if I answer this impulse? Yes. And they are both now laughing probably over the money they have already received, and angry because they did not succeed in their robbery. There is the lake! Gracious! It is a long distance around to the other side. I may see her. Assuredly there will be no folly in ascertaining if she be really suffering. Humanity at least demands that." As he approached, this renewed bias of severity towards the girl increased, and more than once did he accuse himself of folly and threaten to turn back, but still with unfulfilling effect. Coming within sight of the humble dwelling he noticed its poor, yet neat appearance, and was particularly struck with the dark, melancholy gloom of its position amid the dignity of the tall still trees. A small kitchen-garden was growing by the side of the house, but there was no evidence of untidiness about it. The usual pig was not to be seen at all, and if he was anywhere about was probably in some distant pen in sequestered grandeur. And the fowls did not look like negro's fowls at all, but were a respectable addition to the landscape.

The agitation of the young man had quite left him, and he felt thoroughly self-possessed as he walked towards the house. His memory had brought up again to his judgment facts enough respecting the girl to convert his softness of feeling into something like easy indifference even, and the consciousness of performing a humane duty. The real relation between them—he as a powerful young man of the neighborhood, and she an humble yet unscrupulous outcast, whom he was trying to raise from a voluntary degradation—was now fully restored, and he asked at the door to have her informed of his presence, with that feeling simply. Her face was pale as she approached the door in the entry, and she asked him to come in and be seated, in a low voice, in which he thought there was perceptible a slight tremor, of course highly natural.

"No, I will sit on yonder bench under the tree, while I stop," said he. "I wish to speak to you but for a moment, though I came purposely to do so."

He led the way to the rustic seat and they both sat down there together. The old negro lady, who was the only one else in the house, (as her son had taken the old father and Tip upon a ride to town in his white-washing cart,) could not refrain from looking out of the window for a moment in irrepressible curiosity, but being immediately detected by the young girl, was so overcome with the fear of having offended her, that she trotted frantically into the kitchen and made four pies, to keep from temptation during the remainder of the interview.

"I have come to assist you," said Charles, coldly and sternly. "However guilty you may have been, it is not proper that you or your father should suffer from want, even of which your own folly is the cause."

She told him that she would have economized the money which he had given her, but that it had been devoted, together with that which Col. Norcomb had bestowed upon her, to the payment of a debt due the overseer, Baylon, who had loaned them some money upon their needy arrival in the neighborhood, the amount of which had accumulated considerably with the lapse of time. "And in order to meet the future with courage, I consent to be ashamed now," said she, with a laugh. "But why should I be ashamed at accepting money from you?" continued she, looking around at the poverty of the place in which she dwelt.

He said nothing immediately. ("Of course her lover shared it with her. This is charity with a vengeance. And has she not procured money of Warriston?) Does not Rudolph know your want, and has he not been willing to assist you?" continued he aloud, after a pause.

"Yes," said she, blushing, "but let me be a beggar from you alone! I would rather be under obligations to you than any one else."

("She talks of obligations!) and why to me?"

"Because—because it is better for your nature that you should do good to one that you have done wrong towards," said she, passionately. "Won't you beg my pardon?" continued she, earnestly.

"You are not sly at all in your machinations," said

the young man, sceptically; "you carry the day by bold attacks. Now listen to me, Dinah! Facts are soldiers that will not serve in a bad cause. It has been tried over and over again to get them into the field under evil banners, but they always rebel—yet I will beg your pardon."

"But you may not for what facts teach you," said she, in bitterness. "Yes, it is well to accuse me of falsehood, yet not in reference to Mr. Warriston. I have told you a bitter lie," continued she, astonishing the young man by this confession. "Yes, I have wronged you, and it is not you that have erred against me! But God will forgive me and help me, I know. Give me money enough to go away with, and we will go far away from here forever! It is certainly worth the sum to get rid of us," continued she, earnestly. "You shall never hear of us again. Oh, sir, we should not live here. We have no right to live among honest people."

"Now, Dinah, can you relieve my mind from the anxiety which I must feel as a man and a member of society for a young being who is erring at the outset? What is this mystery which overhangs you; which causes this duplicity of earnest emotion? Why not confide it to me! Though it be a tale of degradation—"

She looked at him sternly. But it was almost in carelessness of his presence that a haughty look passed over her face, as if she were defending herself from her trials by a secret consciousness of her own superiority. She replied not, and the singular characteristics of her conduct, especially the impossibility of the insincerity of such feelings as she had just betrayed, and the firmness with which she resisted him once more in his desire that she should make him her confidant, only served to renew his old interest in her, in spite of her degradation, while it aroused his fancy.

The romances of old came up to his mind in which young earthly beings, pure and unstained, were delivered into the power of evil beings, that they might redeem the latter from restless wandering and misery through the tortures of their own inoffensive natures. He had coldly told her that he would despatch the charity which she had accepted from him, but on rising from the interview he sought an excuse to be his own messenger. As he bade her adieu, he asked her in a natural manner the best spots to fish upon on the borders of the lake. "Upon the other side, I think," said she, pointing towards the opposite shore of the magnificent lake, with a laugh. Her equanimity had been quickly restored, and her old way of satire seemed to have come upon her again. She knew he was seeking an excuse to come again, and for the moment could not refrain from plaguing him.

"Say!" said she, when he was about leaving; "will you please say nothing to father about me? Will you, please?" continued she, slowly, and turning her eyes tenderly into his face.

Whatever her relations were, her passionate earnestness gave tokens that her father knew naught respecting them.

CHAPTER XLVI.

DINAH REVEALS A SECRET TO CHARLES.—AN ACCIDENT.

"LET me see, in about a week from now I will go over there again," ejaculated Charles on his return. "To-morrow I must be with Laura. The dear girl with her warm heart has defended Dinah, although she feels that she is guilty of criminal intentions. This girl is certainly occupying more of my attention than I ought to give to her affairs. Yes, about a week from to-morrow, say!"

On his arrival at his house, meeting his mother, she gently accosted him with an inquiry as to the direction of his walk. "Towards the lake," said he, carelessly.

The mother looked at him steadily, but refrained at the moment from uttering her thoughts. Whatever they were, her son felt that she would certainly disapprove of his changed intentions with regard to the girl, and he concluded not to mention them to her.

When the next morning came, it was a bright day, and a prospect of fine weather for the next three or four days being indicated, he mentally shortened the period which he had fixed for visiting the girl, and resolved that he would go in about three days.

Towards noon, he stole out of the back gate, and sought the woods with a chuckle of self-gratulation, and a slight sense of conscience, as boys who run away from school. He was playing truant from his intention, under the self-deception that a row on the lake would be especially pleasant on that day. He soon reached the side of the lake opposite the house in which Dinah lived, and could see far off the diminutive opening of the road, which wound by it down to the lake-side.

The wind scarcely stirred, and would not perhaps have been perceptible, had it not a gentle purling sweep there across the lake's broad bosom. The young man, after being seated upon a rock for a few moments, resolved to betake himself to an old boat which was anchored by a stone to the shore near by, and was swaying under the influence of the slight swell. It was a red-painted, flat-bottom thing, with fixed oars of pine, rudely contrived by some farmer who left it on the shore for common use of the fishers. Ere he departed upon his proposed pleasure tour around the island above, he turned his eyes to the sky and the landscape, and noticed with pleasure the effect of light and shade on hill and dale, near and afar off. At some distance from him, sitting upon a log which projected from the dark and shaded water upon the shore, was a frog enjoying the pleasures of solitude, and bawling at the top of his raucous voice, his love of the liquid element. A pleasure party of mud-turtles also visited for a moment the shore at the young man's feet, and wheeled to seek other spots for the organization of their aquatic picnic.

Having pushed off from the shore, he arrayed himself for his pleasure cruise; but noticing at the moment, that the wind was unfavorable, he concluded that he would experience sufficient muscular excitement, were he to push the rude gondola across the lake, instead of smiting the waves which rolled around the little island above. The more he tugged, the more the desire of a slight refreshment, such, for instance, as a glass of milk, grew upon him; and on arriving after a vigorous pull for half an hour on the other side, his thirst was so exorbitant, that he immediately started off for the desired refreshment to the nearest habitation, which happened to be the negro house. Thus in innocent unconsciousness, was he brought the next day after his interview with the girl, to her threshold again.

He had been engaged in conversation but a moment, and it was ere she received the pittance of benevolence from his hands, that she folded hers in temporary refusal, and said with rapid accents, but yet with composure, "I possess a secret which is rather your right than mine, and I have determined to impart it to you at once, however much you may blame me for not having done so ere this!" (The young man's heart began to beat.) "In the record of the deed to the property which formerly composed the original estate of Mr. Pompney, and by which it passed out of his hands thirty years ago, a flaw exists, of such a nature that the title to the whole of Pompney Place, and a part also of other farms about, still rests in the heirs of the Pompney family." Charles uttered a natural exclamation of deep astonishment. "An error in the description, by which the boundary of the tract intended to be sold was altered in such a manner as to omit this portion."

"But how is it, that this defect, after escaping the notice of those interested for so long a period, has now been suddenly brought to light?" interrupted he, quickly, with almost a sneer, under the influence of his incredulity.

She suggested as well as she could, in reply to his

suspicion, the careless manner in which records were then probably made, the insignificance of a figure or two, and the musty reliance upon the correctness of the parent document, in the few searches which may have been made.

"But—but Colonel Pompney had no heirs!" continued he, astounded at this singular development from a young sixteen year old, respecting his own affairs. It would have been more appropriate from some lawyer of years of pettifogging. "And besides that, the time of prescription has run and—"

"No! The time is not yet out, and Colonel Pompney has an heir living. I am his granddaughter!" said the girl, quietly.

Charles started. ("By Heaven! she is of the blood of the old pioneer, and he has—) But how—how are you his granddaughter?" stammered he, in his wonder.

The girl quickly answered him. She seemed anxious to hasten to an end. Her grandfather Pompney's daughter, a wild girl in her youth, became enamored of his overseer. She secretly married him, and the two were dismissed in unbruited disgrace from the parent's presence.

"Although this record is not right, sir, the original deed is. That is in your possession, and you should have it recorded again," continued she, quickly, and immediately, though still in a quiet way, "Thank God, I have done my duty!"

A thrill passed over the young man. It was because he recalled, while he thought of the scene before the cabinet, with those deeds torn and scattered upon the floor, the inexplicable voice of his dream.

Had the spirit of the pioneer unsuccessfully possessed his descendant with this human chicanery, to recover back into his line the home of his founding?

The girl then reverted to the history of her father; how he had won her grandfather's confidence by the composition of traditions about his ancestors, and how he assisted to lay out his grounds, and the final winning of the affections of his daughter, and the subsequent rage of the Colonel; their wandering in distant places; the Colonel's losses in money matters, and his final death in the arms of his daughter, after he had parted with his estate. Charles recalled the corroborative reminiscences of Colonel Pompney, often the theme of his aunt.

"But why did not your father promulgate his relationship when he returned to this place?" asked he, on observing that the girl appeared disinclined to proceed with a farther relation of the history of her family.

"Because we were—" she stopped and blushed, and Charles recollected that he had again forgotten their degradation.

"No one cared enough about him. What reason had we to—" continued she, weariedly.

"But such a fact, when known among the villagers, might have assisted you."

"No—no; not one of them knew it then, much less now, and would they have believed it? Oh, no! At any rate, father would not do it. He would not have it mentioned. My—my mother's gravestone has not her family's inscription."

"Is it possible," thought he, "that, in the midst of all their dishonor, they have felt this delicacy? Even his crime may have been brought about by suffering and want, which maddened him."

"But he knows nothing about this. It was only I who—" She stopped and blushed deeply.

Charles suddenly reflected that there had been no positive proof that the girl intended to rob the cabinet of its contents, and that the sole evidence that there had been any other person than she in the library on that occasion, was the recurrence of the singular voice. Impelled by this new development, so favorable to his inclination to trust in her purity and honor, he reached an old conclusion by a new chain of thought, referring to all the events with which he had connected her, whose links were passed in rapid unconsciousness, whose links were singular but infallible; and while he would not disbelieve the evidence of his royal sense, his vision, he was forced to slight the humbler sense of hearing. Yes, he believed that it was an exaggeration of Rudolph's voice he had heard upon the lake, of some sot's in the graveyard, lastly, of Gluckinson's cry; and to believe that this singular repetition might be referable to some subjective disorder, was preferable to believing in supernatural visitations, which seemed his only alternative, when he remembered that the same voice was that of a night-horse—of the unreal creature of a dream. Dinah, on yesterday, had acknowledged that she had been guilty of deception in her statement.

Yes, it appeared clear to him now. Becoming possessed of the secret of the faulty record, she had indulged her curiosity, or perhaps the baser appeals of interest at the expense of honor, which however she had nobly withstood, and noticing the frequency with which the cabinet was unlocked, had attempted to examine at a secret hour, those papers which related to property once in the possession of her ancestor. Taken by surprise, in the moment of confusion she had endeavored to restore them to the drawer with partial success. Fear and shame had induced her to fabricate her tale of the night's occurrence, and the inability of her nature to sustain her in it, had led to the consequences which followed.

Diana noticing his reflective silence, and without doubt, conjecturing the thoughts which were passing in his mind, blushed as if at the ideas which were attached to her, and conjured him at this point to have confidence in her, when she stated that she did not intend to despoil the safe of the important deed or any other of its contents, and in a manner wherein her subtlety, if she had any, was quite concealed by her agitation, asked him if she had not done all she could to make reparation, even had she any such base intentions.

Charles was satisfied by her earnest, honorable manner, that she was truthful. Indeed, there was something which made him long so forcibly to reburnish his sympathy with her, that he felt willing to be duped by her, if she were not. The manner in which she had become possessed of the secret, was now the absorbent of his fanciful marvel. As he was resistlessly about to question her respecting it, she seemed again to divine his thoughts, and such was the increased tremor which shook her frame, that he was dissuaded by an emotion which first bore the romantic form, but afterwards transformed itself into a species of downright shame, at the absurdities of his own imagination, connected with this ridiculous voice. "Without doubt, she learned it of her father in some way, and she honorably, creditably, desires to shield him from the slightest suspicion. Yes, and I will not even suspect her purity, or even cause her to think that I suspect it by asking her!"

He rose to leave her with a species of triumph which is of the highest order, the rejoicing of an honest nature, to find the clouds of suspicion removed from another. In his exultation, he asked her to return with her father once more to the household of his mother.

"No! no! I cannot. I do not desire to," said she, in a low voice. "We can get along well enough here, and indeed we have no claim to be admitted into any one's family." Perhaps the thought of the degradation of her family and name, was moving in her mind all the time; but Charles thought it was singular she should not wish to recommence the course, which was the easiest to remove that stain. He knew that his mother would be slightly opposed to the return of the girl of course, and if the girl acted on that consideration, under all the circumstances she was entitled to the credit of great delicacy, rather than the discredit of excessive pride and obstinacy.

And now as he bade her a cheerful adieu, he did not relax in his design of assisting her, not only in the physical wants, which her youth, the age of her father, and their position created, but also in a moral reëstablishment of the two upon an honest footing in the world. Aye, at least for the honor of old Pompney and his blood.

Four or five hours had been expended by him since he left his residence, and he concluded it to be wise to return in the shortened manner by which he came.

The wind had risen considerably, and as he embarked in the fragile boat, he noticed that the waves of the lake dashed up with force against the shores, while the little vessel itself was thumping with a heavy sound against the rocks. It was past the hour of sunset, and the thickly clouded heavens precluded the possibility of witnessing the lingering spectacle of a golden twilight. However, he commenced to pull upon the oars on his way back. Dinah, bareheaded, had walked down upon the road leading around the lake, to meet her father returning in the cart from town. As Charles watched the receding shore from his position, he noticed her form, now visible in an open space, and now disappearing behind a clump of trees or intervening rocks. Her hair was short and irregular in front like a boy's, but behind it was long and fell thickly upon her neck. This he could distinguish, as the wind played naughtily with it, and he observed that now and then she turned her vision towards him. A drop or two of rain soon fell with a dash on the red paint of the oar-handles, and struck his hand. Birds were flying fitfully and irregularly in the air above him, and the crows, particularly, were squalling in an unusually ill-boding manner.

He now thought that Dinah was right, when she told him to stick to the land and an umbrella if he didn't want to get wet through. A September storm was commencing with the shades of the evening, and the harbinger drops were commencing to be followed by a driven rain sweeping on the bosom of the lake before a rising blast. He saw the girl running back quickly in the direction of the house, under the shelter of the trees, and soon he observed her on the banks of the lake at the point which he left, crouching against the pelting rain, and waving her handkerchief as if by way of command to return. He acknowledged in pantomime her act, and let on a flood of vigor. Just then, a sudden blast carried his hat high into the air, and resting for a moment on one oar to point humorously at its abandoned flight, he proceeded again with a vigorous dash. The girl now seemed irritated. He could see that she stamped her foot, and no doubt she was ejaculating that trite but expressive phrase, "What a fool!" But he was under the impression that he could reach the other shore before it became quite dark, and after that, he might borrow an umbrella at some of the farm-houses, and trudge homeward on foot, inspirited by the incident. The boat was a rickety little concern, and he was under the exasperating necessity of arresting his progress now and then, to use the rusty tin dipper kept therein for bailing emergencies, and at each of these periods, he drifted around helter-skelter, bouncing up and down on the dancing waves.

He was throwing a tin full of the water in irritation high into the air, when he noticed the girl putting her hands to her mouth after the manner of youthful individuals, making an impromptu speaking trumpet. The round full tones borne on the blast, fell in a moment on his ear like the cry from a boy's lips. She had lowered her voice, and drawled out each word to a great length to make him hear; but he observed with peculiar emotions above the clearness of the tone, and the confusion and indistinctness of the articulation, that his eccentric imagination, without doubt excited by the late divulgement, had clothed the peculiarity of her effort with a startling resemblance to the dream-set voice of her ancestor, the old pioneer, and, indeed, proved its own disorder.

The night and the mist had closed down upon the lake, and the land was fading in the distant driving rain. His position might be rendered slightly uncomfortable if he did not point his course to some point of the lake which he could speedily reach, for it was the season of shortening days, and the storm had brought on darkness before he had anticipated. Under the veering inspiration of this reflection, he gave such an energetic pull that he heard a slight snap in one of his oars. After that and two or three pulls, it tranquilly parted, and there was he upon the bosom of a storm-shrouded lake, in a leaky half-appointed craft, laid up perhaps for the night. His rude efforts at sculling were aimless, melancholy, and slow; and a calculation of the respective distances from his position of different parts of the shore, which he could still dimly distinguish, brought the philosophical conclusion that each of them was a little more remote than the others.

"I can't tell where I am. If I had a match, I would smoke," said he. "But as it is, I don't see that I shall have any other means of passing the coming night, than such alternate amusement as bailing and reflection may afford. I could try my lord Byron's feat, but it would be an ignominious ending to bring up in the mud-flats, instead of the pebbly shore. I have been a fool several times in my life. This is an addition to the number of infatuated epochs."

The distant, dim blackness of the mountains was now shut out by the clouds, which seemed to have been precipitated upon the lake—mist, fog, and rain altogether. For about a quarter of an hour, he had been hoping that the evening light of one or two farm-houses might soon throw their faint beams through the fog and darkness, to guide his irregular way, when he was rejoiced to observe in one direction, a small light, as if his hopes had been speedily answered, and as it grew upon the darkness, and usurped with its general effulgence, without a seeming nucleus, a portion of the horizon, he saw that it was no light from a household. The girl had manifested her sense by lighting a beacon-fire upon the shore. It was all the young man wanted. He divested himself at once of his boots, his coat, and his cravat, and leaving them with sentiments of cheerfulness in the unmanageable boat, plunged into the waves and struck out boldly in the direction of the illumination. He could vie at swimming with the latest invented fish of the imagination, possessing three banks of fins, (thirty-eight on a side,) and felt that his distance from the light could not be over a mile.

But the maiden replenished the sacred fire for the swimming god several times ere he struck the shore, and when he did so, he made a mechanical attempt to bow himself on his knees, to thank One superior to all, and he fell senseless upon the pebbles.

What occurred within the next three or four minutes, he knew not; but there was a little Herculean maiden, who dragged him in her energy like a dead ox, to the fire—who chafed his limbs, wiped the resulting blood of his folly from his nostrils, and placing her warm lips against his, breathed into his mouth. He turned wearily as he revived, and saw bent over him a noble face, expressive of a natural soul, and the full large eyes which had been looking wistfully into his own, were filled with a brighter light.

"You don't know what I was thinking of, when I had to pull the water about my ears in that absurd manner out there," said he, smiling feebly after some time of silence.

He had thought, as his consciousness spent before his energies, that in vain had the young maiden tried to save him from the evil, jealous powers of an enchantment with which he was interfering.

"It is an easy, slipping-down kind of action when one commences to drown, isn't it?" said the girl.

The fire burnt up brightly in spite of the industrious rain. His head was sustained against her bosom, and they were both as wet as two drowned butterflies.

"I made eleven distinct and consecutive efforts," continued he, "eleven of them! Why should such a useless dog as I am be spared," continued he, turning his eyes feebly up to hers in his weakness.

"I don't know, unless you were born to be hung, I suppose."

"There is such plain common sense about you, I like you," said the weak young man. "That is what I call sensible talk."

Though she now appeared as composed and gentle as ever, Charles noticed that she bent over carefully to shelter his face from the drops and spray-driving drizzle of the rain. His shirt had been spread open, displaying a manly chest, and she pulled it together.

The old father and the negro had returned, and directed by the partial intelligence of the old lady, and by the light of the fire, the colored man soon reached the two thus seated upon the shore.

The young man rose after a while, and leaning upon the stout negro, both of them pretty decent Apollos, a black one and a white one, walked slowly amid the rain over the dank grass, or through the little running torrents on the road, treading on the soaked chips and fallen twigs from the trees, Dinah leading the way in front with a fire-brand. It illuminated for a while her solemn face, which appeared unusually serious, despite the pretty lines of roundness which her wet hair brought over her shoulders produced.

CHAPTER XLVII.

DINAH CONFESSES HER LOVE.

Charles thought it rational to remain at the negro cottage that night, and retiring to a neat bed with clean linen, slept soundly until the morrow. His constitution was a strong one, and the physical results of his adventure, if any lingered, were soon made a matter of private attention solely.

In the morning he bade a temporary farewell to the humble but hospitable abode, and repaired leisurely to his own dwelling. Here he recounted to his mother and aunt the singular mishap which had occurred to him, not without obeying, however, an inclination which he had, to conceal certain parts thereof as unnecessary to the narrative. He then discovered to them the extraordinary developments which had been made by the girl of her relationship with the Pompney family, and of the flaw in the record. They were both overcome with astonishment thereat, and the aunt, after many confirmatory memories of Pompney, joined with Charles in approval of the girl's final conduct, and urged the immediate recording of the old deed, which had been produced for inspection. But it was far otherwise with the mother. She coldly intimated that she saw no other feature in this divulgement, even were it reliable, than an additional evidence of the wiliness of the girl, who had evidently reasoned that this was the most she could do, as she had failed in abstracting it, and had no further opportunity of doing so. Although he rejected it, this theory struck coldness to Charles's heart, for it seemed to discover a certain fixed antipathy in his mother's bosom towards the girl.

Charles soon drove to Miss Wellwood's residence, and narrated to her his latest experience with Dinah. His affection for Laura mounted the higher as she gave token of her sympathy with him in thought and feeling upon this subject. She approved his plans of assisting the girl in her evident efforts towards self-rescue from the miseries of poverty and dishonor.

"Why not have her put in as mistress of the north district school; the present mistress is going away in two weeks, and the selectmen are soon to have a meeting, to appoint another! But that, perhaps, would be wrong. The neighbors would certainly make an outcry against the girl because she is the daughter of a criminal."

"Let them," said Charles, with symptoms of gall; "I don't believe in this hunting of the innocent for the crimes of others! I will do it."

"But then if she should happen to be —" said Laura, hesitatingly.

Charles thought in a moment of the girl's relations with the young man, Rudolph, which had been unexplained by her. "She is pure," thought he, "and she cannot love him, but she still receives his visits."

Whether Laura's doubt was the result of a woman's weakness, (and a man's too, for that matter,) which she could not resist, or whether it was caused by a just sense of the right of the mothers and fathers of young children, it had the effect upon Charles again to reconsider the problem of the girl's character with suspicion of an error in his conclusions, but for a moment only. Was it not evident that Laura had cut off her own suspicions with regard to Dinah, not rooted them out of her bosom, for otherwise would she not in her warmheartedness have even before this, proposed the taking of the young girl into her own household? No; perhaps a deference to the mother's opinions had prevented her.

"At any rate," said Laura, "it is our duty towards this young girl, whether she loves him or not, to distract her attention from this neighbor of ours, for even were he to marry her, her happiness would be as short-lived as his sensual passion." The little parenthetical doubt of the existence of Dinah's love towards Rudolph was a singular matter of satisfaction to Charles, for it temporarily drove away a growing fear.

It pleased him thus to have a common object with Laura, for the exercise of the finer feelings of human nature in his fixed intimacy with her, and he started off to visit the girl again with his mind filled with her suggestions.

The scenery about the old negro house, the natural music of the forest, and the odors of the humble flowers, all seemed to him to belong to the young girl. The old unreservedness and natural trust appeared again to characterize their conversation, and he even began to blame her in a ludicrous manner, as having been the wrong one in the quarrel.

There was an unusual expression of sadness about her mouth; then she finally said, "I shall be grateful to you forever for your kindness to me. I cannot repay it now, and yet I must—I must go away from here."

He felt a chill from her very earnestness, and after a moment he asked in a tone of kind deprecation: "Why do you wish to go away, Dinah?"

"I pray you do not ask me now. It must be my own secret. Yes, no one has a right to demand it of me. I would not displease you, or throw away the kindness which you have bestowed upon me, but—"

"Come, Dinah, tell me."

"I cannot—cannot," said she, with a blush.

"But you must. I do not like to wait," said he, even with a slight air of irritation. "Dinah, you must not destroy the confiding interest which Laura and I have united in bestowing upon you. It is now even a part of our happiness to—"

The girl concealed her agitation with a master effort. "Indeed, indeed, I would love to tell it to her," said she in a passion, "and why should I not to you? Yes, I will reveal my folly. It is a girl's romance, and will you not respect me if I but tell you that there is one to whom nature has given a power over my feelings, which I can hardly define? Oh, sir, I shall always hear the sweet sound of his coming step in memory as long as I live. I shall always see his smile, and even when his voice has been raised in bitterness and irritation towards me, it has startled echoes in my heart which will never die. I love him, I love him!" She paused for a moment, and recklessly gave herself up to an emotion which she cared not to conceal.

"Dinah," said Charles, in a low, trembling voice, "your pure attachment should bless this being and bring happiness to you."

"Oh, sir, but will you respect me if I tell you that its revelation to him would be but to incite him to outrage the laws of society, of honor? Never can it be. The torment of its concealment shall be my happiness."

("Its revelation to him would—what folly is this of mine? She loves him. His locket upon her neck, the stolen meetings, and now at last she confesses her love for the miserable Rudolph!) But, Dinah, would you nurse a passion which would be criminal in its hope?" exclaimed Charles, with the bitterness of an honest heart.

"Criminal! yes, it is criminal," continued she, overpowered with self-reproach.

("Thank God! she sees his miserable sensuality; and though she loves him, would shield her honor with the robe of Nessus, with the wretchedness of despair.")

"Let me say no more," said the girl, standing erect as if recovering herself. "You will spurn me from your good esteem with scorn and contempt even if I stay here, and I wish to go away from hither for ever."

"No, Dinah, no! it shall not be so," said the young man. "I am older than you, and believe my experience in the philosophy of our feelings, that there is no grief so profound, nor misfortune so great, that reason cannot soften the one and overcome the other. Banish from your being the sentiments which are your misery while concealed, and would be your dishonor if gratified. But fly not his presence; I will be your aid and counsel, in combating your own unhappy love, and here you may have one to whom to fly when you are driven by your misery to wish for your dishonor. Dinah, I was an insensate, a fool, when I once insulted you with my evil suspicions of your purity and youth, but do not for that think I can ever again suspect your honor. Stay here, and you shall have a protector in me from yourself, and in my family from the world."

The degradation of the girl's name may have once had its weight with his interest in her, but it never pressed so heavily upon his heart as seemed now to him this revelation of her infatuation. And why did he suddenly feel that it was not love he bore Miss Wellwood? Even then, perhaps, was his protégeé praising God for the approaching blessing to him and to Laura.

CHAPTER XLVIII.

DINAH IS APPOINTED SCHOOLMISTRESS.

The selectmen of the town of Templeville sat in solemn silence, like the Roman senators awaiting the Gauls, while Nat explained to them the fitness of the young girl to take care of the young, from the purity of her heart, the fineness of her intellect, and particularly a peculiar amount of patience, all of which were vouched for by the richest and most powerful of the neighbors, the young master of Pompney Place. They had held a secret consultation in executive session, and, headed by Pithkin, were unanimously in favor of rejecting her claims to the humble place for which her name was proposed, when Nat mentioned the desire of the family at Pompney Place in connection with this matter. The result was that, headed by Pithkin again, they turned around and, giving an unanimous vote in her favor, rushed hurriedly home to tell their wives. "The daughter of a criminal!" Sometime afterwards, it was found that one of the selectmen had been confined in his garret in a faint condition, from a continuous deprivation of food for a week after this event. The indignation of his spouse having continued for that length of time, he was released with an indelible impression created in his being that an elephant resided in the pit of his stomach. This, however, was about all the harm that was done by this appointment, for by the conspiracy of Nat and Charles, and the unconscious aid of the great Pithkin, the town was speedily overwhelmed with such an amount of public opinion manufactured in favor of the new appointee, that the lady aforesaid seriously contemplated adding another animal to her unfortunate husband's internal menagerie, by incarcerating him again, because he said he was sorry!

Charles alluded to their success, in a conversation which he subsequently had with Judge Pithkin, on inviting him to dinner.

"Yes, they seldom repent of having taken my advice," said the judge. "More particularly when I'm wrong, for then they can lay all the blame on me."

After paying himself this extraordinary tribute, he looked forcibly at the young man, who immediately thanked him heartily for executing his wishes in this matter.

"Certainly, I can afford to be magnanimous! She laughed at me once when I was tipped out of a buggy head foremost; but all I want is your friendship, gratitude, and a pinch of snuff."

Charles went over to the negro cottage the next day, to inform Dinah of her appointment, and it was the first she heard of it. In a moment she seemed to comprehend his delicate generosity, and at the same time the delicate position in which she was placed towards the villagers by his endeavors thus to remove from her the stigma of social degradation. She murmured something about "one having such generosity in his bosom must have many other virtues there to keep it company."

"I wish this action would tell you, Dinah," said he, "that I am the best friend you have; and yet I know I am a better friend to myself than to you when I aid you, for—"

"You can ever accuse yourself of selfishness," said Dinah, "but if the world is to judge of your friendship, it will only convict you of a misapplication of it, I guess."

"For shame, Dinah; when you were a dependent you didn't dare say that. Now you are your own mistress, you can plague me by depreciating your own right."

There seemed something after all sorrowful in the young girl's countenance, and in spite of the sincerity with which she quietly expressed to him her gratitude on account of herself and her father, there appeared to be this melancholy air about her, as if revealing a resignation to a presentiment within. What was it that struck his soul too, other than an indefinable feeling of some unhappiness which was near him and her? Was it not rather the putting to death, by the order of potent common sense, the criminal thoughts which were rioting in his mind like bacchanals around his drunken will, and which led it on in intoxicated infatuation to the violation of his duties towards himself, society, his mother, to Laura, and even to the girl herself; the hopes of his mother, the love of Laura, the demands of society, the avowal of the girl's attachment to another, the stain upon her name. They were all stern thoughts, but one was more powerful than all the rest to scare the joyous band of revellers from his bosom, and sober his will. It was the embassador to his mind of the girl's avowed love for another. He thought of the worthless wretch upon whom she bestowed her love. Dinah saw his melancholy irritation. But she always forgave and passed over any impatient petulance on his part, for she seemed instinctively to know how impossible it is to supply wants as fast as an idle imagination may be able to demand them, or to remove inconveniences by which elegance, refined into fastidiousness, may be offended in the circumstances of the hour.

The bushes were still filled with unfolding buds of the prairie rose, and the air was perfumed with their delicate fragrance. As he came up, he had plucked one from the hedge and given it to her, and she held it in her hand as she sat by him on the rustic seat. Soon, while speaking of her new relations with the school, he referred to his coming absence from the neighborhood, upon a proposed visit to the White Hills, and when she asked him if he would return soon, there was a wistfulness in her face, which was sententious. The air of the evening was too bracing to the thin blood coursing slowly in the veins of such as the old father, who was now by the side of the kitchen fire, in company with the old lady and Tip, but the young blood of his daughter and her benefactor was hardly touched by it. In the distance, by the neat barn, the colored head of the house had finished his lacteal operations, and left the large pan of milk resting upon a bench without, while engaged in throwing down a slight October repast to the milky mother.

A calf was wandering in antics upon the open sward, and had twice been driven away from the glowing pan by the uncalculating negro, when Dinah, placing the rose in her bosom, ran to bring it to the house. Charles followed her down, and as he met her with the milk, refreshed the bitterness that was within him by suddenly uttering, in affected indifference, a half-muttered allusion to women and their love. Dinah looked at him incredulously, and, with an air of momentary superiority or pity, exculpated, whitewashed, and acquitted him from his own immediate judgment, by honeyed words of gentle reasoning upon his own nature, which she said was so much like a woman's. The rampant calf had rushed at the rose hedge, and commenced to demolish a bush in an attempt to get at a green pumpkin behind.

"Chase him!" said the girl.

"No," said Charles, "the thorns will drive him off."

"Chase him, or hold the pan," said she, stamping her little foot.

"Eh? I'll hold the pan." He was very lazy.

"You have spilt the milk!" said she, on returning from the pursuit.

"So I have, by Jove!" said he, in an humble way.

A confusion of thought had suddenly come over her, and she trembled as she took the pan to carry it to the house. He saw not the tear that dropped upon her cheek as she went, and when she returned she said, "I beg your pardon." Perhaps he had seemed so much like a brother to her, she had forgotten for a moment the distance between them.

"Dinah, you insult me by your thought," said Charles, in a lively manner; "and when a woman insults a man, you remember what you told me her punishment should be." He tried to kiss her, but in the midst of her confusion, she showed her loyal heart to him and his duties to another. Although she did not allude to Laura, he was reminded by her look, and a deep shade of melancholy passed over his countenance. She looked into his face piercingly.

"It is right, Dinah," said he. But why, in the tumult of his actions, had he seized a little bow that had fallen from her neck, and thrust it into his bosom, and why did he give himself up to sweet reflections as he left her?

"Oh! can it be that she loves not this—but let me think. Her hand trembled when I bade her adieu, and to the rose I gave her, she once seemed to bow her lips, when she thought I saw her not."

CHAPTER XLIX.

SINGULAR INCIDENTS.

NAT was returning from a visit to Miss Wellwood. She had asked a favor of him! The young lady had observed that the overseer Baylon was frequently tormenting Dinah by his presence, probably on account of the relations of his employer Rudolph; and although the girl laughed it off, had asked Nat to investigate the matter, and immediately commenced to abuse him, to conceal her pleasure at his alacrity.

"This mission shows her kindness," reflected Nat as he proceeded along the road; "but she certainly intrusted me with it, something in the way in which the great Mogul treats his embassador to a foreign country. He vituperates him before he goes, and apologizes for it, by stating he may forget it after he returns. I've a good notion not to do it. However, I suppose I must."

"There goes the rascal now!" he exclaimed, as he suddenly descried the overseer walking in the middle of an open field of short grass adjacent. "By George! I will commence at once to watch him. Perhaps he may have come out here to cut his throat, which will be an agreeable sight, and will repay me for my temporary delay."

He looked again into the field. There was no overseer there! He rubbed his eyes and looked again. On the distant side, were four cows slowly emanating from a wood. They were the only living creatures to be seen. Such a singular impossible disappearance had the usual effect upon him. He commenced to philosophize; that is, he began to wonder, which is the first step therein, but he did not get any farther. Overwhelmed with astonishment, he turned immediately, and rushed back to Laura in breathless haste.

"Why didn't you stop and investigate the matter?" asked she, also in astonishment.

"It was so extraordinary, I couldn't keep it for that length of time! There is no doubt about it, he is a villain endowed by Satan with the supernatural power of disappearing from the presence of others!"

"Other villains? It is certainly remarkable. There was no place he could conceal himself? No tree—no—"

"None!"

"Curse her!" soliloquized Baylon. "They might have got the property, and I might have got it from them, if I had only had any power over her then! I am going to drive her off." However, the marm can do it, I guess! He! he! There is more drudgery for the proud lady. What the son does, she will patiently undo. I hate 'em all. Go to the devil everybody!"

He was exasperated at the young maiden, and now proposed paying her a visit. This time on meeting her as she was walking towards home from her labors in the town, he was no longer enabled to assume the mask of friendship; yet furious as he was there was something else besides his knowledge of Charles's interest in her, which made him refrain from threatening her as he wished. It was in silence that he listened to her words, which pleaded with him, not for herself, but for his sake. And while she still scornfully warned him that his persecution would recoil upon himself, she begged him to become a good man, and brightened into the eloquence which comes of that fulness of heart which a superior being feels towards an inferior he must pity, while he despises; for even such lofty friendship towards this man appeared then to fill her breast, in the hope that he would reform his plan. His tendency towards the humorous, which seemed to have been given to him as the only successful method by which he was permitted to gratify his hatred towards virtue or sacred things, did not fail to assert itself after he left her presence. "She no doubt," said he, "cried for Christ when she was an infant! I must to chapel."

While walking across the fields on uncertain legs, at a certain point therein, a new freak took possession of those maniac members. They went into the earth with lightning-like rapidity. Thought is quicker than lightning, and he proposed to let them go. But as he recollected with horror that his body would in all probability follow, taking with it his individuality, he made a convulsive grasp at something which spanned the abyss. Had the earth yawned at last to swallow him up? Four cows, followed by the innocent Gluckinson, were wending their way slowly in the field from a distant wood.

The overseer drew himself up after the manner of the gymnastic scholar with the horizontal bar, so that his top-knot projected above the infernal shaft, which bore a remarkable likeness to some old, disused well. He gave a terrible yell, and immediately disappeared.

The youth stopped his whistling, and looked with astonishment into a cloud just over him. A repetition of the cry directed his attention and footsteps to the aperture to the lower world, upon the brink of which the unfortunate Obadiah hung.

"Oh, help me, for God's sake!" said the latter, with another desperate tug at the beam.

"Hallo! is that you?" asked the youth, in an easy, affable manner.

"Good God! what a question. Help me, quick!"

James appeared lost for the moment in a profound philosophical revery.

"Damn you!" roared the convulsed Baylon, in his fearful peril. "I'll lick you like the devil—Oh, dear Mr. Gluckinson for God's sake—I'll give you money—any thing—fifty cents—a new hat—any thing! It's deep. I can't see the bottom, and I can't hold on much longer. Damn you! Don't you see you are committing murder, you murderous jackass! I'll have you indicted for murder, you infernal scoundrel. Heaven will bless you, my dear friend, give me your hand!"

The young man smiled a demoniac smile, and with a yell of agony, the wretched overseer relaxed in faintness his hold.

For two or three days after this, the youth Gluckinson was accustomed to steal out of the house at a certian hour, with small articles of nourishment, and disappear in the adjoining scenery. However, at the end of that period, feeling that the habit was observed, he was forced, apparently against his will, to cease the practice. Soon after that, a great excitement was caused in the neighborhood, and much alarm among his friends, by the unexpected absence of the young lawyer, Mr. Bonney, from the village and from many important engagements which he had contracted. At the moment of continued suspense, when an immediate search had been resolved upon, he suddenly re-appeared with mysteriously soiled and torn vestments, and without any shirt whatever. Singular to say, it was about the same time that the overseer Baylon, who had not been seen for some time, also made his appearance in a similar state, but with the addition of a remarkable emaciation of person, and a peculiar blood-shot appearance about the eyes, as if he had been drawn out of some place legs foremost, with a rope. In answer to questions respecting this singular matter, the young lawyer seemed disposed to maintain a strict silence, and between him and the overseer, there appeared some mysterious subject of common thought, which they were not disposed to allude to in public.

As a general thing, Nat was remarkably unfortunate in accomplishing the wishes of Miss Wellwood. However, in spite of fortune, he ever had the same will to persist.

CHAPTER L.

ON A VISIT TO THE WHITE HILLS.

A party had been made up to visit the White Mountains at the most beautiful season of the year, when nature puts on her gaudiest attire, like a desperate coquette, whose season is over.

It was on this tour that Charles resolved to divulge to Laura the fact that he loved her not, and had been guilty of deception and dishonor in inducing her to bestow her affections upon him, when he knew they could not be returned. He felt the stain, and though he was conscious of his coming degradation, he chose shame in preference to a life-long lie upon his part, or misery upon hers. "But alas! she loves me! And I have fanned that flame by my own folly. Is it not my duty to sacrifice my own happiness by retaining the secret forever in my bosom? No, I cannot. Sooner or later the energy of duty would fail me, and then when it is too late, she would discover my fatal hypocrisy!"

The party consisted of Charles's mother, Laura, Squire Wellwood, and himself. The aunt having declined, as Judge Pithkin represented his inability to leave, Squire Wellwood proposed that an invitation should be extended to his friend, Nathaniel Bonney; but his daughter seeming enraged thereat, he concluded not to promulgate it.

On the way to the mountains, time and again the young man reflected upon his false position towards the sweet and unsuspecting girl, and hated himself. On these occasions, he seated himself by the side of the squire, and listened in silence to his partially related anecdotes. He wished that their pastor, Dr. Fuffles, could have accompanied them, for he longed for some one to whose sympathy he might open his bosom in confidence. Still he knew that it was without aid that he had to undergo the task of rendering an innocent girl unhappy, to save her from the double condition of misery and servitude.

They visited the various localities, which the tourist does not generally select, and Charles's homage to nature was colored with the sense of unworthiness of the religious Hindoo. Returning, they crossed into the territory of Vermont, and reached, after much molestation from the hospitality of the generous inhabitants, a notable summer resort, situated amid a group of wood-encircled lakes, upon the New York boundary thereof.

It was at this hotel, long celebrated in the stage-driving annals of times gone by, that they stopped to visit the lakes in the environs, and enjoy the well-known courtesy of the affable host; (of whose extraordinary politeness, it was related to Squire Wellwood by an admiring neighbor, that having discovered a strange dog, on one occasion, lying upon his flower-bed, he requested him to leave in such courteous tones, that the dog turned over, and died upon the spot from remorse.) Charles and Laura taking a buck-board, (which is a singular vehicle, especially contrived for ease in tipping over, belonging particularly to this region,) proposed to view the scenery of the lake Hortonia before dinner.

As they neared the lake, Charles reined in the horse. Both Laura and he had been plunged in a profound silence.

"Laura," said he, "it is well that you should know me. You do not. You have not studied my character enough, and I would not take advantage of your affection for me to hide my faults from you for the world."

"Eh?" said Laura, looking inquisitively at him.

"You do not know it, for I have carefully concealed it from you; but a terrible irritability has lately developed itself in my character, which often leads me to absolute violence. Such is my rage, would you think it, that I often—I often wreak my vengeance upon unoffending pieces of furniture, and that, too, on slight provocation, such as the absence of a shirt button or—"

"Oh, I like that! Give me the man of spirit! The man of excitable temperament, whose sensitive organization thus vehemently demonstrates its power. None of your tame, unresisting pieces of clay. I am so glad you told me, Charles."

("Eh! oh dear!) Yes, yes. I thought you would be gratified with that. But that is not exactly what I wish particularly to explain to you in my character just now. You will be surprised when I divulge it to you, and I here beg you earnestly, mention not to a living soul the fatal infirmity. I am—I am," continued he, leaning round to her in a mysterious manner, and pointing to his head, "at times I am weak here! Be prudent and keep it secret; now you know the secret."

"Why, how is that, Charles? What do you mean?"

"Well may you ask! I shut myself up when the fits come on. But enough of the unhappy subject. I think it was owing to having been hit on the head at school when I was a boy, and—"

"Oh how I can nurse you! How I can attend to your wants in those moments of weakened nature, and cheer you by my presence and unceasing attention."

("Heaven! she considers the ferocity of a savage an evidence of spirit, and idiocy in a husband an agreeable dispensation for strengthening the wife's love. I am reduced to having an incurable ulcer in one of my legs. Confound it, I can't go that. I'll try on constitutional lameness.) Your generosity merits my gratitude, especially in this particular of growing imbecility, of a tendency towards idiocy, I say," continued he in a louder tone. "Yet knowing as I do that you might overlook that in your kindness and affection towards me, what can I ask of you, when I tell you, that at any moment I may be laid up for years, with rheumatism in my chest!"

"Oh, that is nothing, dear Charlie; when you are imbecile, you will not be conscious of the rheumatism, and when you have the rheumatism you cannot do any harm by your temper."

("It is of no use. I have run through my mental, moral, and physical condition. I have got to break it to her!) My dear friend," said he after some moments of pause, with his lips slightly compressed, "unite all your forces now; bring up all your courage!"

"Gracious heaven! how pale he looks. What is it?"

"I—I know not how to tell you."

"Oh Charles, you scare me. Why the gloom of this ride, the self-crimination, and now, this sudden agitation. Pray go on."

There was a certain bitterness in the expression of the young man's face. "Laura—"

"I pray you, beseech you, go on!"

"Laura!—I love another."

The girl started with great suddenness, and then buried her face in her hands.

"Yes!" continued he, gloomily, "I've been a liar and a hypocrite to you in our intercourse, but thank God, I've told you now that I have been such."

Laura still concealed her countenance, and in the increase of her agitation, her bosom rapidly heaved.

("Heavens! I've crushed her soul! I've broken her

heart. Scoundrel—wretch, that I am!) Oh Laura, let me still swear that I will be devoted to you—be faithful, though—"

"Ha! ha! ha!" cried she, throwing back her head, and bursting into laughter.

("Good Heaven! Delirious! She's going crazy!) It is false! It is false! Yes, now I know you love me, dear," said the alarmed young man, attempting to conceal his rashness in a futile appearance of triumph. "Oh try and be calm. Know that it was but a foolish ruse of my jealousy to try your affection."

"Ha! ha! ha!"

("Gracious! the violence of the shock has shaken her mind.) Ever, ever will I love you, and hate myself—that is, for this folly, I mean. Do but restore yourself to quiet, and I'll go through fire and water for you—I'll—"

"I am better now; you say you love me!"

"Oh yes. I am so relieved. To think of my wishing to make you believe I didn't," said Charles, laughing feebly at the ridiculousness of the idea. "How absurd! But you know better, don't you?"

"Yes, Charles; but it was so unexpected."

("Oh dear! all hope is over.")

"However, I shall be well presently."

"Oh yes, you are even better now. (Jove! I begin to wish I had stuck to it.) But after such violence as that which I have been guilty of, you must hate me, I know you do. Will you not hate me forever? (If she only would!")

"Oh no, no. I shall always love you just as much as ever," said the girl, demurely, but with great firmness.

The iron of this announcement went to the very centre of his soul. He turned his head away in bitterness to conceal his gloom, unwilling then to disturb further the happiness of the light-hearted young girl.

"Don't you think we have ridden far enough?" said he, after a lengthened pause. "How flat the scenery is here. The sky isn't worth a glance."

"Yes, let us return," said the girl, looking out of the corners of her eyes at him, and biting her lips.

They drove on some way in silence on their return, but as they were approaching the inn, Laura finally turned to him, and said, "Charles! I too—wish to intrust you with a secret." There was an appearance of sadness upon her face, and her agitation certainly seemed profound. "Yet though I also, as you will see, have been a hypocrite, I can be truthful to you now, without fear of wounding your nature or hopes. But still it is best, perhaps, to summon your courage and unite all your energies. I too—love another! and this is a parting kiss to our engagement!" said she, turning around and kissing him with ardor.

In his surprise and bewilderment, he kissed her three or four times, and then they shook each other's hands, and both burst out into a loud and unrestrained laugh. Laura then unfolded to the young man how she had secretly felt a growing attachment to the young lawyer, Mr. Bonney, without hardly knowing whether it was love or not, but that she was now sure it was something else besides admiration for his warmheartedness, and other virtues. "But don't you tell him," said she. And Charles now, in his turn, confided to her all of his secret. It struck her with a soft rage, but soon brought the bestowal of another kiss upon his lips. And so with mutual confidence and renewal of temporary secrecy, they arrived at the inn. Such was the happiness and merriment in their looks as they alighted, that Laura's worthy parent immediately rushed down into the office, and treated eleven wayfarers whom he found there, under the firm conviction that heretofore he had been mistaken, but this time the proposal and engagement had surely been made. As each of these, by a strict social intercussation of etiquette, extended their courtesy in return, he was obliged to drink one hundred and twenty-one times, and was then put to bed.

CHAPTER LI.

THE SCHOOL.

DINAH went on in industrious attention to the fulfillment of her duties in the little school, and more and more the scholars were coming to like her. Two little fellows might be seen every day sitting on the front bench together, looking into their spelling-books with a busy noise, or furtively turning their heads towards the other boys. Their little hearts were joined in love for each other, and they already looked up to their sweet mistress almost as a mother. They were orphans.

One day, the young lawyer Nathaniel was turning a corner near the school, when a brick-bat struck him in the stomach. It came in the midst of a shower of stones and smaller missiles, and he had time to observe the retreating overseer Obadiah, bending against the hail of rocks with bruised hat, ere his attention was exclusively absorbed by the personal anguish of the accident.

"Hallo! hallo! What is this?" gasped he, after a while, looking around. A great noise had greeted his ear, and in the disturbed distance there appeared an approaching mob of children. "What is this? Do you want to knock people's eyes out, and break all the windows in the neighborhood, eh?"

"Hurrah for the mistress! We'll fight for our mistress forever!" cried the little fellows, immediately, crowding around Nat in triumph, and to hear what he thought of the affair.

"Hooray, Square Nat," said Gluckinson, appearing in their midst, in hoarse excitement. "We've beat him off! He's been tryin' to make 'em disobedient, and we've stoned him. He's running away. Hooray!"

Three days before this occurrence, two youthful members of Dinah's school had swerved from the path of rectitude in the most unaccountable manner, and, boldly announcing that the pursuit of liberty was an inalienable right, stated that they were not going to be made to do any more sums. The next day, one of them suddenly absented himself at an unauthorized hour from the school-house. Hushed whispering was immediately prevalent among the children, and it was observed that they had become very inattentive to their lessons, and frequently bent their eyes in a dark manner towards an adjoining wood-shed. Late in the afternoon of the same day, intense excitement was caused by the sudden and voluntary appearance of the truant before the mistress in tears, and with a distended stomach. He had been hanging about the wood-shed all day, eating varied delicacies in solitary ecstasy, until satiety came, bringing with it penitence. It was then that, with a puff of excitement, the conspiracy came to light, and each of the boys related with deep feelings of importance and awe, the fact that this youth had lately been seen in frequent conversation with the overseer Baylon, that sticks of candy and sugar cookies were observable in his possession in remarkable recurrency, and that he had frequently advised them to be naughty, as they would get as many sweetmeats as they wanted by it!

Dinah gave them quiet commands of obedience, and the look of honesty and honor from her eyes was enough. Unknown to her, a counterplot was formed. It reached Gluckinson's ears by a rapid telegraph, and gallantly led on by him, they assailed the unsuspecting Obadiah at an opportune moment with a rocky tribute. At one period during the attack, as the enemy attempted to turn and pursue his assailants, Gluckinson blenching slightly, danced behind the little band armed with rocks, (appearing like Gulliver among the Lilliputs;) but he soon recovered his equanimity, and taking the lead again in a brilliant manner, the enemy was put to a base and speedy flight amid the triumphant cries of the assailants.

The devotion of the little fellows, and of the simple but honest Gluckinson, fighting for their puissant lady, was approved of by Nat with sparkling eyes. "Here, boys! Here's a dollar. I see your mistress coming after you. Run and spend half of it to-day, and the other half to-morrow, and then I'll give you some more. I breathe a little more regularly now, but still a large circle of friends and admirers will be pained to know of my condition. It did execution. You projected that missile, didn't you, Jim?"

Jim had. Taking a severe aim, and determined to inflict a terrible and lasting vengeance upon the person of his enemy, he had thrown the brick with all the energy which his tended muscle was capable of, and it had landed directly in the pit of Nat's stomach.

The boys rushed to the candy-seller's, wild with joy at this immediate reward of their fealty, and a grand feast of molasses candy was immediately inaugurated in front of the astounded and rejoiced old woman's; forty-five boys being ranged along in silence on the curb-stone, each energetically dissolving, with working jaws and steadfast gaze into vacancy, immense lumps of the saccharine joy.

Nat having paid his salutations to Dinah, and conversed with her cheerfully for some time, went away to his office accompanied by James. On the way, he observed that Gluckinson's vivacity had all left him, and he became melancholy once more.

"The cook licked me again this morning, Mr. Nat," said he, finally. "I don't know what to do. Won't you tell me? Baylon used to advise me, but that's before I began to hate him. He told me I'd better join the church."

"By the way, that reminds me; that's a good idea," said Nat, "just the thing, James. The boy who blows the bellows at Dr. Fuffles's, has been discharged for paying more attention to blowing his nose. You can join, and take his place Sundays, and in that way you can get religion and strength at the same time, don't you see?"

The next Sunday, the youth was duly installed with the consent of his mistress, as assistant-organist, and pumped way, under the recollection of the causes of his acceptance, with a devotion of inexpressible profundity.

In a few days after the occurrence related, in accordance with the usual custom, the advancement of the school was shown up to the parents of the neighborhood, in a fall examination. The young schoolmistress welcomed them to what hospitality the place afforded, with an old-fashioned wave of the hand and bow and blush. Judge Pithkin, though conscious of his celebrity and the grandeur of his position as presiding spirit, sat on the stage as calm and unmoved as a prize pumpkin at a country fair, the object of admiring curiosity. The examination advanced, and the scholars being generally found to know more than the committees who examined them, it was pronounced quite satisfactory.

The usual characteristics of such a gathering displayed themselves. Thus, during the recitation of the class in mythology: "Who was Calchas?" asked the little schoolmistress, mechanically.

Boy. "A celebrated soothsayer, who died of grief at being unable to tell how many figs there were upon a certain tree, some one else having mentioned the exact number!"

Dinah. "Yes! that is correct."

Then Dr. Fuffles to Dinah, in a patronizing manner: "Does not history inform us rather, that he died from having eaten too many of the figs in a fit of spleen, consequent upon finding his superior in divination? I think you will find it so. Yes, perhaps that is more precise!"

Then Dinah's attention would be called for a moment to Judge Pithkin. He had been eyeing a boy for some time, with symptoms of growing alarm. "Gods of heaven! that boy has got the measles! I haven't had 'em!" said he. "Take him out! Lead him away! I insist on it!"

"Oh, no, sir!" said Dinah, quieting him. "It is only his natural complexion."

"Eh? you are sure of it, are you? Fond of beef, eh?" continued the Judge, resuming in confidence his expression of grandeur, and looking down upon the audience.

He was much concerned about this time, however, by an extraordinary and continuous succession of smiles which the spinster aunt bestowed upon him. In fact, well knowing love to be a plant, to which was necessary the sunshine of smiles, and observing that his was naturally of very slow growth, she had suddenly resolved to apply the hot-house pressure to it. It put him out, more especially as he was just commencing to con in secret a speech which Nat had written for him, to be delivered on this important occasion. After a short period, he was relieved, however; for observing that he appeared to be wandering, and being attracted to the old father of Dinah, modestly seated in a distant and obscure corner, she went at the latter, and caused his old heart to beat with violence from the kind words which fell from her lips about his daughter.

Under a desire to be exceedingly affable, the spinster proceeded to discourse with the old man upon other and more abstruse subjects, which he listened to in humbleness, although he didn't understand a word of it. "Your head is weak, my friend," she would say, "but I know you are nevertheless acquainted with all the secret, aye, mysterious workings of that dark and inscrutable enigma, the human heart, and I honor you for your appreciation of it!" All of which only made the old man more undecided than ever.

Then, after a while, the judge is forced by an idea of his own importance, to come down for a moment from the stage, and examine a spelling class. One boy is laboring under a fatal hallucination. All words commencing with an *f*, he spells with *ph*, and *vice versa*.

"Now, *fat*, sir. Don't bully me, sir," says the judge, sternly. "Don't attempt to bully me. Spell *fat*, sir, and without *ph!*"

"*F—a—t*—then!" said the boy, driven to the verge of distraction. "You are a fat old rascal!"

"Eh! this argues insubordination in the school, and bad rule! What is this, eh?" says the judge, with severity, shaking his head, while the apothecary, who has lately been elected selectman, makes the extraordinary remark, "Cert'nly, these are the ones she encourages. Hows'ever, she can't help favoring wickedness, because she naturally has a fellow feeling for it!"

A half smile parts the disdainful lips of the young girl, as she hears the deliberate insult, but her serious countenance returns to its repose, as she defends herself without excitement. "Sir, for the same reason, perhaps, your fellow-citizens may have favored you with the position which shields you from reply."

Here all the visitors laugh forcibly at the apothecary, and Pithkin, observing that his brother selectman stumbles grammatically in his desire to reply, says to him, to relieve him of his agony, "Sit down!" The apothecary thereupon pretends to be engaged in an important conversation with the justice; but the latter will not be humbugged, and tells him also, "to hold his tongue," which, on the whole, he is glad to do, and go away shortly, as he had brought himself into an uncomfortable position before the elite, by wagging it.

Then the boys commence to recite the usual exciting harangues, calculated by the compilers of elocutionary books to test the constitutional ability of youths to withstand pulmonary complaints. One informs the audience in shrill tones, that he has a vocal organ which remains entirely bellicose in its nature; while another, intending to ask the assemblage if a deliberaative body of Romans could waste any great period of time in unprofitably discussing a certain matter, converts the question into a supposed petition by some Roman to the heathen powers, to flay alive the Congress of his country. "Gods, skin a Roman Senate," and overpowered by the idea without doubt, is immediately withdrawn in tears from the stage, without proceeding farther. However, none find fault with these exercises, or if they do, they cannot lay it at Dinah's door, because the high-school master teaches elocution throughout all the institutions. And now at last the time has come when a few remarks are expected from Judge Pithkin and others, on the state and advancement of educational matters.

The judge, having risen upon this occasion, immediately commenced in great style upon the prosperity of the school, and proceeded to express himself in a concise but fervent manner, by affirming it to be his deliberate conviction, that all the prosperity of this and the other institutions, was owing to his sole efforts, and whatever drawbacks there were, were to be laid to some one else. This idea pleased him so much, that he was unable to entertain any other, and he was fain to repeat it from the commencement. A faint chuckle was heard in the audience, and this overpowered him completely, so that not a single idea was left in his memory. He then pulled Nat's notes from his pocket, and commenced to read them from beginning to end, directions and all, with great fidelity and determination not to lose one drop of them, all of which resulted in a great success, and he was generally congratulated upon the happiness of his effort; although it may have sounded somewhat singular to many, to hear him say in a coherent and straightforward manner—

"Yes, gentlemen and ladies, we have cause to be satisfied with this advancement in educational interests, and I felicitate you all. Allude then, ladies and gentlemen, to the necessity of taking charge of tender youths, and call the attention of the assemblage to the duties of parents in assisting the teacher in discipline of conduct; and you can put in a joke or two in reference to their having been children once themselves—the old birchen rod—times being different now from then—but manners of mind the same—necessity of this ground touched upon slightly. Another joke here—and then ladies and gentlemen, wind up the whole with an allusion to our country, just before they commence to applaud!"

CHAPTER LII.

PURE LOVE.

CHARLES, as soon as he returned on the following Saturday, rushed on the wings of his infatuation to seek the presence of the young girl whose character exercised such an influence over his feelings, and now his hopes.

On his way he met the colored folks and the old father of Dinah going to chapel for the coming evening, and they passed him with respectful bows.

Charles stopped at the turn of the road which brought the house in view, for he saw Dinah seated upon the bench beneath the tree before it, engaged apparently in an absorbed reading. Her back was turned towards him, her arm rested on the rail of the bench, her forehead upon her arm, the book was on the seat beside her, and in this lazy attitude she was perusing its pages. He stole across the road, and came up towards her as slily as a cat upon a mouse, treading softly upon the grass that his footsteps might not betray his presence. Reaching the broad old tree, against the other side of which the bench rested, he observed her attention was still apparently engaged upon the pages of the book. So near now that he held his breath for fear of discovery, and she quietly said, sitting up in a natural way, "I am glad you have come back."

He took his seat beside her, and shook both of her hands, which she willingly rested in his. If there ever was pure friendship and gratitude, it beamed from her eyes as she welcomed him back again into her humble presence. He asked about the progress of her school, and seemed to take further delight in making her tell him all about her own affairs during his absence. The feelings with which he had now approached her, relieved of the dishonor of double-dealing, were the feelings of the discharged prisoner enjoying the sunlight of heaven. The thought of her avowed passion for Warriston now seemed hardly to have any weight with him. He felt that her love for his neighbor was but the confused echo which is ever awakened in woman's bosom by a true or even false call of affection, and he felt that those calls must—must soon be shut out from her pure soul. But as he continued in pleasure to question her upon her humble affairs, in which he now took more interest than any thing in the world, and referred to the advantages she would derive from a continuance in the school, he noticed that a faltering look came over her face. Aye, she listened in silence as he fondly predicted in terms of glowing friendship her future career of happiness and usefulness, and a thought, which was silently denying what he said, seemed to have more weight than all his warm and hopeful words. She suddenly rose. There was an energy about her actions, and a nervous firmness in her tones, as she briefly said:

"I did not tell the truth when I said I was glad that you had come back. I am sorry—indeed sorry, that you come hither. It cannot be. You must not. Every one is wronged, but above all you are—deceiving yourself."

"Dinah," said the young man, after a moment, "these words do not bring me happiness. They rudely strike the soul of a friend."

"Pshaw!" said she; there was a trifling indifference to his feeling apparent in her manner. "You will always be unhappy. It is because you are lazy."

"No, no. It is not. It is because I fear to lose the reality of possessing a genuine friend. One who can sympathize with me, as if she were myself," continued the young man, repressing his feelings.

"What!" said she, turning towards him sharply. "Is it I you wish to be as yourself to you? Certainly. You wish to act as if you were beside yourself when you are beside me," continued she, summoning up her old way of irony.

"Dinah! I felt alone until I saw you. Do not move away from me. Yes! it was you alone who awakened in my heart those—"

"Oh, where are your feelings of honor, of decency, sir? Where is your trusted love for Laura?"

"Dinah, I love her not," said he in a low voice.

"Yes! yes! I thought so," muttered the young girl in suppressed energy. "Well, sir," continued she shortly, rousing herself, "her happiness is now your only dutiful thought, and I will not be an accomplice in your desire to violate it."

("I have indeed deceived myself with my own stupidity,") said the young man with a melancholy laugh. "Dinah, if not your words, at least your manner seems to tell me that you are seeking an excuse to break our friendship without revealing its real cause. Yes, you are right, and it is perhaps idle now to tell you that she would willingly sever the ties which bind me to her."

The girl looked at him suddenly with glittering eyes.

"But though you can feel no return for my love,

you shall now know of its existence and its power. Dinah, I naturally and necessarily love you; and though we should part to-night forever, let me not leave in your soul the thought that mine has been but a dull block in its intercourse with you, that I have not lived a growing life in the sunshine of your darling face, that returning echoes have not been awakened by the sound of the voice which poured forth the expressions of a natural and a vigorous intellect, that no thrill has trembled along my fibres at the light touch of your hand."

The girl stretched herself convulsively towards heaven, as the vehemence of the young man's emotion shut up for a moment his lips.

"Yes, Dinah! though you now would leave me for one whom the mysterious dispensations of Providence drive you towards, leave me not without the homage which my nature owes to yours; leave me not, saying that you cannot see or feel my love, e'en though you love another. (By God! if she will love him, he shall marry her and love her, or I will send his soul to hell!")

"What has told you that I love another?" she asked rapidly.

"Your own confession!"

"For whom—for whom?"

"My neighbor Rudolph. Oh, infatuated love!"

"Yes, yes! Infatuated love is mine, but it shall have its eternal way. What!" said she, in a kind of sudden, abstracted passion, "think they that I am born without human rights? Shall not my soul stand up for its honor? Am I not a woman with a heart to love, like the rich, the proud, the lofty of the land?

Have I not a head to plan and hands to work, and shall I idly bear to have torn away from my being the only energy which would impel them in their usefulness. Never. Whilst thus I lean upon my friend, will I defy with his dear love the world and all its rudeness!"

She threw herself into the arms of the young man, and laid her head upon his shoulder. What joyous delirium seized him as he pressed her closer to his breast, and placed his lips to hers.

"'Tis I! 'tis I she loves! Thank God!" murmured he. "Fool that I have been. Oh, Dinah, how can I return such pure, such honoring love!" continued the young man, as he reverted in memory to the time when she had revealed her secret love, and deemed it dishonorable, because he had deceived her with his apparent love for Laura.

"Mine! mine now. No one can part us," said he, again straining her to his bosom, and placing a kiss upon her returning lips.

"God says it is right, and He will not part us! No! No! They cannot part us!" murmured she. "Am I not his to make him useful in the world. I will live and die but to that end, for it is my destiny." And yet a sadness seemed strangely in her words.

The shadows of twilight were darkening over the amphitheatre. The winds of the decaying year swept up fitfully through the dark forest, from whence the sound of the mourning dove issued to mingle with the long clarion notes of the cock, as he crowed his final parting to the day.

CHAPTER LIII.

DINAH AT LAURA'S RESIDENCE.

Laura, in furtherance of her desire to promote the happiness of Dinah, extended a formal invitation to the young schoolmistress to spend a week at her house, during the fall vacation.

Dinah and Laura are walking together in the garden, and, in unreserved confidence, but half express the affection which they bear each other, for they cannot. An agitation seizes the former's frame, and the mingled radiance of fear and joy, which is designated as bashfulness, spreads upon her face; for her heart, quicker than her vision, tells her Charles is near. After a while, Laura, pretending that she hears wheels upon the distant side of the house, abruptly runs away from the two lovers; and a few moments thereafter, the sound of a waving musical romance from the piano lulls their auditory sense. Charmed by its affluence, they also wander to the house, and sit them down in a little back parlor, looking out upon the loaded fruit trees.

Charles took her hand respectfully, and sat down in a chair in front of the sofa, against the arm of which she rested.

They then entered into a conversation, in which their sympathies were more unfolded, and their souls came nearer together, as it progressed through the flowery field of English poetry. He soon came to dwell upon the hopes which his mother had entertained with regard to him, and expressed frankly the unpleasantness of shocking her, and apparently dashing those hopes by a sudden revelation to her of his new attachment; and although he alluded to the meanness of secrecy, and the false position in which the receiver of his love was placed, the latter knew that time would have to be expended in softening his parent's mind towards her, before such a divulgement could be made without causing pain, which might thus be avoided.

A sad air came upon Dinah's face again, and a sigh escaped her lips; but she quickly concealed them from the young man.

"And, Dinah," said the young man, in prophetic exultation, "the bestowal of a mother's love upon you will soon fall from her lips, mingled with a praise to her Maker for this blessing of her son. Oh, darling, you may not blame me if then I become peevish and moping, because—because I shall be jealous of her!"

"Hush! hush!" said she, tenderly, putting her hand upon his mouth; "hush! some one is coming."

A hand was upon the door. "In this room, dear?" asked a well-known voice.

"Yes, you will find it upon the table," cried Laura, from the staircase above. The tutelary girl was anxious about the foolish children, wandering in the park, and was cunningly dressing for a divergent drive with her visitor.

"Heavens! my mother is here!" cried Charles. Dinah rose and placed herself with a rapid adjustment of her dress in front of the young man, who had been kneeling by her hand, and hid him with its folds, as she stood against the sofa. She appeared quite tall and stately as she assumed this position, like her godmother the huntress, when she has returned from the chase; and he was like her brother Apollo, skylarking behind his favorite sister. As the mother entered, although she had been made aware of the young schoolmistress's hospitable presence in the house, she stopped in surprise, and it was after a moment that she acknowledged the bow with which her entrance was saluted. In the girl's erect position she thought she saw again too apparent that boldness of character, aye, the effrontery so unbecoming her youthful years, which was more abandoned than the natural hypocrisy which could not conceal it. In her bitterness and pride, as the thought of the girl's artful disposition towards her son rushed upon her mind, she violated the rights which the roof, under which they were both guests, afforded the girl, and in reproachful terms, yet with a sincerity of sadness, soon came to ask her plainly by what fatuity she had thought to forget the return which she owed her benefactor, and lead his honor into the infatuated dishonor of embittering the hopes of his parents—with what palliation to usurp the happiness of the unsuspecting girl, under whose roof she was now a guest.

She thus confessed the power which her listener possessed, and naturally desired to exercise over her son; and although she did not believe that the latter could be so infatuated with her as to succumb to that power, it was a bitter truth to know that he would be estranged from Laura's affection, or at least was preparing the way by his disposition towards this girl, for a just discarding aversion in the mind of his affianced. She had lately received bitter proofs of the growth of this disposition, and prospected in sadness the hopes for his future thus crushed by an idle whim of his fancy.

But yet such a sadness had been concealed, and why did she fear even to speak to him frankly of this subject, or reproach him with a mother's right for his folly? Amid the contending emotions of that proud heart, a feeling almost of guiltiness had seized her, and yet she knew not why. Dinah stood in a motionless position, listening to her reproachful words, and replied not until the mother asked her with increased agitation if she dared to meet her son alone.

"He honors me with his love," said Dinah; "mine shall not dishonor him!" She put her hand behind her, which the young man seized and pressed to his lips. There was a melancholy tenderness in her voice, and a renewed weariness appeared to come over her spirit.

"Let us be seated!" said the mother in her hope. As she advanced towards the girl in a conciliatory way, she discovered her son still on his bended knee behind the robe of the former, holding her hand in affection, and a smile upon his lips! The faltering of Dinah's voice had touched him, and set up a thrill of exquisite pleasure within him. The mother had known the steadfast honor of her son, and exclaimed in overpowered tones: "Horror! my son concealing his shame behind the robe of the cunning daughter of a criminal!"

"Yes! my mother! I love her!" said he.

"Would you be estranged from me forever?" cried she, in her discontent; and she sank upon the chair and covered her face with her hands.

CHAPTER LIV.

THE SINGULAR COURSE OF MR. BONNEY'S AFFECTION.

Charles's aunt and Mr. Bonney, seated upon the top of two firm and well-made ladders, placed at a comfortable proximity for colloquial purposes, were engaged in an interesting conversation.

"Yes, it is now definitely settled, Mr. Bonney," said the former. "Would you think it? Yes, she intrusted it to a father's solicitude. It is to take place on the twentieth of December next."

Nat made a convulsive movement, and came near falling from his eminent position, but managed to recover himself.

"And I will tell you, but say nothing about it. Would you think it, I—te-hee—instituted—te-hee—the most ingenious stratagem. It caused him to make the proposal at once. At a moment when they were becoming inattentive, causing him to believe that she was indifferent to him, I roused his pride. It was like a box on the ears of his purpose, and now they are to be married on the approaching twentieth of December."

("Oh the devil!) I did the same thing. I did the same thing to Laura! After sixteen industrious hours of unexampled lying on different occasions, I succeeded in making her believe that he rather preferred eating his breakfast to marriage with her, and it has had the same effect upon her, hang me if it hasn't!"

"Oh, dear, disinterested Mr. Bonney, did you?"

"Ha! what fatality is this which attends me?"

asked Mr. Bonney, in a low voice, sternly interrogating his interior oracle. "I try this unfailing principle of human nature in two cases: In my own, for the first and only time it at once works backwards! Deluded by the overpowering argument of personal experience, I try it in my rival's, and it resumes with fatal vigor its accustomed course! It will be the same thing with the law of gravity! The end of the pursuit of my affection will be my extinguishment. I shall break my neck by falling up to the top of a four-story house, while running after her."

"And you must be thanked for your kind effort, indeed, Mr. Bonney."

"And you also, I think. (I can afford to say that. If the principle had worked stern foremost in his case as in mine, her efforts would have been in my favor at any rate. But let me be prudent. If I was deluded by the personal experience of this supernatural reversion of general principles, it determines me. I am in the claws of a crab-like fate, and from this moment, whatever I ought to do in the brief period before me, I will do backwards, confound me if I don't.")

"Do you know, at one time, I thought you were inclined to pay her attentions, Mr. Bonney. Indeed, I really did, would you think it?"

"Hey! Has she ever said any thing about that?"

"Oh no, no; of course not. You know, being taken up with Charles, you know, at the time."

"Certainly! Certainly. The idea was totally unfounded, of course! And I now authorize you to deny it for me firmly and peremptorily on all occasions upon which it may or may not be mentioned," said Nat, tumbling off his ladder in his vehemence.

It was inadvertently omitted to be mentioned at the commencement of this chapter, that this brief conversation took place in an alcove of the circulating library of Templeville, where the parties were hunting for books.

It may also be stated that, during the same day, a great change suddenly came over Miss Wellwood's manner, which had been of an exceeding liveliness, amounting almost to a continuous exultation. The commencement of this change was manifested in a flood of tears, which lasted for half an hour, and after that it was observable she expended the remainder of the evening in contemplating her finger nails in a blue manner.

CHAPTER LV.

THE MOTHER IS SHOCKED.

Some ladies of the neighborhood, calling upon Charles's mother on her usual reception day, caused the saloon to resound with their loquacity. One, after many inquiries respecting Charles's father, travelling upon business in Europe and the expected period of his return, with lively abruptness called the attention of the room to the melancholy of Miss Wellwood, who was present, and then with the same pleasant versatility turned her conversation towards the kind interest which her hostess's son, Charles, had lately manifested in the district school of young children.

"And do you know," said she, glancing at Laura, coolly, certainly with a refreshing intention, "I think the susceptibilities, too, of my young friend's nature seek this fair wild flower of the woods, in preference to the cultivated society of the more refined." She was possessed of six daughters, whose prospects for matrimony were lessening with each passing hour. "What eccentricity, that he should pretend to find extraordinary qualities in this fair maid—late of your milking pail, ha! ha! But that is just his way, to be sure. Yes, he will amuse himself with this new idea for a while, and make a model of perfection of his Florimel, by an ardent application of his lively imagination, and then quietly relapse into ennui. However, the girl is not vulgar in her manners at all, though I understand she naturally possesses a kind of unscrupulous disposition. But, indeed, one would really think, ha! ha! he takes such an extraordinary interest in her that he was really in love with her!"

The singular idea thus emitted by the female Thersites was not canvassed at all by those interested, although much blushing took place, particularly on the part of Laura, who certainly, of all, had a right to consider the intention of the lady as an insult.

After the ladies had extended their valedictory salutations and requests, and Charles's aunt and mother were left alone, there were some minutes of silence. The former was suddenly struck with a new idea in her surprise. "Can it be that he wished to enjoy over again that moment of ecstasy, and has proposed to Dinah also?"

The mother rose with a stern look, and left her sister alone. She ordered her carriage soon after, and paid a solitary visit to her pastor, Dr. Fuffles.

"—Yes, it seemed to me," continued she, in her conversation with the blushing doctor, "that I saw in that flashing eye and distended nostril the consciousness of her power; and in the suppression of that spirit, thus not altogether concealed, the depth of her artifice. Thus that very gentleness of manner and willingness of disposition by which she extends her power over those with whom she comes in contact, is to me but the mask of the hypocrite. I do not speak from prejudice; I acknowledge that she has many fine traits of character; but how natural it is that in an ambition to raise herself above her condition, how almost pardonable it is, that she should use those admirable qualities in an improper manner."

"Is it possible that you can believe that the warmth of disposition which appears in one so young is assumed? Great Heaven! what a horrible sepulchre of goodness must any heart be, that can assume a virtue for a vicious purpose. I cannot believe it in one so young!"

"Oh no. It is not that. She is by nature really of an affectionate disposition, and I think is disposed to do rightly. Only in the error of her ambition to rise above her station in life she pardons unconsciously to herself the wrong she would inflict upon others, and the artifice of the means she would thus use, in what appears to be the holiness of the aim. Her virtues are but so many misfortunes to her, for she will use them for a bad purpose. Indeed, such is the fascinating power of some elements of her character, that with all my desire to be perfectly just I have at times forgotten the shadow and see nothing but brightness. It is, alas! too true. She cannot be trusted, and is more to be feared because her artifice is so imperceptible.

She is certainly unfit to be a teacher of young children."

She paused, and leaned her head for a moment upon her hand, as if overcome with the bitterness of her thoughts. The education of rare refinement and politeness had taken out from her soul altogether the passion of anger, but in the midst of all her feelings of justice and desire to be right, something like unconscious hate for a moment took possession of her bosom. But not a shade passed over her countenance of the emotion within. It was ever the mixed expression, of regret that such were the circumstances, of compassion for the girl, and of a determination that it should be broken up.

The doctor felt that Charles's mother was always just, and guarded against doing violence to the interests of others. He knew how far-seeing her nature was, the depth of her power of perceiving character, and a conviction of the painful truth came over him. "What dark springs the human bosom contains!" said he. "If each of us had a window in our bosoms to disclose those secret springs, we would close the shutters immediately!"

CHAPTER LVI.

THE UNEXPECTED ADVERTISEMENT.

Dinah had returned from Laura's residence to the humble house by the side of the lake, where the honest colored people, with their instincts of servitude, were only too happy to constitute her as their mistress. Often did she run along into the wood, or across the fields, almost as lightly as Camilla, to meet the embrace of her lover. Often did she await with listening ear, in some bowered outpost, to the coming footfalls of his honorable step, to throw her arms about his neck. And yet on those sweet occasions of expectation, why ought not her soul to have been altogether happy? Why did she often sigh or mutter, "I will to-day or to-morrow"? It was not the bitterness of the mother's feelings towards her, for that they had talked about with a noble hope and patient resolve to win her to their happiness.

One evening they had wandered in the groves towards the lake, and sat them down upon a broad stone. There, taking her hand, he diverted the hour with a simple melody, or with what she loved better, with pompous talk about what he intended to do in the great future before them.

In his gladness he had become swollen and arrogant, consenting now and then to smile at her, and looking upon her with great benignity. The hour was still pleasant and warm for the season.

"Look at yon moonlight upon the lake through the trees," said she, musing, with her elbows on her knees, regarding the magnificent scene.

"You are a lunatic, darling, like all the rest of them," said he.

"Yes," replied she, with a short, nervous laugh. She held down her head and muttered something.

"What did you say?" asked he.

"Oh, nothing."

A pause.

"Don't you think, Charles, as I am a member of the human family, I have a right to all the common chances of happiness?" said she.

"Singular question!" thought Charles. "Eh? I don't know what you mean. You are wandering slightly, I think. You are delirious with the moon, milk-and-water girl!"

"Yes! yes! I am," cried she, suddenly arousing. "Say, Charlie, if I lived in a tree like a dryad, you would come philandering by moonlight like this, and serenade me, would you not? Come, tell me about your future."

Charles commenced to unfold his plans in reference to his proposed career as a merchant, and the wishes of his father that he should succeed him in business. He noticed, while thus talking to her, that she passed her hand over her brow, as if she were oppressed with some thought, or imagining, some indefinite feeling.

She said nothing to him in reply, and there was another pause—she again in resistless abstraction, and he somewhat puzzled at her peculiar manner. She commenced soon, however, but in a strange, disinterested way, to allude, with her youthful but clear discrimination, to the increasing honor which was becoming attached to the mercantile character. She had gotten the correct idea that, out of the circumstances of the age and the peculiar elements of American society, there was growing a noble merchant character, such as once existed in Venice and Germany, but qualified by the superior intelligence and advanced civilization of the present age. This ideal commercial character she placed with her naturally strong imagination like a thing of beauty and honor before the young man.

More and more was she becoming his idol, his very being. The sympathy between them seemed to him to be as eternal as it was natural, though sometimes he felt a presentiment that she might be torn away from him forever. He gazed at the planet, that light which every solemn spirit worships, and the indefinite fear which had taken possession of him heightened his sentiment almost to romance. She saw his agitation. Her lips rested upon his, and she gently returned his warm kisses of affection. By and by the sensible creature pretended to sleep in his arms, and to awake only as his voice heightened at the climax of his words of love; and then she pretended to conceal an embarrassment in her caresses. It is to be hoped that such tender words generally have more attentive listeners.

"Come, Harlequin, Columbine is going home," said she. She had forgotten her melancholy, and commenced to plague him.

There was no noise in the woods of winds, or birds, or of any moving thing save themselves, and they heard only the crackling of the dry fagots as they advanced slowly towards her house. What voice was that which suddenly swelled upon the still night air?

"Di—come wake up, Di!—I have come again!" it sang rather than spoke, in those tones which were now so familiar to the startled young man. The shout thus appeared to come, with an unearthly ring, from the forests away from the lake, and towards the Indian maid's fountain. The echo of the side of the lake answered once or twice in dying confusion, and then an idle, defiant whoop awoke it to further reply.

The girl clasped Charles's shoulder quickly, and stood in apparent trembling and fear, as if it were a startling summons. She cast a beseeching look into his face, and then awaited the return of the cry with a shudder.

"Heavens! What is it?" said the young man, as he heard her name thus uttered, and saw her agitation.

"Hush! hush!" said she, quickly. "He won't come here!"

They both stood still to await a renewal of the voice.

"Ha! some farmer singing a rude song to awake the echo!" said the young girl, moving.

"No! no!" denied the bewildered young man. "Heard you not—heard you not—your name, Dinah? It cried your name!"

"To the moon—to Dian—who crazes him with her effulgence," said the girl, quickly. "Come! let us go! We are half-crazed, too! Pshaw! what a fool I was to be frightened! If he does it again, we will frighten him, Charlie. I will be the goddess, and cry on the stillness my distant warning to this mortal for his temerity."

But there was no further interruption from this mysterious voice. The usual silence had resumed its reign; and they soon reached the house, as the young girl seemed to insensibly quicken her step.

Charles bade her adieu. On his way home, the silence seemed to increase; and he meditated upon the surest way of solving the mystery. He had wisely laughed with her at their being startled, but his thoughts were far otherwise than in the train which the laugh would indicate. Again the absurd idea of a relation existing between the young girl and some supernatural being took possession of his disturbed fancy.

The singularity of her character now seemed for the moment unearthly. Her connection by descent, too, with the ill-blooded race of Pompney and the murdered pioneer, that whose wilfulness of disposition in life should make him still walk the earth, was the argument of an implicit tradition. While receiving the exciting blows of his varied emotions upon his nervous system, he scarcely knew or cared whither he strayed. The singular mystery which had now become firmly attached to her character, was a cause of his restlessness and cogitation; but it checked not the movement of love as the principal in his frame. He determined to solve this mystery, and yet he had the natural fears akin to jealousy which deterred him, and thus distracted his being. Even the want of confidence, which the existence of this secret in the bosom of the girl proved to him, was enough to make him feel all the misery of that worst of passions, without the prospective enjoyment of satisfaction by vengeance. The supernatural then left him, and the old and strong theory with regard to this matter came back with corroborated force—that of her having a lover, who met her in secret, and who possessed power enough over her young nature to make her forget honor in hypocrisy, and use her bright faculties in the extraordinary cunning of a feigned passion for him, the wealthy dupe. Then the horror, the sacrilege, the impiety of these terrible thoughts seized his soul, and he felt as if some fiend was cunningly devising these circumstances to break his love and his life from Dinah. To the honor of that love, and as a proof of its purity, these feelings of distrust and suspicion, founded on extrinsic facts, failed to usurp the place of her pure character's essential influence. It is not sufficient to say he loved her still, and that he could not love her without a confidence in her purity; for he would have followed her to the end of time, were it but for her hypocrisy, so consummate it was, if it were deceit. But, independent of that love, the innate honor of her character kept its sway in his bosom.

The hypothesis that Dinah was concealing relations with Rudolph in this secret was immediately dismissed from his thoughts as untenable. Warriston had left the neighborhood and gone to Paris. Convinced of the hopelessness of a reciprocation of his passion, he had sullenly sought other scenes; for that passion conquered not the perversity of temper which made him paradoxically wound his own wishes. Or, perhaps, in thus going away, a kind of honor glimmered in his nature. He may thus have tried to atone for the baseness of his intentions towards Dinah. Indeed, before he went, he acknowledged the influence which she had over him, and which she had generously exerted to make him a better man.

Charles, upon this occasion, shook the hand of his neighbor with the warmth of a friend, though this expression was received with remnants of the accustomed sullenness.

As Charles neared the scene of the churchyard, a sense of awe again came over him, and drove away completely the base theory attached to the mystery of the voice. That sense of the supernatural, at first, was, perhaps, nothing more than the result of his reflections upon the peculiar power of the imagination, which thus played with such an airy thing as a sound; but with the stillness of the scenery reigning about him, and beneath the soft phrensy of the moon's resplendent influence, which was now hallowing tree, and spire, and tomb, the witchery of Dian's goddaughter's involuntary connection with unearthly rioting took him in trembling possession.

CHAPTER LVII.

DINAH IS TOLD THAT SHE MUST RESIGN.

JUDGE PITHKIN was weak. Dr. Fuffles, though ever reverencing the dreams of his youth, succeeded in giving to the magistrate an upright and impartial statement respecting Dinah.

"I think the mother has a juster estimate of the circumstances than the son, perhaps. It may, indeed, be the misfortune of the girl's circumstances rather than of her nature, but it is somehow improper, and indeed you know the Madame has a more fixed project of beneficence in view. She proposes to buy a little place in the West for these unfortunate people, and make them permanently happy."

"Certainly," said Mr. Pithkin, "that strikes me as correct. I have thought so frequently before this, but I must have forgotten it. I have never seen any thing improper in the girl, excepting when I was—but I believe in the re-establishment of the good old principle which holds a man guilty till he proves himself innocent. Besides that, the parish demands that my time shall not be taken up with bothering about little girls, especially as the Madame will give her a better place. That must be done, hang me, if it musn't, you know."

When the young girl heard by whose will the selectmen had been swayed, she bowed her head. Come, let us build a theory upon that simple action, of one submitted to these earthly trials. May she not have thought that the indignity and injustice was done her by one whom she wished to honor and love? Her nature may at first have been confused by feelings which were new to her bosom, except as she had felt the latent power of them, and for a while she may have stood, as it were, unprotected against herself, against the earthly possibilities of her soul. But it was a gentle feeling of injury, no doubt—an anger rather akin to grief. The thunderbolts of passion purify the atmosphere of most souls, but her anger should have been a brilliant electrical refulgence in her being. She could now be rewarded with the exquisite happiness of forgiving without injustice to herself, for the feelings of anger which she felt were experienced by her not because a wrong had been done to her, but because it had been done. She could feel a pity for her who had done it. Indeed, for a moment, a fierce pleasure takes possession of her, as she curiously wishes that it might be she who would have to atone for the wrong. Yes, were it possible she could bear upon her own shoulders the sin which had been committed against her. The Saviour taught this eternally true and thorough forgiveness, founded in comprehensive justice.

Thus apart from the feelings of her heart, receiving the approval of her intellect, it may have caused her to rise from her reflecting attitude with firmer love in her bosom for her injurer; for one whom she knew to be such only because she could not fortify herself against the fond sophistry of pride and prejudice, or see the consequent distortion of her judgment. And was this forgiveness and love, shown to Charles's mother, separated from the young girl's relation with the son? Such an energy of right could show the source whence flowed her power over others, the unreflected consciousness of a moral independence of being, the assured possession of a spiritual destiny with which no will could meddle but the one in her own bosom. If Dinah thus felt patient at being the object of an antipathy, and if to the repulsion of her warm desire to dispel it, she meekly submitted with hope, she exemplified the philosophy as well as the honor of Christianity. What are the idiotic errors of human admiration! The men of history who have most ruthlessly sacrificed the happiness of others to secure their own, are the characters that are really spoken of with the greatest awe. The frail child seemed prouder and more erect in spirit than ever.

CHAPTER LVIII.

THE FATHER.

An old merchant of New York sat in his counting-house in Pine Street. In spite of the negligent manner in which he tossed his hair, it still fell gracefully upon his forehead, and his coat, which he seemed to delight in handling roughly, unfailingly made out to vindicate its elegance. He had but then arrived from a prolonged business visit abroad, and was perusing the last epistle which his wife, sequestered amid the wheaten scenes of autumn and unconscious of his return, had sent to be forwarded to him. He looked up from the letter and called his chief clerk.

"Mr. Brown, I dislike to confide any thing to a married man, with injunctions of secrecy. It subjects him to the extreme torture of being tempted to reveal it to his wife. My dear Brown, I fear a crash, and we must protect ourselves—but there is a more painful subject to which I refer." Here he endeavored to look unconcerned, walked away into the street, and by and by returned.

"Brown, I shall go into the country this afternoon. I wish to surprise them. You probably remember, Mr. Brown, the follies and dissipation of my son Charles, while in the city here?"

"Well, sir, candidly I do not."

"How can you say that, Mr. Brown, when you know that he went to the country satiated with the extravagant follies which make up the existence of the young men of the present day?"

"Well, perhaps he did bend to a few improprieties to which youth is liable, but you know—"

"Hey, have you authority for that remark, Mr. Brown? Are you not aware that many of my friends have been accustomed to congratulate me upon his conduct as unexceptionable?"

"Yes, and I say, sir, I never had any other idea myself, but—"

"Of course, I see. It is from want of knowledge in this matter that you cannot speak. But let me tell you now of a new field of viciousness that he has entered upon. Mr. Brown, he wishes to compromise the honor of his family, and his mother's happiness and mine! My wife gives me the painful intelligence that he has become entangled in his follies even to a proposal of marriage with some person far below him, and of dishonorable reputation. Now, Mr. Brown, can you blame me if I should dismiss him forever from my presence, from my house?"

"Oh, sir! such conduct is certainly inexcusable."

"Hah! What?" continued the troubled but affectionate father, much alarmed. "Eh, do you know any thing about the young female? Have you heard any thing about his conduct in the matter that should warrant you in saying that?"

"Oh no, sir, and I could not think it possible that he would act with dishonor, but—"

"How can you defend him, Mr. Brown, in this outrage upon his parents and society? Has not his mother here written to me that he is about to become a willing victim to the intrigues of some low and artful creature, who—and that too when—but disinheritance must be his penalty, and would you not advise me, my friend, to such an act of justice?"

"Such a measure I should certainly approve, if—"

"Would you, Mr. Brown? Would you see me embitter the existence of my own offspring by driving him upon the charity of the world without friends?"

"Oh no, sir, he shall always have friends. I, myself, would—"

"No, sir. He shall not have one. He will deserve to have none, and he shall feel what it is to trifle thus idly with those that are nearest to him. But say no more, Mr. Brown, say no more. I am going to investigate it," continued he, mournfully. "I'll put on a clean shirt and go incognito. They don't expect me, and it is a good opportunity. Heavens! the folly and disobedience, and frippery of the young men of the present day!"

CHAPTER LIX.

NAT AND HIS FELLOW-PASSENGER.

Prompted by an inspiration which yet whispered hope to him, Nat had desperately sought the scenes of New York. He had heard of the power of absence, and went with the sole intention of awaking Laura's soul in melancholy and then to love, by a prolonged absence. It had lasted for four days, but unable to endure it himself any longer, he was now returning. Taking his seat in the cars, he shut down the window for composure to a melancholy revery.

"You may open that window," said a well-dressed elderly gentleman opposite him, thus manifesting the innate affability of his disposition.

"Eh, did you speak?" said Nat, somewhat surprised.

"I say you may open that window!"

"This one? Why this window? There are others open, and—"

"I want that window open," said the elderly stranger, resolutely. ("It is my duty to teach the boys of this age to respect the wants of their elders, and I commence from this moment!) Where do you stop, young man?"

"Templeville, my native heath. Name, Bonney."

"Eh! what! Do you know a family there, residing

at—let me see—Pompney Place? The young man, I believe, is an idle, dissipated—"

"No, sir. No, sir. Not at all. I know him well. That is, perhaps, he may be rather radical in his views. He smokes meaner cigars and more of 'em, for instance, than any man in the neighborhood, and he has studied more and learned less than any man of his age and standing in society, but—"

"Eh! What! Studied more and learned less?"

"I meant, to be sure, learned less and studied more. How stupid I am!"

"That is just what I told Brown," muttered the elderly gentleman. "I told Brown people thought so."

"Did you?" asked Nat. "Who is Brown; let me see, do I know him?"

"How am I able to say?" asked the other, distractedly.

"But I must say you were wrong. In fact I may say his faults are not at all the faults of intellect. However," continued the young lawyer, after a pause of apparent melancholy reflection on both sides, "whatever they are, they may, perhaps, be attributed to the example of his father, who they say is a worthless old dog. (I'll cheer him up with a little scandal. It will relieve my own feelings also, by George!")

"Eh! God bless me! What is that?" asked the other, starting. "What do they say?"

"They say that he has the misfortune to have one of the most miserable wretches for a father that ever breathed," proceeded Nat, vivaciously. "To be sure, his character does not seem to have been very badly influenced by him, but it is often remarked what he might have been had he had a respectable progenitor, or even one respectably informed, for they say his parent is as illiterate as he is unprincipled."

Nat had certainly succeeded in instituting a change in the nature of the old gentleman's feelings, for he shuddered at these words, and a cold perspiration stood upon his brow. The terrible power of scandal had never before struck him so forcibly perhaps.

"They say he is a fearfully ugly man in personal appearance," said Nat, artlessly, after a pause.

"Good! I like that. But put up the window, young man. You can put up the window. You laugh? Why merriment, sir?"

"Ha! ha! a good thing," continued Nat, recklessly. "They say he is henpecked, too, so that he cannot live with his wife at all. He certainly has not been up there since they have come to live at the Place."

("Oh, I feel as if this were more than I should be called upon by fate to endure! I have a good mind to swear. I could damn something,") said the other, turning away violently to look out of the window, and muttering an indistinct ejaculation.

"Heavens! what have I said?" asked Nat internally, seized with a sudden remorse. "But I don't believe it, sir, I don't believe it, at least the last particular. The others, perhaps, may be true," continued he, aloud. "You see, I heard them in Templeville, and I considered it my duty to reissue them with the usual improvements, ha! ha! Confound it, a man has a right to repeat any thing he hears, derogatory of his rival's relatives, at least. There is some power, however, which won't permit me to do it without taking it all back, hang it," continued the ardent young lover, gloomily.

"What! your rival?"

"He is my rival, and chiefly the fine effect of his quiet, gentlemanly ways is overpowering, and his presence caused by a very fine mustache, you know—"

"Oh, pshaw! Let him have it off. (What is this! This young man, too, mad upon the same subject, and for the same cunning, intriguing object. The folly and frippery of young men, nowadays. Heavens! However keep cool and extricate them both.) Young man, I know that young girl better than you do. Why, why should you wish foolishly to wed a girl who in the first place hasn't a cent in the world, and in the second place—"

"That is the worst of it," said Nat, gloomily. "Why, her expectations are immense, sir, while the only expectation I have is that she won't have me."

"Oh she has been deceiving you, young man. She hasn't a cent. Not a cent, sir. The ill-founded expectations she had are vanished. She hasn't a cent, and never will have, sir, I know it."

"Oh, are you sure? Hurrah!" cried Nat, spiritedly; "now I must have her, I must and will have her."

("He appears to be insane. It is useless to try to rescue him, and as that is the case, it is my duty to employ him at once in rescuing Charles. Certainly.) You persist, young man? Well, I can help you. I am now going there, and I have no doubt I can bring it about. Yes, I can and I will, if you say so."

"Oh, if you could but approach Miss Wellwood in this delicate matter and—"

"What?" said the elderly gentleman, suddenly losing his entire propriety of demeanor. "I can't, sir, and what is more, I shan't. How dare you ask me to do it? How dare you?"

("Well!" said the slightly astonished Nat, "I have an idea that he is inclined to be unhappy and contradictory at times. First he wished to have the windows open, and then to have them shut. Now he volunteers his aid to me, and immediately afterwards changes his mind even into rage. Oh, I will decline his assistance.) Very well, very well. The important fact which you have given me that she is not wealthy is sufficient, and—"

"Not wealthy! not wealthy, sir! What do you mean?" said the other, who had loosely surrendered himself to his increasing irritation. "She has a million if she has a cent. Oh, pshaw!"

("There he is again. Confound me if I say another word to him. I'll leave him alone with his perversity. He's becoming really ugly.") And although thereafter, the elderly gentleman hunted for him at various periods during the journey, under a strong desire to renew their conversation, it was not until they reached Templeville that Nat emerged from among the trunks in the baggage car, where he had smoked and thought himself into a frenzy.

CHAPTER LX.

CHARLES'S FATHER AT HOME.

The meeting between Charles's father and his mother was very affecting, as also between Charles himself and his returned parent. All the hopes and fears, even the present happiness, of that couple were centred in his, and thus the unpromising aspect of business which they were forced to consider was carefully kept for a while from his thought, and indeed any allusions to his unhappy and irritating entanglement with his humble friend, his father refrained from making before his obstinate will. Though just anger was in their bosoms for that which only seemed ingratitude for their care, the hope of the ephemerality of his infatuation repressed it. Now more than ever did his union with Laura seem their chief and immediate aim. Laura's father was a frequent adviser upon the subject of business, and the result of their conferences was a bent unison upon the immediate necessity of a union of the two families.

The mother still kept her cool and unruffled exterior, and carefully guarded the anxiety and unhappiness of the father from displaying itself to the son, and the unconscious Charles thought he saw the time was coming when she would relent to his love.

The father was judicious enough to go no farther than a slight reference to the matter, showing a half-considered incredulity, although it annihilated now his inmost and most passionate wishes. Even Charles's aunt kept her estimation of his conduct apart. On one occasion, however, she asked him very naively if he had proposed, endeavoring to draw him out by alluding to proposals in general as being good things. His singular conduct on that occasion led her to believe more than ever that it was of no use. She now had a presentiment that he could not be made to marry Laura, just as strong as the one in which she foresaw her own union with Pithkin. She kept it locked in her own bosom, however. During these days, Squire Wellwood was constantly with his old friend, Charles's father, and commenced and left unfinished as many as two hundred anecdotes, about one hundred and fifty of which Nat was doomed to listen to, as he dined frequently at one house or the other. On discovering the identity of his late fellow-passenger, Nat had neutralized, with prompt sagacity and by a most brilliant manœuvre, the discovery which he had made to him of his secret love for Miss Wellwood. Ere it was recalled to memory, indeed, by the parent in his distraction, the intrigue-loving aunt alluded to the strategic arrangement which she had made with the young lawyer, and by which he was to enact the part of rival. And the predilection which the old gentleman had experienced from the commencement for him was now being freely developed.

In the many argumentations with which the elders beguiled themselves upon subjects of a political or religious nature, they were continually contradicting each other. Laura's father, under an unusual pressure of feeling, tried to play off excessive coldness and politeness of demeanor at first, but finding it very laborious and unsuccessful, gracefully returned to his former manner. It was also quite a common occurrence with Nat, to see Charles's father in his temporary irritation giving up to an uncharacteristic rage, and crying out to the old squire, "Now keep cool, you've lost your temper;" or at the conclusion of some story, to hear him say, "Indeed that may be interesting, but the story I told was true!" Or to observe him carelessly requesting the other to produce proofs of his tales, more excruciating in their invention than the narratives themselves. On one occasion, when Judge Pithkin and Dr. Fuffles were present, the young lawyer saw all four of these gentlemen in a rage at once, which he thought was the most unique scene he had ever witnessed.

But the argumentation between the two parents was the most exemplary species of social intercourse Nat thought he had ever witnessed, and he impartially assisted both parties, invariably urging them to the verge of infuriation by taking sides with the one most in the wrong.

"If you will just listen to what I have to say," Charles's father, a prey to his continual irritation, would remark, "and will admit the reasons I've advanced, you will see there is nothing for you to say."

Whereupon Nat would immediately add, "In fact, no reply can be made to that at least."

Or Laura's parent would gasp out, "But all I want at this moment is—don't go out of the question—which is that you are wrong and I am right."

"Certainly a philosophic and pertinent statement of the subject," interposes Nat, encouragingly.

CHAPTER LXI.

THE TARDY REPARATION.

The next day after Charles's visit to Dinah, his father had arrived at the place, and in the natural flow of filial gladness the day was passed by the son; but when the evening came, and the hour brought over his soul a renewal of yesterday night's feelings, he seized a proper opportunity to seek the side of Dinah for a short hour.

Again the bright moonlight, the stillness of the woods, and the beating heart perplexed with doubt and shadowy misgivings. He soon reached her threshold. It was the early hour of nine. Dinah was absent from home. The colored lady looked at the young man inquiringly. She had supposed that her young mistress was taking the usual pleasant walk with him by the lake or through the grove. Charles said carelessly that he would tarry a little while.

"Oh, yes! maybe she's gone to Missus Wellwood's, Mas'r Charles. She isn't afraid; she often goes out in these yer woods alone! She likes the woods, and trees, and flowers, and those yer things, 'specially at night!"

Charles held his peace. Suspicions of increasing weight pressed upon his heart, and it seemed as though the cold state of inanimation were coming over it. He soon made an effort, however. Wisely unwilling to alarm the occupants of her home, by suggesting fears of insecurity from such habits, he manufactured upon the spot an ingenuous air which should be reported to his darling with the fact of his call, which had been unexpected, perhaps, from a knowledge of his father's arrival. As he did not wish, upon that evening, to be noticeably absent from his own hearthstone, he returned to its side, and sought to drown his care in the social specialities of blood relationship. But his care increased in power as the hours wore away, and even when the rest of the house were buried in sleep, he sat at his window, peering foolishly into the woods and the sky, and longing to unlock from somewhere—from the air—the secret, the existence of which was annoying him with the presentiment of future misery. The hour was about the same as the noticeable one of yesternight. The moon shone with the same monotonous lustre; the small, ragged clouds hung around almost in the same spots, and the unwelcome breeze had the same chilling power. Misery appeared in the elements of the landscape, and his heart's grief was beginning to tarnish the outer world. Yes—the hour, the scene, the unhappiness were the same as when the corroding suspicion broke over his love, and he would rise and seek Dinah's side, and ask her to take away this disorder from his pulses. He would beg her for that confidence, without which his brains would be good for nothing to make him happiness in the future. Yes, she would show him the honor of her past concealment, and—Heavens! what a cry! It was dull from the distance, but like a dying cry, enamelled with the namby-pamby romance of his cursed imagination. His heart leaped towards the depths of the park, for "Charles!" he heard his own name in a clearer way. It was a small tone from the distance; but the solemnity as of despairing reliance upon the power of his name against evil, struck him with exalted fury, for it was uttered in the well-known and beloved tones of his darling!

"Charles! Charles! Oh, come!" quickly cried that voice again, and then broke off abruptly, as if this cry for his aid had been instinctive, and its desperation had struck the anguished utterer to fatal silence.

The young man did not surrender his being to a moment's bewilderment, though, if a phantom were then deluding him with a mocking cry to the shadowy halls of another existence, he would have chased her in his pity to the discordant gates; but it was love that lent him sagacity. In the groves of the park, upon a certain dark patch made in the pale flood by a broad-spreading and prominent elm, the merry men and elves had stopped their dance; affrighted, some had fled, while others cowered in an adjacent place. What beings of violence and wrong were they who had come there to usurp the green ring of the little fairies' peace-honoring festivity? As Charles reached this spot, with a faithful memory of whence came that heart-striking appeal, he saw lying upon the grass a young man, enfeebled with a bloody wound—a tall, lithe form; and while the beauty of the countenance, amid the stupidity and pallor of the ghastly sickness, failed not to manifest itself, those features, which the observer well remembered to have seen in the graveyard, struck him, now more determinedly, with their resemblance to the traditional lineaments of the old pioneer. Over them was bent a woman's form.

"Oh! Guy, Guy, darling!" cried she; yet it was in despair; and she convulsively raised his languid head and placed it upon her arm. She turned her face away as if in wretchedness, too, and the young lover saw, indeed, the lines of earthly beauty which he had loved to trace upon a beloved face. He ran to her side. The look which she had bestowed upon his approach was not of some unearthly being's unconsciousness of his presence, but the steady appeal for aid from his well-known hands in behalf of earthly anguish.

A thought of some tragic culmination of human passion and suffering, superior to the rubbish of his imagination, thrilled his heart. He lifted the form of the prostrate man, and held his drooping head against his own bosom, as the young girl, while pressing her robe against a stanchless wound, uttered the sorrow-stricken, revealing words: "Oh, Guy, my brother, what madness was in your brain? Heaven! it is too late to save him!"

The wounded brother revived, and Iris waited for a moment by command of the justice-loving gods, ere she cut loose his soul. With an effort he raised his form to an erecter posture, and, with singular gaze and outstretched arms, fiercely exclaimed: "A disgrace to life, I have got my deserts from my own hand!" The tones faltered, and then rose again. "Father, father—Dinah, save his honor from my cowardly guilt!" One alone of all those to whom he wished to tell the secret, shuddered as the hale command came from the sinking man's lungs with the momentary energy of absent delirium and recovered virtue. His head fell back, and, as he looked towards the sky, Charles saw that the traces of bad passions were gone from his face, and something of his sister's soft look was appearing there.

CHAPTER LXII.

THE CRIMINAL BROTHER'S WRONG.

When the sombre effect of the stranger's self-sought death had relaxed its sway over Charles's heart, it was with deep surprise that he reflected upon the fact that, for the first time in his intimate intercourse with her, Dinah had now pronounced the familiar name of "brother."

Amid the confusion and excitement which naturally attended the discovery, first to his own household, and then to the neighborhood, of the committal of such a fatal deed with its immediate circumstances, and in deference to the profound grief of the father and sister of the unhappy suicide, Charles repressed his desire of an explanation of the mystery attending the event, and resolved to await an appropriate time therefor, after the usual judicial investigation had taken place, and the sad valediction of interment was rendered to the remains.

The removal of the inanimate form by Charles's domestics from the park to the humble cottage by the lake, there to lie for a brief period amid the honor of a home, was the commencement of an aged father's anguish which lasted through many days. But the hours of consolation which the daughter devoted to that grief were not expended without the gratification of her pious wish, for she soon saw it change its form, and saw his tears flow but as those of humble resignation to the will of Providence. It was now that she exposed to Charles's sympathy the past history of her unfortunate brother. Her looks of varied emotions so well interpreted by Charles, perfected with appropriate adornment a terse recital, for she seemed indisposed to dwell long upon the retrospection of the hours of misery her brother had passed through, and of sorrow which he had caused for others.

Seated in her humble parlor by her lover's side, she recapitulated in low tones and with a smile of affection the life of her parents in their early days and their attachment; her father's gentle manners, and disposition towards letters; and her mother's wildness of love. But she changed her manner to a rapid rehearsal as she was forced to mention their subsequent misfortunes, commencing with her grandfather's displeasure and proceeding through his bankruptcy and dotage, towards his death in their poverty-stricken household. After this, the facts in her personal narrative were of a nature which made her blush for one whose portrait still hung next to a heart beating with kindred affection. Though she mentioned them not, Charles felt the hours of sorrow upon the part of the upright father and the too fond mother, as they watched that son's wilful career, and saw his blindness to the selfish cruelty of his life.

Whilst poverty daily scattered with her skinny fingers their hard-earned pittance, crime had been beckoning him with her false allurements to follow her. The gratification of his personal desires had been his business, the procuration of the means he seemed to think the business of his friends. The gambler's unholy trade, and the accompanying bowl, were great helps in the march from mere self-indulgence to infamy. One day, and Providence, kindly for all, ordered that it should be after the death of the too affectionate mother, the horror came. Sunk to a degradation which took away even his manliness, he had become not the dupe, but the creature of creatures, male and female; and this too, ere the fresh hue of youth was robbed of its early bloom. And yet at times those fits of repentance, those tears of bitterness, when he would seek the hearth side of his home, had seemed to give evidence that his degradation was a result only of the wilfulness of the Pompney blood, joined with destitution of circumstances, and did not usurp entirely his being. But the virtuous characteristics of the father and mother descended to him, were subordinate to this monstrous impelling power of his character, which drove him back continually to his old courses of vice. The longings of vengeance and the promptings of rage against peers in vice, in the ceaseless and necessary quarrelling which constitutes a part of such wicked scenes, filled up his bosom from day to day when it was unoccupied with greed or lower sensuality. The father occupied the moments undevoted to the battle against poverty, in stern endeavors to rescue his offspring. Aye, even while bending his form in the humble employment of sweeping the streets, he was forced to occupy a mind, educated for refinement, with dubious plans for his son's future; to submit a heart, made for love and affection, to bitterness and anger against his blood. He soon lost his lowly position; his patron, a political wretch, was forced to visit the State's prison for a term of years. Soon after this the mother died.

Dinah paused in her narrative and bowed her head. A few sacred moments were devoted by her to the cherished memory of her beloved mother. As Charles saw those filial tears trickle upon her cheek, his heart melted in sharing the honor of their presence, and he turned his face in instinctive reverence towards heaven.

The moment was come when she had to repeat the story of her family's dishonor. Guy forged the endorsement of a person in whose service, at various periods, his father's penmanship had been extraordinarily employed. It was in the precedented, though exaggerated form of a note by the latter, anticipatory of his salary, whose reverend name and honest shifts, with the recklessness of honor, which characterizes the novice in crime, he had thus also impiously counterfeited. But indeed his cruelty was not yet so mean, as to cause him thus to deliberately expose his father. No; the circumstances were such as to lend to the guilty son's consideration of the transaction, the hope, not uncommon as an element in such deeds, of successfully covering the crime ere it was detected. The note was successfully negotiated through specious falsehood. The hour of its payment came. In the confusion of honor the father acknowledged it. He had hoarded a few dollars, with the fond hope of removing with his offspring and the remains of his wife, to the scenes of his glad boyhood. These in partial payment delayed the exposure by protest, but ere the recreant son could be found, it came, and the unhappy parent permitted himself to be incarcerated upon the terrible charge. Yes, it was not until he was seated in the prisoner's box, that his sense of justice and his duty to his dear daughter overcame the distracting wish to save the son at his own honor and liberty's expense. From that degraded seat he sternly proclaimed aloud that he was innocent, and that his own offspring was the malefactor. The accustomed indifference of the attorneys to such declarations was manifested then, and with the usual jocose allusions to the cunning of shifting the burden to one who was beyond the pale of justice, procured his conviction by the jury, although the penitence which he had manifested in returning part of the ill-gotten money was recommended to them by the judge.

Guy had now absconded from the face of the law and the stern love of justice of his father, with the ready belief that, while the latter could clear his parent's honor in a statement of the truth, he, the real victim, would escape in his flight, the punishment due him from the former. But even when he heard in his retreat of the blow of dishonor inflicted thus meanly upon his own father, he delayed from day to day to approach and sacrifice his own liberty. Soon he heard of his father's pardon, and then more than ever he lingered. Night by night he plunged in the crazed crowds of degradation and dissipation for temporary relief from the stings of shame. And he succeeded; the deed was done; the sacrifice was a thing of the past. New alliances with crime in more degraded rounds were productive to him of immediate excitement. Shame was leaving his bosom altogether, and he became an object of suspicion to the police of the distant western city to which he had fled. His father disowned him from the period of his conviction of his impiety, and sternly prayed that his name should not be mentioned to him again, but with purification by his active penance or his death.

As Obadiah Baylon's name at this point fell from the lips of the pure young girl, Charles started with vehemence and anticipatory anger. He seemed to feel it was necessarily receiving an honor that it did not merit.

The overseer of Warriston's property in obedience to his natural disposition, perhaps idly, was one day examining the records of the young man's possessions, when the spiritual master he served placed before his evil nature the flaw in the record of the original Pompney deed. With the cunning and secrecy of one to whom cunning and secrecy are always loved means, he soon discovered the true circumstances of the case. He remembered that his former master, Rudolph's uncle, had often spoken in drunken jest of the cause of Pompney's latter eccentricities, lying in the fact that his wild hoyden daughter home for the holidays from her French boarding-school had married his valet. The estate was still in Pompney's heirs, and heirs perhaps were still in living line. He traced in hope that line through a long time and wide space, and found the father emerged from a felon's residence. The children were the heirs, and while he loaned the father money to pay the criminal debt and to remove to Templeville, he smiled upon the daughter, and through his former companions in dissipation discovered the abiding place of the son.

Guy was the fitted agent for his machinations. He caused him to believe that he was a rich man, and entered into a secret compact with him to share his coming estate for putting him in possession thereof. Under the terror of the law for a new pecuniary offence, the wretched young man readily consented to the proposition of Baylon, that he should sink his existence in oblivion until such time as those difficulties could be settled, and circumstances should be ready for him and his sister to come forward and lay claim to the estate. Those circumstances lay wholly in the necessity of the abstraction of the original deed from the depository of Charles's family, in which he had discovered it existed, and, by a strategic production therefrom, and a discreet inspection, had also discovered a correctness in its details fatal to his eager expectancy.

Aware of the stern sense of duty of the father, which still manifested itself amid the evidences of a declining spirit, Baylon wisely refrained from developing his plan to him. The young girl was a necessary party, and her mind was to be prepared, through her brother, to sustain her part as claimant. Thus, when Guy was carefully brought up to the neighborhood of Pompney Place, and secreted in the old hut in the woods, he was secure from the police and the opposition of the father, and adjacent to his sister, who would give him her loving aid, while he should rejoice her with the prospect of future wealth and happiness.

The misery of the wretched young man was so profound, the degradation of his servility to Baylon so shameful and irresistible, that the sister kept the secret of his proximity from the suffering heart of the father, until an amelioration should take place in the wretched young man's condition, which she would strive to produce. It was during this period that the delirium of his excess at times renewed itself, invariably possessing the elements of a sorrowing desire to see his mother, and a fearing aversion for his father. It was the natural result of his education; for it said that, in this delirium, the mind seeks for protection against imagined foes, from those they most love; and it was his mother who fondly shielded him from punishment, from the sternness of the father, which constituted him, on the other hand, as the imaginary enemy. The filial awe and reverence was erected into fear, and the imagined enemy of delirious wickedness would naturally be such. The father had manifested his feelings to his son, not by blows, but by sorrowful looks and words of principle; and such punishment of the young man's soul was reinforced by the blow of dishonor which he knew that he had given his parent, reacting upon his own conscïence; though it was no longer able to rescue him from a slavery of habits and of thought, which prevented his atonement of that bitter wrong.

On the occasion of Charles's dream, then, the wretched brother, being in the wood and hiding from the presence of men, wandered in semi-aberration to Dinah, but still in the cunning of his fear of approaching his father, seeking her with a secret call. It was late. Knowing the power of her father's name to keep him quiet, she resolved to conceal him in her room until early daylight, and then return with him to his hiding-place. To beguile his thoughts, she diverted them to the channel into which they easily flowed, and told him such facts as she had learned of her father, about her mother's young life in that very house, her favorite room, and its romance. Physically wearied, and her young soul, too, seeking relief, she fell asleep when he began to rest. She awoke to find him absent, and glided quickly down-stairs. In the corridor, as she was attracted by the noise of the cat, she bethought herself of her mother's room at the distant end. He had indeed sought it, and she discovered him seated there in fortunate quiet, produced by the sorrow of his hallucination. Charles recalled her motionless attitude of circumspection, and reflected upon the curious though natural working of his brain, which had transformed this reality into a romance. She led her brother away to the room above, and stopped his inquiry by an appeal to her father's name; and while they two stood motionless upon the staircase above, Charles sought the halls below. While the young man now remembered the wild feelings which followed the belief that he had experienced a supernatural vision of the past, he was beginning to feel emotions which were deeper, sadder, and more romantic even than they.

Although the sister warned Guy not to come from his secrecy in the hours of daylight, he at times appeared recklessly in places to which his excited fancy drove him. Thus, after high-wrought conversations with Baylon, he would visit the scene of his possessions, and view it from the park, or from prominent points in the adjacent landscape. Upon one occasion, puffed up with his prospective affluence, and mad with liquor, he proposed to himself to visit a scene of festivity in the village, (to which Baylon had referred in his presence,) proudly conscious that he was of the Pompney blood, and better than all of them, despite his rags! Baylon met him emerging from his hiding-place at evening, and after useless dissuasion, received with violence, sought the aid of Dinah's influence. Interrupted by Mrs. Norcomb, she quickly assigned a place of meeting in the town with Baylon, and thus reached the festive gardens before him.

"I soon searched and found my brother there, secluded amid the foliage of the park, and afraid to go into the hall. Still, when I strove to urge him away, he attacked me with—with bitterness, and said I was ashamed of my blood. At last I reached Obadiah, with whom, after a while, Guy consented to go away, as he was wearied with the rain and the darkness."

"By the double power of threats of delivering Guy to the police, and appeals to my friendship, Obadiah hoped to manage me, even after he saw that I was opposed to his apparent professions of interest. I had not yet learned the secret of the existence of the truthful deed, although he had confided to me, as well as to Guy, a knowledge of the defective record. He soon discovered that his scheme seemed to me, even under those circumstances, an outrage; for I plainly proposed that Guy and I should transfer our right, if any should appear to exist, to those who had given a value for the property, and should not be subjected to pecuniary annoyance from a technicality of the letter. He threatened Guy's exposure in answer to this, and commenced his attempt to drive me from your honorable mansion, and from the support in my opposition to him, which I would be gaining in resting there. His power was sufficient to keep me silent, and I waited from day to day for a brighter hour, when I might relieve my brother from his fatal position. The money I then received from Mrs. Norcomb, I felt easily justified in taking from her, for it was for a good cause. One element of Obadiah's power over us I lessened by it."

"With Guy I passed many bitter hours, for his mind was thoroughly abased to his wicked friend's plans. Still I watched him with all the care I could bestow upon him. I met him at night, and rowed about upon the pleasant lake, or walked with him in the woods; and when I could refrain from entreating him to rouse and free himself from the horrible snares about him, I endeavored to insinuate into his wishes promises of happiness from a virtuous future. But it was in vain. Urged by Baylon, who saw it could be an easy matter, in spite of Guy's reckless habits of dissipation, and a safe one for himself, Guy attempted to abstract—to steal the deed from the cabinet. From some angered remarks, defiantly uttered in partial intoxication, I had been forewarned by his own wilful lips of an indefinite horror of this nature. I watched, and he came in a still hour of the night. I prevented the perpetration of this additional crime by the hands of my brother, but he was mad—he was delirious with wine and evil thoughts! He wounded me as I resisted him. Oh, Guy, my brother!"—She paused. "No, no, he could not have been so base, he could not have meant it, with all his frenzy and anger!"

"Obadiah had absented himself from prudence, or in pleasing expectation. I had often before this, and especially when your dear kindness sought for my confidence, longed to reveal to you the troubles which were upon us; for, in spite of the fears that Baylon might forge some successful counter-tale, I felt," continued she, blushing while she attempted to conceal with a pleasantry the existence of her love at that period, "I felt that one who was not remarkable for saying any thing worth listening to, Charlie, ought to possess the opposite virtue, at least, of discreetly managing a secret. But now I felt it to be my duty towards you and your family to tell the story of our shame. While I delayed, from day to day, the consciousness that I was each moment hiding a wrong haunted me. But still, the thought of the threats of Obadiah, the annihilation of hopes of Guy's reformation by his exposure, and my father's coming anguish, deterred me. Charles, was I right? I was young; my judgment may have been disturbed by my heart; but wasn't I—wasn't I right?"

When Charles saw this young girl pleading for his decision to sustain her own delicate sense of her behavior, he felt as though he would have died to take back his past. He now saw that her confusion and distraction, which in his blindness, upon the day before her dismissal from the house, he had taken to be an acknowledgment of guilt, was distraction caused by her very honor, by a distracted desire to protect her father and brother, and yet the interests of her employer. He turned away in self-shame. Dinah said naught respecting that occasion, and at this point, as she noticed his manner, she cast a melting look into his eyes, and rising, threw her arms about his neck and kissed his lips.

"Obadiah now threatened to deliver up Guy, if I disclosed a word respecting the deed. My threats, in return, of criminating him were of small avail, but I still thought by secrecy to save my father from wretchedness, to free my brother from his voluntary submission to Baylon's influence. Obadiah had still hope of obtaining the deed after Guy's attempt, either by taking away my power by dismissal, or through Guy's interference with my resolve. A month elapsed. I had paid him the remainder of his debt with the money which you gave me, and when I resolved to take the additional sum which your kindness, dear friend, offered to our poverty, it was with the resolve to tell you as much of the hidden fact as should protect your interests. I clothed Guy in a new suit of clothes. I had revealed the secret to one friend alone, the faithful colored girl, Judith, and she had assisted me in attending to Guy's wants in the old charcoal-burner's deserted hut, which successfully served as his refuge from the unusual facilities for detection of the present day. But at this period she went away to Canada."

"I now defied the wickedness of Obadiah. In the midst of his anger, he knew that I had a powerful and believing friend in you, and soon also became frightened with the fear that I might interfere with his relations with his employer. Indeed, he saw that a divulgement of Guy's presence would only be an act of revenge which would injure himself as well as our family. But with the sight of money, Guy appeared to brighten up from his sullied degradation. Instead of abuse uttered against those whom he said were his persecutors, he quietly acceded to my proposition, that as much money as we could spare should be devoted to refunding the money of false pretence, for which he had become legally amenable. He seemed, indeed, to be resisting his own habits, and to be awakening to the true character of Obadiah. With fitful bravery he even proposed to make the requital to father, by offering himself now to the course of the law. But while he cried and persisted in promising it to his honor, he shuddered, more perhaps at his own shame, than from any prospect of losing his liberty. He wished, at least ere he saw his father, to venture to his friends in Rochester, who would assist him, he said, and in answer to my entreaties and opposition, he chided me with bitter taunts of a want of love. I foolishly permitted him to go. Perhaps I could not have helped it. I may not have done better."

"It was but the other night, even while a conviction

of his continued degradation, prophetic of his future, pressed upon my happiness, that he announced his return in the eccentric tones of intemperance, and I started from your side in fear of a new flight by him from the consequences of crime. I took him that night to our home, to his injured father's presence, who bent over him in forgiveness. The excesses of a delirious life had permanently maddened his nature. Remorse and wild defiant hope shared possession of him after that interview. He insisted upon proudly seeing the rightful possessions of his mother, and there he—Charles, darling, I kept the secret of his dishonor from you, from the world, until I might save him from his habits, but it was too late—it was too late! Yet when my father looked upon his face so much like dear mother's, he had been spared the—the—"

Charles sought to wipe away the tears from her eyes, and held her hand in honoring silence. He would fain then occupy his mind with an approving contemplation of her judgment in guarding the sorrowful secret, for her self-denial, thus shown to be so noble in its unconscious bravery, pained his bosom with a fear that he was unworthy of one who could possess such.

CHAPTER LXIII.

THE MOTHER VISITS DINAH.

The community was aroused to an unusual excitement, both by the promulgation of the event and the subsequent knowledge of the past history of the unfortunate young man. But after a judicial examination of the affair and the nine days were elapsed, it became the cause of but common-place emotions in the neighboring mind. The usual compassionate horror was shown for the rash deed by which he deprived himself of earthly existence, but a virtuous indignation at the life of dissipation which it ended, soon usurped its place.

Though the father would have had the secret of his son's dishonor buried with his mortal being, the facts elicited from Charles, as the witness of his death, were necessarily followed by an exposition of the boy's life of guilt and dissipation ; and above all, of the crime of impiety of which he had been guilty. While many a bosom swelled with sympathy for the aged man who had thus been obliged to bear the cross of social expiation for his offspring, the discussion of the circumstances often relieved pity of its force in producing the argument of parental shiftlessness and neglect of training.

Charles had ere this exerted himself to remove the imputation which had rested upon Dinah's own character, in connection with the midnight occurrence in the library of his house, by making use of the mere palliative plea of a natural curiosity on her part to examine ancestral papers. But the believing or unbelieving minds of those who had been cognizant of that event and of the subsequent trial, nevertheless contained a prejudice against her, great enough to corroborate their comprehensive conclusion, that the family, though of respectable derivation on one side, had sunk into a kind of social recklessness and degradation with the weight of poverty. And now, besides the repugnance of Dinah's feelings as a sister to the publication of that event as a criminal attempt of her brother's, the knowledge of the eccentric instincts of human nature in the mass would have been enough perhaps to deter Charles therefrom. Dinah, at least, well knew that a greater stain would in all probability come upon her thus indirectly than the one she now bore from the public misapprehension, lying either in the addition to the atrocity of Guy's character, or in her wrongful attempt to shield him in his crimes from lawful punishment.

This was indeed the weaker stuff made of human prejudice and inevitable circumstance, which time might possibly unravel. The supposed wrongs inflicted upon society by the parent had been required as a foundation, too, for the character of unreliability and moral recklessness, into which this woof of imputation, made by Dinah's attempt to rescue her brother from misery, had been worked, chiefly perhaps, by the antipathetic but self-justified measures of Charles's mother. But in the incessant weaving of popular opinion, human nature did not fail in the firm reconstruction of this prejudice, rendered necessary by the late events, and in spite of a certain amount of honor which was acknowledged to be attached to them. The brother's wickedness, at least, was rightful material to be used.

Time wore away. The recital of Dinah had filled Charles with feelings which he would not profane by anger in her presence, for her manner taught him something of that spirit which is the quintessence of womanliness, akin to an angelic nature. When he recounted that narrative of honor to his mother, her love for her offspring and her pride of heart received rude blows from his impulsive work, though she saw his filial respect. The honor which he paid his theme was the source of her self-shame, and even if he made no angry mention, as he once had, of the deeds of her active antipathy, she well knew that they lent energy to his earnest appeal to admire, to love the young girl. Her admiration she gave, for it was by the cold command of her intellect; but no love yet warmed her heart for one who, though sincere and honorable, was still a stumbling block of fate in the path of her child's future. What was this recital to her, after her pity recovered its balance, but a change in the form of the social degradation which was attached to the girl's name.

Yes, while the memory of the son and brother seemed more sullying than any thing before, perhaps the father's innocence and the child's heroism were outbalanced in her mind simply by a prophetic thought of the sneer with which society would hear of their self-told virtue; the unspoken accusation that they were willing to comparatively hide their own disrepute by blackening the character of their suicide, unanswering relative.

Recent events connected with the financial condition of her family fortified her inclinations with a sense of duty, and while Charles sternly discussed the proper methods of effectually punishing the scoundrel, Baylon, or observed with pleasure the degree of respect which was paid, amid the natural flow of social intercourse, in his father's household, to his sympathy with Dinah's sorrow, his mother thought in secret in another way.

She saw, indeed, that it remained only to appeal to the young girl to save her son from what she would have deemed a dishonor to him, even were it not a misfortune. She rose in energy, and ordering her carriage drove to the humble cottage in which Dinah lived, at an hour when her son was not there.

Her manner upon this visit would have led one to designate her going and coming as a stealing to and away from the house. Were those two beings who met on this occasion equals, or which was the superior and to whom was owed the courteous bow? They were both actuated by their love for one object, although the blush upon Dinah's face would have revealed another, had not its object's moral vision been blinded by the darkness of a mother's pride.

With all the energy of her last hope, she commenced to appeal in sincere and heart-felt tones to the girl to give up her son. She would confess the bitter infatuation of his passionate nature, which would lead him even to sacrifice the future happiness of his parents and his own to its temporary sway. A smile, almost of scorn, passed over her listener's face, as she suggested the evanescence of her son's passion. She might fondly wish to believe that his love was not eternal, but Dinah deemed she possessed no right to use this thought as a means to her end, however justifiable the latter may have been. Surely it was not her love for her son which prompted her here, but the erring weakness, the wilful harshness of her pride, which refused to concede even that he loved Dinah, for she seemed sincere. She touched delicately, however, upon the position of Dinah, which resulted from the criminal stain upon her family, and perhaps she might have been spared the unhappiness of recapitulating the various evil results which would flow therefrom upon the future of her son, in the event of this misalliance; for how often had her young listener gone wearily over the same imagined ground, and how often had she stopped at bitter conclusions before her.

But the mother proceeded to allude to the natural centralization in Charles, of all the hopes which animated her breast and that of his father; the hope of an honorable future for him; a high, irreproachable station in society, doing good to himself and the world through the dignity of his position. She then referred to the prospective state of his circumstances, should she not release him from his infatuation but carry it to a union. He would be estranged forever from his parents and their love. How could it be righteously otherwise, when they saw the return for their years of care and anxiety, an insensate, selfish blasting of their only hopes? Should they not rightly drive him from their doors for the selfish gratification of his passion? Though her listener cared not defiantly to discuss this question, she saw the consequent misery which would be felt by Charles, were such a measure executed.

The mother then proceeded to refer to the unwritten laws which society enforces with perhaps more rigidity than its written ones. However harsh and unjust it might seem that the sins of an individual should be visited upon the reputation and social standing of his innocent kin, it was nevertheless true that they were; and no matter how high-spirited the victim of atonement might be, he had to succumb. Society knew nothing about the atoning features of the criminal aspect of their reputations. Charles and his children would have to bear the quiet taunt of society at his marriage with the near relative of a criminal, though he furiously denied its right to utter that taunt. Society would regard his right to its respect for the purity of his love, only so far as that right did not interfere with its own. And in another way would society punish him, (reasoned she, earnestly.) It would punish him for his selfish sacrifice of his parents' happiness to his own; for, with its unfailing severity of logic, it would reflect that he had no right to force upon them the consequences of a stained alliance, though he himself might be willing to bear the spot. Though his parents were wrong in every other way, they here had a right which society would sustain them in. Society (continued she) would also visit evil consequences upon him in return for the impaired usefulness of career which would probably be the result of this marriage. And in this manner, while unfolding various cross relations of the rights and duties of Charles, his parents and society, she did not fail at the conclusion of each consideration to show the evil consequence which would result to her son.

If Dinah then banished from her mind the consideration of these bitter and truthful conclusions as no matter of conscience for her, she well knew her love could not fill up these shortcomings in his happiness; for what would be its power over him when he had to bear all these sacrifices, and knew that she had deliberately and selfishly called for them?

"But am I not wronging his love, and will not my love be a compensation for all" cried she, in her distraction.

The mother now said that it was not her intention to force Charles by any threats of disinheritance, nor would she now appeal for their own feelings, but only for Charles's future they thought to oppose his union with her. While she spoke, an agitation which she could not control seemed suddenly to seize her, and in a low tone she spoke with hesitation of a point which she had hitherto concealed. She had not referred at all, upon the present occasion, to the ardent desire which she had long had, that a union should take place between her son and the daughter of her neighbor, Wellwood; and now, when she brought up the subject of that union, she did not produce her desire therefor, as a subject for Dinah's consideration, but stated with much confusion and abashment that the marriage between Charles and Laura had now become a matter of necessity to his future. For some time past in mercantile circles, strange convulsions had been taking place, by which the oldest firms in America had been shaken; among these (and she stated this without any injunction of confidence, for she knew the honor of the girl's character) was her husband's house. Bankruptcy stared them in the face, and but one expedient appeared which would save them from pecuniary ruin. Her husband in conference with Laura's father upon the union of their children, had revealed the precarious condition of his affairs, with the foreboding of a situation which he had once laughed at as impossible. Laura's father then more urgently pressed the immediate union between his daughter and Charles. The business of the father would be the chief inheritance of the son, and once married the interest of the husband would become the firm and whole-souled interest of the wife. Her money might then be hazarded in protecting that interest, and he very reasonably showed that however great the friendship between the two families, and however slight the risk, it would be violating his duty as a parent to permit such a disposition of its use, in any other case.

"Charles does not love her!" cried the girl, in a kind of horror.

"Dinah," said the mother, earnestly, "he loves her—loves her, and would marry her, could he forget you. And she would love him. Oh, Dinah! think of the misery he will be put to, from which he might be saved!"

The young girl hunted with the eagerness of imprisoned hope over these circumstances, thus arrayed around her, to find some flaw from which they would fall to pieces with reason's touch. But this last thought of impending disaster to Charles rendered her reason helpless in rescuing her. She was no longer the antagonist of the mother or of any human being, but of fate. Even had she lightly considered ere this the social stain, she now felt that when years of passion were over which it should help to embitter, those of toil would continue which it would help to aggravate. The love of his nearest and most loved friends would rightfully be taken from him, and the incessant vexation of these results, of his selfish folly and her selfish wickedness, would wear away in bitterness and unhappiness years which could have been devoted to cheerful usefulness, and over which her love would be powerless.

"Yes, yes," thought the girl, in a kind of sympathetic energy, though she bowed her head in silence, "if it were I only to suffer! But how will he have to work his hands in the unaccustomed labor of some miserable routine, to rack his thoughts in bitter calculation. And what for, but to provide the heartless cause of his suffering with her daily food and raiment. And what right have I to break the heart of his father, or sadden the life of this mother, whôse love for her child is so great, that she could err even to protect his happiness which she thinks in danger. But oh, cannot—cannot I share his love with them? No, it must not be. Oh be true to yourself and conquer these feelings. It is for his sake. I won't be a fool! He will be better off, and those whom he loves will be saved from misery. Yes," said she, and there was a kind of strange cheerfulness in her soul, "and in the varied scenes of life, and with the new enjoyments and excitements which his honorable ambition will bring in a useful career, the feelings of regret will wear away, and I shall be his beloved friend and the friend of those whom he loves, and all will be well. For do I not now feel that I am able to give him up, and it is but for a few short years, and then God will make it right, if it be not so now."

The mother, in fine, endeavoring to extract a promise from her, which she refused to utter and bitterly denied the right to extort, went away with disappointment and irritated misgiving, but yet with a hope.

The hour after she left was the Thermopylæ of the girl's existence. In her high-wrought vehemence, she poured out to her Friend in a kind of heart-welling way, her irrepressible and stanchless feelings. Afterwards came the solemn heart's ease and peace of mind of purity.

This was the first love of a young heart, and characterized by the high honor and exquisite delicacy of first love. If she erred, she erred for his sake. Unselfishness was the rule of her life, or if it was not, she had a cunning insight into the hopes beyond life for reward.

CHAPTER LXIV.

THE COURSE OF LOVE.

The thoughts which now passed in Dinah's mind were such as were to be borne in silent anguish in the present, without the hope that their poignancy would diminish with the progress of time. In her lonely moments the horrid darkness which seemed to involve her fate was preferable to the radiance of her lover's presence, which struck a delirium to her heart; but yet upon one occasion she fled wildly from that darkness and cried aloud for his coming. As she spurned the solitude of her chamber with dizzy step and fainting sight, she fell not to the cold floor but upon the bosom of her gay-hearted friend, who had usurped the glory of liveliness for his daily manner.

"Why, darling!" said he. "What a jump you gave. I crept to your door, and stood ere I knocked, and you've paid me for my eaves-dropping. How silent you have been!"

She rose vehemently from his embrace. "Yes, I was tired," said she after a moment, in a dull, listless manner, yawning.

"Eh, what! little girl. Have you been following in the fields the setting sun?" said he, "as though you would not have him leave you in darkness."

"Do you think I am afraid to be left in the shadows? No. Even in the deepest night is there not always some reflection, some dim remembrance of the glorious light of day? Oh yes!"

"Dinah, what is this? you are weeping? My child, oh keep not a sister's grief from one who—"

"Charles, Guy's memory is incorporated with my daily prayers, and they breathe a pleasant hope. I should not weep his death now, should I? And I am not weeping for him now; my tears are the tears of selfishness. I am but crying like a philosophic baby to dissipate a general melancholy, my friend," continued she, with her accustomed smile.

"You conjure up a foolish melancholy, in order that you may enjoy a philosophical dissipation of it," replied he, in a lively manner. "Yes, an ingenious pastime. You women somehow have a great knack of crying about trifles, and—"

"Stop it! I won't have you talk so. Why, Charles, how can you say that—and stop it, sir, stop it immediately," replied she, sharply. There was a look in her eyes as if she felt a knife rankling in her inmost heart.

"Eh? I will, foolish creature, but it is a compliment, you know. To have a soft heart is quite a different affair from having a soft head, and—"

"Charles, I am sick as death. I feel faint, and will you not go away now, will you not, dear? I wish to lie down."

"Cannot I assist you. May not I be—"

"Oh no, I must have rest and quiet, Charles. It is sleep I want; and go away, and come again by and by."

"Well I will, dear; but soon—soon the time will

come when I shall have the right—when my love shall be your guard against exposure, your support in illness—and oh tell me now, Dinah, ere I go; that day is not far distant, is it, from this?"

"How is it for me to answer now? How can I say? Do not be so fast, silly fellow. There is plenty of time before us, and—"

"What! By heaven, you shall be taken to a home of your own within the week, away from this cabin of poverty and solitude, though you fondly love to linger here. But forgive me, dear, forgive me; I have been wrong in distracting you at this moment of weariness and fatigue, and—and I am going. Good-bye."

She moved herself suddenly. "You are so rash and passionate, Charles! Why don't you try to curb your feelings?" said she. "They only make you fretful, and indeed—I must say—sometimes they cause me to feel an inclination to be—to be trivial. It is only their continued flow I fear. You see I'm afraid our intercourse will become monotonous if it is uninterrupted. And now I will tell you what I wish to have you do, just for a trial. You must not come to see me so often, you know, and I will now forbid you returning hither for at least three days. Just think of it, sir, three whole days! What an unendurable punishment! But it must be so, I positively command you. Ha! ha! It is my august vermilion edict. Go—go—say not a word; good-bye, and there is a seal to it," said she, kissing him violently.

"But I—I—" stammered the young man, stricken by each of these singular words, as if they had been blows.

"Sir, have I not commanded you, and have I not

the right to? Not a word, sir, and leave me now," continued she, violently and sharply.

"Why, darling—but—but—has not—" said the young man, with a slight shudder; "has not my love a right—oh, do you—"

"Your love!" Her manner, indeed, seemed like a terrible, serious scorn. "What about your love? I am tired of this nonsense, Charles. We have both been like a couple of fools for the past three weeks. Let us begin and act like reasonable creatures, for a while at least. You are sensible and so am I, and let us assert our natures. Come, I'll make a treaty with you not to utter that word of love for a week, if you will."

An appalling sensation fell upon her listener's spirit. She stood looking steadily at him, and even an easy indifference was apparent in her looks and her manner.

"Great God, Dinah! What means this horrible lightness of speech. This sudden change; these unweighed words so abhorrent to your nature? Heavens! Does my sense garble its work—"

"By the great canopy which o'erhangs us I scarce can tell myself, ha! ha!" said she, with a dull distracted laugh. "I believe I am crazy. But go away. Leave me. It is my foolishness, cannot you see? Why, how scared you look! Come, this is our parting! Good-bye. But remember. You are not to come back for three days. I mean it. I am serious."

"Ha! ha! yes—well, good-bye," said the bewildered young man, lingering to look at her in trembling astonishment as she withdrew into her chamber.

CHAPTER LXV.

WOUNDED LOVE.

THERE was a rude violence in his manner. The hot words of abuse and revilement fell from his lips. Amid that passionate reproach, he could not feel that the last remnant of self-respect was oozing away.

"Sit down here," said he, roughly. "You shall hear me!" and he took her violently by the hand and forced her down upon the sofa.

"It is a strange opinion I have of you," said he, suppressing his anger in an ugly sneer, "and, perhaps, as you already delight in intellectual amusement, you may take some pleasure in hearing your own character drawn by the victim, ha! ha! the fool, who you thought could never read its ugly lineaments. I know you. I know your miserable soul to its most secret springs, and you first shall hear its description, though it be to you but a monotonous iteration of unholiness!" Beneath his thick utterance was still a beseeching tone, and the light of love was flashing irregularly in his eyes.

"There can be no joy for me henceforth, nor affliction, either, by God," muttered he, in a suppressed way, "and it is to you—to you—(raising his voice) miserable, that I owe this double exemption. How can I ever repay you. Come, sit still, you shall hear me. I cannot publish your perfidy to the world; for in proclaiming you the wretch and hypocrite, I should but proclaim myself the fool and dupe. But perhaps it might render good to both of us. I might obtain the puling sympathy of other such love-sick sentimental fools as I am, and you the praise of your peers in hypocrisy; and perhaps these ugly gifts would out-balance for both of us the scorn and ridicule which we would each receive from sensible men and women."

"Listen to me. When I came from the city to this place with sense enough left to seek reformation for the weak, unhappy habits of my foolish, lazy heart, I thought to find it in nature. It was her breath I thought would fan once more the expiring flame of manliness and common sense in my bosom; so did I almost hate then my kind, I never thought a human being could give to my soul any other emotion than that of weariness and disgust. The sickness of my soul was no imaginary one. I will tell you, Dinah; I was grovelling in wretchedness without knowing how I became so low or how to rise again. It was then I met a creature, so fair in body and soul, she seemed to come from heaven as a special dispensation for me. What was this new sensation that seized me? I watched you. I could not bear to have you out of my sight. Your presence became the sweet chastener of my degraded silliness, and the cloud of wilful neglect was clearing away from my purpose."

"Some one told me that you were wicked. That that look of gentleness was the cunning sweetness of hereditary hypocrisy. At first I laughed to scorn the improper thought, and I—I do now; indeed I do. Oh, Dinah, let us be friends again! Try! try! You will love me in the end. With you to inspire me, I can be a god." The muscles of his frame seemed to raise perceptibly in their tension, and his eye glittered temporarily with the lofty thought of future existence with her. His nostrils dilated, and he stood something like Hercules, when counting his labors to win heaven.

The young girl made no movement, but kept her head bowed while her heart shuddered anew.

"Enough! I have deceived myself, ha! ha! I have been fancying that I am a lovable creature. I don't blame you for not loving me, but what did you let your eyes lie to me for? You need not hang your head, Dinah. There is no need of a show of shame. Come, I have been sad with you in the midst of hope, and now you must be gay with me. Great God! to think how that sunlight of your soul was my sunlight then, and your clouds were my clouds. I thought I should die with joy to be the slave of your sweetness, and now, oh infamy—"

"Well, Dinah, you have told me you cannot love me. Riches have pinions, eh? I may lose my wealth. You have heard of that, and you would await another rich booby."

He had ere this risen, and taken her hand as it were to chain her to his passion, but now he released it with a scornful thrust from him, and she sank upon the floor at his feet. With a mechanical air, she half upturned her face to him, and lifted her hands in deprecation of his violence.

"Oh darling, forgive me, forgive me," cried he, as he recovered her from her position and pressed her to his bosom. Despair has its embrace. "What have I said? Oh Di—dear, let us be friends, let us—"

She seemingly relented, and made a motion as if to throw herself upon his neck, but it ended in an erect posture, and she said sharply and quickly, "No, it can never be. Friends we may be, but no more. My soul is my own. My word is passed." She neither saw nor heard any thing for some time. When she rose from the sofa to which she had sunk again, he was no longer there. His love had driven him in wildness from the horror of her firmness.

"He has gone, and his happiness is saved to him, dear, dear friend. Oh thank God it is past!"

"Now for flight. It is better he should have seen me ere I went. But quick, he will come back and I cannot—cannot—" She thrust her things into the old and worn portmanteau which she had concealed as he entered the room, and her hands worked fast to help her in flying from her own happiness. All was silent about the house save her own light footsteps as she gathered her little treasures and put them into the carpet-bag. Her father had gone into the woods with the negroes to gather autumnal fruits, and with necessary apparel she packed his trunk, which would be conveyed to the depot by the deceived colored man. Rich maidens inherit jewels from generation to generation. Some old stubborn Puritan ancestor of hers bequeathed to his race no earthy stuff, but the energy which urged him to scorn his martyring torture amid the burning fagots. There was an ore of heaven in her blood.

The passion of her passionate heart still burned in the same steady, bright, unchanging flame, and when her heart was to be torn in pieces, its last throb would be for the one whom she loved.

CHAPTER LXVI.

CHARLES DISCOVERS THE FLIGHT OF DINAH.

It was the close of the beautiful season of the Indian summer, and the melancholy shades of the imbrowned woods were fading rapidly to bleakness with the incessant falling of the many-tribed leaves. The forest paths were filled with the little innumerable mats, and the wind whistling through the trees was blowing the decadent foliage in thinner showers to the ground, as the dejected Charles passed along the rustling way in silent communion with his bitterness, towards the residence of Dinah. The oft-drawn pictures of future felicity in his union with her were now forced upon his mind in bitter contrast to his hope, which still sprang wretchedly within his bosom, and the careful retrospect of his intercourse with her displayed to him the consummate artifice of her hypocrisy, when it did not belie this last falsity of her soul towards him. The falsity and fickleness of woman he knew was a proverb, and he saw the shrewdness of her heartlessness in releasing herself ere poverty was upon him. But he still had hope. Her soul was but tarnished with the education of poverty, and with the continued manifestation of his love it would brighten to its original purity. The disaster of his own ruin had not yet come, (he weakly thought;) and, too, it was not as if she already loved another.

Tully, the negro, showed some wonder at Charles's inquiry. Did he not know that she had gone away? Charles sought her room with rapid footsteps, and its deserted appearance went farther than the negro's statement in revealing the truth which led him to despair. No letter, no token of farewell to one whom she had promised at least to be a friend. She had fled from the neighborhood of one whom she had wronged, to seek in some securer quarter a more advantageous exercise of her artifice and her charms. Heavens! had she gone to pursue Warriston's footsteps and bring his willing affections back to her? Had she secretly kept up her relations with him, and was he now awaiting her in some distant place?

"No! no! Hypocrite, liar as she is," cried he, passionately lifting his head from his distraction, "she could not have falsely denied that. She loves no one yet. She must love me, even if it be the work of my life to make her, and quick I will discover her and bring her back!"

No time elapsed ere he took measures to discover the direction of her flight, and he soon was convinced that she had sought the great metropolis. He knew, too, from indubitable evidence that Rudolph had taken the European steamer, and reasonably conjectured that her temporary relations were not with him.

CHAPTER LXVII.

DR. FUFFLES GOES WITH CHARLES TO THE CITY.

In obedience to the absorbing will of his heart, Charles endeavored to follow the footsteps of the young fugitive. At times her farewell to him and the scenes of their intercourse seemed not heartless but delicate.

At times he felt not the strength, but feared the weakness of her self-reliance in conquering her way through the world.

The wild distraction which characterized his first essay to discover her was chastened by its want of success, and without relinquishing hope, he returned from the city to the country-mansion, (at which his mother had resolved to stay during the winter,) with a subdued gloom.

The sweet religious days which comprise the anniversary of our Lord's advent came and passed; the dark evergreens, which adorned the way-side church, with their united light and shade were emblematic of suffering, and yet of hope. The anthems chanted in the loft, accompanied by the trumpets of the village band, filled his heart with sensuous glory and yet with melancholy.

Quickly, with the new year's coming, he returned again to the city. The measures which he had first taken were still unproductive in their results, and the impulse to continue his personal efforts to discover her was undying and resistless. In the mean time, the delicacy of his position towards Laura, as understood by his parents, was a matter of sorrowful misgiving to them, although as the hour of danger to the business of his father had been postponed by an extension of paper, they did not yet wish to ask the devotion of his thoughts to those important interests.

To accompany Charles upon his renewed visit to town, Dr. Fuffles applied for leave of absence from his charge. A special meeting of the vestry was held, at which the subject of the temporary loss of their beloved pastor was debated with deep upheaval of emotions and a storm of words; but the doctor having finally alluded to his intention of paying his own expenses, they immediately yielded to his desires, and with great unanimity resolved to let him go.

The doctor was desirous of accompanying Charles to the great metropolis, not only that he might offer the young man that sympathy which was due him in his bitter pursuit of Dinah, but also that he might more conveniently invite publishers to treat with him for the publication of his great work now in manuscript, "The Poetical Exegesis of the Revelations." In the construction of this work, the doctor had been too partial, perhaps, to the established rhetorical rule of flattering the reader by leaving him something in each one of them to puzzle over and discover for himself; and, in fact, the work might be said to have been generally more unintelligible than the great mystery which it was intended to explain. However, it possessed at least one indubitable evidence of inspiration, which was manifested in a consciousness of its immortality by the author, who boasted of it in eleven different places after the manner of the old poets.

The clergyman of the city, with whom the doctor exchanged upon this occasion, was equally celebrated with him, and to a certain degree, of a similar style of mind—the only difference, perhaps, being that while the former was accustomed to preach on those mysterious and metaphysical subjects which were generally beyond the comprehension of his parishioners, the doctor entirely carried off the palm by holding forth upon matters which not only his flock didn't understand, but he didn't himself. This friend of the doctor had formerly been a Presbyterian, but having engaged in a public controversy on the merits of their respective religions with an Episcopalian bishop, a curious result took place: the Presbyterian became an Episcopalian, and the Episcopalian became a Presbyterian.

As the doctor was an infrequent traveller, it is natural to suppose that the excitement of the journey should have been characterized at the outset by a little timidity. However, nothing occurred to mar its pleasantness, excepting perhaps a momentary cumulation of feeling upon one occasion, when the doctor emerging at a station for the procuration of refreshments was informed, while returning, by a seedy gentleman, who was evidently the life of the large party of natives, devoting their daily energies to hanging about the landing-place, that he would have his body carefully returned to his place of residence, if it could be recognized, and if he would only be kind enough to leave his address. The doctor, horror-stricken at the insinuation of the benevolent stranger, rushed distractedly to Charles's side; but his fears were soon dissipated by a gentleman occupying the seat in front, who informed him in a pompous manner that there would be no danger, and deduced this conclusion simply from the fact that he was aboard. He was the mayor of the town at which they stopped. His visit to the metropolis was private and incognito, but as he looked around severely upon the other occupants of the car, he indulged in gratifying pictures of the reception which the citizens would give him were it official. As how the right of the city would be given up for the formation of the firemen and civic societies, and the left be devoted to the military, while the drunken "citizens on horseback" would be enticed towards Harlem under the impression that he would be coming in that way.

The hours lagged in weariness to the restless young man, urged by the powerful impulses of his passion, and with nervous joy he saw the lights of the city in the distance ahead. He soon drove up with his fatigued friend to the mansion of his father in Jefferson Square, one of those architectural ornaments to the city, which are said (especially by persons who have never been out of America) to resemble in a striking manner, some of the gorgeous palaces of the resplendent clime of Italy, and which, perhaps, do in every thing except the dirt. Charles awaited not the coming of the day, but leaving his respected friend beneath his roof to retire to the black-curtained feathery pavilion of Somnus, commenced his search for Dinah with mingled hope and misgiving. The approaching rigor of the weather, the financial stringency, the youth of the young girl, the helplessness of her aged father, her ignorance of the ways of such an assemblage of human beings, all conspired to lend a desolate, gray tinge to his emotions, but they only made his energy greater. When the morning came, the warning which he had given that he might not return, proved true. He was taking the proper measures to discover her, and all of them in his power.

Dr. Fuffles sallied forth in the morning, filled with architectural admiration at the splendid city, and resolving to occupy the hours of his temporary stay, undevoted to business or sociality, in the impartial criticism of an unassisted examination thereof. A plan, accommodated to the brevity of his sojourn, in which he proposed to examine all the streets of the city, to look down into all the cellars, inspect the tops of all the houses, call into every corner grocery, and ride in all the omnibuses, was soon put into execution. Some few hours at the commencement were devoted to lamentation for the loss of the "Exegesis," the manuscript of which had mysteriously disappeared from his pocket within five minutes after he left the mansion on the first day. As it was but a copy of the original at home, however, he soon recovered his spirits, and it is satisfactory to know that his surprise and chagrin were quite offset by the thief's upon discovering the nature of his booty.

It would be tedious to relate here the various incidents which occurred in the doctor's ramifications, but a few may, perhaps, be alluded to from their singularity. For instance, upon one occasion while crossing one of the streets, and closing his umbrella which he had hoisted instinctively in proceeding under a building in process of erection near by, he became involved in a roaring, tearing assemblage of people turning the corner with an engine behind them. By some process or other he got inside of the ropes, and was compelled to run for his life for over a half mile, surrounded by the cordon of frantic, whooping demons on their way to the conflagration. At the end of that distance, the announcement being made that there was no fire, he was released, not without a difficulty however with one of the firemen, who was mildewing for a personal contest, and who rubbed up against him for some time with the hope of producing exasperation, while making use of such expressions as these—"Where yer shovin' to, sa-ay? I'll just tuck and I'll—" etc.

Although he soon recovered his hat, and his temper

which he had temporarily lost in endeavoring to find the former, he presented a very disordered appearance, which no doubt was the cause of the reply made by a passing gentleman in answer to his inquiring desire to go to Broadway: "Well, I am sure I have no objection," said the hurrying merchant. "You have my permission, if that is what you want."

"He must be a Bostonian," reflected the doctor, philosophically. Another individual told him "to go away, that he had nothing for him;" but he at last succeeded in finding the great picture gallery, and was carried along amidst the throng of beauty and elegance towards Union Square. When he arrived there the lamps were being lighted, and after a short admiration of the tall bronze horse on the paved square, he proceeded towards dinner and Charles's mansion.

Still filled with the ardor of investigation, he stopped upon one of the cross streets down which he was walking, overcome with the thought that he might lose something worth seeing were he not to look into an area gate of one of the houses which happened to be open. At this point, he observed a mysterious individual standing near a tree box, who had commenced winking at him, and now slowly approached him.

"One go in for the daddles, the other watch and flab the nabbers," said this person quickly, in a whisper.

"Dear me! nab the flabbers!" exclaimed the doctor, in astonishment.

"Meet at 36th street and 12th avenue, and divide."

"Eh? my friend, I don't understand you," said the doctor.

"Oh you needn't come that on me: It's my lay any how. I was here before you."

The doctor looked about him. He knew not but that the eccentric stranger was seeking for some printed ballad which he had dropped, or was awaiting the deposition by some favorite hen of her treasure, and was fearful of its being rudely snatched from him, but he saw evidences of neither.

"Lay! what do you mean by that?" asked the doctor, sharply.

"There's a coat, a poll-parrot, two umbrellas, and the half of a boiled ham in there. You take the poll-parrot and umbrellas, and give me the coat and ham. I must have the ham," said the man, shivering, "for I am hungry. Be quick about it, they are all at dinner. I'll whistle if the nabbers turns the corner."

"This is most extraordinary!" ejaculated the doctor.

"Go in! Go in quick," urged the ragamuffin, swearing violently, "if you're going to do it."

"D—n it, I will, d—n it!" exclaimed the doctor, mechanically, confused to imitation with the frequent "d—n its" of the stranger, and walking bewilderedly into the yard.

A stately policeman had turned the corner, with a relaxed drunken man hanging over his arm, whom he was taking to the station-house. The doctor emanated from the gate, and observed the eccentric stranger tearing rapidly down the street. A fearful thought came over him with regard to his hat and clothes, still crushed and soiled.

"Ha!" said the policeman, who had hanged the drunken man quickly over the railing of the house,

"I've got you, have I?" With one pounce he grasped the doctor. It was a more exciting affair than that of the inebriated specimen of dereliction whom he left hanging upon the railing. Twisting his hand into the neckcloth of the doctor he slammed him against a tree box, and then against the fences of the little courtyards as he dragged him along. The doctor's legs were in the air the greater part of the time. That evening he spent looking through a grating at a lamp hanging in a dim corridor, or in keeping off, with his umbrella, a demoniac Irishwoman in the cell with him; and next morning, although he was discharged by the magistrate in the matter of theft, upon the explanation of Charles, he was fined five dollars for fighting the policeman, and general disorderly conduct on the way to the station-house

"Well, this, I suppose, is city life, isn't it?" said he to Charles, after a long silence, as they rode home.

Upon another occasion it fell to the doctor's lot to witness one of those pugilistic contests, common to the overflowing energies of great cities, which was of unusual interest. In spite of the foregoing mishaps which had occurred to him, he bravely ventured out again to complete his inquisitorial tour of the metropolis. Having arrived in his wanderings opposite an open lot in some sparsely settled suburbs, he was overcome with astonishment to observe therein, what seemed to his subjectively confused vision, nothing but a mass of legs and arms twisted up in intertwined motions.

It was a prize-fight which had become general, and contained among other singularities a wooden-legged being, whose crutch might be seen rising into the air and falling with the regularity of machinery upon the devoted heads of those about him. At some distance, also, upon the outside, was an individual who, hesitating to go in, with that bashful fear of excess of pleasure so common to some modest natures, but infected by the general enthusiasm, and gifted with a brilliant imagination, was defending himself against an imaginary enemy which he saw before him in the air. Suddenly observing, however, the attenuated form and emotional absorption of the doctor, who stood speechless upon the other side of the street, he immediately directed his footsteps in a sly and circuitous manner to the rear of the unconscious clergyman. Having arrived there, he proceeded to kick him with such awakening force, as to cause him not only to reflect upon the present with increased astonishment, but to anticipate the future with fear. If it was done facetiously, the doctor was only another instance of the philosophic rule, that men of profound reason and clear judgment are rarely remarkable for quickness in the appreciation of humor.

"I am somewhat emaciated, but I must protect myself," said the doctor, desirous of immediate reparation, though dimly conscious of the distance between his wishes and powers. He turned around, but was astonished to observe that his aggressor was running down the street with rapid steps; and not only he, but a greater part of the crowd, the ringleaders even slinking away, with hasty looks at the recent scene of their combat. They had been dispersed by the unexpected appearance among them of a benevolent individual, soliciting contributions for the erection of a church, and it was not until they were out of his reach that they assembled again, and promised to have another good time in some spot less liable to such harrowing interruptions.

With such episodes as these, was the doctor's personal examination of the great city made, and the rest of his hours were devoted to the pleasant duties and sociality of his clerical exchange. As Charles was almost continually absent in his ceaseless search, the doctor was frequently forced to dine alone, often being reduced even to the society of the turkey upon the board. Upon these occasions, he managed, however, to be very much enlivened by the presence of the latter, and they generally had a fine time together.

Charles searched in vain for his beloved, but with sleepless energy. The doctor in all his little journeys kept the thought of her discovery in his mind. He knew and appreciated the eternalness of love.

Upon one occasion, wayfarers passing by "the Principal Depot for Mrs. Piper's Celebrated Domestic Pies," were astonished to observe an elderly gentleman, without any hat, and with a considerable piece of pie in his hand, emanate violently therefrom, and drive recklessly across the street. It was supposed by many that he had become temporarily frenzied with intoxicating materials contained in his luncheon, and the proprietor of a Teutonic establishment opposite, whose rivalry to Mrs. Piper's emporium was vindicated by its prominent sign of "Restauration with Pie," was wildly exulting in a malignant hope founded upon a sinister theory, when it was discovered that the elderly gentleman was only pursuing the retreating form of a young girl with whom he thought he was acquainted.

It was a beautiful day, though severely cold, when they left for home again. The young man had discovered, indeed, that Dinah had been in the city, and employed as a seamstress in one of the cheap clothing houses. With the want of demand she had been dismissed from employ, and although the proprietor had known naught respecting her residence, nor whither she had gone, he recalled to memory a remark which she had made, referring to a conditional return to the country. These facts cheered him, at least, with the total dissipation of his fears respecting her relations with Warriston, but with a thousand distracting conjectures and increased uneasiness, he again temporarily sought his home.

CHAPTER LXVIII.

WINTER.

When Dinah concluded to withdraw the influence of her presence from her lover and become but an object of memory to his being, she knew that she had to furnish new thoughts to his mind ere she went, which would by their very violence and horror heal the wound which she was making in his spirit. The days of this trial to herself were few, and as soon as she had exhibited to him the feigned release of her feelings from a temporary attachment to him, she prepared to fly. On the very occasion when she was thus actively engaged, he had returned in his distraction to heap upon her a scorn, which she felt at the time was not so harrowing as the mingled exhibition of his sorrow. Her soul was chiefly called upon to suffer in witnessing the latter, but her principle was firm against her self-reproach.

With what seemed a necessary falsehood to the kind

colored people, a part of which was to make them believe in the coming brevity of her absence, she succeeded in quietly leaving the neighborhood; and in accordance with the previous determination of her judgment, which suggested the solitude of a great city, and the facility therein of procuring steady employment, sought immediately to hide herself in New York. Fortune favored her efforts. Within a day after she arrived, she had procured through the agency of a small intelligence office a situation as seamstress in an obscure yet populous street, with a privilege of performing her functions at her own lodgings, which was conditional upon her advancing from her humble means the value of the material upon which she was engaged. The Hebrew, thus fortified, accepted some natural excuse which she made respecting this matter, and thus she felt quite isolated from human relations. The humble room which she rented was situated at some distance from this quarter, and she was accustomed to make the necessary visit to her employer's establishment at an evening hour. Though who shall blame that heart if, at times, it dared recklessly to forget the measures of this cruel care?

The old father was quite happy when the worthy desire of remunerative work did not stir up uneasy emotions in his aged breast. He wished to perform his share, and felt that the world was losing a considerable amount of advantage which it might derive from the activity of his energies. On these occasions, Dinah used to despatch him upon imaginary errands, in which great haste and precipitation was demanded; such as immediate inquiries of a distant grocer respecting the price of potatoes, or visits to Laurens Square, to take the time from St. Catherine's steeple, all the neighboring clocks being out of repair and quite unreliable, or to recover Tip from the infatuating society of other dogs in the streets. Once, in order to please him, she permitted him to go in her place to her employer's store with a newly finished shirt, and receive the week's wages. He returned with a cross-cut saw, two chisels, a hammer, and no money, having expended the whole of the week's stipend to a penny, in this carpenter's outfit.

"Why, father, what have you done?" said Dinah, as the truth struck upon her.

"I—didn't mean to do wrong, Diney; I can earn some money now!" said the old man, noticing the look of disappointment and anxiety on his daughter's face. He thought she might be vexed, and bursting into tears, fell upon her neck like a little child.

"Never mind, father dear, it is right," said she, soothing him with a filial kiss, while her own tears dropped. "We can get along without this money. I intended it for foolishness, indeed, and you have got something of use and value with it. Perhaps, in a few days, too, when it is better weather and there is more business, you can get some work to employ them on."

Time rolled by, and the country was in the depth of winter; Dinah worked steadily and cheerfully in her little garret-room, the small grate of which threw out a comfortable warmth, yet spared her little stock of coals. Sometimes her father amused himself with the unfortunate tools he had purchased, and walked about the room pounding the doors, unscrewing the hinges, fiercely examining the windows, which were a sight to fire the glazing eye, or piling the musty drawers of the old closet in the middle of the room to inspect their deficiencies. When he became wearied with this occupation, he would sit down by his daughter at the window and read his Bible, or engage in a fond conversation with her, who generally managed to make him laugh heartily and forget the harrowing subject of want of work, in the pleasant way in which she caused him to look at every thing. Now and then he expressed a desire to go back to Templeville, but then he said he was glad they came away after all, and he would only like to go there again after they had improved their estate a little. He knew that they had been unpopular there, and seemed to understand that there was something improper in the position which his child would have had to hold had they remained, and he approved of her choice in leaving, although he could not make out the chief reasons of her sending away her friend Charles. Still, whatever she did was right to him, and he patted her head or pressed her to his bent form with an expression of love and confidence.

As she sat thus in her working hours plying her needle, what thoughts, and how many, in the silent moments passed through the mind of that pure-hearted child. Again and again did the scenes which she had passed in the society of Charles come back upon her memory. Perhaps in relief of the thought that he was suffering from the abscission of those ties which she had so abruptly sundered, she thought of the brief space in which their sympathy had grown into an affection, and with a sinking hope reflected that perhaps reason after a while would restore equanimity and happiness to him, when he thought of the profitlessness, folly, and temporary hallucination of having bestowed his love upon one who had thus assured him it could never be returned.

"Oh heavens, have I done wrong!" thought she, in terror at herself almost, as the consciousness of the eternity of her own love towards him now made her feel that her reasoning might perhaps be fallacious. "It was for his good, and yet his desire to have me with him may never die, his love may always be as strong as it is now. If it is so," she would say, rising in triumph from her chair, "I will fly to him. Who has a right to keep us asunder. Yes, it is so," she would continue, singing her words, and grasping the clothes of her astonished old father. "How can I love him in the way I do, unless he loves me in the same way? He can't live without me. He'll suffer and be miserable. Yes! I have done him the wrong to think his love was not as strong as mine! It is not too late! I can go back to him this very day—now, on the hour—and we shall be—happy—happy, and together forever. My love became morbid, and I was a fool. When I am older I shall see what a fool I have been, and how criminal has been my folly! When it is too late and he has become soured and disgusted with the world, and perhaps has—died, oh heaven!" The gushing thoughts thus pouring quickly through her mind would momentarily overwhelm her young soul. "Pshaw! He die for me!" she would continue, after wiping away her tears. "He has not known me six months. It is only a temporary affection he has for me. Yes, his dear mother indeed was right. He has met a young girl in his idleness, and become attached to her for the moment. And Laura, darling, will love him, and she will feel that it has not been a matter of cold necessity—she will feel that the strength of family friendship has but commanded this duty, to give to her a life of pure happiness in his pure love."

Thus over and over again she revolved the step which she had already taken, and warred against the strivings of her love to make her undo it. Sometimes she was strong and sometimes she was weak, but the plain common sense which appeared always to characterize her nature and chasten her sentimentality, dulled the force of the only reason for returning to his love which she could bring against herself—the conjecture of his suffering permanently for the want of her love.

At best it was a late and temporary affection engrafted on his being. How absurd to suppose that it could not be lopped off without danger or damage to that being, and how foolish and criminal not to cut it away when the older branches of his affection, of long standing, the growth of years, and even inherent and necessary to his very happiness, were to be sacrificed for it.

The stringency which had been for some time existing in the money market, had time and again warned the merchant of the coming disaster, which now came in the midst of winter. One day, the proprietor of the shop for whom she worked told her that he liked her workmanship, her steady habits, and industrious manner, but the times obliged him to discharge her as well as others. The announcement caused a serious pang in her bosom, but hope was strong there. She could seek employment, as she had already saved sufficient money from her wages to enable her with proper economy to devote nearly a month to that object, and certainly by that time, in the recuperative energy which Americans, even when children, feel to belong to their race, she trusted that the scarcity of places would be diminished, and the equilibrium of affairs reëstablished. The contemplation of seeking the aid of Laura and her father was yet unadmitted, for she felt that it would be fatal to her duty of weaning the affections of Charles, should he obtain the clue to her situation or location, which it would certainly give to him. No, the time had not yet come when she could safely accost her friends in Templeville. And even when taking into consideration her father's welfare, she saw no reason why she could not postpone such beggary for some time.

As the medium of the intelligence office had become almost useless at this time, she commenced her new career of personally soliciting employment in the various walks of life, wherein she thought she might fulfil her duty. Carefully concealing from her father the dissolution of her connection with the shirt establishment, she expended a part of her little store in purchasing linen, and occupied a part of each day with the usual industrious application of her needle. When the hour came at which he was accustomed to lie down and refresh his aged limbs with slumber, she would darken the window with an old shawl, and covering him in comfort would leave him on tip-toe with a kiss on his sleeping lips, praying the benevolent care, during her absence, of a wealthy Irish lady on the floor below, whose daughter was the heiress expectant of as high as seventeen pigs and their posterity, then on board in the country. Upon these occasions she generally encountered Tip sauntering about in a pleasant manner two or three blocks distant from his house, whom she was accustomed to send back with a severe reprimand, to lie at the attic door. With dashed hopes the chagrined animal would turn towards his residence, his speed insensibly lessening as the sway of his inclination to skulk after her increased. As it was a matter of uncertainty, when he did go home, whether he stayed up stairs over ten minutes or not, owing to fitful impressions in his mind of dogs passing in the street, she at last permitted him to follow her; and as he had an innate sense of delicacy with regard to entering strange doors, not knowing but that his exit therefrom in some cases might be rendered uncomfortably precipitous owing to popular prejudices, his presence did not at all interfere with her designs.

But now time wore away in unsuccess. She saw her store gradually decreasing, as the intensity of the weather and the pressure of the times increased. The month of February had nearly elapsed. She had been forced to tell her father of her want of work, and had expended the whole of each of her days in its eager pursuit. At many a night-fall did she return from her bitter struggle with limbs aching, and oppressed with fear that her father might yet be brought to suffering from the step she had taken. On the afternoon of one of those cold days, as she was turned away by a manifestation of churlishness from a store door, she drew her shawl closely around her, and walked along indulging in a species of melancholy entertainment, in speculating upon which of her toes was the coldest, and being at the time quite a disciple of Zoroaster. Even Tip now felt the severity of the crisis. No bones were longer to be picked up at ease in the streets, and no idle dogs to play with were to be seen about. His appearance began to assume a lankness, and the expression of his countenance, when it was not frozen up or blinded with driving snow, was that of unmitigated disgust. He stuck to her bravely, however, and followed her wherever she went.

Dinah felt her chance for employment diminishing with her money. Starvation for her father, her dog, and herself, or the violation of her duty towards Charles, stood before her. She blamed her folly for not writing to Laura, while such a step still seemed forbidden to her. She had felt that Charles in his first disappointment would seek for her, and knowing nature would direct his inquiries to the great city. But now, while she expended the whole day in the thoroughfares she had no fear of discovery, as she reasoned upon the probable result of the acknowledgment of her heartlessness. Yet there was a hope which she could not conquer, living in her breast, though it actuated not her actions, that she might see his face once again—but to fly from him forever, and hide in more profound secrecy from his loved presence. "No, I need not fear his discovering me in this great city. Indeed, if he would seek me he has already done so, and now, perhaps, his mind and soul are turning towards Laura, and renewing his friendship with her. Her society is effacing the inciting remembrance of me, and what a wretch would I be were I to write now to her."

"She would surely reveal it to him, and my concealment would be thus exposed. He might furbish up his infatuation again, and I should assist him towards a listless future; and what for? Because I was hungry one day. You shall not suffer at any rate, father. I have money enough to return to Tully's. I will not touch that, it is sacred. Judy will receive us again, and we can keep in secret there until the winter and the crisis be passed. Then for a glorious summer of work. He'll be married and will assist me to a situation, and—Gracious, the idea! it makes me sick! Oh dear! it makes my soul sick to think of him! Why don't he come and tear me from this wretchedness? Dare he forget me! I am his equal! I am—pshaw—a fool, and he is my peer, if he thinks of me now."

Her measures were soon taken. The money which she had gotten by the disposal of the tools, with two or three dollars added, she hoarded with a miser's greed in her bosom. In case of need she could thus return to the negroes; though, perhaps, her misgivings of their ability to sustain them, at least a hope of bettering her condition herself, postponed the execution of the reluctant determination. With the rest of the money, which hardly amounted to three dollars, she purchased a stock of pocket books and pen-knives. Her father she kept in warmth and food, but who shall know the physical misery of cold and hunger which she passed through the next few days with her attempt at becoming a New York street merchant. Who shall know all the bitterness of soul she experienced before she gave up. "I'll stand it as long as I can. No one else is interfered with, and I have a right to do as I please," said she to herself wilfully. "But I will not let father suffer. Charles may marry whom he pleases, and take care of his own affairs! He wouldn't exactly expect me to murder my father! What a sentimental idea! that he's so fond of me I can't trust myself in his neighborhood without endangering his prospects. One day more, and if I can't sell any thing, I'll break into my treasury and then write to somebody—Nat—Laura—for more. If they tell, it isn't my fault." And she did break into her treasury. Shilling after shilling went in the cause of filial solicitude. One day she stood with her little stock by the railings of a noble house in a by-street. Tip had got in between her dress and the fence. His head was slightly emerged over the basket in his hungry reflections, and he was contemplating the amount of nourishment which might probably be extracted from one or two pocket-books, and regarded the bone-handles of the two knives with a wistful eye. A well-dressed gentleman stopped and spoke some words to Dinah, and Tip knew he was a rascal. He darted out and barked at him furiously, but received the coward's blow, which caused him to retreat to the other side of the street and lift his voice on high for a short space in canine sorrow. The gentleman, rebuked by the pallor of the girl's face at his infamous words, walked on quickly, while she called to her side her humble but scared protector, yet trembling with his fright and the pain of his contusion. She had eaten nothing since yesterday at that hour, and the cold was increasing. Leaving the hated spot, the two creatures walked in desperation to the sunny side of another and more frequented street.

No answer had come to the consecutive letters which she had been forced at last to write to Laura and to Nat, and her last dollar was gone. "I must go. Great God! my father will suffer. I will beg, I will steal enough to carry us back. They shall buy. They must want pocket-books for their tailor's bills, if not for their money. They must have knives to cut their throats, if not to mend their pens," cried she, in the irony of misery, standing up near a shop door as the people went by. She had tried and tried in vain. Two men came along. She took up a pocket-book and pen-knife, and trotted along after them.

"Go away!" said one of them, peremptorily. "Yes, run away, young girl," joined in the other. "We can't attend to you now."

"You must buy one," said she, almost fiercely.

"Eh!" replied the affable man, noticing her face as they walked quickly along. "Well, I'll be along to-morrow. We are in a hurry now. I'll buy one to-morrow."

"But you must buy one now," said she, in weary persistence. "Oh do, please! I tell you, you must," continued she, with a kind of laugh of despair.

She stopped and turned away. The stern man had persuaded the weaker one that he was a fool, and had spoken such a bewildering word to her that it sealed her disappointment. Just then her wandering eye fell upon the open window of a carriage, with a trunk, rolling rapidly by.

"Heavens! Charles!" she cried wildly, and stumbled forward to the curb-stone. One or two passengers noticed her idly, but she had recovered from her temporary agitation. Where then was the eternal sympathy of hearts that it did not hear that loving appeal? The carriage passed on, and turned a distant corner. "He is going! He is going away. He came to seek me. He cannot give me up, and I cannot give him up. Hypocrite, liar as I am, he would take me to him. God made me for him.—Thank heaven, he heard me not!" continued she, and bowed her head. "Oh dear, what is this weakness? I am not going to be sick!"

She was so tired she could not help sleeping that night, but it was only with deep sleep that his form was effaced from her imagination. The remnant of the loaf was left for the morrow. There were other people in want in the house. If she had asked for a bone for Tip, her neighbors would have asked her why she did not drive him into the street. "To-morrow I beg, and if that will not do, I'll go straight to Pine Street and bolt into the counting house, and demand my rights as a friend of the family. Or else I will seek admission to the work-house."

The next day she turned away from the post-office with heavy heart, and started off in her distraction to Wall street. An old gentleman, who had been into a bank to receive his dividends, was entering a carriage with outriders. In the carriage was a sweet face underneath beautiful hair, inclining to the Roman idea of highest beauty. This hair was the only trouble of that young girl's existence. She had even been called "carrot-top" by her schoolmates in excited moments. She was a proud girl and did not fancy beggars, but she said something to her father.

"Look at her hair? Buy her whole stock? It is not worth any thing," said he. "Set up for myself, eh, ha! ha! You will not spend the money for liquor, will you?" continued he, addressing Dinah suspiciously. "But what of that; Dr. Sommers tells us to keep up charity on Paley's plan. Yes. Here are two dollars. No, it is a five, by the U. S. 6's! Well, you needn't think to get any more, and you can run away at once. I request you, in fact, to go away as—"

"Hold your tongue, papa," said the ruddy-locked girl.

"Eh, I—" continued the parent.

"Come here, dear," continued the young lady, with an eccentric design in the desperation of her desire. "I live at 440 14th street, between the 4th and 5th avenues. (Fright has often a singular effect in changing the color of the hair!) May be—may be—you know a housebreaker; if so, tell him our house is a good place. He can find lots of things there," said she, naively. "Now go away. (I can't bear to look at her hair.") The carriage moved away, and Dinah saw the heiress smiling an adieu of fond envy from the window to her locks.

What were her feelings? The gratitude which had welled up in her heart lasted till the carriage was gone, and then gave place to nabob feelings. She almost ran as she returned to her father and Tip. Her plan was quickly made. They took their bundles, the rent of the miserable little half-furnished garret was paid, and placing the key in the hands of the Dutch grocery man, they bade adieu to the house, and wended their way to the Hudson cars. She had money enough to take her to within forty miles of home, and she was trusting in God.

She hoped all the while for secrecy. The last twenty-five miles they walked. They then met with some rebuffs, for they started out on the high road and were without money. It was the road of the trampers to Canada, and the people were suspicious enough to make no discriminations. On one occasion, they encountered one of those fresh natures not yet sordid enough to calculate the chances of deception. He was a kind-hearted farmer who came to his door, and after many sentiments of pity, extended his benevolence in showing the journeyers a house in the distance, where he said he thought they might obtain a night's lodging. That night, after dark, they stole into a barn, Tip having succeeded, after a furious wagging of tails, in fascinating with his debonair character a bull-dog who guarded the premises. The father was comfortable and pleased. They had not walked far, owing to one or two lifts in carts, and she had kept his body warm, perhaps at her own expense, and his mind cheerful by all the little artful devices of her filial piety. At the last place they stopped, she had unobservedly put half the meal which had been given her, in her pocket for him. They all three slept together huddled up in the hay, the bull-dog having quietly retired to his kennel to meditate upon a variety of diversions with which he hospitably proposed on the morrow to entertain Tip as his guest. The seeds of the hay got into Tip's eyes very frequently, he was very hungry, and on one or two occasions was much alarmed by a sudden and fearful increase in the deep-chested snoring of the oxen, but otherwise he enjoyed it very much.

Fearful of abuse, Dinah roused her father just at the dawn, to start again. The remnant of the meal which she had reserved for her father was given to him. Tip, with some difficult manœuvring, captured for himself an old bone from his friend, whose hospitable feelings were temporarily impaired by the jealousy of his instincts with regard to food. On the floor of the barn were a few pieces of turnips and pumpkins half cut up for the oxen, which had carelessly been dropped from the shovel when offered to them. As there was a slight nervous irritation produced in Dinah's system by hunger, she did not think it worth while to attempt the stringy and frozen vegetables themselves, but she ate the seeds of the pumpkins, and from the wintry tops of the turnips she culled several little tender appetizing leaves which sufficed for her silent morning meal. It had been growing colder in the night, and she felt also a singular lassitude. "I might as well lie down again for a moment and think. It is winter now and they won't get up early," said she to herself. She thought of how near home they were, and how easily they could get there before dark without fatiguing her father, when her eyelids closed and nature again asserted its sway over her tired young limbs.

When she awoke she found two females standing over her, one a middle-aged girl, the other an old lady, without doubt her mother. With the sweet cunning which women have and men have not, they seemed to know the state of the case. The younger threw her arms around Dinah. In spite of her suffering, that look of ease, grace, and dignity, mingled with her accustomed dreamy expression, still maintained its position in the countenance and frame of the latter.

"What are you crying for, my daughter," said the old lady, severely, to the younger one. She immediately blew her nose with a noise like C in the bagpipe to conceal the sudden ebullition of her own feelings, and darting at the confused old gentleman, followed her daughter's example by falling upon his neck with an honorable embrace. They saw the devotion of the young girl to her father. She had taken off her flannel petticoat to wrap it around him, and he was now sitting up merely, quite unable to get any further, owing to the complicated manner in which his legs had been swathed against the night's rigor. The old lady led them into the house, and gave them a pleasant meal. She told them her goodman had gone away, and she said that they had made her blush because they had thought her house was not made to shelter poor but honest folks.

Dinah satisfied their honest curiosity, and yet she kept her secret from them, and especially her destination. Their generous entreaties to accept further hospitalities such as their own humble condition afforded, she answered by the kind look of gratitude and the silent prayer that happiness might be their store. The old lady having noticed that Dinah coughed somewhat, told her that a mixture of rum and molasses, and hog's lard, held before the fire till it simmered, was a good thing. Her old man took it whenever he caught cold, although in a somewhat peculiar manner, as in cases of enrheumed necessity he was accustomed to grease his nose with the lard, eat the molasses on hot cakes in the morning, and drink the rum all day. By evening he generally managed to get himself into a perspiration and a desire to go to bed.

A bitter icy blast blew at intervals, and flakes of blinding snow were driven into the faces of the three humble journeyers, as at last they walked up the familiar road. In the distance stood out dimly upon the leaden sky and lost in its heaviness, the honorable spire of God's house, and on this side nearly concealed by the multitude of intervening trees might be dimly seen the chimneys of the lofty mansion at Pompney Place, once the home of her mother, and now of her beloved

Charles. It was dark as they passed by the iron railings of the park, and the bare and aged elms and the evergreen firs uttered a mournful sound with their branches. Dinah turned her face towards the lights of the house, and then quickened her step forward to a rapid pace. Her dizziness soon went away, but she could not refrain from telling her feelings to some one.

"Tip," said she, "I am sick, Tip."

They soon reached the clergyman's house. "We must stop here. Do not forsake us. I cannot go any farther," murmured she, weakly, as if communing with her Master.

They knocked at the door, and all three entered the hall and stood there in silence together, awaiting the return of the summons. Her lips were thin and her face sharp, but the old beautiful look was still on her countenance. There was a noise of voices. Charles and Dr. Fuffles emerged from the dining-room to cross to the study.

"Great Heaven!" cried the young man, and rushed forward. She sank gently at his feet with a murmur of feebleness, for the brave heart had at last given out. That bosom, exposed to the snowy blasts of winter, he pressed to his own in his joy and his passion. Dr. Fuffles had caught the old father, and jerking the unfortunate being from his legs dragged him with strangling energy to the large fire in the library, and commenced to violently remove the things which Dinah had wrapped about him. Gluckinson, who had driven Charles over, rushed excitedly into the room. "Hooray, Doctor!" said he in his joy. "Three cheers! Hooray! Dinah's come!"

"Three cheers!" said the doctor, getting up into a chair wildly.

"Hurrah!" said they together in hoarse unison.

CHAPTER LXIX.

THE FELICITY OF THALASSIUS FOR NAT.—BAYLON ABSCONDS.

Nat had tried so often the unsuccessful manifestations of his affections that he would still have kept up his eccentric course towards Miss Wellwood, had not Charles violated his pledge of secrecy to his young neighbor, and revealed to the young advocate, ere he renewed his pursuit of Dinah, the name of the true object of Laura's sweet affection. In the moments of ecstasy, as he grasped Charles's hand, which warmly returned his pressure, he probably experienced some such sweet suffocation as Glaucus did when he was smothered in a cask of honey. It was certain that he remained speechless for a few moments, but the impulsive kiss which he then placed upon Charles's pallid cheek, told his sympathy with his friend's sorrow, while it completely manifested his own exquisite happiness.

Laura with her father had gone to Albany. The gloom which was spread over Charles's household lent a horror to her own unhappy feelings, and she sought relief in a visit to the gay scenes which generally attend the assembling of the legislature. To say that Nathaniel flew towards the capital would be perhaps to use an inadequate expression. Suffice it to say that he soon drew up before Laura's hotel in a horrid hack and a terrible flutter.

One moment to inquire of the clerk, the next to bound up stairs towards Laura's parlor. The old gentleman was coming along the hall. He grasped the young lawyer in intense excitement. "He's here! In this very hotel. He's eating crabs and drinking milk in the ladies' ordinary. Run in to Laura there! I'll be back presently. I must find out what he's here for."

The young lady sank upon a sofa overcome with surprise.

"I had to come. I had to come—on court business," exclaimed Nat, wildly. "I met papa outside and he told me—Oh Laura," continued the melting lover, sinking down upon his knees and seizing her hand, which he covered with kisses.

"He's gone up stairs. He's gone up stairs," said the squire, rushing wildly into the room. "Hollo! what's that?"

"I'll wager you now," said the delirious Nat—"I'll wager you saw me holding her hand, ha! ha!"

"Oh the devil! Why you are holding it now."

"It is paste, papa! Mr. Bonney says the jeweller has deceived you," said the young lady, quickly.

"Oh yes! and the rest of it pinchbeck. I'll wager my head it's pinchbeck and your daughter may hold the stakes."

"He's gone up to his room, Nat, he's gone up. I must watch him closely. It's opposite mine in the area. I can look into his window," said the parent, unable to stop longer and diving frantically into an adjoining bedchamber. "By the way, what the devil is that," said he, suddenly, compelled to pause by a startling noise behind him. "It sounded like kissing. Confound me if it didn't. Hollo! What is that?"

"He's gone down stairs! He's gone across the street, whoever he is," said Nat, with temporary presence of mind in the midst of his absorption.

"Down and after him," said the old gentleman, bolting in renewed excitement for the staircase.

"He is gone. Close the doors, Nathaniel, else we may perchance be interrupted. Are they all closed?"

"No. The door of the bookcase is not," said the lover in his delirium.

"Never mind. But, Nathaniel, ere you speak, I wish first to confess to you—"

"No, he hasn't gone out! He hasn't gone out! He's in the barber shop," exclaimed the squire, looking in and rapidly disappearing again.

("Heavens! At this moment! It is the only moment. The fates may change their mind.) Do you see that plethoric individual?" said Nat, briefly, to the waiter in the hall; "keep him away from here for fifteen minutes, and I'll give you five dollars. Tell him any thing. He's after somebody. Tell him he went away in a horse—just now, in a horse and wagon."

Thus placing the waiter upon guard, he no doubt reminded him of the fate of Alectryon, (whom Mars turned into a cock for not keeping Vulcan away from his soft interview with Venus.) At any rate he told him he would "wring his neck for him, if he didn't keep his eyes open." The waiter was a man of Napoleonic comprehension and forecast.

"He's gone up on the roof, sir, to look at the skaters

on the river," said he, running after the squire and pulling his coat.

"Eh? Has he? You know him? Say nothing. Lead me up that way. Lead me up."

"Yes, sir. Follow me, sir. Follow me," said the waiter, rushing along dark corridors and mounting unknown staircases. "Here, sir, here!" continued he to the panting old gentleman, as they arrived upon the garret floor. "In here;" and he gave the exhausted squire a forcible shove into a small unfurnished chamber, turned the key upon him, and fled to the head of the staircase.

"Fifteen minutes are almost up. I can afford to get kicked, and he wears patent leathers;" soliloquized he, as a deadened sound of scuffling, pounding, and cries for release now emanated from the deserted chamber.

"It wasn't me. It wasn't me. I was ordered to do it," continued he, as the exasperated squire grasped him by the hair.

"Who! Who was it? The fat man? The fat man?" said he, quickly.

"Yes, sir, yes," said the imperilled waiter, with great promptness. "Yes, sir. In the bar room. He told me to do it."

It was by this happy time that Laura had finished her murmured confession of love, and was now explaining with the eloquence of affection the singular attitude of her friendship for Charles, and his towards her, which, under the influence of the friendship and hopes of their respective families, they had mutually supposed was love for each other. And now Charles's love for Dinah seemed no longer to the young advocate a passing infatuation. At least his sudden want of love for Laura seemed no longer mysterious, and they both momentarily prayed that he might find her speedily, for it would add to their joy.

"And I knew it," said Nat, as Laura exclaimed that she must have loved him all the while, from the very moment when she first saw him. "I knew it, but I thought it was only admiration for my intellect."

"Oh no, Nat, no!" replied Laura, artlessly, and turning up her face towards his again. "That never once troubled me, indeed."

"Oh yes, as we never had any need of using our intellects in our conversations, you never saw the brilliancy of mine." And he gave her one of those ineffable kisses which resound in the heart of a female like a thunderbolt in a thick forest.

("I cannot bear so much happiness all at once!") said the young lady. "Run away for a moment, Nathaniel. Run and find papa, dear. Oh, he may become suspicious."

"Oh yes, dear, but soon I will always be with you. Then I never—I'll never leave you. No, not for one moment," said the impassioned lover, with intense romance. "I swear!"

"Oh don't. It would be too much. And run now, there's a dear," said the sensible girl.

"Gracious! I forgot. Who's this he is running after so? What makes him so—"

"And oh dear, so did I. A person arrived here last night, and his presence has appeared to set papa wild. He says he must find out what he is doing here and—his name is Mudgeon."

"Mudgeon! I know, I know. Back quickly. Oh

my Laura, good-bye!" continued the young lawyer with a wild embrace, lasting nine minutes.

On coming below, opposite an ante-room, a singular sight presented itself to the young advocate's vision. Two fat men in personal combat stood clinched together therein, each unable to move farther, and in deadly silence, excepting the sound of their fitful respiration. One of them was his father-in-law. The other, he saw, was the ancient enemy, Mudgeon. As he arrived, the latter fell down suddenly, and the squire fell on top of him and then rolled over on his back, and they both remained arrayed in this manner for a few exhausted moments, like a couple of mammoth turtles.

"What—the devil—What the devil!" here exclaimed at last the astonished Mudgeon.

"Ha! I threw him," exclaimed the squire, breathing heavily, but in triumph. "I threw him down. I got the better of him."

"My lumbago! my lumbago! You couldn't have done it, if it hadn't been for my lumbago," gasped the other.

"Lift 'em up," said Nat to the waiters who had gathered around. "Lift 'em up. Remove that one. I'll take charge of this one."

"He wanted to murder me and get my property sold. He attempted to assassinate me," cried the retreating Mudgeon, as they carried him off.

"I didn't!" indignantly denied the other. "He locked me up. He bribed a waiter to lock me up! In a garret, with an ugly-tempered cat, who had six kittens."

"Hey!" said Nat.

"But you won't get it. You won't get it. I won't

sell it," cried Mudgeon, tauntingly. "You'll hear what I'm going to do with it. You'll hear, ha! ha!"

"Where's your lumbago? Why didn't it hurt you? You haven't got any. I knew you never had it," said the other, hurling back an equal exasperation.

They both made a superhuman effort to rush at each other again. But a self-possessed waiter with a sofa cushion quietly knocked Mudgeon into an armchair where he was fain to remain seated, while his opponent, with a few rash attempts at gesticulations of defiance, was hustled excitedly from the room by Nat and the other waiters.

Mudgeon sat up all the next night, in order to have it noised about, so as to reach his enemy's ears, that he couldn't lie down owing to his lumbago, and then left the hotel in triumph. Deprived of the excitement of his presence, and failing to derive poignance from the revival of his anecdotic powers, the old gentleman immediately longed for another intrigue of the matchmaking order, and Nat gratified him. With great caution and a studied circumlocution, he at once revealed to him that he had come expressly to Albany to arrange a concealed affair of long standing; that he had already enlisted his daughter's sympathy, and that he now sought his aid to intercede for him with the friends of the young lady as he was cruelly opposed by them, especially by the father, who had other views in prospect for his daughter.

"He shall renounce them! I will talk to the rascal. We'll see whether he can stand our powers of diplomacy, eh, Nat? Tell me the miscreant's name, and you may consider it as settled."

Nat, upon hearing this warm speech, concluded it

to be a felicitous moment to divulge. He did so, and the old gentleman immediately mounted to his apartments and broke every piece of furniture which stood therein. Having performed this feat, he paid his bill in a dignified manner and walked off to the cars with his unhappy daughter, Nat following in intense excitement, breaking his suspenders in his energetic efforts to mend the ties of friendship, and losing his hat in endeavoring to gain a re-entrance to the outraged parent's esteem.

"I can't support it! I can't support it!" exclaimed the latter, distractedly assisting the porter with the trunks, while he accused the pathetic Nat of treachery.

"Well, drap it then! Drap it!" said the accommodating porter.

"It's only a temporary fancy of Charles, I tell you," said the old gentleman. "Besides, it's an unequal match. You are poor and she is—"

"I know it. I know it," replied Nat in desperation. "But splendor with her is preferable to poverty with another."

"But I've promised her money to Charles. They've as good as got it. You won't get any money. There's no money."

"Good! Hurrah!" said Nat, in suppressed excitement, following the old gentleman into the car.

"But you must give her up! You must give her up!"

"She told me she loved me. It is a little too much to expect that human nature should be insensible to the flattery of affection."

"Well, I'll see, I'll see," said the parent inanely.

This last remark was made after they arrived at Templeville, Nat and the old gentleman having wrangled for five hours on the interesting subject in various parts of the train, to which the latter restlessly shifted himself.

"Oh my father, receive your son's blessing," cried the joyous Laura.

"And be happy in your new child," said Nat, making a rash attempt to kneel.

"You'll be handy for me to tell stories to, Nat!"

When they arrived home, they learned with feelings of joy the return of Dinah, for they had heard with admiration the cause of her flight. But with sorrow they heard, also, of the illness which she had contracted in her noble struggle.

A day or two after, Nat experienced much surprise in receiving a letter from Rudolph still abroad, containing a power of attorney, and asking him to employ his legal knowledge in settling his overseer Baylon's accounts, and discharging him from his situation.

As a tribute to Dinah's suggestive estimate of the latter's character, he had perhaps concluded to take this step. Perhaps it was a return to common sense. It was not altogether too late, but it is worthy of note, however, to remark, that the amiable overseer upon hearing the news, did not wait to surrender his books to the young lawyer, but fled incontinently to seek impunity for their discrepancies in the troubled and semi-sealed regions of the South, taking with him to pay his expenses the strong box of his absent and long-deluded employer.

CHAPTER LXX.

REMORSE.—THE FADING FLOWER.

As she entered the room of her home in which the suffering girl lay, the mother thought of how, from the first moment in which she saw her, she had been kept by Providence, (as if unworthy on account of the bitter prejudice of her heart,) from seeing and being exalted by the purity of her character. Her high imagination, which once did its work for those prejudices, now seemed to play with the mingled elements of the anguish of her remorse, and the pleasure which she had in knowing that those prejudices were dead. She assumed an erecter position as she entered, as if the fiend of pride within her in its expiring struggle, towered for a moment. But she moved from the statue's stillness towards the bedside. Quickly placing her hands upon her bosom she cried with bitter emotion, "Dear Dinah, forgive me, forgive me for what I have done!" The light of Dinah's goodness thus breaking in a dazzling flood over her spirit, she fell in a cringing, abased attitude by her side. Had she dared, she would have pressed the pallid hand of her whom she had been persecuting, but in the freshening degradation of her remorse, it seemed almost like an impious sacrilege. She felt that hand seek her own in gentle kindness, and heard the murmur of tranquil delight and sorrowful love from the lips of the adjacent sufferer. She knew it was but the sweet echo of the pardon which had long since been made—made as soon as that bright intellect had conceived the persecution. The sin of her pride was conquered forever by her remorse, and the grand, joyous science of goodness was mastered by a contemplation of the young girl's sacrifice. She even felt a proud pleasure in offering up to Dinah's spotless character the exposure of her own infirmities of heart.

"I knew she could not wrong a human being," said Dr. Fuffles, in triumph.

The powers of the young girl now worked fiercely in their endeavors to destroy the frame which they once had animated, but if they were to succeed, her physical appearance was still so fair that hardly a trace of their work discovered itself, and her soul seemed secretly, rather than openly, to be busy filing off its chains, like a prisoner. Who shall tell the unutterable love which filled her bosom for the bowed spirit of the aged father, who sat hour by hour at her side, and listened yet with hope to her filial words? Charles would come into the room at morn, and she would say, "How do you do, sir?" in the old stately way which was natural to her, and smile on him in the courtesy of her noble ideas. Or a robin, the red-breasted darling of children and men, would come to the window and fly away as they opened it, and she would laugh at Charles's frantic efforts to catch him. Returning to her bedside, and taking her hand, he would laugh too, and try to plague her, but all the while with the smile on his lip, there was something gnawing at his soul as he looked in her face. One day she called herself foolish in not having written to him when she got into trouble. She said it was silly, stupid—"I was like Penelope who stood thinking in confusion, and put a veil over her face because she couldn't decide between her father and her husband." As he saw that young creature chastising her own innocence of plan, and looked in her honest face, his lip quivered, and under the pretence of getting an orange, or stirring a bowl, he turned away to weep scalding tears.

More than once did he thus turn away. She would then move restlessly on her pillow, and seek the quiet for her frame which would not come. Charles's mother with her ever bitter repentance hastening her steps in their labor of love, and Laura and Adeline, with their pleasant faces, gladdened the girl's dear wishes, and gladdened all the household with the hopes which they now and then carried from the sick chamber. Pithkin, who liked Dinah vehemently ever since he had done her a favor, gave the aunt many opportunities of sympathetic conversation with him about the young sufferer, and all through that household reigned the quiet of hope and of fear.

But one day her strength appeared to be rapidly failing her, and seemingly conscious of it herself she had been talking with Charles in a serious, earnest way, about what he must do as long as he lived on earth, for himself, for the poor, for society, and all for God.

"I thought I might stay. I could have wished to," said she. The tears flowed quietly from her eyes. She rose in her bed as if she were trying her strength. With sudden power she placed her feet upon the floor and stumbled towards her lover and her father. "Charles! Father!" cried she, quickly. The young man caught her ere she fell, and as he sustained her she faintly attempted to kiss his hand, and clasped it to her bosom. The father bowed his sorrowful head. A languid color reddened her cheek like a sunset hue in a morning sky, and a smile was on her face as she reclined again on the pillow.

A heavy sense came over them all. The young man felt condensed into the moment all the future of melancholy and love which her memory could carry with it, but on his noble face there was not a trace of emotion, unless, perhaps, the shadow of a melancholy smile. His thoughts and his hopes were evidently in the heaven to which she had departed. The faint odor of the flowers of spring was wafted through the apartment from the open casement, and outside the songs of the birds might be heard, and the bark of the faithful friend and humble companion of the girl's wanderings, with the happy unconsciousness of his limited nature racing over the sward with another humble member of his species. With the other domestics at the door of the chamber, the earnest Gluckinson stood. His head rested against the wall, and his tears flowed in unrestrained honor.

Nat entered the room the next day to look at that form, once animated by a soul which did honor to humanity. He principally saw two pale feet and the diamond ring of her wedding yet flashing upon her slender finger. And again the sweet look of resignation so familiar in life seemed to be meekly fashioning the lineaments of her countenance, as though the spirit of her suffering, accompanying her soul to heaven and thrust from its gates, had sought again to animate her body. As he choked down his emotion while withdrawing, Nat felt a fierce repining at the existence of sorrow and misery in the world, but he knew that

God is just in afflictions and he earnestly blessed his Name.

There were no carriages, but the young men of the village bore her in quiet to the churchyard. The maidens went before with flowers, and the old men followed behind bowed in silence. The dog in his glimmering intelligence sat near the park gate and looked wistfully into the faces of the mourners as they passed.

The recollection of Dinah heightened the mother's love for her son, and she shared with him his unfailing sorrow. One day of the spring they visited her grave together. There was an air of gentleness about the spot, and they found the old father there. He had stuck flowers in grotesque anxiety, like pins in a pincushion, upon the mounds raised over his wife and son, and in his hands he held a bunch of violets he had tired his aged limbs in lonely happiness to gather for the adornment of his darling girl's grave. He cried in bitterness, and fell upon the mother's neck, but they supported his tottering steps to the family carriage, and cheered his trialed soul. Sometimes he lives at Laura's, but he loves Charles's home, where his wife and daughter once lived.

In the weary watches of the night when his soul sighs for relief, Charles often rises, and opening his drawer gazes upon something which he treasures with a miser's selfishness—a pair of exquisite slippers, half worn, which once adorned her darling feet. How often has he seen their diminutive points thrust from beneath her rustling gown. By their side is a piece of paper with the word "Dinah" written in several places, up hill and down, in a large hand with grand flourishes about them. He had found it in the little room which she once occupied as a dependant in the house, and in which she had probably been trying her pen in idle fancy.

CHAPTER LXXI.

CONCLUSION.

Some time after the occurrences related in the last chapter, Charles and Mr. Bonney each received an epistle from their old friends, Col. Norcomb and his wife, indited at their plantation near Charleston. The letter to Charles bore a black seal, for even in such ways did the warm-hearted Southerners endeavor to show their respect for the memory of the dead girl, and sympathy with her lover. Amidst the tributary sorrow of friendship which tinged their words, they could not refrain from dwelling upon the fact that they had always felt the nobleness and purity of her character. That rather than believe otherwise, they had even determinedly suppressed but as a work of his fancy, an incident which occurred to the Colonel on the night of the brother's attempt to abstract the deed, when he imagined, as he approached along the hall, a strange retreating voice crying "Dinah!" with a curse; an incident which was now so sorrowfully explained to be a truth. The letter conveyed news to Charles of the birth of two lovely twin daughters to them, to be named Dinah and Laura, and wound up with a hope that he would soon see them come to reside permanently in a part of the Union which was free from the great political curse.

The letter to Nat thus commenced: "I herewith despatch to you the overseer Baylon, in charge of a constable! He was taken in a swamp by my niggers, who, for the first time ever known, gratified me by laboring zealously to capture him. * * * * My neighbors, insisting upon it that he was an abolitionist, immediately issued to distant friends cards of invitation to assist at a burning, and it was with difficulty I saved him for you. Such was his gratitude to me, that he made a confession of all his misdeeds, and I think if that profound jurist, Pithkin, has not any thing to do with his trial you can easily gratify the desperate Obadiah's wish to retire awhile to some pleasant monastery from the care and solicitude of earthly existence."

Nat's approaching marriage was the theme of many happy wishes, and the advent of the little twins, (one of whom was to be named Laura Nathaniel,) of many playful allusions to Mrs. Norcomb's fondness for her sex, and of the father's determination to bring them up into that womanliness which should render them worthy of such love, apart from a mother's feelings.

It is sufficient to say here, briefly, that Obadiah was tried in due time for his crime before Judge Pithkin, who had now become an associate Justice of the Court of Sessions, and Nat as District Attorney succeeded in convicting him in spite of the Colonel's fears. In his ardor, in fact, the judge sentenced the overseer "to be hung by his neck until he was dead," but on being reminded that the prisoner was not convicted of a capital crime, he merely sent him to the penitentiary for twelve years. One night late in a cell adjoining that in which

Baylon was incarcerated, the prisoners heard a peculiar noise within the solitary chamber of the latter, and deadened by the thick walls which intervened. On its being entered, he was found without life. The satyr for money had turned in upon his bed, and died, it being his last humorous effort, and one which made for him many genial acquaintances in a new sphere. As for his friend, the apothecary, nothing remarkable has yet taken place in his personal experience, excepting, perhaps, an accident which occurred to him upon the last Fourth of July, when he was severely wounded by an extraordinary burst of eloquence from a village orator, it being entirely in a moral way and referring to the peculiar envy of his existence.

One day last year, being in company with Judge Pithkin and young Nat, the spinster deliberately proposed to the former, being the first case of the kind on record, and thus inaugurating a new era in matrimonial affairs which will be hailed with satisfaction by every one. Mr. Pithkin was unable to gasp a single word to the lady in reply, but he shouted fearfully to Nat for aid, on the principle, perhaps, that in any great emotion we can speak better to those whom we are not particularly interested in, than to those in whom we are. He afterwards murmured something about being unwell. "My prognostications have been fearfully realized," said he finally, with a ghastly smile. "I have one consolation, however. I have the satisfaction of knowing I am a true prophet." He was married soon afterwards to her by Dr. Fuffles, who at first refused to perform the ceremony, intimating his fears, that as he was a single man, the lady might take it into her head to prefer him. There was no difficulty, however, upon that occasion, excepting a little distraction on the bride's part, caused by an overwhelming desire to stand at one side and see the ceremony On his marriage tour, Pithkin tried to lose her, but being unsuccessful he has settled down and gets along very well with her, except on occasions of extraordinary excitement in the neighborhood, such as dress balls, musters, and the like, when she excites him by proposing apparent impossibilities to be executed on their part, and afterwards filling him with admiration by achieving them. On the last of these occasions she astounded him by proposing to go to a fancy ball as an animated hour-glass, and actually triumphed in dressing for this character by putting on two crinoline petticoats, one expanding upward and the other downward. There is also another slight cause of excitement in the judge's mind with regard to his wife, consisting in a singular mystery which seems to be connected in her thoughts with the name of the gallant Southerner. As he often feels compelled to relieve his antipathy to the Colonel by alluding to him in an opprobrious manner, he observes on these occasions that his wife invariably ejaculates something about "a fatal blow," connected with the Southerner's experience, which he as yet has been wholly unable to discover the exact species of—whether a blow on the nose of the latter, or a high wind in which he was involved, he knows not.

Having accompanied the family to the metropolis lately and witnessed a tragedy, she resolved to write one on returning home. Although her figures ran sadly into one another and she found it utterly impossible to control her imagination, she got as far as the last of the fourth act with it, but having unfortunately killed off all the characters but one fellow, she was unable to go on any further because he had no one to talk to. However, it was enacted with great success at the village Lyceum, the place of the fifth act being supplied by performances on a tight rope, the artist being also tight. On the third night of the run, however, the performances were brought to an abrupt and unfinished conclusion, and it was afterwards understood that the play had been suppressed by the authorities as being too exciting.

The honest Gluckinson has been appointed coachman to Mrs. Pithkin, and may now be seen every fine day issuing from the gates of the Pithkin manor in the Pithkin carriage, with Mrs. Pithkin seated behind in great pomp, on her way to visit the sick and poor of the parish. Very lately, however, he has frequently expressed his regrets at not having been "born of respectable parents in New Orleans," and it is supposed that the piratical tendencies of his nature at times create a strong desire in his bosom to be hung. His enemy the cook has become Mrs. Sucker, and the devoted Sucker has taken his place in the peculiar relations which existed between them.

Whenever Squire Wellwood scolds Nat's wife, as he thinks it his duty as her parent to keep up that practice, Nat takes his revenge in scolding his daughter. Just after his marriage, Nat was very much distracted with the question as to how he should raise his children; whether he should let them associate with other boys, or keep them in on the secluded principle; and as he hasn't got enough of 'em yet, having only one up to the present moment, the question is not yet settled. The Squire frequently alludes in admiration to

Dinah's life. "She was a noble girl. But just think of it, Nat, if she had only said nothing about the deed, we might have captured Mudgeon. However, what's the use repining?" The relentless Mudgeon, considering the times, contemplates establishing a cannon factory upon the Gosling farms, and already the sound of an indefinite number of future pieces of ordnance is reverberating in the prospective imagination of the enraged parent. He relieves himself, however, in the usual manner of the Arabian Nights. The mother extended her benevolence to the faithful negroes, now in Canada, who had protected Dinah in her suffering, and the request that the little orphans should be cared for was not forgotten.

Dinah's character was goodness ever, but in that there can be no monotony. The remembrance of her in the neighborhood is not more spiritual and poetic than was her life, and the sculptured angel with folded wings which stands over her tomb may well be considered as a representation of the girl herself, as she stood through life, bending in heavenly resignation over her own hopes.

THE END.

www.ingramcontent.com/pod-product-compliance
Lightning Source LLC
LaVergne TN
LVHW020936110826
845150LV00004B/880

* 9 7 8 1 4 2 5 5 5 2 0 8 4 *